A
GAINSVILLE
NOVEL

Also by Kelley Armstrong

BETRAYALS

KELLEY ARMSTRONG

VINTAGE CANADA

VINTAGE CANADA EDITION, 2017

Copyright © 2016 K.L.A. Fricke

Published by Vintage Canada, a division of Penguin Random House Canada Limited, in 2017. Originally published in hardcover by Random House Canada, a division of Penguin Random House Canada Limited, in 2016. Distributed in Canada by Penguin Random House Canada Limited, Toronto.

Vintage Canada with colophon is a registered trademark.

www.penguinrandomhouse.ca

Library and Archives Canada Cataloguing in Publication

Armstrong, Kelley, author
Betrayals / Kelley Armstrong.

(A Cainsville novel)

ISBN 978-0-345-81521-7
eBook ISBN 978-0-345-81522-4

I. Title. II. Series: Armstrong, Kelley. Cainsville series.

PS8551.R7637B38 2017   C813'.6   C2015-908564-0

Text and cover design by Terri Nimmo

Cover images: (hound) © Alexandre Cappellari / Arcangel Images; (sign) © Clipart Design / Dreamstime.com

Text images: (bird silhouette, p. i) © Ozmedia, (bird silhouette, p. 420) © Lhfgraphics, (sign) © Clipart Design, all Dreamstime.com

Printed and bound in the United States of America

2 4 6 8 9 7 5 3 1

VINTAGE CANADA | Penguin Random House

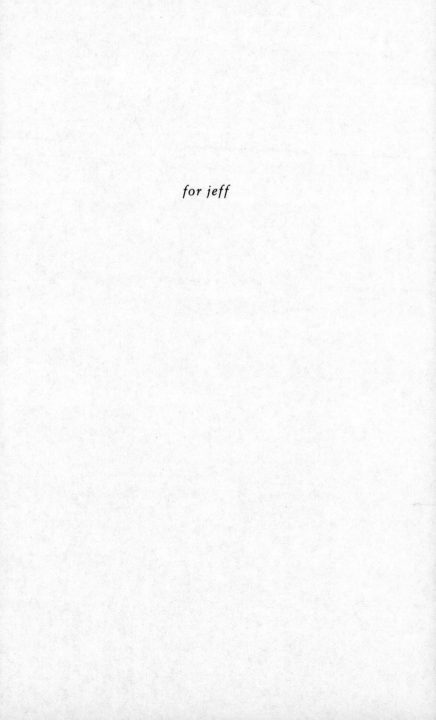

for jeff

BETRAYALS

CHAPTER ONE

I woke to the sound of horses. It took a moment for me to remember where I was—in the forest behind the Saints' clubhouse. I'd gone for a walk with Ricky which had turned into a chase that turned into victory sex and an exhausted drop into sleep on the forest floor.

I reached for him. When my fingers thumped down on cold earth, I scrambled up. "Ricky?"

Don't panic.

He wouldn't have wandered off. That was our pact after the last time I woke up alone in these woods, when Ricky had been lured away and nearly killed.

As I yanked on my clothing, a hound's baying cut through the night. I spun and caught a flicker of distant fire.

A scream sounded deep in the forest. A man's scream. I yanked my switchblade from my pocket and—

"Liv?"

Ricky's groggy voice. Then his hand on my calf, and I looked down to see him on the ground where we'd been sleeping.

"You weren't there," I said, and he knew exactly what I meant, rising with a curse as he reached for his jeans.

When a low growl reverberated through the air, I strained but saw nothing.

"Is that a hound?" I whispered. "A *cŵn*?"

One glance at Ricky's face told me he hadn't heard anything.

"I heard a man scream," I said. "And now growling. There was baying earlier. It think it's one of the—"

A snarl. Then another cry, and I turned fast, catching a glint of red eyes and the faint outline of a giant black dog.

"Over there," I whispered. "It's—"

Ricky had disappeared.

"Damn it, *no*."

Something crashed through undergrowth, running away, but I blocked it out, squeezed my eyes shut, and focused. "Ricky."

"Here." Warm fingers clasped mine. "Hold hands for safety. Just like in kindergarten."

I told him what I was seeing and hearing. Pinpointing the source was impossible—it would come from the north, then the southeast, then the west.

"I think someone's been cornered by the hound," I said.

Now the woods had gone silent. Eerily silent. I clutched Ricky's hand.

"I'm still here," he said. "Oh, and when we went out for lunch yesterday, you said your brownie tasted like it'd been dredged in sawdust, so I dropped off one from Uppercrust for your afternoon break."

He was proving it was really him I was talking to. "Thanks."

"Covering all the bases. Was the brownie good?"

"It was awesome."

"And the dude being menaced by the giant hell-hound?"

"Apparently gone."

"Huh. Do you want to go grab another brownie?"

"It's after ten."

"Is that a challenge? I can find—"

His voice faded, and his figure shimmered against a backdrop of rubble.

There was no rubble in this forest.

I could still feel his hand, though, so I gripped it tighter, and his figure came clear again.

"Did I go somewhere?" he asked.

"You started to."

"Huh." He peered out into the night. As I looked around, he said, "Still nothing?"

I shook my head.

"We know it's not the actual Hunt. I'd hear it if it was." Ricky had Cŵn Annwn blood himself and recognized the sound of them. "It's a vision, which means you have a message pending. So do you want to get it? Or leave it on vision-mail for a while?"

When I didn't respond, he said, "I'd rather you got it. I know the fevers are easing off, but I still don't like you having visions when you're alone."

"In other words, just get it over with."

"Take it slow. Keep hold of my hand. If you can't hear my voice, come back. And if you can talk, tell me what's going on so I know everything's okay."

I nodded. Then I stared out into the forest, picturing what I'd seen a few minutes ago—rubble amidst the trees, nature reclaiming a human encroachment. Like the abandoned psych hospital. Like Villa Tuscana. Two other places where I'd seen fae visions. Ruined places, rich with fae energy, stolen by humans then falling to rubble, Nature slowly reclaiming what was hers, restoring balance.

When I heard a childish giggle, I turned, expecting to see the little girl who was so often my guide in the visions.

"Are you here?" I asked.

A laugh answered. Still girlish, but different from the first. I looked around. Piles of brick and stone and crushed mortar littered ground already blanketed in moss and vines. When I turned toward Ricky, I could see him faintly and feel the pressure of his hand. I told him what I saw as I led him toward that girlish laughter.

"Pou eísai?" a girl said, and though I didn't recognize the words, I knew they meant *Where are you?*

The other girl answered in the same language, telling her companion that the point of the game was to *find* her. The first girl let out a victory laugh, hearing her target, who shrieked as she realized she'd given herself away.

I stepped around a half-crumbled wall and saw a campsite—sleeping bags and backpacks—tucked into what remained of a room, the roof mostly intact. When I came closer, I saw more bags. Not a camp but a squat for the homeless.

The girls laughed again. One darted past. She was in her late teens, older than I expected, given the games and the giggling. Another girl zoomed from a hiding place. She launched herself at the first, and they fell, tumbling together and laughing.

Then they went still. Absolutely, unnaturally still. That youthful joy vanished in a blink, and when I looked into their faces, I saw two other girls—prostitutes—sitting on a bench. I'd spotted them six months ago while searching for an apartment. When they'd looked at me, I'd seen that emptiness in their gaze.

These were the same girls, recognizable now only as they presented that soulless gaze to the world. Then that disappeared, and the girls looked normal, though still solemn, their eyes dark with worry and concern.

"He's found us," the second one said in that foreign tongue.

The first girl made a noise in her throat, an odd rattle, as her sharp gaze darted about. "Go warn the others," she whispered.

The second one shook her head vehemently. "I won't leave—"

The first girl spun and grabbed her by the throat, and when she spoke, her words came carried on a hiss. "I said go." She gave the second one a shove.

Still the girl hesitated, but her companion stomped in her direction with an urgent "Go!" and she took off through the trees. The first one watched her and whispered, "Be safe, little sister." Then she turned and, once again, her gaze emptied. She took a step toward the forest.

"I know you're there," she said, speaking English now. "I have what you want." Her voice took on a coy lilt. "I have everything you want. You need only come and take it."

She stepped toward the forest, her hips swaying, and when my gaze lowered to those hips, I saw her belt. Snakeskin, like she'd been wearing the last time.

The girl walked into the forest, still calling to whomever she sensed there. I hurried after her, but when I stepped into the forest, all that was left was her voice, and even that was growing faint.

I stopped to listen and—

A scream. A horrible scream.

Like those of the fae. The dying fae on the grounds of Villa Tuscana.

Dragging Ricky, I ran toward the sound. I heard a hiss. I caught a glint of scale and of fang. A man howled. Then he cursed. That scream came again from all around me, and I spun, but there was nothing to see, nothing more to hear, just that terrible scream.

A thump, like a body hitting the ground. An odd rasp, like a death rattle. Silence.

I kept walking, kept listening. Breathing. A soft scrape. A grunt. The whisper of fabric. The smell of blood.

My hand tightened on Ricky's. A single moonbeam swept the clearing, like a peephole into another world, and I spotted a foot. The girl's foot. Bare. Her toenails painted red. The beam moved over her supine body. Her leg. Her snakeskin belt. Then her torso, her shirt pushed up, stomach painted as red as her nails, a slash of crimson that split her belly in two. A hand reached into her stomach, and I fell back as the moonbeam moved up a man's bloodstained arm. I could see the girl, dead on the ground, but I focused on him, as that light passed over his shoulder, to his head, fixed on the girl. Then he turned, and I saw the face of a man maybe thirty, fair-haired and bearded.

The moonbeam passed and the scene went dark. I hurried forward, hanging on to Ricky, and found myself in an empty clearing. A sob sounded to my left. Another joined it, rising to a keening cry.

I was back at the ruined building. The dead girl had been laid out in the grass, her ripped stomach covered with a jacket. Four teenaged girls ringed her. All wore those snakeskin belts. They wept and they wailed and they gnashed their teeth, and when they did, I saw fangs, growing and retracting, as they cursed the girl's killer in that foreign tongue.

"Why do you wait?" a voice asked, and I turned to see the youngest girl. She was small and thin, with pupils that kept contracting sideways into slits.

"Are you talking to me?" I asked.

"Who else is there? You wait and you stall and you play, and we die. They say you do not care. That we cannot expect you to care, and even if you did, you cannot help. You never can. You never do."

"I don't understand."

"Do you try?"

"I'm not good with riddles. You need to be clear."

She pointed at the dead girl. "Is that not clear enough? You stall and you play and you tell yourself this isn't your business, and so we die." Those strange eyes met mine. "Pick a side."

I inhaled sharply. "You mean the fae and the Hunt. I have no idea which one—"

"We don't care which you pick. Just choose and be done with it. The longer you stall, the more they are distracted and the more of us die. Fae are being murdered." She waved at the dead girl. "And where are the Cŵn Annwn?"

"I heard them. I know I heard—"

"A half-hearted attempt. They are distracted. By you. The rest of us? We do not matter. Lost girls never matter."

"Tell me what—" I began, but she disappeared, leaving me standing in a forest, holding tight to Ricky's hand.

Ricky and I were alone in a back room of the clubhouse as I downed my second shot of Scotch.

"So the young girls are fae," he said. "The same type you saw when you were looking for the apartment. The same two girls even."

"I think so."

"And they're associated with snakes—the belts and the hissing and the rattling and the slitted eyes. If we can pin-point the language, that'll help."

He attacked the problem as rationally as if fae them-selves *were* a perfectly rational phenomenon. As a child, he'd embraced his grandmother's tales of fae and the Hunt, in some way recognizing them as stories of his past, his heritage.

"We'll work on the language," Ricky continued. "I'm wondering if that's why they don't care which side you pick—because they aren't Welsh fae. As for the Cŵn Annwn being distracted . . . I honestly can't imagine your situation would distract them so much they'd shirk their duties. I think they're having trouble catching this guy. Which opens another avenue of investigation. Before all that, though, you need to tell Gabriel. Loop him in. Pronto. Otherwise . . ."

He'll feel slighted.

He already feels slighted.

One would think Ricky'd be happy that I was spending less time with Gabriel. But even before we knew the parts we played in our ancient drama, I would tell him Gabriel had crashed at my place and he'd only joke that the couch must be more comfortable than it seemed. I'd asked him once, point-blank, if my friendship with Gabriel bothered him.

"You were friends with him before you met me," Ricky had said.

"I wouldn't exactly say friends . . ."

"You were. And I won't interfere with that, because that's how this all goes to shit, Liv. Arawn and Gwynn and Matilda. When they make Matilda choose, everything goes wrong, for all of them, and we aren't going to do that. It is what it is. I understand that."

"It is what it is? What does that mean?"

He'd shrugged and changed the subject.

I checked my watch. "It's late."

"It's not even midnight. You know he's up, Liv."

"It can wait." I got to my feet. "We're supposed to be at the club tonight to socialize, and it'll look bad if we're hanging out back here."

He opened his mouth, and I knew he was going to push me to call Gabriel, so I picked up the pace and was out the door before he could say another word.

CHAPTER TWO

The choice the fae girl mentioned was one I'd been putting off because, as I'd told her, I had absolutely no idea which side I would choose. Until six months ago, I would have laughed my ass off at the very thought of such a choice, so obviously straight out of a fairy tale. Which it was, quite literally.

I was the living embodiment of Matilda of the Hunt. Matilda of the Night. Mallt-y-nos. In Welsh myth, Matilda was a noblewoman who refused to give up her love of the hunt, even for her bridegroom, and so was cursed to ride with the Cŵn Annwn—the Wild Hunt—forever.

In reality, Matilda was a *dynes hysbys*—a cunning woman or witch—born with blood from both the Huntsmen and Tylwyth Teg, the Welsh fae. The two kingdoms shared the girl, who'd grown up friends with the princes of both, Arawn and Gwynn ap Nudd. To avoid conflict, the young men had agreed not to court her. Arawn kept his word. Gwynn did not. In the fallout, the two made a deal. If Matilda went to Arawn on her wedding day, she'd be his, and the world of the fae closed to her forever. If she stayed with Gwynn, the world of the Hunt would close instead. Of course, neither told Matilda about the pact.

The night before her wedding, Matilda left for one last hunt with her old friend, Arawn. As she saw the gates to the fae world close, she raced back, only to be consumed by the fiery abyss. Unable to save her, both young men blamed themselves and each other, and their worlds had been at odds ever since.

The story doesn't end there. There was no end, no satisfactory conclusion. So the cycle keeps repeating. New players are born to take over the roles—not reincarnations, but humans from the proper bloodline and with memories of those distant ancestors. Whichever side possesses Matilda will win the battle for survival. Each has its champion: Arawn and Gwynn, who are supposed to woo her to their side. Ricky is Arawn. And Gwynn in this particular round? That would be Gabriel.

So that's the story, and the direction our lives are supposed to take. The champions do battle for the hand of the maiden, and the winning side takes all, gaining the most precious gift for the fae: the power to survive in the modern world.

A nice story . . . for someone else.

We've decided we don't particularly like our roles. Gabriel isn't the jealous and treacherous Gwynn. Ricky isn't the reckless and impetuous Arawn. And I'm sure as hell not the hapless and helpless Matilda.

We've told the Cŵn Annwn and Tylwyth Teg to back the hell off or they're going to make enemies of all three of us. That's how we can stand against them: by sticking together as the original three could not.

The two sides haven't abandoned their hopes. They can't, because their continued existence depends on my eventual choice. As civilization consumes nature and pollutes the elements, the fae lose the natural energy they need to survive. Having a Matilda cleanses their land. But I don't have enough mojo to go around—hence the need to choose. The Tylwyth Teg and Cŵn Annwn had given me half a year to come to terms with both my role and my powers. I had two months left. Then the battle was set to begin.

Except now someone was trying to change the timetable.

———

Ricky and I were heading out to spend the night in my Cainsville apartment. We left the clubhouse at one. I was on the back of Ricky's bike, enjoying the buzz from three shots of Scotch and the vibrations from the Harley's motor, my fingers slipping around Ricky and up his thighs, his chuckle rippling through me.

He pointed to the countryside whipping past and then at the road ahead. Asking if I wanted to pull over or keep going. I tapped his leg, which meant it was up to him. He gunned the bike and then moved my hand further down his thigh. In other words, if I was okay with not stopping for sex right away, he'd take a little more of what I'd started.

I smiled, my hand sliding to his crotch, rubbing as he accelerated—

He hit the brakes so fast I lurched, and his hand moved to my leg, steadying me and squeezing in apology. Then I saw what he had—a dark car with its lights off, almost hidden in a tree-shrouded drive.

Ricky would have noticed if it'd been here when we drove in. He was the son of a biker gang leader. He was also a member of that gang. The future leader of that gang. He did not miss anything so near his clubhouse. Sure enough, as we drew near, the car pitched forward. Then lights flashed . . . and Ricky relaxed.

I had to smile at that. In his world, if someone was lying in wait on an empty country road, he *hoped* it was the police.

He pulled to the shoulder and I hopped off the bike, removing my helmet as he did the same. He put up the kickstand and had his ID waiting before the cops even got out of the car.

They were plainclothes officers, which suggested detectives, as did the unmarked car. I reached into my pocket, fingers hitting buttons on my phone.

The senior partner took Ricky's ID without a word. He examined it and then said, "Had anything to drink tonight, *Richard*?" twisting the name, suggesting he knew full well that wasn't what Ricky went by.

"A beer at eight when we arrived at the clubhouse. Another at about eleven-thirty. I don't think I finished that one, but you're welcome to test me."

Ricky was right about the drinks. His father, Don, had strict rules about drinking and driving, mainly because it gave the cops one more reason to hassle them. Ricky kept further under his limit, even if it meant resorting to tricks like exchanging a half bottle of beer for a fresh one so the guys wouldn't rib him.

"And you?" The officer shone his flashlight full in my face.

Ricky tensed, but he only said, "She's a passenger, so her blood alcohol doesn't matter. Yes, she's been drinking. Three shots of Scotch since about eleven-thirty, which puts her over the legal limit."

"That's dangerous, on the back of a bike."

"She hangs on tight."

I managed not to crack a smile at that and said, "I'm nowhere near the level for public intoxication."

"We'll call an officer to drive you home. We're going to need to speak to your 'date' down at the station."

"She's my girlfriend, not my hookup," Ricky said. "As for leaving . . ." He glanced at me and I stepped forward, my hand extended.

"Olivia Taylor-Jones. I work for Gabriel Walsh, legal representative for Mr. Gallagher."

"Did you say Taylor . . .?"

"Yes. *That* Olivia Taylor-Jones. Formerly Eden Larsen. You mentioned questioning. May I ask what it is in regards to?"

The detective pulled himself up to his full height, which fell below mine. I'm only five-eight, but my boots added extra inches.

"Are you a lawyer?" he asked.

"No," his heretofore-silent younger partner said. "She's a private investigator who works for Walsh. She has a master's degree from Yale. English major, I think. But she got her PI license recently."

The lead gave him a look, and the younger one mumbled, "It was in the papers."

"He's correct," I said. "Unless you have a warrant to arrest Ricky, any questioning you need to do can be done at our office . . . after Mr. Walsh arrives."

"We don't need—"

"Gabriel?" I said, lifting my phone from my pocket and hitting the speaker button. "Did you get all that?"

"Yes." His deep voice sounded across the line, the clink of keys telling me he was on his way even before he said, "I'll meet you there."

CHAPTER THREE

W hen we arrived, Gabriel was already at the office. He hassled the senior partner—Detective Amos— about the pull-over and the middle-of-the-night questioning. Setting the tone, much as Ricky had. The biker was a reasonable guy; his lawyer was the asshole. That wasn't an act, either.

Gabriel is one of the best defense attorneys in Chicago. One of the most infamous, too—blackmail, intimidation, and extortion were just a few tricks in his bag. A lawyer is supposed to represent his client to the best of his ability, and Gabriel really can, because he doesn't worry about pesky obstacles like ethics and conscience.

If you put them side by side, and asked which was the biker, most people would guess Gabriel. Yes, he's about six-four and built like a linebacker. But it's more than that. Gabriel is that moment before a storm when everything seems preternaturally calm but you can feel the electricity in the air, and know you'll get no exact warning when danger and destruction comes. Ricky is as warm and calm as a summer's day, and while there can be storms, you'll get plenty of warning, and it'll be a flash of lightning and a crack of thunder, passing quickly, the sun blazing bright again.

Only when Gabriel decided he'd suitably reprimanded Amos for his missteps did he usher us all into the meeting room.

As soon as we took our seats, Amos slapped down a

photo of Ricky in a bar. Someone sat across from him—me. I recognized the sleeve of my jacket. Amos laid out three more photos. One was of Ricky getting off his bike. One was of him leaving a lecture hall. The last was of him sitting under a tree with me again, my back to the camera.

"It seems someone has my client under surveillance," Gabriel said. "I presume this is your work?"

"No, it's his."

The detective laid down another photo. I took one look at the man in the photo and inhaled involuntarily, catching a sharp look from Gabriel and a confused one from Ricky.

"You know this man, Miss Larsen?" Amos asked.

"It's Taylor-Jones," Gabriel rumbled. "And Ms. is preferred. Olivia is not the subject of this interview, so please do not question her."

"But . . ." I began. "That's Matt, isn't it? The barista down the road?"

Another glimmer of confusion from Ricky. Gabriel, though, understood in a heartbeat. Yes, there was a barista named Matt at our regular coffee shop. Yes, like this guy, he was around thirty, light-haired, and bearded. But I'd only made the comment to cover my initial reaction. Gabriel smoothly went on to say that yes, this man resembled our barista but he didn't think it was. Perhaps Detective Amos could confirm that?

As Amos answered, I had to fight to keep from staring at the picture. Because I did indeed recognize the subject. He was the killer in my vision earlier that evening.

". . . name is Ciro Halloran," Amos was saying when I forced my attention back on track.

"And this was the man taking photos of Mr. Gallagher?" Gabriel said.

"That's right. Halloran disappeared three days ago. A friend suspected foul play, saying Halloran had been investigating someone dangerous. When we went to Halloran's apartment, we found these." He waved at the photos. "It became clear who Halloran's target was."

"And in what capacity was Mr. Halloran 'investigating' my client?" Gabriel asked.

Amos said nothing, which meant he didn't know.

"You identified Ricky as the person Mr. Halloran feared based solely on the fact you found these photos in his apartment. Is that correct?"

"If you expect me to answer your questions, your client had better be ready to answer mine."

"So I'll assume Mr. Halloran's friend did *not* identify Mr. Gallagher as the man Halloran was worried about. You arrived at that conclusion based solely on finding these photos." Gabriel's expression said that was flimsy grounds for stopping Ricky and that he was being generous when he finally said, "All right, ask your questions."

The questions were exactly what one might anticipate. Did Ricky know Ciro Halloran? Did he know why Halloran would be taking photos of him? As I'm sure Amos expected: the answers were no, no, and no. Gabriel had asked him to wrap up the interview when Amos's phone rang. When the detective got off the call, he said, "That was the judge. The search warrant's signed. Let's move this chat to your apartment, Richard."

Gabriel argued against the search, but not strenuously. Ricky knew better than to keep anything incriminating in his apartment. If he needed prescription medicine, he'd have a copy of the script on file. He didn't own a gun, legal or otherwise. As for alcohol or cash, the police wouldn't find more than a six-pack of beer in his fridge and a hundred bucks in his sock drawer.

As we left the office, I murmured to Gabriel, "Can I ride with you?"

"Should we both?" Ricky asked, too low for the detectives to hear.

Gabriel shook his head. "Don wouldn't want you leaving your bike here. We'll meet you at the apartment."

We climbed into Gabriel's Jag. The moment he'd reversed onto the road, he said, "Who is Ciro Halloran?" and I told him.

"So you had a vision tonight?" he said when I finished.

I winced. I'd been telling myself Gabriel wouldn't expect me to call him at midnight to report a vision. I'd been wrong. I knew I'd been wrong. I just . . .

"I didn't want to bother you," I said. "It was late. I figured it could wait until morning."

Gabriel said nothing for the rest of the drive.

The detectives had called in officers to help with the search. Too many officers, given that Ricky's student apartment was maybe four hundred square feet. They were being assholes, making a scene where he lived. Except he didn't really live there. He spent more time at my apartment or his dad's house. This was just his legal address. We didn't tell the cops that. We simply waited in the living room while they searched.

They'd been at it nearly an hour when Amos slapped down a pile of unopened mail in front of Ricky.

"Care to explain this?" he said.

"I hate paying bills?" Ricky said. "Nah, I have a busy schedule and that's my triage system. I tackle the stuff I recognize right away—like bills. I toss out the obvious junk mail. If I'm not sure what it is, I pile it up until I can go through it."

"Go through it now."

"No," Gabriel said. "That's an invasion of privacy. If you saw something in there you'd like to discuss—"

Amos plucked out an envelope and slapped it on top of the pile. It was a personal letter, hand-addressed to "Rick Gallagher." The return address was illegible, the envelope having gotten wet, the ink badly smeared.

"You don't open *personal* letters?" Amos said.

"People think they can make contact with the club through me. I've also been in the papers lately, with Liv, which means even more unwanted mail."

"That return address isn't water damaged," Amos said. "It's just an ink smear, deliberately done. That's suspicious, which is grounds for me to ask you to open it."

Ricky glanced at Gabriel, who gave a reluctant nod. Ricky opened the envelope and took out a single page, also handwritten, unaddressed and unsigned. He read it aloud:

I know what you did. I've been watching you. You're going to screw up, and when you do, I'll be there to make sure you pay.

Ricky snorted a laugh.

"You find that amusing, Richard?"

"It's like a bad movie script." Ricky put the letter down. "I'm sure you're going to say this is from Halloran. With the part about watching me, it might very well be. So go ahead and do your handwriting analysis or whatever. Even if it's him, I have no idea what he's talking about. I've never met the guy. Never heard of him."

"Are you sure?"

Gabriel cut in. "It would not be the first time my client has been harassed by a stranger for his membership in the Saints motorcycle club. Citizens looking to exercise a tendency toward violence often focus their attention on perceived law-breakers, in hopes of provoking a confrontation. Such individuals are almost always in need of psychiatric care. The fact Mr. Halloran has disappeared suggests he is one of them."

"Or that your client is responsible for his disappearance."

Gabriel's voice dropped, dangerously. "Perhaps you should clarify, Detective. If you are accusing Mr. Gallagher of a crime, I would like that stated, so I know where we stand."

"Are you familiar with the murder of Lucy Madole?"

Gabriel's blank expression answered for him. At one time I'm sure he'd tracked every local murder, ready to leap and offer his services when a suspect was arrested. He no longer needed to do that. If a suspect wanted him, they knew his name.

I *was* familiar with the case. Lucy Madole was a doctor, only two years older than me, who had been murdered in a neighborhood where no one should be wandering around at night.

I'd paid attention because the *Post*'s articles had pissed me off, suggesting Madole might have been in that neighborhood selling prescription drugs to "former associates." Not because the suburban-raised, Harvard-educated doctor had known gang ties. Rather, the insinuation seemed based solely on the dark tone of her skin.

"I know the case," I said. "As for what it has to do with this letter . . ."

"Dr. Madole left behind a husband."

"Sure. I remember that."

"She didn't take her husband's name. Women nowadays don't seem to like doing that. Madole was her birth name. Her husband was Ciro Halloran."

The vision flashed again in my mind. Ciro Halloran carving up a young fae.

Lucy Madole had been beaten and knifed to death.

"I presume there's a point here, Detective?" Gabriel said.

"Oh, I think you see my point, Walsh. Dr. Madole was killed in a part of town she'd never have visited on her own. A part she was obviously lured to. As a doctor, she had access to drugs. Your client sells—"

"If you are going to finish that accusation, you had better be able to support it with evidence."

"We both know he does. His family business does anyway, and the rest is hair-splitting. Dr. Madole was no dope dealer. But she was young, with heavy college debts. And your client? There are a couple of ladies at the precinct who get all giggly when his picture's in the paper. So apparently he's the kinda young man who might have been able to persuade Dr. Madole to sell him a few pills. The kind who might also get pissy if she feels guilty and tries to stop selling them to him." He turned to me. "Wasn't your fiancé killed a few months ago? Beaten and stabbed to death?"

"Her ex-fiancé, James Morgan, was beaten and strangled," Gabriel cut in quickly before I could react. "Which I know well, as the person accused of his murder. A charge that was dismissed when the real killer, Tristan Crouch, turned himself in. You are very clearly suggesting that my client murdered Dr. Madole. I presume you have the evidence to charge him."

Amos said nothing.

"No? Then I believe we are done here. Please conclude your search, and if you have further questions for my client, I'll expect them to come with an arrest warrant."

Gabriel left when the police did, and he glanced at me, his mouth tightening when he realized I wasn't following him. He gave a slight chin jerk, telling me to come along . . . and I looked away. After he was gone, I texted him, saying I'd tell Ricky about Halloran and work the case tomorrow. If he wanted to talk then, let me know.

He didn't text back.

I told Ricky that it'd been Halloran in my vision, killing fae.

"Gabriel should be here," he said. "We should all be discussing this."

"He knows. He's fine."

"I just think—"

"He's fine. I'll talk to him tomorrow."

Ricky shook his head and picked up a textbook as I settled in at my laptop. He drifted off to sleep shortly after that. When he woke at five, seeing me still at my laptop, he said,

"You do realize there's no point in both you and Gabriel being up all night researching the exact same things."

"I'm sure he's asleep by now."

"You know he's not. You two—"

"Tomorrow's Saturday."

He took a deep breath and then met my gaze. "I'm not saying I'm worried about Amos tying me to this murder, but I'd kinda like both of you working this. Together."

He held out my phone. I took it.

WAITING GAME

Gabriel had been home for an hour now, and for nearly that long he'd been standing in front of his fifty-fifth-floor window, staring out at the city with a tumbler of Scotch. He hadn't touched the drink. He wouldn't, even if he'd never wanted it more in his life.

No, that wasn't true. There'd been one other time he'd wanted it this badly, one other night he'd spent holding a glass, staring out this window. When Olivia left.

She'd only been away for two weeks, and he'd known she was going. It was a motorcycle trip with Ricky, a much-needed vacation after they broke the case against her parents, discovering that Pamela had indeed murdered four people and Todd let himself also be convicted for the crimes, because she'd done it for Olivia, as part of a deal with the Cŵn Annwn to cure Olivia's spina bifida.

It was not surprising that Olivia had needed to get away after that. But it hadn't felt as if she was fleeing Pamela as much as fleeing him. Getting him out of her sight after he'd abandoned her when she needed him most.

It was a mistake.

Except it hadn't been. Not really. The mistake had been that he hadn't listened to her messages and known she was in trouble. But the reason he hadn't been listening? That was no mistake.

Tristan had just told Gabriel that he was Gwynn, and

he'd refused to believe it. Matilda's jealous lover? The man who'd betrayed both her and Arawn? Dishonored their friendships? The man who'd brought about Matilda's death through his own selfishness and blindness and arrogance? Gabriel was *not* that man.

He'd rejected the idea. And then he'd rejected Olivia. He'd laughed at her suggestion that they were friends. Left her standing by the roadside in one of Chicago's worst neighborhoods. Told her not to come into work the next day.

Later, when Ricky had come by the office, trying to set things right, Gabriel had sent him away.

A few nights before that, Olivia had woken from a nightmare vision of being alone and trapped and needing Gabriel and he would not come, and he had said he'd never do that. He would be there for her. Always. And when she called, alone and trapped and needing him, where had he been? In his bed, ignoring her calls, wallowing in a pit of jealousy and selfishness and arrogance.

No, he was not Gwynn at all.

His hand tightened on the glass. He looked down, swirled it, considered. Squeezed his eyes shut and saw Olivia that morning before she left. Showing Lydia her new tattoo. A moon for Ricky. A moon for Arawn.

Gabriel had followed her out the door and thought, *I won't let her leave. I'll say something.* Then his gaze had dropped to her ankle, where her boots covered the tattoo.

She's made her choice. Branded it on her skin. And it's the right choice. The one that makes her happy.

The trip had lasted exactly as long as it was supposed to, and when it ended, she'd come back to work with him, as it had been.

Only not as it had been.

He'd started losing her when he'd laughed at the notion they were friends. When he left her on that roadside. Then he'd sealed the loss when she'd called and called and, yes, he did come—came running as soon as he heard her messages—but it'd been too little, too late.

He'd spent the intervening months telling himself it was better this way. What was the alternative? That he keep jealously consuming her time and attention with no intention of taking more, of *giving* more?

In that moment, at the office, as she'd been leaving and he'd wanted to speak, it wasn't just the tattoo that stopped him. He'd wanted to say, "Stay," and nothing more, because he didn't know what more to say.

I don't want you to go. I want . . . I want to try . . .

I want to go back to the beach. Before Tristan came. I want that moment again, and I want more than that. I want you to tell Ricky goodbye. Be free of him so I can try to make this more. But I can't guarantee anything. I can't guarantee it'll work or that I'm capable of more, capable of being anything you need, capable of knowing what you need, of making you happy. I probably can't.

I'll try and I'll make a mess of it, and you'll leave for good, finally say "Enough" and walk out.

Gabriel had never had a relationship with a woman that lasted beyond a night. No person had ever gotten as close to him as Olivia already was, and he'd screwed that up time after time, which proved he really wasn't cut out for more, was deluding himself if he thought otherwise.

But the bigger delusion? The past four months of telling himself this distance was for the best.

He was right to leave her with Ricky. To not interfere. That wasn't easy—Gabriel was accustomed to getting what he wanted, and having admitted that he wanted Olivia, doing nothing about it went against everything in his nature. But if he cared about her, then he could do that. He had to.

If he was being honest, it was not so much selflessness as an exercise in delayed gratification, a concept he was more familiar with: working toward a goal with systematic forethought. He was not saying he'd leave her with Ricky *forever*. He was stepping back to reassess and determine exactly how to win her.

To that end, he'd accepted the fact that he was not happy about this schism between them. No, let's be honest. To say he was "not happy" understated the matter entirely. He'd had something and he'd lost it and he wanted it back, even if "it" was only more of that evening on the beach, the feeling that he could stay in that moment forever, like a peasant caught in a fae dance, not caring if the rest of the world continued on without him. For now, *that* would be enough. To get back what they had.

He'd known it would take effort. He had lost Olivia before, so he knew how to proceed, with care and caution. Yet this time, none of that was working.

He brought her mochas, made exactly the way she liked them, and they'd sit barely touched on her desk. He'd offered to take her to the lessons required for her concealed carry permit, but she'd gone with Ricky instead. He'd convinced her to start driving her father's Maserati and then hinted at taking rides along the coast, teased that he could get her out of speeding tickets, but she'd only laughed. He would take her to lunch at her favorite restaurants and they'd talk nothing but business. He'd make dinner reservations at "their" steakhouse, but she was always too busy, seemed annoyed by his presumption.

Olivia didn't appear to be actively blocking him. Simply oblivious.

No, simply uninterested.

He'd been about to make his most desperate play: suggest they visit the Carew house. It was her great-great-grandmother's home, and the site of most of Olivia's visions, and while that made him nervous, the house fascinated her as few things did. He would find some excuse and they'd go back and maybe there they'd recapture something they'd lost.

Then came the call tonight, and with it he'd seen another way. A mystery to be solved, Ricky was in danger, Olivia would rely on Gabriel to help her save him. They'd spend the night investigating this threat and, for the first time in months, they'd work together as partners. Instead, she'd stayed in Ricky's apartment and sent Gabriel a text saying they could talk tomorrow. He read that text and he knew what it really said. That this break could not be repaired. He'd lost her trust, and he would not get it back this time.

He swirled the Scotch again. Gabriel did not drink. A conscious decision, made with full forethought and understanding. The understanding being that he came from a family prone to addiction, apparently a by-product of human blood mingled with fae. He'd grown up with a mother who'd lost herself to those demons.

No, *lost* implied there'd been a fight. He'd seen a woman who gave herself over with glee to the bottle and the needle, her young son a distraction to be suffered as little as possible.

So he did not drink. Never recalled even feeling the urge until the night after Olivia left, and he'd realized it wasn't strength that kept him from imbibing: it was the simple fact he'd never felt any need to. He hadn't had pain to dull.

He went to bed shortly after that. Or, that is, he went to the couch, setting aside the untouched drink and stretching out to rest before he got to work, certain there would be no sleep that night. The next thing he knew, he was waking to his phone, and the moment he heard Liv's jaunty little ring tone, his heart rammed into his throat as he thought, *I've done it again. She called, and I didn't answer—*

The phone stopped. He looked down and realized it hadn't been ringing at all. It was just a text message.

Call me.

She'd changed her mind. She hadn't been able to sleep and— His fingers paused on the keys as he looked to see dawn seeping through the darkness. Not night, then. But it was early. Very early.

He hit her number. She answered on the second ring.

"That was fast," she said. "Did you even go to bed?"

"I heard the text."

"Ah, sorry. I was trying not to disturb you. I . . . uh, I've been doing some research. Not really turning up anything, but I thought . . . maybe we could talk? We didn't get a chance last night and—"

"Yes."

"Perfect. I know it's Saturday. Do you plan to go by the office? It's not urgent, so I'm not rushing you."

"Come to the apartment. I'll make breakfast."

When she hesitated, he pushed on. "You're going to want to speak to Rose about the fae in your vision, particularly with the connection to Ricky's situation. There's no sense going to the office only to leave again. We can talk here and then drive to Cainsville."

Still she didn't answer, and as the seconds ticked past, he waited for her to come up with an excuse.

"That makes sense," she said finally. "Ricky can drive me over. What time?"

"As soon as you can get here." He felt the compulsion to make an excuse for that, to say that he had a busy day and therefore had to get this interruption over with. A few months ago, that's exactly what he would have done so she didn't think he was eager to see her. Now he held his tongue and let the words hang there.

"Give me thirty," she said, and signed off.

There. Thirty minutes. He only had to wait thirty more minutes.

CHAPTER FOUR

B y nine, Gabriel and I were pulling into town. My town. Cainsville. Founded by Tylwyth Teg, Welsh fae.

There are no tiny winged creatures flitting about Cainsville. The fae look human, and while that's a glamour, I've seen some of their true forms. Most look like the supermodel version of humans—taller, thinner, with flawless symmetry of feature and form. There's also a glow, like a backlight, and I can be a smart-ass and call it pixie dust, but otherwise there's no resemblance to Tinker Bell.

The Tylwyth Teg founded Cainsville centuries ago, as they escaped persecution and the dwindling wilderness in the old country. Here they built a town, surrounded by that wilderness, where they could coexist with humans. Part of coexisting means spreading their DNA through the local human population, allowing them the extra control of fae compulsion.

Gabriel parked in front of Rose's tiny Victorian. There was another car in the drive. A client's, presumably. Rose is a psychic, though she uses her Walsh con artist skills as much as her actual second sight.

I looked at the client's car. "Guess we should have called first."

Gabriel checked his watch. Rose's sessions always started on the hour, meaning she'd be tied up until ten.

"My place?" I said, and he nodded.

My landlord, Grace, was sitting on the front stoop of my three-story walk-up, right across from Rose's house. Grace is a bogart, which is a type of fae connected to specific locations, especially homes. Or that's the theory. I think she must be at least part troll. She perches her wizened ass on that stoop and glowers at the world, daring them to cross her threshold without paying the toll. That morning, though, she was engaged in a stare-down with a small black cat sitting on the railing post.

"Keep it up, TC," I said to the cat as I climbed the stairs. "You've almost got her beat."

Grace turned her glower on me. "I never should have let you install that cat door."

"But you did. And you can't change your mind now, because I have an official copy of my rental agreement stipulating that the door is permitted."

"Only because someone"—that look swung to Gabriel—"blackmailed me into it."

"Blackmail is a strong word," Gabriel said. "Also slanderous."

She rolled her eyes, but there was no real resentment in it. Gabriel was the Tylwyth Teg's golden boy. While they'd prefer he didn't turn his more ruthless talents against them, they understood and valued those talents.

"I'm guessing that's a client?" I said, waving at the car in Rose's drive.

"Could be a new girlfriend, but she didn't look like Rose's type." Grace glanced at Gabriel. "Trouble with the boy?"

That's what they called Ricky. *The boy*. The Cainsville elders rankled at the thought of a Cŵn Annwn descendant riding in and out of their town whenever he pleased. With Grace, though, there was no condescension. She liked Ricky, at least as much as she liked anyone.

"We're fine," I said. "He'll probably be around later."

"Tell him to bring me one of those lemon scones from the city."

"He always does."

She gave a satisfied smirk and leaned back in her chair. Gabriel and I went inside, with TC trailing along after me. Yes, I have a cat. I refused to acknowledge it for a long time, even calling him TC as a short form for "the cat." But he's mine, as much as Cainsville is. As might be expected in Cainsville, he's not exactly an ordinary feline. As for what he is, I have no idea. Part of my bargain with the Tylwyth Teg is that they won't share any of Cainsville's secrets until they're allowed to court me to their side. They're hoping curiosity will break me. It won't. TC may not be the cuddliest cat in the world, but he watches out for me and he's not evil. Or no more evil than the average feline. That's all I need to know.

Gabriel headed for my kitchen and started the coffee machine as the cat wound around his feet.

"Can you feed him?" I asked. "I'm going to walk over to the diner, see if I can get one of the elders to talk about what I saw last night."

"Do you think that's a good idea?"

"I'm allowed to ask general fae questions. Just nothing Cainsville specific."

"And you wish to do that alone."

"Just so you can speak to Rose if I'm not back by ten. We'll divide the work and get you back to Chicago by lunchtime. I'm sure you have better things to do with your Saturday."

He turned, his gaze cool. "If you would prefer to investigate alone, Olivia, I'd appreciate it if you'd say so. I'm hardly going to the gym to swim laps while one of my primary clients is under threat of arrest." He turned off the coffeemaker. "I would prefer to accompany you, but I won't insist. And yes, I'll feed your cat."

"You don't have to," I said. "He'll just be less of a pain in the ass if you do."

Gabriel didn't return my smile. He just headed to the cupboard and took out a can of cat food. As I opened the front door, TC raced out and nearly tripped me. Then he sat in my path and fixed me with a baleful stare.

"The food is that way," I said, pointing.

More staring. When I tried to walk around him, he darted into my path again and planted himself there.

I sighed. "You want me to take Gabriel."

TC lifted a paw, cleaning it, as if to say, *Whatever do you mean? I'm just a cat.*

"Nice try," I said. "But I'm not snubbing him. I'm just . . ."

I looked at the apartment door. Then I went back in, with TC trotting at my heels.

"Okay, I lied," I said as I walked into the kitchen, where Gabriel was throwing out the cat food tin. I took it from the trash and rinsed it. "I want to talk to Patrick." I tossed the can into the recycling bin. "I want to look at his books. See if I can find the answer there."

"The books that gave you visions the last time?"

"Yes, and I didn't want you trying to stop me. Also, the last time we did this, you decked Patrick, which I suspect is a very bad idea."

"So is asking to use his library, which puts you in his debt. As for the visions, while it's true that I don't like you encouraging them, I would hope that if you plan to do so, you would take along someone who might actually help you if you collapse unconscious on the floor again. Because Patrick will not."

True. While Patrick wouldn't let me die of fever on his floor, if I fell and banged my head, he'd calmly observe the results and then wander off when that proved dull.

"I think it's worth the risk." I paused and added, "And I'd like you to come."

He set the cat's dish down and followed me out the door.

CHAPTER FIVE

W e found Patrick in the diner. He's almost always there, writing at a table, playing his role as Cainsville's resident novelist. He's been published in several genres, under multiple pen names. Currently, he's Patricia Rees, writing paranormal romance. I don't comment on that. I wouldn't know where to begin.

The other Cainsville elders usually affect the guise of, well, the elderly. There's a distinct advantage to that. One could grow up in Cainsville and never realize the elders weren't aging, which is exactly what Gabriel had done. They'd been old when he was a child; they were still old. He had never stopped to consider exactly how old they might be. I remember a teacher I hated in second grade. In my memory, she was ancient, and then I met her a few years ago and discovered she was only now nearing retirement.

Presumably, the Cainsville elders will occasionally abandon their guise to live as younger residents. I suspect it's tough to seduce the local ladies when you look like you'd need a whole bottle of Viagra. But most times, they're seniors. The exception is Patrick, who appears somewhere between my age and Gabriel's. As for why no one notices that he doesn't age, chalk that up partly to fae compulsion and partly to the human brain's need to find explanations. Before we knew about the Tylwyth Teg, Gabriel had told me he remembered a man who'd taken an interest in him as a boy. In his memory, it was Patrick, but as an adult, Gabriel had realized that was impossible and decided the man must have been a relative of Patrick's instead.

Patrick is a hobgoblin. I remember the first time Rose said the word, and I made the mistake of equating it with "goblin." She'd been quick to correct me. She said I should think of Puck from *A Midsummer Night's Dream*. Which is exactly who Patrick reminds me of. An arrogant, self-serving trickster who isn't nearly as clever or as interesting or as charming as he thinks he is. Of course, I may be biased, having discovered a few months ago that Patrick is the father who abandoned Gabriel to his hellish life with Seanna.

We got three steps into the diner before the place went silent, every aging pair of eyes turning our way.

The first to react was Ida Clark, de facto leader of the Cainsville Tylwyth Teg. She rose to greet us, along with her consort, Walhter.

"Olivia," she said. "And Gabriel. We haven't seen either of you in a while."

"And we haven't seen you together in even longer," said Veronica, beaming at us from her table.

"We're together plenty," I said. "I work for him, remember? Now, if you'll excuse us, we have a case—"

Walter perked up. "You're working on a case together?"

"We are," I said. "Ricky's in trouble, and Gabriel's helping me fix it."

Did I take some pleasure in seeing their faces fall as I mentioned that dreaded name? Maybe.

I walked to the counter, and said hi to Larry—the cook and owner. I'd worked here for a few months after I arrived, and contrary to what the elders claimed, I did still stop by quite often. I just didn't talk to *them*.

I motioned to the server—Susie—that I was going to take the coffee pot. Then I carried it over to the dark-haired guy banging away on his laptop. Patrick didn't even let me draw up alongside his table before he lifted his mug.

He smiled as I filled it. "Hello, Liv. Good to see you."

Gabriel took the pot from me and returned it as Patrick said, "You, too, Gabriel. The old folks are right. You don't come by nearly often enough these days."

I took the seat across from Patrick.

"Pleasantries complete, one-sided though they may be," Patrick said. "Liv wants to get down to business. How may I help you, Olivia? I presume that's what brings you to my office. You want something."

"Of course."

"And in return?"

Quid pro quo. That's how all fae operate on some level, but it's more overt with a hobgoblin.

"In return I will tell you what we're investigating," I said. "And you can decide how much of it you want to pass on to the other elders."

The old folks heard that perfectly well, and they were not pleased. Patrick's eyes glittered as he sipped his coffee.

I glanced around. Other than the elders, there were no other customers. Susie and Larry had gone into the back, like bartenders sensing a brawl brewing.

"Is that a reasonable deal?" I asked Patrick.

"It is."

"No." Ida got to her feet again. "It is not."

She started toward me. Gabriel stepped into her path.

"I want to speak to Liv," Ida said. "I am allowed that, under the terms—"

"Under the terms of our agreement, you are allowed to speak to her, but not to interfere. She wishes to consult with Patrick. You are attempting to interfere."

"Patrick isn't the one she should speak to."

"Perhaps, but he is the one she *chooses* to speak to."

"He cannot be trusted—"

"None of you can."

Ida stepped closer. "We are trying, Gabriel. Mistakes were made. If you and Olivia would just put aside this nonsense—"

"It isn't nonsense to us. Olivia wishes to speak to Patrick. Please allow her to do so. I'm sure he'll share the story with you afterward."

"I might," Patrick said.

Gabriel gave him a look. Patrick might play the rebel, but he didn't antagonize the others unnecessarily.

"Can we move this conversation to your place?" I asked Patrick.

"You kids go on ahead. I'll finish my coffee and catch up."

Ida didn't try to follow us out of the diner, and while I hate to give Patrick credit, I think he sent us on ahead so he could deal with them while we escaped.

Patrick's house wasn't hard to find. The town is arranged in a grid pattern. All commercial and public buildings are in the downtown core. Beyond that, it's houses, houses, and more houses. Besides Grace's walk-up, there are no townhouses or apartments. And there are very few buildings—residential or commercial—less than a hundred years old.

That is strange, when you think about it, but unless you *do* think about it, Cainsville settles comfortably in the mind, as if this is how towns should look. No rundown corner stores with barred windows and cigarette ads. No tawdry McMansions on streets of stately Tudors. There aren't even many stop signs—you're expected to follow the common courtesy of slowing down and checking before turning or crossing an intersection.

Cainsville is a town of unspoken rules and unconscious compliance. For someone like me, who chafes under restrictions and expectations—or Gabriel, who refuses to acknowledge them at all—that should be hell on earth. But it isn't.

It's not fae compulsion that draws us here. We don't balk at natural rules, like slowing down to watch for children. It's the larger, more institutional ones we struggle with, and there's no sense here that we're unwelcome if we don't conform to the laws enforced beyond the town borders. Only what happens within the confines of Cainsville counts in Cainsville.

We were walking past the school when I thought I spotted a gargoyle. That shouldn't be surprising, considering how many there are in the town. But they appear and disappear, and there's even a May Day contest to find them all. The local children submit their lists to the elders and win prizes for the most found. If they locate them all, they get a special award: a gargoyle made in their likeness. The last child to win that was the guy walking beside me.

The gargoyle I'd just spotted wouldn't have done much good as a waterspout. It was tucked under a bush beside the school's front gates. I hadn't noticed it before, so I stopped . . . and saw nothing. The gargoyle had vanished. I took a step back. Still nothing.

I glanced at Gabriel. He just stood there, waiting. I crouched beside the bush and pushed the leaves aside. Behind them I saw a rock. Just a regular gray rock. Despite the rough and jagged surface, no matter which way I looked at it, I couldn't find a face.

"I did see one, right?" I said.

"Possibly."

"Can I get a hint?" I asked.

"You're the detective."

"Spoilsport."

"No, I'd be spoiling your sport if I told you. The clues are there. Follow them."

I touched the rock.

"I wouldn't do that," Gabriel said. "It bites."

I shook my head. Holding the branch aside, I tried looking again from every angle. No shape took form.

The clues are there.

I let go of the branch and eased back. That's when I saw another branch, higher up, the bark almost worn away in one spot. I tugged it, and there was the gargoyle. Or, more accurately, a baby gargoyle. That's what it looked like—an infant in swaddling clothes, with twisted and exaggerated features, its face contorted in a wail. I reached out to touch it . . . and let out a yelp, drawing back to see a drop of blood welling on my fingertip.

"Didn't I warn you?" Gabriel said.

"Ha-ha. There must be a thorn . . ." I leaned in further, seeing no thorns . . . and a smear of red on the gargoyle's tiny jagged teeth.

"You weren't joking," I said.

"Do I ever?"

I sat back on my haunches and looked up at him and thought, *Where's yours?* Where was his gargoyle?

"Ah," said a voice behind Gabriel. "I see you've found one of our most popular gargoyles. The cranky baby."

I looked over at Patrick. "It bites."

"Of course it does. The children wouldn't love it nearly as much if it didn't. That's why it's at the school."

"That makes no sense."

"Then you, my dear, don't know children."

"What's their purpose?" I asked as I stood.

"Children? No idea. It appears to be simply an inconvenient stage between birth and usefulness."

"I mean the gargoyles," I said.

"They divert water from buildings, reducing wear on the stonework."

I shook my head. "I know they can scare away the Cŵn Annwn's ravens, but this one couldn't do that—or divert water. The gargoyles must serve a greater purpose."

"They do." He leaned in conspiratorially. "Would you like to know what it is?"

"Yes."

He straightened. "Then you have to ask the other elders, because solving the mysteries of Cainsville for you is a line I will not cross."

I looked at Gabriel.

"You already know what I was told," he said. "They ward off the Black Death."

"There's never been an outbreak of bubonic plague in Illinois."

"So apparently they work," Patrick said. "Now come along, kids. I still have another chapter to write today."

CHAPTER SIX

atrick's house was typical for the town: a one-and-a-half-story Gothic Revival. Inside, it was typical for *him*, far more concerned with personal comfort and amusement than historicity. In the living room, walls had been ripped down to create a large area that was half entertainment center and half library. We sat in the library end.

"I had a vision," I said. "The details are unimportant, but—"

"Details are always important."

"I just want to know what kind of fae I saw."

"And I want the details. Start at the beginning." When I hesitated, he said, "Liv . . ." as if I were a child being difficult for the sake of being difficult. I don't know how to deal with Patrick. He's useful, and he's not unpleasant to be around. I could like him, as an ally. But I cannot get past what he did to Gabriel. Patrick was Gabriel's father and—fae or not—he left him in unconscionable circumstances with Seanna.

"Olivia?" Gabriel said, glancing over, wondering why I was balking when I'd *wanted* to speak to Patrick. He didn't know Patrick was his father, and I was in no rush to tell him.

I told Patrick the whole story, starting with hearing the Wild Hunt, through the death of the girl, to the others mourning her and the youngest's words to me.

"Lamiae," he said. "Greek fae."

"Like Lamia from the myth?" When Gabriel arched his brows, I said, "She was a Libyan queen Zeus fell in love with. Hera punished her—because, clearly, if your husband screws around, it's the other woman who needs punishing. Hera turned her into a snake-woman and forced her to devour her own children. She also made Lamia unable to close her eyes, so she'd forever relive her children's horrible deaths."

"Charming."

"Oh, but Zeus came to the rescue. He made it so she could take out her eyes. Which solved *all* her problems. Then she went mad and started devouring random children." I looked at Patrick. "Other than the snake part, I'm not getting the connection."

"Folklore and myth is a muddled mess," he said, easing into lecture mode. "Stories are told and retold, passed on and altered according to each storyteller's proclivities and imagination. Take Matilda—there are clearly elements of her true story in the myth. Same with Arawn. Gwynn ap Nudd, though . . ."

Gabriel flinched. Patrick didn't notice and continued. "The legends of Gwynn bear little resemblance to the truth other than the fact he was king of the Tylwyth Teg. In some lore, he's confused with Arawn, making him lord of the Hunt. Then there's his part in the Arthurian legend cycle. Yet his real role—in the Matilda myth—was stricken from the records. The simple fact is that the stories you'll find in human collections rarely have more than a nodding acquaintance with the truth. Which is understandable."

"Because they come from humans."

"History is written by the victors."

An odd choice of quote. Was that what humans were to fae? The victors? Driving them from their homes and destroying their lands?

I pushed back on track. "So the lamiae?"

"A similar mess. You have the Libyan queen of myth. A half-snake monster who devours children. Later she's not so much devouring them as sucking their blood, becoming a form of vampire. Then, rather than being half snake, she's a beautiful young woman, often depicted with snakeskin around her waist."

"The belts I saw."

He nodded. "And by that point, she isn't targeting children at all—she's going after men. Seducing them and stealing their life force."

"Making her a variation on the succubus."

"Exactly. Go a step farther and you don't have a single monster named Lamia, you have a monstrous subtype called lamiae, young women with snakelike traits who seduce men and consume their life force."

"Which is closest to what I saw. Are they descendants of Lamia, then?"

He shook his head. "Remember what I said about the records getting mucked up? Flip it around the other way and you have something closer to your answer."

"The fae known as lamiae culturally evolved into the story of the Libyan queen."

"Either the story changed with the times—folklore giving way to myth—or two separate stories got mashed together. The point is that what you saw are lamiae, a Greek fae subtype."

"Show me," I said, nodding at his bookcase.

He smiled, not at all perturbed by my lack of trust. "You want the truth straight from the source? Good girl." He glanced at Gabriel. "You won't hit me again, will you?"

"That depends on whether you do something to deserve it."

"I would strongly advise against hitting me, Gabriel."

"Then I would strongly advise against giving me cause."

Patrick shook his head and went to the bookshelf. The tattered and worn tomes mended at his touch, the leather so new I swore I could smell it. He selected one and motioned me over. I took the chair he offered at a desk. Gabriel positioned himself at my shoulder. Patrick set the book in front of me.

"*Fae of Foreign Lands*," I said.

"You've been learning Welsh."

"It seemed prudent."

He chuckled and flipped open the book. It was hand-written, like many of his volumes—bound journals rather than printed books. The black ink gleamed so brightly it shone, and the words wriggled like eels, slipping and sliding across the page.

"Focus," he said.

"I am."

"*Boinne-fala*," he said. "As impatient as the children you are."

"What does that mean?" I asked.

"That you lack the patience of—"

"*Boinne-fala*," I said. "The fae use the term for humans, but the translation is 'a drop of blood.' Which makes no sense."

"Doesn't it?"

"I could see if you used the term for those with fae in their bloodline. For the *disgynyddion*—descendants—rather than *epil*—offspring. We do have a drop of fae blood."

"You have far more than a drop, Liv. You may not be a direct *epil*, but you have enough Tylwyth Teg and Cŵn Annwn to make you more fae than human. To fae, *boinne-fala* is a disparaging term, meaning one who has no more than a drop of Old Blood. A base and mortal creature. So, when I call you *boinne-fala* . . ."

"You're mocking me."

He smiled. "Exactly."

I shook my head but did take his point about my lack of patience. I concentrated on the ink squiggles, on catching them and forcing them to be still. Soon they settled and turned into Welsh words. I started to translate.

"They appear as young maidens just past the cusp of womanhood, of marriageable age and . . ."

The words shimmered and bled into one another, and I struggled to pull them apart again, but they kept running across the page, turning it into a pit of black ink, and then . . .

I was on a hill. Ahead stood a small marble temple. I climbed the hill to see the temple columns wound with snakes.

I stepped inside. A mosaic covered the nearest wall. I had to squint in the candlelight to see it, but when I did, I could make out a woman in bed with a man who was half snake. Olympias and Zeus, if my classical mythology was correct. History claimed that the mother of Alexander the Great had been part of a snake-handling cult devoted to Dionysus. Mythology further claimed that she'd been impregnated by Zeus himself in snake form. As for the second mosaic . . . well, I recalled that both snakes and Dionysus were associated with fertility, and that next mosaic certainly suggested that. Let's just say there were a whole lotta young men and young women and snakes having a whole lotta fun. Well, the men and women seemed to be enjoying themselves. It was tougher to tell with the snakes.

"May I help you?" a high voice asked.

I turned to see a girl, maybe sixteen, dressed modestly in a linen *peplos*—the gown so often depicted on women of ancient Greece, a long tubelike affair, fastened with clasps at the shoulders, leaving her arms bare. A belt cinched the waist. A snakeskin belt.

"May I help you?" she repeated, but she wasn't addressing me. A man stood in the temple doorway. Perhaps twenty, with a military bearing, though he wasn't in uniform. He looked about the temple uneasily, his brown face darkening with a blush as he saw the mosaics.

The girl smiled. "I am afraid we cannot offer entertainments such as that."

"N-no," he stammered. "Of course not. I . . . I simply wish to pay my regards . . . That is, I wish to honor . . ."

"You came to pay your respects," she said. "And to honor the gods with me."

He nodded and held out his hand, coins in the palm. The girl smiled and motioned for him to deposit them into the mouth of a carved snake. Then she took his hand and led him to a room in the back.

The scene went dark, and I heard a girlish giggle. I turned to see dim light filtering through a crack in a stone wall. I followed it and came out in a room, unlit by anything except that seeping light. Another giggle. Then I spotted a girl in a simple Edwardian-era garb, suggesting she was a maid or of similar station. A well-dressed young man bore down on her as she danced away.

"Do you want something, my lord?" she asked.

"You know I do."

He lunged again and she feinted, and eluded his grasp for a few minutes, only to be captured when he faked another charge. He pushed her up against the wall, fumbling with her petticoats. When he shoved them up, I saw a belt of snakeskin around her waist. He got his trousers down and was inside her so fast she gasped. Then she wrapped her hands in his hair, pulling him against her as he thrust.

"You're good to me, Anna," he said.

She smiled. "We're good to each other, my lord."

The scene darkened again. Nighttime now. I heard whispered voices—a man saying, "I don't usually do this," and a girl's laughing reply, "That's okay. Neither do I."

After a moment, I could pick up just enough light to make out what seemed to be an alley. A very dark, very dirty alley. Music boomed from a nearby club. Footsteps sounded and I saw a girl in a miniskirt with a snakeskin belt, cropped leather jacket and leg warmers, her hair teased a mile high. She led a man by the hand. He had to be in his forties, wearing what looked like eighties-style club clothes meant for a guy half his age. A middle-aged divorcee—or not-so-divorced—out for a night on the town. As for the girl, despite the outfit, she didn't look more than sixteen.

As I thought that, he said, "You are eighteen, right, babe?"

She giggled and replied, "Sure I am," in a way that said both of them knew better. He knew what he was getting. He wanted what he was getting.

"So, uh, how much?" he asked.

"Fifty."

"Isn't that a little steep?" He looked down the alley. "I mean, I'm no expert, but this isn't a night at the Ritz."

"I can give you a night at the Ritz . . . for five hundred." She tugged him closer. "Don't be cheap. I'm quality goods. For men with quality tastes."

He nodded and pulled two twenties and a ten from his wallet. She took it and stuffed it in her pocket.

"The problem, you see, is one of sociological evolution," a voice said behind me.

I turned to see Patrick sitting on a trash bin.

"Yes, you aren't the only one who gets the dramatic recreation version," he said. "So much more interesting than merely reading the words, isn't it?"

"You said something about evolution."

He hopped off the can and started walking down the alley, away from the rutting couple. "Precisely. Look at the lamiae. How old do they appear?"

"Teenagers," I said as I followed him to the street.

"In the modern period, yes. They're teens—a stage of life that was created in the twentieth century to deal with the problem of prolonged adolescence."

"Because in earlier times, you went straight from childhood to adulthood. Betrothed at twelve. Married at fourteen. Usually to a guy at least a decade older."

"Which makes sense from a biological point of view. Nature isn't kind to women. They're at their most fertile in their youth. But times changed, and young women demanded more, not unreasonably. So society accommodated. Today, the average age of a first marriage for Western women is twenty-six. You have evolved, sociologically. The lamiae cannot."

"Why not just change their glamour? Be twenty-five instead and hang out in singles' bars."

"Not all fae have that freedom. The lamiae have only two forms: the girl and the snake."

"So they look like teenage girls, and they need to have sex. They'd find plenty of teen boys willing to oblige."

"Boys are a poor source of what lamiae need. They're too young, too unstable, still coming into their full life power. Ideally, the lamiae need regular and reliable access to adult men. And as society changed, that became increasingly difficult to get in any safe and acceptable way. They go from priestesses to ladies' maids to prostitutes. From power and privilege . . ."

"To destitution and danger."

CHAPTER SEVEN

O ur next stop was Rose's place. The woman who answered Gabriel's knock was obviously a relative of his. The same pale skin and the same black hair with the same widow's peak. Admittedly, the tall and sturdy build flattered the male Walshes better, but Rose's full figure denied any hint of masculinity. She had light blue eyes, too, though hers were darker, well within the realm of normal.

Rose doesn't smile much more than her great-nephew does, but when she opened the door, she looked pleased.

"I saw the car," she said. "I was hoping you'd pay me a visit."

"Something up?" I asked.

She waved us into the parlor. "The cards suggest someone might be in a bit of trouble. Nothing serious—or I would have called."

"Let me guess," I said. "Is it Ricky?"

She glanced over.

"If you saw them this morning," I said, "you're running on a bit of a delay. That's what we're here about: trouble involving Ricky, which involves fae and possibly the Cŵn Annwn."

Gabriel said, "I'll make tea," giving me time to poke around the room. There's always something to discover in Rose's parlor. Today it was the underside of a turtle shell.

"Scapulimancy," Rose said. "Shoulder bones are also used, as the name suggests, but I'd rather have that on my shelf. It was a method of divination in ancient China. Heat the underside of the shell until it cracks and then read the future from those cracks."

"Huh." I bent to examine the shell cracks. "This one seems to say that it's destined to spend a very long time on a psychic's shelf, where it will eventually acquire a thick layer of dust."

Rose shook her head and waved me to the desk. We settled, and I told her what had happened and about my visit to Patrick. She pulled a few books off her own shelf. Hers were human folklore, which meant they only mentioned Lamia as the Libyan queen and lamiae as a Greek vampire or succubus subtype.

"What I couldn't ask Patrick was about the Cŵn Annwn," I said. "I heard the Hunt right before my vision, and Ricky didn't."

"Meaning it was another part of your vision," Rose said.

"Apparently. The Cŵn Annwn were hunting someone. What I saw suggests that this Ciro Halloran guy is killing lamiae. The province of the Cŵn Annwn is hunting killers whose crimes are connected to the fae."

"In other words, Halloran would be a prime target."

"And now that he's disappeared . . ."

"You're thinking the Hunt took him."

"Right. Which means the next step is to confirm it with the Huntsmen, ensure that there's no way of linking Ricky to Halloran's death, and tidy up any loose ends. Case solved."

"You have a method of contact for the Huntsmen, do you not?" Gabriel asked as he brought in the tea.

"Ioan gave me one." Ioan was the leader of the local Cŵn Annwn.

"Is it a complicated process?" Rose asked.

"Kind of. It needs to be done while standing in a forest clearing flooded with moonlight. Then I face east, chant a few lines in Welsh, and, at the stroke of midnight, dial Ioan's cell phone number." I reached for a cookie. "Or I could just call him."

"Call," Gabriel said. "We can have lunch in town and then meet with him."

I paused with the cookie at my lips and then said, "I should take Ricky to see Ioan. He's their champion. It's like you and the Cainsville Tylwyth Teg."

"She's right," Rose said. "This Ioan is much more likely to talk with Ricky there."

Gabriel gave a curt nod. "Understood."

"I'd totally go for lunch, though," I said. "If that offer still stands."

His jaw worked, as if ready to say, *No, it does not.* I'd rejected an overture. He would retreat behind his wall. That's how it always went. But after a moment he said, "Of course it does."

Lunch with Gabriel went well enough. We talked about work. Safe and easy conversation. After it, he suggested I go visit my father in prison. I hate that. No, let me be clearer. I love seeing Todd; I hate seeing him in there.

Todd Larsen has spent the best years of his life in a maximum-security facility for crimes he didn't commit. I hear about stuff like that on the news. I see it as a plot in books and movies. But until I found out about my dad, I'd never really thought about what it means. My father was a year younger than I am now when he went to jail. He has slept in a cell for twenty-two years. Eaten prison food for twenty-two years. Dealt with whatever horrors befall a good-looking young prisoner. Dealt with whatever shit befalls a convicted serial killer.

I've heard he spent a lot of that time in solitary, and while part of me is glad he was shielded from the other prisoners, at least temporarily, I cannot actually fathom what that would be like, either, living for weeks with little to no human contact. He tells me it hasn't been so bad for him—I suspect the Cŵn Annwn had something to do with that—but the fact remains that he has spent half his lifetime in prison, wrongly convicted. I've known that for months now and yet I can't get him out. Some days, the sheer frustration threatens to drive me mad.

We sat on our respective sides of the Plexiglas barrier. There was a speaker between us, meaning anyone around could eavesdrop on our conversation. Todd didn't care. He was just happy to have me there, and that was why I kept coming, as much as it hurt.

Todd and I discussed books, as we often did, sharing a love of mysteries. And, yes, in my mind I still refer to him as Todd. I had a dad growing up, and it feels disloyal to grant that title to someone else, however deserving. But I do call Todd "Dad" to his face because I know how much it means to him.

As he talked with me, I could see him relax. Where Pamela looks every one of her forty-five years, my father could pass for late thirties. The age is there, in crow's feet and faint lines around his mouth, but his blond hair is untouched by gray, and while his build is slight, he obviously spends time in the prison gym.

"So I'm guessing a PI impersonating a cop is out of the question," he said, about a private-eye novel he was reading.

"Yep," I said. "Although, if someone *mistakes* me for a police detective because of how I dress that day? Or my manner, or my choice of words? That's fair game. I can't really pull it off, though. I don't have the right look, as someone loves to remind me."

Todd glanced at Gabriel. "Much easier for you, I suspect."

"True," Gabriel said. "It's hardly my fault if my size leads some to draw the conclusion that I work in a different area of the law. Or, occasionally, on the other side of it, which can be even more useful."

Todd laughed, and we continued dissecting the book until the visit was down to the last ten minutes.

Gabriel stepped in then and provided an update on Todd's appeal, admitting we hadn't yet been able to find Imogen Seale. Imogen was the one person who knew my parents hadn't committed the first pair of murders, but she'd been on the run for months now.

"Our prospects aren't as encouraging as I'd like," he said, "but proving innocence is difficult when innocence is not the case for all parties." He chose his words with care, given the semi-public nature of the setting. "I will not ask you to change your mind about turning against her. We've been through that often enough."

I shifted in my seat.

Todd's gaze met mine. "I can't, Liv. I'm sorry. She's still the woman who went to prison so our child could walk."

"Then she should have taken the fall and left me my father."

"I wouldn't have allowed that."

"Bullshit. The DNA was hers."

Gabriel cleared his throat, reminding me to watch my words.

I looked at Todd. "I want you out."

"I will get out, eventually. You don't need your daddy anymore, Liv. You're doing fine. If the appeal doesn't work, I will tell the truth. That's our deal. But you agreed to let me try it my way."

"I didn't agree. You refused to do anything else."

"It's still a deal." He gave me a quarter smile. As much as I seethed, arguing with Todd was like battering a foam wall. It seemed soft and yielding, but I couldn't break through, no matter how hard I tried.

I stayed silent for the rest of the visit. I said my goodbyes as genuinely as I could, not wanting to storm off in anger, but the minute the visiting room door closed, I strode ahead, leaving Gabriel to catch up.

He said nothing until we were in the car. Then it was, "You're upset."

"Let's just go," I said.

He sat there, one hand on the steering wheel, those damned shades covering his eyes. He was eager to be gone but clearly felt some unwelcome obligation to pursue this.

"It upsets you," he said finally, and I almost snapped a reply, but managed instead to say, "I don't want to talk about it."

He gave an abrupt nod, and what sounded like a sigh of relief. Anyone else would have prodded, made sure I wasn't holding back. Gabriel couldn't get that car in gear fast enough. He'd fulfilled his obligation by acknowledging that I was "upset"—not once but twice—and I'd let him off the hook. That was enough.

We didn't talk for the rest of the ride.

DANGEROUS GAME

Lunch with Olivia had not gone well. Not as well as their lunches used to go. It was perfectly cordial. Like eating with Don or another long-term client. Not like having lunch with someone who'd been a friend, a good one. Simply working a case together wasn't going to bring Olivia back to him.

He'd suggested they go visit Todd because he knew she loved seeing her father. Gabriel was proving he understood her, could provide what she wanted. Except it hadn't been what she wanted at all. It only reminded her of Todd's situation.

He had to go further. Had to take a risk. Had to do whatever it took to give her the one thing she wanted most right now.

Gabriel had betrayed Olivia's trust three times since they'd met, which would not be nearly so grievous a track record if that first encounter hadn't been a mere six months ago. And now, as they struggled to recover from the third misstep, he decided to attempt to fix it with . . . another betrayal. A measured risk in the hope of solving a problem he knew she desperately wanted solved.

First, though, he would do something he'd never done in his life: get advice.

Rose answered on the third ring.

"I need to speak to you," he said, "about something that Olivia has forbidden me to do."

Rose's response came slowly, as if she was bracing herself. "All right . . ."

"I've decided to do it anyway."

He could have sworn he heard the thump of Rose falling into a chair. Her breath hissed along the line. "Please tell me that's a joke."

"I never joke."

"Tell me you've started trying. It's a poor effort, but —"

"I don't appreciate being mocked."

"It isn't mocking. It's praying, by whatever gods one might pray to, that you are attempting a little levity, because the only other possible excuse would be that you've fallen down the stairs and hit your head."

"I am in full possession of my senses."

"Not if you're considering betraying Liv again. I know patience is not your strong suit, and yes, it's been a few months, but if you really are ready to give up, then may I suggest you just step back. Don't vent your frustrations on her."

"That's not what I have in mind," he said, his voice chilling. "At all."

"You've used up your chances with Liv, Gabriel, and—"

"I wanted your opinion on what I am about to do. On whether my reasoning is sound."

She went quiet. Then, "You want my support."

"What?"

"You want me to tell you that whatever you have planned, it's perfectly all right, and she'll have no reason to be angry."

Gabriel gripped the phone tighter, his words brittle now. "I was calling to ask your opinion, because you have, in the past, suggested that, before I do something imprudent where Olivia is concerned."

"You're right. I'm sorry. I—"

"No, *I'm* sorry. This was a mistake. The decision is, of course, my own, as are the consequences, and I did not intend to shift blame. I apologize for bothering you."

He hung up. Rose called back. He let voice mail answer. She called again. Then she texted. He shut off his phone, pulled on his jacket, and headed out.

Gabriel sat at the table, his hands folded on the top, gaze fixed on the door. It opened, and a guard prodded a woman in.

News reports claimed Olivia looked like her mother, but Gabriel saw a resemblance only in gestures and expressions. Olivia's jaw would set, and he'd glimpse Pamela. Or her eyes would ignite with a spark of ruthlessness, and there, too, lay her mother. Flares only, rising and falling away. It was the same with her father. Those moments when she'd be carefree and childlike, that was Todd. Or when she'd dig in her heels, her expression warning him there was no sense pushing. Mostly, though, he saw only Olivia, her own person, untethered to either parent.

When Pamela spotted her visitor, she stopped short. He waited, his hands still folded, gaze on her, no challenge in it. Yet there *was* challenge there. He'd told the desk that Pamela had rehired him, and now all she had to do was deny the ruse and this meeting would be at an end.

She looked at him. Then she nodded for the guard to leave.

"Misrepresenting yourself, Gabriel?" she said as she sat. "I shouldn't be surprised. I *am* surprised it took you so long to come." She leaned back in her seat. "Go ahead. Tell me exactly how you feel about me."

Pamela let the silence stretch until she shifted, unable to hold it. "Let me guess—it took so long because you were trying to figure out a way to make me pay, legally. To prove that I tried to have you framed for murder. Failing that, you've come to tell me that I'll pay, one way or the other."

He stayed exactly as he was, hands folded, gaze resting on her.

"Stop that," she snapped.

"I'm waiting for you to finish speculating on the nature of this visit. You seem to be enjoying it, so I will indulge you, though I must warn that, as you know, our time is limited."

"What do you want, Gabriel?"

"The question is what *you* want."

"What *do* I want?"

"Me."

A harsh laugh. "Your head on a pike, I suppose? No, sorry to disappoint. I want you out of my daughter's life, but it appears I can only wait until she comes to her senses and sees you for the manipulative son of a bitch you are."

"You want freedom," he said. "What do you need for that, Pamela?"

Her jaw set in a way he knew well.

"What do you need, Pamela?" he repeated.

Her jaw clenched so hard he heard her teeth grind. She barely pried her mouth open enough to spit, "Bastard. You enjoy this, don't you?"

"It's not pleasure. It's control."

"You take pleasure in control."

"No, I take comfort in it. It makes life easier. You need me. My counsel. My services. You need me to represent you—along with Todd—in your appeal. It's your only chance of seeing the outside of this prison."

"If your appeal frees Todd, it will free me."

Gabriel eased back, hands falling to his lap. "Not necessarily. That's what Todd wants, but if you think it's what your daughter wants, you are sadly mistaken. If you cannot be tried for James Morgan's death, she'll happily see you stay in here. What she wants is Todd's freedom. What I want to give her is Todd's freedom." He straightened, hands on the table again. "It's not going as well as I'd hoped."

"Are you actually admitting—?"

"You will wonder why I'm offering to represent you, and that is the answer. The last time I saw you, you said that if I took your case again, you might be able to recall more useful answers to our questions. I presume that still holds true?"

"It does."

"Then it seems . . ." He met her gaze. "That you win this round."

CHAPTER EIGHT

oan had asked us to meet him at an address in the Loop. I figured it was a high-rent residence there—Gabriel's own condo was nearby. But when I told Ricky the address, he said, "That's office space." He was right—it led to a skyscraper a few blocks from James's corporate offices. The route would have taken us right past, but Ricky detoured, saving me from those memories.

"I'm sure I wrote the address down right," I said as we looked up at the building.

"I'm sure you did, too. I'm wondering if we're being sent on a wild goose chase."

The building was dead quiet on a Saturday afternoon. Inside, we told the guard who we were there to see, and he sent us up to the twenty-third floor.

As we stepped from the elevator, we saw a corporate sign.

"Gwylio Consulting," Ricky read. "Welsh, I take it?"

"It means 'to watch, to look out for.' And the correct pronunciation is *guh-wi-luh-ee-oh*."

"Easy for you to say."

"Actually, it is. Once you know the pronunciation of the letters and the diphthongs, you can say any word, because—unlike English—there's only one way of pronouncing them."

"I'll take your word for it. The question is what Gwylio Consulting actually does. That sign's not giving me any clues. Nor is this." He waved at the reception area beyond the glass doors, which looked like any upscale corporate office.

"Security," said a voice.

We turned to see a man approaching. Early sixties. Physically fit and handsome enough that he still turned heads. Ioan emanated money and charm and good breeding, from his stance to his smile to his suit. Not exactly the kind of guy you'd picture riding a flaming black steed and dragging souls to the afterlife.

"What kind of security?" I asked.

Ioan's smile grew. "Whatever you need."

"Right now, I need answers."

"Then you've come to the right place, as I've been telling you for a while, Olivia." He led us to the door he'd come through. "It's good to see you, Ricky," Ioan said as he ushered us through.

Ricky nodded, and I could see Ioan's gaze following him, disappointed by his apparent lack of interest. Ricky *was* interested in his Cŵn Annwn heritage, but to betray that would give them the advantage.

As we walked down a row of offices, I looked through the glass walls. Nice offices, all of them. Executive sized, executive furnished. Tidy, but not unduly so.

"It looks real," I said.

"Hmm?" Ioan glanced over his shoulder at me.

"The offices. You've done a good job of making them look like they're actually being used."

"Probably because they are. It's a legitimate business. How else do we afford to live, if we do not work?"

With the exception of Patrick, the Tylwyth Teg didn't work. When I'd thought they were human, I'd presumed they lived off retirement savings and social security.

"They have nest eggs of a sort," Ioan said.

I shot him a glare. "You aren't supposed to do that."

"I'm not trying. But sometimes, if your thoughts are articulated clearly enough, I hear them anyway."

"How do we block that?" Ricky asked.

Ioan paused at a door and arched his brows.

"Yeah," Ricky said. "It's like the rabbit asking the wolf how to avoid being eaten. Except in this case, it's in the wolf's best interest to keep the rabbit happy."

"Is that how you think of yourself? Rabbits to our wolves?"

Ricky considered. "More like foxes to your wolves. Which means we're still in danger of being chomped."

"But you also have the hope of outwitting the larger predator."

"Outwit. Outrun. Whatever works to keep us one step ahead of you."

Ricky walked past as Ioan held open the door to an office. This one was huge, spacious, and well-appointed, with a sitting area outside the office proper. We took seats on a leather sofa.

"So the mind reading," Ricky said. "From what you suggested, we can prevent it by not forming clear thoughts. What's your range?"

Ioan only smiled at him indulgently.

"Short," I said. "I've only seen him do it when I'm right beside him."

"All right, then," Ricky said. "Short range. Difficult to maintain. Works best on clear thoughts. Got it." He looked at Ioan. "Thanks for your help."

Ioan's composure rippled, a trace of consternation showing through. After a moment he said, "The tusks."

Ricky took his out. We both had one—the tip of a boar's tusk, carved with writing too old to be deciphered. There were symbols, too. Mine had a sun and moon intertwined. Matilda's symbol—Cŵn Annwn and fae mingled. Ricky's had just the moon.

"Hold it," Ioan said.

Ricky clutched his tusk.

"There," Ioan said. "You're blocked. Now, back to the subject of employment. The Cainsville Tylwyth Teg do live primarily on their investments—investments from illegitimate capital gains. You're familiar with the Walsh family. You know how most of them make a living. Let's just say they come by their skills naturally. The fae have never met a human they couldn't fleece, and their sense of superiority makes them feel perfectly justified in doing so. The Cŵn Annwn prefer to earn a living as honestly as possible."

He took a seat. "However, as I realize that sounds like ethical superiority, I will also allow that we find interaction with humans more tolerable than do the Tylwyth Teg. We can assimilate more easily. That means something like this"—he waved around the office—"is easier for us to accomplish."

"And the fact that you don't age?" I said.

"We do. Or, more precisely, we age our glamours." He turned a frame on a table to face me. In it was a photo of a boy. "This is my son, also named Ioan. He's eleven. He lives in Florida with his mother. We're still close—or as close as we can be, living across the country. He'll go to college there, get a business degree there. When he is twenty-four, I will be taken by a sudden heart attack. He will come to the funeral. My associates—also my Cŵn Annwn pack— will convince him to stay on in the company, where he will quickly rise to my position."

"Because he *is* you," I said. "Your son is a fiction until you're old enough to be expected to retire, and then you'll appear *as* him and continue on."

"It's an elaborate ruse, but variations on it have worked for us for centuries." He eased back. "I *do* have a son, quite a bit older than this one. He does run his own business, though. Quite successfully. Though in his case, his fae blood might be a little more prominent, his line of business not quite so legitimate."

"My father," Ricky said.

Ioan went still. "Someone told you?"

"No, I suspected. You just clinched it. Now, Liv has questions—"

"You're angry that I didn't tell you sooner."

"No, I'm moving on."

Despite his demeanor, Ricky was pissed. He may have suspected this, but he wouldn't like hearing it confirmed and was trying to act as if it didn't matter. He wanted it to not matter, so I said, "Ricky's in trouble."

That got Ioan back on track. "Yes, of course. That's why you're here. What seems to be the problem?"

"The police are investigating Ricky in the disappearance of a man who was stalking him. A man who seems to be the target of the Cŵn Annwn."

Ioan frowned. Before he could ask, I explained. When I finished, Ioan leaned back in his chair and said, "Ciro Halloran . . ."

"Never heard of him?"

"No, I certainly have. He's been doing exactly what you saw in your vision: killing lamiae."

"Lamiae? Plural?"

"Two so far, we believe. That does put him in our crosshairs, so to speak. We haven't been able to catch him, though."

"Is it really that hard?"

"The Cŵn Annwn . . ." He straightened. "Explaining further might be seen as a violation of our contract. May I explain, on the understanding that your willingness to listen does not mean you are nullifying the agreement?" When I hesitated, impatience crept into his voice. "I'm not trying to trick you, Liv. That's their way, not ours."

I glanced at Ricky. He nodded, and I said, "All right."

"Good. Now, you know the Cŵn Annwn pursue killers who murder those with fae blood. There are additional restrictions. We are hunters, not assassins. We must set the hounds on our prey. We cannot take lives ourselves. Nor can we set the hounds on them in any milieu other than a traditional Hunt."

"So you need to lure your prey into the forest? That's a little complicated, isn't it?"

"We have ways. Charms and compulsions, like the Tylwyth Teg. They do not always work, so we have sought other methods. Loopholes, if you will."

"The brainwashing experiments with Chandler."

Ioan's lips tightened. "Not one of our finer moments. The theory was sound, allowing us to turn murderous partners against one another. It would also have allowed us to target those without a fae connection."

"Why?"

He looked surprised. "Because it's justice. The purpose of our existence."

And that, I suppose, was the only answer I'd get. The only one he could give. Their jurisdiction might be limited to crimes with a fae connection, but that did not keep them from seeing injustice elsewhere and wanting to correct the balance. Which is why they'd made the deal with my mother to kill murderers they couldn't touch.

Ioan continued. "My dealings with Chandler bore fruit, as you know, but they also caused the deaths of innocent people. I will not forgive myself for that. No more than I forgive myself for the danger he put you in. I knew Chandler was not a righteous man, but I thought he could be controlled. I allowed my zealousness to overwhelm my prudence. It won't happen again."

"And Halloran?"

"He appears immune to our compulsions. We've been seeking other remedies."

"But I had a vision of him being pursued by you guys."

Ioan frowned and then said, "We haven't caught up to him. Possibly that's a prognostic vision? Have you had those?"

"No, just visions of the past."

"I don't know what to say, then. I can only hope that it *is* a vision of the future, and we'll catch up to him soon. As for his interest in Ricky, though, that's very concerning. It seems—"

"Awfully coincidental?" I said. "Yep. Whatever's going on, though, I am going to investigate, because I can't take the chance of ignoring it. I'm here to ask for everything you know about Ciro Halloran."

"What about him?"

"Whatever you learned in the course of your investigation. Background info, current info, anything pertinent."

"None of that is pertinent," Ioan said. "He's killing fae. That is an undisputed fact. Details would simply get in the way. I can provide his home address, though."

"Already got it. How about the crimes, then? Begin with motivation. Why'd he do it?"

Ioan looked confused. "We're not a court, Liv. We know he's guilty. *Why* he's done it is meaningless."

"Can you tell me *anything* about the murders?"

"The facts, yes."

"Do that, then."

It was two blocks back to where Ricky had found street parking. He was quiet as we walked. When we reached the bike, I caught his hand, and he looked over and said, "I'm okay." When I kept giving him a look, he pulled me into a hug and whispered, "I'll *be* okay."

I eased back. "I know you suspected Ioan was your grandfather, but having it confirmed is a different thing."

Ricky made a face. "Yeah. Not in the way he thinks . . ."

"What's pissing you off is what he did to your grandmother and your father. He helped them financially, but there's more to supporting your kid than that. Which is a lesson your father learned well." Don had raised Ricky from birth, letting his mother continue med school and then go on to lead her own life and build her own family.

Ricky said, "When guys screw around and leave a kid behind, it's a thoughtless, stupid mistake. But the Cŵn Annwn do it intentionally, and I can't wrap my head about that. My grandmother was an unwed mom in the sixties. Ioan fucked up her life, and now he stands there, telling me the truth like I'm going to get all misty-eyed. I wanted to—" He broke off.

I hooked my fingers in his belt loops and tugged him closer. "You're angry. You have a right to be angry. Accept it. Redirect it." I leaned to his ear and whispered, "I kinda like the way you redirect it." I reached into the saddlebags and waggled a skirt I kept stuffed in there. "Ride?"

He chuckled and nodded.

We lay in a patch of forest, the temperature plummeting as the sun dropped. Ricky pulled me against him, his warmth wrapping around me.

We weren't dozing. The sex hadn't been strenuous enough for that. We just rested, as we usually did, finding a bit of forest and catching our breath, enjoying each other's company. The last time we'd been out, Ricky had joked that we should squeeze a blanket into the saddlebags, as the days grew shorter, autumn settling in to winter. I would, too, if it meant holding on to these moments for a few weeks longer.

As Ricky returned texts from his dad, I made a call. Gabriel didn't answer until the fourth ring. That gave me pause, but we'd parted on good terms, no need for concern. That's what it's like with Gabriel—even a moment's delay and I'm racking my brain, worrying that I've annoyed him in some way.

"Hey," I said. "Just calling with the post-Ioan update."

More silence, and when he replied, it seemed grudging. "Did it go smoothly?"

"As smoothly as can be expected with the Cŵn Annwn," I said, adding an extra note of brightness, as if that could even the balance. "I was going to suggest we pop by and update you, but you sound busy."

"I am."

I started to ask, *Is everything okay?* then bit my tongue. I could tell it wasn't, as easily as I could tell with Ricky earlier, but with Gabriel, asking even once makes me feel like a court-ordered therapist nagging him to share his feelings.

"We haven't heard anything from the police, have we? About Ricky?"

"I would tell you both immediately if I did."

"Okay, then," I said. "Do you want to wait until Monday?"

"Yes. Monday will be fine."

"All right. I'll see you at the office—"

"No," he said abruptly. "We should talk tomorrow. Will you be in the city?"

"We planned to spend the night in Cainsville."

"There, then. Ten tomorrow morning?"

"Is everything okay?" The words came before I could stop them, and I winced as they left my mouth, but even then I scolded myself for being so dramatic, always expecting the worst with Gabriel. There was nothing wrong with asking—

"Yes, of course," he said, his words clipped and cool.

"Right, well . . . I'll see you at ten."

He said something that was probably a goodbye but sounded more like a grunt before he hung up.

ARAWN'S MISTAKE

Ricky woke sharply. He lay there, in the darkness, listening hard, hearing only the sound of Liv's breathing. She slept with her back to him, his hand resting on her hip, her body close enough for him to feel the heat of it against the night breeze fluttering in through the open apartment window.

He'd close the window in a moment, but for now he snuggled against her back, settling whatever unease had woken him.

Ricky did not consider himself a troubled guy. His path might be unusual, but it was the only one that led anyplace he wanted to go. Sure, there'd always been the vague sense he was missing something important, but he wasn't the type to dwell on it. He'd set his course, and he'd hit the gas, and he'd roared headlong toward the goal. Then he met Liv. And he'd stopped for her. He couldn't help it. Stopped and circled back, and found something he hadn't been expecting. Clarity. A strange word to use, but when he was with her, the ride stopped in a freeze-frame, the world snapping into perfect focus.

He didn't understand how it worked with Arawn and Matilda and Gwynn. Were they destined to find one another? Or was it pure happenstance? Either way, he *had* been looking, even if he'd never realized it. Looking for something he needed. She was it, and Arawn was it. The answers to his unasked questions.

Liv often said that theirs was the most comfortable relationship she'd ever had. Again, maybe an odd choice of words, seemingly underwhelming. But there was no overestimating the importance of being completely comfortable with another person. No stress. No expectations. No sense that the other person would like you even better if you changed this or that.

There were, of course, stronger words he could use to describe their relationship. A crazy-giddy, mad-about-you, can't-wait-to-see-you romance that hadn't gotten any less crazy-giddy, mad-about-you, can't-wait-to-see-you after six months.

There was also the sex. There was absolutely no overestimating the sex. Liv was very sure of what she wanted and not afraid to ask for it, and also very eager to reciprocate. Confident and uninhibited, with an appetite to match his own. No, he couldn't overestimate the sex, and the thought of it had him kissing the back of her neck, his fingers sliding to her thighs.

The trick to waking a girl for sex was consideration. Kissing and touching, stroking her thighs, fingers moving up, waiting for a response. Too deeply asleep, and there'd be no reaction, which was a red light. But as he teased Liv's inner thighs, she sighed in sleep, her legs parting, and that was a green. Well, a yellow. Proceed with caution, because if she didn't wake, it meant she needed sleep more than sex. He eased his fingers up, stroking until she shifted more, and he slid his fingers into her and she sighed again, deeper now, snuggling back against him. Still asleep, but having very pleasant dreams and—

A yowl cut through the night.

Ricky stopped, and Liv made a noise in her sleep, clearly not pleased at the interruption to her dream. He pushed upright, peering around the dim room, his eyes adjusted enough to make out everything.

"TC?" he whispered.

The cat usually slept on the foot of Liv's bed. Even if things got raucous, he'd only glower at them and move farther from the epicenter of the disruption. The yowl came again, through the open window, distant, with a plaintive note.

TC had been inside when they went to bed. Ricky always got the impression he liked to stick close to Liv while she slept, watching over her.

The yowl came again.

"Lousy timing, cat," Ricky muttered. He leaned over and planted a kiss on Liv's shoulder, and then carefully slid from bed.

TC was not out front. Nor was he waiting at the rear door. Ricky checked anyway, twice, and then stood on the front porch, shivering in only his jeans as he surveyed the empty street. The yowl came again, muffled. TC was inside somewhere.

The cat had gone missing once before. He'd been trapped in the basement of the Carew house. Purposely trapped there, Tristan putting him in that basement so he could get into Liv's apartment undisturbed.

Which meant Ricky needed to get back to Liv, and they'd find the cat together. Yet when he reached the stairwell, TC yowled again, right on the other side of the wall.

Ricky walked to that apartment door and rapped. He wasn't surprised when no one answered. They'd never met one of Liv's neighbors. They'd only catch glimpses and hear voices and occasionally soft music.

When Ricky rapped again, TC yowled, and he reached for the knob. The door was unlocked. He eased it open, leaning in to call a hello, and—

A blast of ice-cold air hit him. Arctic cold.

A tinkling sounded, like icicles falling and shattering, and he pushed open the door. The blast of cold hit again, fresh and pure cold, like plunging into icy water, exhilarating and terrifying and—

A wizened hand yanked the door shut.

"What do you think you're doing, Mr. Gallagher?" Grace crossed her arms. "You'd better have a good excuse, poking around my building."

"TC's in there."

"Huh?"

"Liv's cat—"

"I know who TC is. Stupidest name ever. If that damned beast ran off, I can promise you he's not in there."

"I heard him yowling."

"Unless he's learned to pick locks, he's not in that apartment."

"It isn't locked."

She jangled the handle. "Yes, it is."

"Look, I don't care what's in there. Just bring TC out. I won't even peek."

"Peek at what? There's nothing inside but dusty old furniture."

He sighed. "Fine, Grace. Just let the cat out. I can't sleep with him yowling."

Her wrinkled face puckered. "What yowling?"

"Damn it, Grace. Just—"

A meow cut him short. TC came trotting from the stairwell. He saw Ricky and gave another meow, sounding exasperated now, as if to say, *There you are*. He walked over and planted himself in front of Ricky. Then he looked at the stairwell and meowed again.

"Someone's telling you to get back to bed," Grace said.

"He was in there. I heard him." Ricky turned to the apartment door.

Grace reached up and took hold of his chin. He let her tilt his face down to hers as she straightened to her full five feet and squinted up into his eyes.

"You got in after dinner last night," she said.

"Right. You were out front. I brought you a scone."

"I'm not senile, boy. I'm asking if you had dinner first."

"No, you were stating a fact, which I was confirming. A question is worded—"

She gave his chin a sharp shake and glowered up at him, but there was no malice in it, no honest annoyance, either. As if he was a kid mouthing back, and she was glad to see he had spine.

"I'm asking if you had anything to eat or drink in Cainsville."

"Then say that," he said. "No, I didn't."

"And in Olivia's apartment?"

"A beer and half a sandwich. Peanut butter, if that helps."

"Did you speak to anyone when you got here? *Other* than me?"

"No, I—" He stiffened. "Liv."

"Well, I'd hope you'd speak to her, though from the sounds of things you two are usually a little too busy for talking."

He wasn't going to ask how she could hear that from three stories down. He shook it off, said a quick good night, and started down the hall.

Grace was in front of him so fast she seemed to teleport into his path. "You're worried about Olivia. That's what you meant."

"Right." He started around her. "If TC wasn't down here, it was a trick to get me out of her apartment."

"No one will harm her here," Grace said as she followed him up the stairs.

He kept going, climbing two at a time. When he reached the top, he jogged down the hall, nearly tripping over TC, who loped along beside him.

"Fine," Grace called from the stairwell. "Check on her. Then get your ass back out here. We need to talk."

He went into the apartment. Liv lay exactly where he'd left her. TC hopped onto the bed and settled at the end.

Then he looked at Ricky, his eyes narrowed, as if to say, *Well, get in already.*

Ricky searched the apartment as TC wound around his legs, trying to get him back to bed where he belonged.

Ricky checked everything twice. Then he returned to the hall, where Grace waited.

"Satisfied?" she said. "You really are Cŵn Annwn. As faithful as a hound."

When he didn't reply, she peered up at him. "Not going to take offense at that?"

"Nope."

"I knew Arawn," she said. When he looked at her sharply, she gave a croaking laugh. "Oh, that gets a reaction. I was there, back in the day. I've met a couple of his embodiments, too. Pale imitations. I didn't see him in them. I do in you."

"Aspects," he said. "I have things in common with him. I won't deny that. But there are differences. I'm not going to make his mistakes."

"No?"

"Arawn was careless, reckless, and impulsive. Petty and self-absorbed. He couldn't stand to lose Matilda to Gwynn and that was about him, not what was best for her, which ultimately *would* have been best for him, to let Gwynn have her as his wife and keep them both as friends."

"Oh, you are clever. Far too clever for a biker."

"No, just clever enough to be a *good* biker."

She snorted a laugh. "All right, boy. But you're too hard on Arawn. He was young. The young make foolish mistakes for foolish reasons, like a girl they can't live without. You might seem young, too, but you're not. It's the part of you that *is* him that sees his folly, like an old man looking back on his youth."

"So you think I was lured out by someone trying to get to *me*, not Liv?"

"Clever boy."

"Then the upshot is that I need to learn from that. Don't go chasing yowling cats in the night. Question everything that could be luring me into trouble."

She chuckled. "You are indeed Arawn. Good. This will make things very interesting."

"Not sure I want to know what you mean by that."

She reached to squeeze his arm. "I mean that you are not a child, easily led from the path by those who wish to harm you. You are Arawn. Lord of the Otherworld."

"Thanks. I think." He glanced at the apartment door.

"Yes, yes. Your girl waits. But before you go, you said you won't make Arawn's mistake. What do you think that was?"

He told her.

She studied him. "And you think you can avoid that? That when the time comes, you'll be able to do it?"

"I'll have to, won't I?"

She nodded and let him go into the apartment.

CHAPTER NINE

The next morning, after I'd enjoyed a very pleasant wake-up, Ricky told me about his night's adventure.

"I hate to give you an extra reason to worry about me," he said. "But I figure you'd want to know."

"You figured right." I stretched and rolled out of bed. "Let's continue this conversation in the kitchen, with caffeine."

"Actually, I was going to suggest we head someplace that has the caffeine premade. Breakfast at the diner?"

"So if any of the elders were behind last night's stunt, they'll see you're well rested and unrattled? Good plan."

"Well, no, I thought you could use a good breakfast before a day of investigating." He pulled on his jeans. "But that's a good idea, too. Though I sometimes wonder if you aren't the one who should be aiming for bike gang leader. You're much better at figuring out the devious angles."

"I take that as a compliment."

"It is."

None of the elders were at the diner, so we had a fine and undisturbed breakfast. Back at my place, we hoped to check out that first-floor apartment, but Grace was already on the porch and followed us inside.

Gabriel arrived at ten. To give Ricky some quiet study time, Gabriel and I walked to the park and sat down to talk. Gabriel's mood from the night before hadn't changed, and finally I had to say, "You don't need to help me with this, Gabriel. Ricky hasn't been charged, so at this point I can dig around on my own. Which is my job." *And you clearly have other places you want to be*, I was tempted to add. That sounded pissy. I felt pissy, though. On Friday he'd wanted me to spend the night working on this together, and not even two days later it felt like discussing the same case was a huge imposition.

"You obviously have other things on your mind," I said.

He blinked hard, as if shaking off sleep. "No, I— Yes, something came up, in regards to . . ."

When he didn't finish, I said, "Something personal. Okay. I won't pry. But if you need to go, I understand."

"Personal?" He frowned, as if not recognizing the word. "No, I was going to say it was in regards to Todd's case. It's a legal matter, nothing to be concerned about, simply something I was working through. We can talk about it later." He pulled off his shades, letting them rest on his knee. "I'm fully engaged in this, and I apologize if it seemed as if I wasn't."

I was about to respond when someone hailed us.

Gabriel rose, murmuring, "I'll handle this. You can head back to the apartment."

"No, we'll get it over with," I said. "Hello, Ida. Walter."

They'd heard about the lamiae deaths and wanted me to stop investigating. Immediately. Which might sound suspicious, but their reasoning was exactly what I'd expect: this didn't concern me, so I shouldn't waste my time with it. I listened, I thanked them for their input, and Gabriel extricated me from the situation as soon as possible.

Back at the apartment, Gabriel fixed coffee and brought a plate of cookies from my freezer. They were Rose's cookies. She liked baking and liked sharing what she baked, handing me a box every other week, without a word, the first time having said only, "I have extra. They freeze well."

Gabriel didn't say, "Hey, do you want me to make a plate of those cookies you have in the freezer?" No more than he said, "Hey, do you guys want coffee?" Like Rose wordlessly handing me those boxes of cookies, this was Gabriel being thoughtful.

We did our research next. I tackled the obvious angle: the murders. According to Ioan, Halloran had killed two lamiae. That meant two teen prostitutes were dead, and I was surprised I hadn't heard about it. Working for years in shelters hadn't turned me into an activist, but it did raise my overall awareness, which means I tend to notice those articles. After an hour of searching, I realized I hadn't missed anything. The bodies apparently hadn't been found.

A social worker had noticed the girls' disappearances, though. I found a reference to that in a blog. A social worker who ran an outreach center for teen prostitutes said other girls had told her the two were missing and had asked for her help getting the police involved. The young woman went to the police but didn't get anywhere. What stopped me in my tracks, though, was the name of that social worker.

Aunika Madole.

Sister of Lucy Madole.

Sister-in-law to Ciro Halloran.

That set me off in a flurry of research. When I had a fuller picture of the Madole family, I shared it with Gabriel and Ricky.

"Their father died when the girls were young," I said. "Cancer. A profile piece on Aunika says insurance screwed them over, and the family was left in debt. Benefactors made sure her mother could continue running a nonprofit clinic for street kids. Their mother died two years ago. Also cancer. By that time, Aunika was working at the clinic full-time after getting her master's in social work."

"Did her sister have any connection to the center?" Ricky asked.

"According to the profile, Aunika said Lucy was 'instrumental' to it, providing donations and medical care."

"And two months ago she was stabbed to death a few blocks from the center," Ricky said. "Where her sister helped lamiae. And now the husband is killing lamiae."

"The obvious link is that Ciro somehow blames the lamiae for his wife's death. Or street girls in general, presuming he doesn't know *what* he's killing. He's murdering them, and his sister-in-law, ironically, is trying to bring those murders to the attention of the police."

"The alternative theory would be that Halloran murdered his wife," Gabriel said. "To do it, he lured her to that part of the city, which is easily accomplished if she has a prior connection to the area."

"The lamiae witnessed the murder, which gives him a motive to kill them. He makes it look ritualistic so their murders seem to *not* be connected to Lucy."

"Possible."

"Which is a working theory to add to any others," I said. "The point right now is that lamiae are dying and their killer is in the wind." I lifted my notebook. "Tomorrow I'll pay a visit to Ms. Aunika Madole."

CHAPTER TEN

I had no luck getting an interview with Aunika Madole during the day—her assistant blocked me—so I went by that evening instead. The drop-in center was in an industrial neighborhood that dated back to the days when the stench of livestock hung over Chicago and the city's gutters ran red with blood from the city's slaughterhouses. It was on the riverside, near equally old and equally empty docks. A tiny district—barely more than a few city blocks—nearly deserted at night but with city life thriving all around it.

From the looks of it, efforts had been made to revitalize this pocket, periodically, for the last hundred years—a building facade redone in a style from the forties, half a bar sign featuring a smoking girl with a sixties bob, long-dead neon from a later nightclub. The most recent effort was one strip of warehouses converted into office space, a weathered For Lease sign suggesting there'd been no new takers for years. Considering the stories I'd heard about the neighborhood, maybe the ghosts of dead mobsters didn't care to share their final resting place with the living.

There were a few lights on in those offices, as well as what looked like one successfully renovated building of condos for the brave and the antisocial. Madole's outreach center was located between the two, in a partially restored building that also housed an AA meeting place and a needle exchange. Cheap space for community services, near areas where those services would be needed.

Fog drifted along the street, the winds swirling it past. I could take that as an omen. It was certainly atmospheric. But the actual atmosphere was to blame for the fog, as a warm fall day gave way to a chilly night. With the window down, I could smell the river, adding to the night's haze.

A light shone from a window in the outreach center. There was also an older pickup truck parked out front. I got out of my car—I used the Jetta on the job, the Maserati not sending quite the right message for a PI. Rose keeps making jokes about some old TV show, calling me Magnum. I have no idea what she's talking about, but I humor her.

As I got out of the car, I realized how quiet and still it was. The surrounding empty buildings should be chock-full of transient residents, but if they were, those residents were as silent as . . . well, as silent as the dead.

As I thought that, a figure moved in the shadows, but when I peered into the foggy darkness, no one was there.

When my phone rang, I jumped like a scalded cat. I didn't recognize the number. I *did* recognize the caller's voice, as soon as she said my name.

"Pamela?" I said. "How did you get this number?"

"I only have a minute. If you really don't want to speak to me, hang up and let me call back to leave a message. I wouldn't contact you if it wasn't urgent."

"You aren't supposed to contact me at all."

"Don't. Please." Her voice was firmer than usual, and I realized there was something else odd about this call—no message warning me I was being contacted from an Illinois penitentiary.

Before I could comment, she said, "I need to see you. I know Ricky is in trouble, and that concerns me."

"Why? Don't you want him dead, too?"

A pause. Then her voice came, tense, as if she was struggling not to snap a reply. "No, I do not. I like Ricky."

"You've never met Ricky."

"I like what he's done for you. He makes you happy."

So did James, once upon a time. So does Gabriel, in his way. I didn't say that. After a while, no matter how valid the reasons, arguing starts to feel like petty bickering. So I told her to just get on with it, and she did. The summary? She'd heard about Ricky and had information. Critical information.

"Really, Pamela? Is that the best you can do?"

I hung up before she could answer. Then I turned off my phone, jogged across the road, and rapped on the door of the drop-in center. It creaked open at my touch.

I backed up and looked around, checking for omens the way other people dip their toes into water. And there it was: a dead crow behind a trash bin. Dead bird equals trouble. A dead *crow* ups the ante.

I took out my gun, and called, "Hello?" I eased through the doorway.

The room was lit by a single bulb, the light wavering. There were posters on the walls. Not cutesy motivational ones, like that damned cat exhorting you to just "hang in there." These were portraits of girls on the street. Half of them were accompanied by later photos of the same girls— one in a graduation cap, one laughing with a toddler, another behind a desk, another in an art studio. Before-and-after shots. Some of the pictures had no second portrait, the girls still on the streets. Two had a different sort of follow-up—a tattered Missing poster for one and a gravestone for the other. Yet even those were beautiful shots, respectful and haunting, reminders of the fates that could befall lost girls.

Lost girls never matter.

As I heard the lamia's words, my gaze fell on one of the portraits. It was the older girl I'd seen die. The photographer had caught her in motion, turning away, wide-eyed, like a rabbit that had thought it was hidden if it stayed perfectly still. A fitting portrait for a kid on the streets, feeling invisible, startled when someone notices her. Equally fitting for a fae, and in that portrait I swore I could see a shimmering glimpse of something not quite human.

"I knew you'd come back," a voice said.

I turned. It was a woman. Tiny—maybe five-two and a hundred pounds. A few years older than me, she wore a cropped leather jacket, faded jeans, and sneakers, her black hair gathered in a ponytail.

"Aunika Madole," I said, tucking my gun into my back pocket. "Yes, I—"

She threw water at me.

I looked down at my dripping jacket and up at her. I thought she mistook me for an intruder and had thrown the only thing she had on hand—a glass or bottle of water. Except she held what looked like an antique metal flask. And she wasn't grabbing her cell phone to call 911. She was staring at me, intently, as if expecting to see something.

"Holy water?" I plucked at my damp shirt. "Seriously? You threw *holy water* at me? Sure, I've heard the demon-spawn jokes, given who my parents are—"

She ran through the doorway. I went after her. In the middle of the room she spun, with a gun in her hand now . . . only to see me holding mine on her. Her gaze dropped to the threshold, and I followed it to see an odd metal plate.

I backed up, crouched, and put my hand on the metal. It felt abnormally chilled, and the tingle ran down my arm. Cold-forged iron. It wouldn't kill faeries on contact, but they'd be unable to cross it. I looked at the metal bottle in her hand. Not holy water. Some other kind of liquid detection.

I took out my switchblade, flicked the penlight part, and shone the beam on my face. "Does better lighting help?"

She went still. Then she backed to the light switch and turned it on. I put away the knife and flipped open my wallet. "Olivia Taylor-Jones."

"Taylor . . ." Her eyes widened. "You're . . ."

"Yeah, hence the demon-spawn jokes. Totally groundless. I'm working as an investigator for Gabriel Walsh."

Her head shot up, her eyes narrowing.

"You know *his* name, then."

"He's the son of a bitch who defended—"

"—some scumbag you think didn't deserve a defense. Yep, that's my boss. Which is not why I'm here. I was going to give you a story about how I was visiting the prison with him and heard some chatter about a guy killing teen prostitutes, but apparently we can cut through that bullshit. You thought I was fae."

"What?"

"Fae. Faeries. You thought—"

She forced a laugh. "A faery? Really?"

"Right, and that"—I pointed at the metal inset under the door—"isn't cold-forged iron. Nor is that flask. You just happen to be throwing water at strangers and seeing if they can cross an iron plate. I passed. I'm not fae. However, those girls who went missing are another story. It's also why you have the plate at the back room and not the front door. Because you don't want to keep *them* out."

"I have no idea what you're talking about."

I sighed and put away my wallet. "So much for cutting through the bullshit. Do you want me to keep pretending I'm investigating these missing girls on a whim?"

"I want you to get the hell out."

"Nope. Sorry. Can we lower the weapons, at least? Please? I suspect you're better at shooting a camera than a revolver."

"Want to test me?"

"I already did. You're holding it wrong, for one thing. You've had some basic training, but I'm pretty sure I'm"—I fired at a wall calendar, putting a bullet through today's square—"a better shot."

"Are you crazy?"

"I'm not the one testing for fae intruders. Maybe we can talk about that."

"Maybe I can tell you to get the hell out of my—"

"You already did. I declined. Now, I understand that this conversation is making you very nervous, but how about we go grab a coffee and talk."

"You're kidding, right?"

"Two girls are missing," I said. "They're dead. I'm sorry if you didn't know that, but they are. I'm trying to stop the guy who's doing it." *I won't mention that it's your brother-in-law.* "If you want to test my motives, go ahead, but I'd really rather do that over coffee. This"—I waved my gun—"is just awkward. And kind of rude."

"I . . ." She trailed off, looking rather like someone who has stepped into a fae realm herself.

"You can check my ID," I said. "But since it could be fake, just take out your phone and google me. You'll get plenty of pictures. Further research will reveal that I've officially solved four murders in the past six months. All were related to that." I pointed at the cold-iron inset. "Which we can talk about, or we can just pretend you know nothing about fae and proceed from there. But I'd really like to get to work finding a killer. So . . . coffee?"

"Twelve hours," she said.

"What?"

"Give me twelve hours to check out your story."

"You don't need—"

"Then we don't talk."

I started to reply when a board creaked overhead.

CHAPTER ELEVEN

A unika and I went still.

"What's up there?" I whispered.

"My apartment."

"And I'm guessing you don't have visitors tonight?"

"Just you." She started backing away, gun still raised, her attention on the ceiling as she tracked the steps. "Get out of here. I can lose them."

"Lose who?"

She didn't answer, just turned and ran, silently, into the next room. When I went after her, she said, "Damn it, girl. You really don't give up."

I lifted both my gun and switchblade. "Whatever this is, I can help."

She loped down the hall. Halfway to the end, she stopped and cocked her head. Then she eased open a closet door, prodded me inside, followed, and shut the door. I was still mid-step when the light went out, and I bashed into a wall. I clicked on my penlight.

"We're hiding in a closet?" I said.

Aunika waved me into the corner and pulled something on the floor. A panel opened.

"You have an escape hatch?" I whispered.

"Doesn't everyone?"

She reached inside, pulled out a flashlight, and started down. I crouched and shone my penlight to see a ladder. I started after her.

"You need to—" she began, then stopped as she saw I was already shutting the hatch behind me.

The ladder only went about six feet. When I stood, I could reach up and touch the ceiling. The dirt floor was damp, and I could smell the river and hear water trickling down a distant wall.

As I looked around, I said, "Shadowy mystery stalkers? Hidden escape hatches? Creepy subterranean tunnels? My mother tried to get me to take social work for my master's. I told her it was boring. I was so wrong."

Aunika snorted and set off, saying, "Keep your voice down."

"Because sound echoes. Radio silence, then."

"Don't strain yourself."

I looked around as we walked. It was indeed a subterranean tunnel. Like *The Count of Monte Cristo*, locked away in a dungeon, digging your way out with a rusty spoon, and creeping along the rat-infested warren of abandoned passages deep below the prison. At least *this* one didn't seem to have rats.

I ogled as we went, touching a rusted metal pipe, leaning into a dark side passage.

"This isn't a sightseeing tour," Aunika whispered back.

"Life is a sightseeing tour," I said. "By the way, do you know how old these tunnels are? They're definitely not part of the original city system for transporting goods to and from the railroad. For those, they had to put in a foot of concrete and run sump pumps to keep them dry." I touched a rivulet, running through a groove at least a half-inch deep, worn by decades of such rivulets. "They really skimped here. Tunnels built for nefarious purposes, I'm guessing. Or by government contract."

She shook her head and continued on. When she heard a beep, she looked back to see me getting out my phone.

"Taking pictures now?" she said.

I shook my head. "Calling my boyfriend."

"You need a guy to come rescue you?"

I waggled my gun. "I have that part covered, but given the situation, I'm going to let someone know where I am. I'm a feminist; I'm not an idiot. And . . . no cell service. Naturally."

A pipe clanged ahead. When I went still, Aunika looked at me and said, "Now what?"

"You didn't hear . . ."

Her expression told me I didn't need to finish that sentence. I started forward, only to catch the whisper of voices. When asked if she heard them, she screwed up her face.

"Shit, you really are crazy, aren't you?"

I was about to answer when another voice came, speaking a language I didn't recognize, but loud enough that there was no way Aunika wouldn't hear. A shadowy figure slid past ahead. When she didn't see that, I cursed under my breath.

"What now?" she said.

"Nothing. Just . . . ignore me."

"I'm trying to. Really, really trying to."

She resumed walking. I caught snatches of voices and saw more streaks of movement as a vision encroached on the world of the living. That was *not* a good omen. It meant I was teetering on the edge of a full-blown vision.

Not now. Please, not now.

I kept my eyes open, as I mentally recited Dickinson's "There Is Another Sky," but stopped short because, well, there was another place here, another world, and I was desperately trying to stay out of it. I switched to Dylan Thomas's "Do Not Go Gently into That Good Night," which seemed thematically appropriate. The voices faded, and I stayed firmly in these subterranean tunnels, my penlight beam shining on Aunika's back.

"You doing okay?" she asked.

I nodded, and she peered at me, as if not quite convinced. "I'm being quiet," I said. "It *is* a strain."

She shook her head. "The exit is just ahead. I'll go up first. Keep the light down and let me make sure it's clear."

We reached another ladder, this one wooden and not nearly as sturdy. As she pushed open the hatch, I moved to the bottom, partly to defend her but also to race up that ladder if she tried to lock me in. But she only went through the hatch and then shone her light around before motioning for me to follow.

We came out in a different building. The night wind whistled through holes in the stonework. That gave me pause. Every abandoned place I've been in lately has spelled fae trouble. But when I looked around, all I saw was a cavernous room with rotting crates and barrels and holes in the roof.

I got about five steps, following Aunika, when I heard the voice again, louder now, a man saying, "Put it over there," and another man, with a younger voice, replying in the other language, which I now recognized as Gaelic.

The first man snapped, "You're in America now. Speak American," and the young man said, "It is called English."

A smack, as if the older man had slapped him. "Don't be smart, you mug. You want to go downstairs, don't you?"

"Yes, sir. I would very much like to go downstairs."

The older man chortled. "I bet you would. Then do as you're told. Finish loading those barrels in the cart and haul them to the wharf. We've got about three hours of night left."

"But it is only midnight."

"And we've only paid the coppers to look the other way until three. Now dry up and move!"

Bottles clinked. Prohibition? The conversation and the slang suggested it, but why the hell would I be getting visions of Prohibition-era smugglers? When I see past events, they're fae memories, locked deep in my brain and poked by my environment.

"We go this way," Aunika whispered, pointing. "And then run across to the building next door. That should get us far enough—"

I cut her short with an impatient wave.

Her eyes narrowed. "I'm trying to . . ." She trailed off as she heard what I had—the sound of actual movement, like a footstep on old concrete.

I pinpointed where the noise came from and took a slow step in reverse. Then another. Backing toward the wall, because there was no place to run.

Aunika saw me and did the same, and when a man slid from the shadows, he had two guns pointed at his chest.

I looked at him and my brain shot out *biker* and *cop*. Yes, there's a world of difference between the two, yet there is an uncomfortable similarity, too. Paramilitary organizations, insular, male-dominated, an edge of machismo, devotion to the job . . . The guy had the military stance and the bold smirk, that preternatural sense of calm from a guy with two guns pointed at him. A man accustomed to having guns pointed at him. From which side of the law, though? A tattoo peeking from under a short sleeve looked military . . .

"Nicely done, girls," the man said. "But you do know you're surrounded, right?"

"Good," I said. "Have your friends step out and say hello."

The shadows stayed still and silent. Aunika snorted. I slid her a look, one that said not to be too certain he was bluffing. My gut told me he wasn't.

"So, little Aunika has a friend herself," the man said. "Or did you hire a bodyguard? If so, you have excellent taste, sweetie."

"Stop talking like you know me," she said. "Like I have the first damned clue what's going on here."

"Don't play the innocent for your friend. We've been in communication for a while, and you know exactly why I'm here."

"Stalking me and leaving cryptic messages is not *communication*. I have no damned idea what you people want, and I'm starting to think you have me mistaken for someone else."

"Aunika Madole. Daughter of Gwen and Grant Madole, both deceased. Sister of Lucy. Also deceased."

Aunika went still. "Does this have something to do with Lucy's murder? I've been trying to get a hold of Ciro for days."

There was a flash and a bang as some kind of strobe hit the floor. Aunika fell back, seeming to move in slow motion with the strobing light. I recovered fast, my gun never wavering, but the guy stumbled himself, as if equally caught off guard.

"Run!" I yelled to Aunika as she got her footing.

I went one way, she went the other. I dove behind barrels, expecting gunfire. The only noise that rang out, though, was footsteps. Two pairs, coming from opposite directions. I kept moving, doubled over, as fast as I could move. When I reached a broken window, I vaulted through it. As usual, my move was a bit less graceful than I might have hoped, but I made it out. Even managed to land without twisting my ankle.

A second building twenty feet away was the obvious choice, but I spotted a broken basement window on the building I'd just come out of. I waited until I heard a set of running footfalls. Then I pitched a chunk of brick toward the neighboring building. A man shouted, "She's next door."

I slid through the broken basement window, back into the building I'd left. A fine escape plan, except that I failed to check before going through. There was enough glass left in the frame to slice open my arm as I dropped. I fell, hissing, and crouched there, cradling my arm.

Shit, it was a good gash. Probably stitch-worthy. I tugged off my jacket and shirt. Backing into the shadows, I kept an ear open as I ripped my shirt and bound the gash. Then took out my phone. I had enough bars to make a call. I went to speed-dial Ricky . . . and my phone vibrated.

Gabriel didn't even wait for a hello. "Did you get a chance to speak to Ms. Madole?"

"Mmm, kind of."

"Good. Can you talk now?"

This wouldn't be the first time he just happened to call when I was in trouble. Gabriel has a sixth sense for trouble, and he would say it's honed from his years on the street, but I suspect there's a sprinkling of fairy dust in it, too.

"I'm in a . . . bit of a spot," I said.

He exhaled, as if in relief. Something *had* prompted him to phone. That relief, of course, only lasted a second, his voice tightening as he said, "Where are you?"

Not *What's wrong?* or *Do you need help?* Simply *Where are you?*

Tell me where you are, and I'll be there.

I eased farther into the room, watching the bars to be sure I still had cell service. Then I gave him a version so condensed that even Ricky would have been asking questions to sort it out. Gabriel only said, "Where are you *precisely?*"

The chime of his car door sounded. The Jag roared to life as he said, "Olivia?"

"An empty building to the left of the drop-in center. Maybe one or two down. I'm in the basement. Text me when you get close."

"Ten minutes."

"It's ten miles through the city."

"Ten minutes. I'll text you."

CHAPTER TWELVE

After I got off the phone, I planned to head back into the tunnels to wait until I could reasonably expect a text from Gabriel. But my room led to another just like it, which in turn led . . . nowhere. There appeared to have been a doorway, at one time, but it had been sealed off by a pile of wood and dirt and brick, as if the ceiling had collapsed.

I climbed onto the mound of debris. My injured arm protested, but it only took a few minutes to clear enough to squeeze through. I poked my penlight through, making sure I wasn't going to drop into a pit. I saw a room with a floor. Good enough. I wriggled through, touched down, and my foot slid, sending me falling backward, arms windmilling uselessly.

I dropped onto something both hard and soft and stinking of mold and mildew, and when I put my hands down, I recoiled as I touched . . . well, I wasn't sure what I'd touched, only that I didn't particularly want to do so again.

I peered down to see the side of a rusted metal bed, and a memory flashed, of the abandoned mental hospital, those rows of metal beds and the woman from my vision—my great-aunt—lying in one of those beds, her eyes gouged, tongue cut out, and the horror of that memory had me leaping up. My foot slid again, and I went back down on the bed, my left hand gripping what I'd touched before—the moldering remains of a thin mattress. My right hand had landed on something hard and knobby. When I saw what I was holding, I yelped and scrambled, shoes sliding on the slimy muck of the floor, and I had to grip the side of the metal bed and propel myself up. Then I stood there and looked down at the bed—at the body in the bed, a skeleton covered in tatters of cloth.

I lifted my penlight and saw two other beds, two other skeletons. I shone my beam over the one I'd landed on. My fall had dislocated the hip bone, and the left leg now lay separate from the body. What I'd grabbed had been the arm, and when I'd jumped, I hadn't let go fast enough and I had pulled that away, too. The ulna and radius bones now hung from the side of the bed. I crouched and lowered my light for a better look, and sucked in breath when I saw why it dangled there.

Enough remnants of flesh remained to hold the forearm and hand bones together, and they hung suspended by manacles. When I shone my light over the other two bodies, I saw each had one hand in a rusted metal manacle.

Handcuffed to the beds.

The nearest body wore a tattered and grayed nightgown. The skull still had long dark hair. I was moving toward it when I tripped over something, and I shone the light down to see another corpse on the floor, also skeletonized, wearing enough clothing for me to suspect this one was male. I crouched beside it. He'd fallen facedown, hands outstretched over his head, as if—

"Well, go on, then," a voice said. "You've earned it, boy. Have your fun."

A door clanged and the body vanished. Beside me, something hissed, and I turned to see a dark-haired girl, no more than seventeen, wearing a thin shift. She sat on the edge of the bed with one hand cuffed to it. She leaned forward, her lips curled back as she hissed.

"Oh, enough with you," a man said as he walked in. He raised a metal baton. At the press of a button, it jolted to life, electricity flashing. The girl pulled her legs up into the bed, her arms wrapping around them as she stared at the man, her eyes black with hate.

Two girls sat on the other beds, both also dark-haired and dressed in shifts. They kept their gazes down, defiance gone, like dogs that have been whipped often enough to know it does no good.

At the sound of dirt under boots, a young man walked in. He was maybe eighteen, light-haired and blue-eyed. He took a step toward the first girl and the man chuckled.

"Not that one, boyo. Wait until you've had some time in the saddle before you ride that filly." The man waved the prod. "Take the little gal there. A good, gentle ride for a virgin."

"I'm not a virgin," the young man said, with a lilting accent.

The man chuckled. "Whatever you say. Just take my word for it and start with her. You can always come back for the others. It'll cost you, though. This is your only free ride, and then you pay." The man winked. "You'll get the employee discount, though."

The young man stepped toward the smallest of the girls. I'd like to say she looked fourteen, but she didn't, and he stopped short, revulsion glimmering in his blue eyes.

"Now, now, boyo," the man said. "This is what you wanted, isn't it? Why you worked so hard loading up the barge? She's not really a child. Not even human." The man reached out and tapped his cattle prod to the smallest girl's bare leg and she jumped, hissing and baring her teeth.

"I know what they are," the young man said.

"Well, you seemed to need a reminder. You don't like seeing them chained up, but they're like dumb animals, without the sense to stay. We give them what they need, and they don't even have the decency to be grateful."

"I'll . . . I'll take the young one."

"Like I said, she's not young. She just looks it. Which you will appreciate a lot more when you're my age." The man cackled and leaned back against the wall. Then he smirked. "Oh, I suppose you want some privacy."

Before the young man could answer, his boss smacked him on the shoulder.

"I know, I know. You don't want an audience. Just holler for me to let you out. We lock them in, just in case. And don't be taking too long or I'll know you're trying for a double."

He opened the door and turned to leave, and the young man lunged, blade in hand, driving it into his boss's back.

The older man gasped. His mouth worked. Then he teetered and toppled face-first to the floor.

"Just because they are not human does not make them animals, you filthy whoremonger," the young man said, bending to pull out the blade. "They are *sidhe*, and if you treated them proper, they would have treated you proper, too. That is how it works." He turned to the girls. "Not that I expect anything for doing this. It is the Christian thing to do."

The girls only stared at him. Then the oldest hissed, lips curling back.

"That's right. You are foreign *sidhe*. You speak a foreign tongue." He laid the blade on the ground and said, slowly, "I am not going to hurt you. I am going to let you go. Do you understand?"

He straightened, his hands out, the lamiae watching him carefully. Behind him, the older man rose, silently pushing up, his face contorted in pain. He held a gun.

"Prosecho!" the oldest lamiae said, pointing.

The other two both shouted warnings, but before the young man could turn, the older one fired. The bullet hit the boy square in the chest, and he went down.

"You stupid shant," the man said, bloody froth flying from his lips. "You hoped if you let them go, you'd get all the free barney-mugging you wanted?"

"No," the boy wheezed. "I just . . . It was right . . . Respect . . ."

The man snorted. "Respect? Them? Dirty little whores?" He toddled to the door, barely able to stay upright. Then he patted his pocket, took out a key, and locked it from the inside. "How's this for respect? May that be your dying thought, you dumb mug. That you just killed your poor little faeries . . . and they are going to take a lot longer to die than you or me."

With that, the man crashed to the ground, and the boy's eyes closed, and the girls started to shriek.

CHAPTER THIRTEEN

The vision snapped, but I still heard the girls shrieking as I spotted a fifth skeleton, that of the older man, slumped just inside the door.

"You hear them, don't you?" a voice whispered at my ear. "Their screams."

I turned to see the young man standing behind me as he gazed at the skeletons of the girls.

"I hope *he* hears them," he said, glaring at the dead old man. "I hope he *still* hears them in hell."

He turned to the door. "Others heard. They came around, hoping to buy a poke, and they found that door locked, and they heard the poor *sidhe*—heard them crying and wailing and begging. And they walked away. Did not want to get involved. And then, after the *sidhe* passed, one returned."

My penlight faded, taking the room into darkness, and when it surged bright again, the boy was gone, and the girls lay in their beds, and—

One glimpse of them and I squeezed my eyes shut and wished for the skeletons again. Cold, expressionless skeletons. Horrifying in their way, but not nearly so much as this, the image burned on the back of my eyelids. The girls, in their beds, contorted in their last agonies of death, chunks ripped from their own arms, as if they'd tried to chew their way free. The two smaller ones with their eyes closed, the smallest's face screwed up as if squeezing her eyes shut against the horror of her own death. The oldest had her eyes wide, hate and defiance, as if she refused to look away, refused to hide from what had happened, faced death snarling, lips curled back in a final hiss, her body pitched forward, throwing herself against her bonds with her last breath.

Then I heard the sound at the door. A low keening that set my hairs on end. It was the same sound I'd heard in the forest, watching the lamiae mourn their dead. I walked to the door, stepping over the body of the man at its base. When I reached for the knob, my fingers passed right through, and I stepped into the hall to see two girls—two lamiae—one crouched outside the door, the other standing with her hands against it, leaning forward, her cheek on the wood.

"We could not find you, sisters," she whispered, first in Greek, the words translating in my mind. "We searched and we searched, and you were lost, and now you are lost forever, and we cannot even get inside to put your bodies at rest."

She scratched her hand down the wood, splinters digging in, trails of blood left behind. Then a distant board creaked. A thump followed and a man called, "Hello?" The girls went still, one choking back a hiss, and when they turned, the grief drained from their eyes, leaving those blank expressions I'd seen on the others.

A man appeared, carrying an old-fashioned flashlight. He saw the girls and stopped.

"Oh," he said. "You're out."

Even seeing the two sets of lamiae for only a few moments, I could tell these weren't the same girls. Considering that he seemed to be one of the johns, I'd sure as hell hope he'd have taken a closer look at the bound and captive girls he was screwing, but I guess that's naive of me.

"Yes." The girl on the floor rose, pulling the word into a sibilant hiss. "He lets us out now. We have learned to appreciate what we have. We were just coming back for the night."

"Oh, well, that's good. So the trouble's over, then." His head bobbed as he put on a false-hearty smile and strode toward them. "Good to hear, good to hear. Even better to hear that you're back for the night." He winked.

The girl smiled. "We are glad to be back. Now that the trouble is over. You heard it, did you not?"

"I . . . came a couple of weeks ago and there was something going on down here."

"Crying. You heard us crying for help."

The man shifted, glancing over his shoulder. "I . . . I don't know what I heard. It's none of my business. You're out now. He's letting you walk around, so whatever it is, it was settled. No harm done."

"No harm done," the girl repeated, slowly, as if tasting the words, and if I'd been the guy, as soon as I heard that tone, I'd have run.

But he only forced an awkward chuckle and said, "Right. Now, is your, uh, boss here?"

"No, he is not." The girl walked over. "He will be, soon. You can wait if you like. But if you do not wish to wait . . ." She laid her hand on his hip. "We will take your money. What you pay him for one, you can pay us for two."

The other girl sidled over, struggling a little more to smile. She walked up on his other side and buried her face— and her expression—against him as both their hands slid to his crotch.

"Both?" he said, breathing hard already.

"Is that a problem?" the girl said.

"N-no, of course not."

"You do not have to do it two times. We will both please you." She unbuttoned his trousers and the other girl reached inside. Then she did the same. "We will both enjoy you. Then you can enjoy both of us. First one and then the other, for as long as you can hold out . . ." She lifted on tiptoes to whisper. "We know ways to help you hold out."

"H-how long will he be gone?"

"About an hour. Is that enough?"

"Y-yes. Please. Yes."

"The room is locked, though. We need to wait for him to open it. If you want to wait for a bed."

"N-no. No. This—this is fine."

"Right here?"

"Anywhere," he moaned. "Anywhere."

She slid her hand from his trousers and pulled them open, then lowered herself to her knees. He tried to look down, but the other girl reached up to kiss him and put his hand under her blouse. Her companion worked on him for a few moments. Then she pulled back, and when she did, I saw her teeth. Sharp white teeth. The other girl stopped kissing his lips and moved down to his neck. Her companion lowered her head to his crotch again, hesitating one split second and then diving in, fangs out.

The man let out a terrible scream, and tried to fling the other girl back, but she dug her own fangs into his neck, ripping out chunks of flesh, tossing them aside, blood spurting and gushing, the man screaming.

"You scream," the one girl said, lifting her bloodied mouth. "Just like they did. You heard them, and you did nothing. Now I hope they hear you. I hope they hear you and they smile."

The scene faded and the young man turned to me. "The *sidhe* are not always kind or good. That is not their way. No more than it is ours sometimes. Hurt them and they hurt you. Help them and they help you back."

"And these ones?" I nodded at the skeletons. "Is there any way to help them now?"

"Put them at rest. In the forest. Their kin will appreciate it."

"And you?"

A wry smile. "I would rather be buried in consecrated ground, but it does not seem to have done me any harm. Look to the little *sidhe*. They did not deserve this."

"Neither did you," I said, but he'd already disappeared.

I staggered back and fell right through the door, into the next room. The girls in the beds were skeletons again, like the two men on the floor.

A thump sounded from the next room. I went still, my gun rising.

"Olivia?"

I climbed back over the rubble to see Gabriel crouched at the basement window, his arm and shoulder through it, knocking against the frame with a glower, as if he could break it wider.

"You won't fit," I said.

He glowered at me, as if the situation was now my fault for choosing too small a window. Then he looked away quickly, and I remembered I was wearing my jacket over my bra. I zipped it up.

"Sorry," I said. "My shirt was sacrificed for emergency first aid."

His gaze traveled over me, assessing. My arm was hidden under the jacket, and he said, "Ms. Madole?"

I made a noise that could be taken as assent. His mouth tightened, as if now annoyed that I'd given up my shirt for an injured stranger.

"Come, then," he said with an impatient wave, and I hesitated, trying to get a better look at his expression. The shadows and the night stole it, leaving my chest tightening, and as I made my way to him, all I could think about was the last time I'd been in trouble and I called him.

But he's here now.

Yes, and he doesn't look pleased about it.

When I walked over, he reached down for me, only to realize his hand fell short. He grumbled and scowled, as he pushed his head and arm through the window.

"I can get out," I said. "Just back up."

He ignored me and reached down far enough for me to

grab his wrist. I started taking it with my right, and a stab of pain reminded me why that wasn't a good idea. I gripped it with my left instead, and used my feet to scramble up the rough wall as he hauled me through.

"Use both hands," he said.

"I—"

He grabbed my other wrist, and I hissed against the wrenching pain. He didn't notice, grunting with exertion as he hauled me out. Once I was through, I bent over, pretending to catch my breath, as I bit my lip and tried not to whimper at the pain.

"What's wrong?" he said.

"Pulled a muscle. Give me a second—"

He took hold of my arm and pulled it straight. His hand closed around my biceps, and a yelp escaped me. He yanked my arm out of my sleeve. It was wet with blood.

"Goddamn—!" He bit the uncharacteristic curse short and took a moment, fingering the makeshift bandage, getting his temper in check before saying, "Next time you are injured, Olivia, please inform me before I inflict additional damage. Do you have anything in the car? A proper first aid kit?"

I shook my head.

He made a noise, like a growl, gripped me by my good arm, and started leading me down the lane like an errant child.

"I'm sorry," I said.

"Considering the number of times we've needed first aid, we should both have a kit in our vehicles. We'll pick those up tomorrow. For now, I have no idea where to find the nearest pharmacy. I don't know this neighborhood, and I suspect you don't, either, so I would appreciate it if you used your phone to search for one while I watch for trouble."

"I meant I'm sorry for calling."

"You did not call. I did."

"I know, but I asked you to come—"

"You did not ask. You did not call or ask."

"You're angry," I said. "Is it—?"

"I understand why you did not call, Olivia. I understand why you did not ask. If I am angry, it is not with you. Now, quickly, please. We cannot be sure your attackers have left, and our voices echo—"

A woman's scream cut him off. I yanked from his grip.

"Aunika," I said.

"Perhaps. If so, let's hope she can take care of herself, because you are injured."

"I'm not leaving if—"

"Yes, you are. She was clearly the target, and I realize you won't like abandoning her to her fate, but it is no more than she did to you. You are injured. She left you."

"I cut my arm on the window after we split up—at my instigation."

"No matter."

He gripped my arm and resumed walking. When I stood my ground, he stopped and glared at me.

"I know you don't care," I said. "I do, but not enough that I'd go tearing after her if I was in danger of bleeding out. My arm is temporarily fine, and I'd like to at least assess the situation before we leave."

"Assess," he said after a moment. "That is all, correct? We assess the situation."

"Umm, the purpose of assessing is to make a decision, meaning it's not actually an end point in itself, Gabriel."

His look said that if he wished it to be an end point, it damned well would be, but he only followed me in the direction of the scream.

CHAPTER FOURTEEN

We wove through the maze of industrial decay, keeping away from the street lights as we headed to the river. The fog made that even tougher, as it settled in, increasingly thicker as we approached the water's edge.

We came out at a rotting wharf, half fallen away. A barge floated past with its lights smothered by the fog. I watched it go by as Gabriel hovered behind me, ready to snatch me back if I leaned closer to the edge.

When I caught the sound of voices, I whispered, "Do you hear that?" and he nodded. I backed up to the building and crept along it toward the voices. Gabriel stayed behind me. The moment one of those voices came clear, though, he had me by the arm and a stifled yelp from me had him whispering something that could have been an apology. He gripped the other arm and pulled me behind him. I peered around him into the night.

"—know what we want," a man was saying. It was the same man we'd pulled our guns on earlier. "Stop playing this game."

"I have no idea what you people want. If you'll just tell me—"

An *oomph*. A yowl of pain and a shout. Then running footfalls and "Damn it. Get her back. Now!"

I looked at Gabriel. His gaze went to my arm.

"It stopped bleeding," I said. "I just want to keep an eye on her. I'm not racing to her rescue."

"Good. Remember that."

We set out at a jog. Aunika had started across a railroad bridge, hunched over, visible only as a shape moving against the fog. "Keep going, Aunika," I murmured. "Don't slow down and—"

A clang. Then an oath echoed through the still night. Aunika disappeared onto the fog-shrouded bridge just as two shapes ran onto it after her. I bounced on the balls of my feet, straining to see, but the figures had vanished into the fog.

"Olivia . . ." Gabriel said.

"I'm just going to get close enough so I can hear her get safely across."

He muttered something but didn't try to stop me. We jogged to the bridge. I grabbed a girder and hauled myself up, wincing at the pain in my arm. Gabriel's hand closed around my calf.

"Two more beams," he said, though I hadn't uttered a word. "Keep your attention on your path, please."

I started to climb. At a grunt from behind me, I knew he'd told me to keep my eyes forward mostly because he didn't want me watching him climb, lest it not be as effortless as he'd like.

I went exactly two more girders. I could still hear the *thump-thump-thump* of footfalls above, and with my eyes shut, I could imagine a train instead, chugging through the fog, those on the bridge feeling the vibration first, then hearing the thumping before the light pierces the haze and they realize there's no way to go but down.

A thud beside me, along with the sound of heavy breathing, partially stifled. Gabriel was there, looking up at the bridge.

"The game's afoot?" I said. And he laughed. It was barely more than a chuckle, but it'd been so long since I'd heard even that. When Gabriel laughs, I *feel* it, a warmth and joy as if I've accomplished something incredible.

"One more," he said.

We climbed two. Above us, one pair of running footfalls slowed. Gabriel and I hung there, nearly at the top, the fog slipping and sliding around us like a living thing, masking all but the metal under our hands.

Gabriel had a grip on the next beam and had already started pulling himself up, his gaze fixed on the bridge. Our nature might not be to protect the innocent, but it is to do this—to get answers, not hide in shadows until the danger passes.

Also, we were climbing an abandoned railroad bridge on a foggy night. To deny ourselves the adventure seemed almost criminal.

When Gabriel paused on the next beam, I passed him. Then I paused, and he passed me, and we continued like that, each wordlessly making sure the other was equally invested.

I got to the top, and reached to help him, but he pretended not to see my hand and stifled a grunt as he heaved himself up.

We crouched, looking out over the fog-veiled bridge. The edges of the fog were fine lace, and over my shoulder I could see the building tops. As I crept forward, though, the fog thickened, and soon I couldn't even see Gabriel. I reached out, tapping him. He moved closer.

He leaned to my ear and whispered, "Stay close," and then gripped my upper arm as we started out. I could make out the basic shape of the bridge, enough to know I couldn't accidentally wander off the edge. If I veered a little, my shoe knocked against the metal rail. Yet that didn't change the fact that I was fifty feet over water on a very narrow fog-shrouded bridge.

I discovered exactly how unsafe this was when I caught a noise ahead and stumbled against the side rail hard enough that I broke Gabriel's light grip.

He grabbed for me; I grabbed back. I caught his hand and that made *him* jump. I started to pull away, but he gripped my hand, murmuring, "No, this is safer."

Then a metallic clang echoed. A yelp, too high-pitched to tell if it was male or female. We picked up speed. Ahead we could hear what sounded like a fight, only the loudest sounds rising over the wind and water. Then a thud. A shout. And a man's scream, a drawn-out scream, growing steadily softer until—

The scream ended in a splash, and Gabriel gripped my hand tight enough to hurt as we listened. No sounds came from below. None from up here, either.

Then we *felt* something, the pounding of footfalls reverberating through the bridge, running fast.

As soon as I saw Gabriel's eyes, I knew there was no question of turning back. His target lay ahead, and he would not abandon it.

We resumed walking. Gabriel loosened his grip on my hand and I waited for him to drop it, but he only adjusted, lacing his fingers with mine. I looked over at him, that profile so achingly familiar, from the set of his jaw to those unnaturally pale eyes. The wind eddied around us, sending his dark hair tumbling over his forehead, and he pushed it back with his free hand, his lips tightening, annoyed by such a petty distraction.

I can't quit you. I thought I'd put all that aside and made my choice, but all it takes is a walk across a railroad bridge in the dark and the fog. There's not a single twinge of romance here. It doesn't matter. I look at you, and all I think is, I want this. Whatever *this is. I want it so bad.*

I tried to loosen my grip on his hand, and he looked over in alarm, his fingers tightening fast, as if I'd tried to leap over the edge.

"Olivia?" he whispered.

I could say my hand ached. That it was getting sweaty. That it just wasn't comfortable. *Here, how about I hold your sleeve instead?*

But if I said any of that, he'd never reach for my hand again.

I murmured, "Sorry, stumbled," and he said, "Careful," and we continued walking.

Three more steps. Then a noise overhead. A raw croak, and a shadow passed, and I couldn't see more than a shape, yet I knew what it was. I opened my mouth to say, "Raven," but Gabriel was yanking me behind him, his gaze fixed on the fog ahead as he released my hand.

Another shape took form. A human one. Gabriel charged. His fist made contact with a crack, and the figure flew back. Gabriel was on him in a second, his hand wrapped in the man's shirtfront, yanking him up and then slamming him onto the tracks.

"Stay down," Gabriel said. "Or the next time I lift you, it'll be to drop you over the side with your confederate. Understood?"

The man nodded.

"My partner has a gun pointed at you." Gabriel didn't need to confirm that. I did indeed have my gun out and aimed. "Now I am going to back up and you are going to—"

"Gabriel!"

The man's hand shot out, aiming for Gabriel's knee, presumably to buckle it. Gabriel stomped on the man's stomach. He yowled and doubled up, and Gabriel reached to grab him. The man flailed, and I said, "Gabriel! Just get back. I have this," because all I could see was one of those flailing limbs knocking Gabriel off the bridge.

He glanced at me, his lips parting, but before he even got out a syllable, he was charging—at me.

I heard a shout from the other end of the bridge, a man's voice booming, "No! Stop!"

I wheeled just as a figure flew from the fog. A knife flashed. I felt it sink into my side as I twisted. Pain ripped through me, and my feet tangled, and a hand knocked my shoulder, as hard as it could. Gabriel grabbed for me, his fingers brushing my jacket as I flew sideways. I tried to twist, felt cold steel skim my fingertips. Then my head hit metal, and everything went black.

FALLING

T he moment Olivia fell past his reach, his fingers skimming her jacket, Gabriel jumped. There was no
moment of indecision. No moment of decision, either.
She fell and he followed, and it was only after he did that he
saw her hit her head on a girder, saw her crumple, unconscious. Yet he felt no flicker of relief that he had jumped after
her because the point was moot. Of course he would jump.

It did not matter whether he thought she was in mortal
danger or simply falling, certain to survive. She fell and he
followed, and all the times he'd told her not to rely on him,
what he'd meant was that he did not want her taking a
chance. Before this, he could not have said whether he'd
have stayed with her at Will Evans's house if she'd been the
one who was hurt when Chandler was trying to kill them.
Whether he'd have climbed into a burning car for her, as she
had done for him. He knew he would not have abandoned
her to her fate. But would he have made her bold and risky
moves? Or found another way, less dangerous to himself?
The question had haunted him. But here was the answer:
she fell and he followed.

Before she'd struck her head, a thousand thoughts had
been running through his. Not mad panic—orderly questions whipping at light speed. How deep was the river? How
high was the bridge? Would they strike bottom? That was
the greatest danger, but almost equal was the force with

which one hit the surface. It was too late to attempt a proper dive and feet down seemed safest and—

And then Olivia struck the girder, and the questions flew from his mind, because all that mattered was that she was now unconscious, plummeting toward the river. While he'd been considering those questions, he knew she'd been doing the same. She could handle this. Now, unconscious, she could not, and he had to see exactly where she hit, because once they struck the water—between the murk and the night—he'd never see her, and if she didn't wake from the force of going under . . .

That was when the panic hit.

The water would almost certainly not wake her, and the river was rushing fast, and there was no one to see her fall, and if Gabriel lost track of her even for a moment . . .

He would not. That was the simple answer. He was right above her, slightly to the left, and he could see the bright glow of a building at exactly the correct trajectory between him and Olivia. When he surfaced, he would see that light and know where to swim for her.

He struck the water. He hit it well, and perhaps there was then some benefit to his distraction, that he'd simply let himself fall. He hit the surface, feet together, and dropped straight down.

It was not painless. As a teen, he'd once leapt from a third-story window, escaping when he'd miscalculated the owner's return during a break-and-enter. This was worse, a flash fire of agony.

He shoved the thought aside, which did not mean the pain stopped, only that he paid it no mind. Get to the surface, breathe, and then find Olivia.

He managed the first with relative ease. He'd landed and could see the faint glow of the city above, and while he'd rarely swum as a child, he'd taken it up in college, when he discovered that, like running, it was a method of exercise that was not only solitary in nature but discouraged interaction in a way that gym activities did not. He was, if not an excellent swimmer, a very good one, and he propelled himself to the surface easily. Then he pushed out of his heavy, sodden jacket as he looked about for Olivia . . . and saw nothing.

He forced back the twinge of panic much the same way he forced back the pain, shoving it aside with annoyance. Like the pain, it was both unnecessary and unproductive. He'd seen Olivia hit the water, and she'd hit it well, her body limp from the lack of consciousness. She would bob to the surface, and with her blond hair and light skin, he'd spot her easily.

He didn't wait for that. He knew where she'd gone under, and he could see which direction the water was flowing, and he had only to swim that way and, when she bobbed up, he'd see her, and if by some chance she did not, he'd still find her, under the water, because it was not that deep nor that murky and he'd see her hair. He would.

Except he didn't. He performed all the logical steps. He headed in the correct direction, and he kept his gaze fixed on it, and he dove under every five feet, looking for her, and as he swam, he calculated trajectory and rate of flow and assessed the variables, and he did everything right. Goddamn it, he did everything *right*, and yet she did not bob to the surface and he did not catch a flash of her blond hair, and that was not possible. *Not* possible.

You've lost her. Again. You'll never save her. You can't.

Gabriel growled and swallowed water, his head barely above the surface. He did not need that now. It was unproductive. None of it was productive except searching for—

You won't find her. This is your fault. Your selfishness. You led her onto a bridge, where you knew there were men who'd harm her if they could. And why did you do it? Because you were enjoying yourself. She was wounded and in danger, and all that mattered was that she was with you and she was happy and you were off on some grand adventure together.

Gabriel threw off Gwynn's voice. Except it wasn't Gwynn's. It was his own, because he *was* to blame for this. He had indeed been thinking only of himself, that as long as Olivia was happy then he'd seize the moment and to hell with the consequences.

He remembered her being pushed from the bridge. Falling. Hitting that girder. Crumpling. Now he looked out at the dark and empty water.

These are the consequences.

Not productive, goddamn it, not productive *at all*.

He thought fast. She should have bobbed up. He should have seen her if she did. Why wouldn't she—

If she couldn't. If she went under and got caught on something.

Gabriel dove. He swam underwater the way he'd come, working harder now against the current. Just swim. Damn it, *swim*. If she's caught, she's been under water.

How long has she been under? Five minutes? Ten? At ten minutes without oxygen, the human brain begins to suffer irreversible brain damage. At fifteen minutes: death.

And that is absolutely goddamn fucking *not productive*. No facts and figures and calculations. Just find her.

As he swam down, though, he kept glancing upward, feeling the urge to surface.

She isn't down here.

He didn't know that.

Yes, you do. She's not down here, Gabriel.

How would he know that? Had he seen an omen? That wasn't his power. Exactly what powers did he have? He could lie and cheat and deceive and manipulate.

Which is how you got into this mess, isn't it? You manipulated her up onto that bridge.

He knew she wasn't down here, just as he knew she'd

been in trouble when he called. Accept that. Get his ass back to the surface and find her.

As soon as his head broke through, his gaze swung left, as if by instinct, and he saw something pale bob up from the water, heading toward a storm drain.

He swam as fast as he could, even if he knew it wasn't necessary. She'd catch on the drain grate and he could get her there. He still put everything he had into those strokes, drawing ever closer to the drain, only to see . . .

There was no grate.

No, that wasn't possible. A storm drain by its very nature ought to be covered.

Not productive. Move your ass, because you have no fucking idea what's in that drain.

A minute later, *he* was in that drain, and moving fast, the current so strong he had to fight to keep his head above water.

Olivia, where is—?

He saw her, caught on something, her body battering against it. He made his way there and found her jacket had snagged on metal rebar jutting from a concrete slab. He had no idea what purpose the wide concrete slab might serve, only that it formed a perfect platform.

He hauled himself onto it. There wasn't more than a few feet between the platform and the curving tunnel roof. He had to lie on his stomach, free Olivia's jacket, and then pull her up beside him. That's when he discovered she wasn't breathing.

When Olivia began seeing visions and losing consciousness, he'd kept thinking, *What if she stops breathing?* The thought had become near obsessive, and the only way to deal with it had been to research the matter. His brain spat back the instructions for CPR now. He laid her flat on her back, knelt beside her, and began with chest compressions. That went well. The mouth-to-mouth did not, and it had nothing to do with the act of putting his lips to Olivia's, because no matter how many times he might have imagined that—unwittingly, of course—in this reality, Olivia was not breathing and that was all that mattered. The problem came when his lips touched hers and hers were ice-cold, and it was as if every fear he'd kept so carefully contained until then escaped, like bats from a cave, overwhelming him.

She's cold. Goddamn it, she's cold.

Of course she was. She'd been in the river. In October.

He squeezed his eyes shut and focused, the worries shooed, annoying but not incapacitating. He performed the rescue breathing and then the chest compressions and then the breathing and—

She coughed. He had his mouth to hers, and he pulled back fast, struck by the ludicrous fear that she'd "catch" him. Yet she lay completely still, as if he'd imagined the cough, and he tilted her head, ready to check her airway to see if anything was blocking it. Then she coughed again, sputtering now, water dribbling from her mouth, and he turned her over, knocking his hand between her shoulder blades, and he wasn't sure if that was the right thing, but it felt right. She coughed up more water. Then he turned her onto her back, and she flopped there, completely still.

He reached for her chin, pulled her face to his, over hers. Her eyelids fluttered. Then they opened. Her lips parted, and she croaked, "Gabriel."

"I'm here. I'm right here. You're safe. We're—"

Her eyes shut again.

"Olivia?" He gripped her shoulder and gave her a shake. "Olivia? You can sleep in a moment. Just tell me you're all right."

Her head lolled to the side.

"*Olivia.*"

He shook her harder while his free hand checked for a pulse, for breathing, and found both. Her eyes opened a sliver.

"Gabriel."

"Yes, right, now stay with me. Just for a moment. Tell me—"

Her eyes closed again.

"Goddamn it!"

He wanted her to sit up, talk to him. She seemed to be all right, but it was difficult to tell with a wet jacket and jeans plastered to her. Taking them off didn't seem wise. When she began shivering, he looked around for something to put on her, which was foolish, of course. They were on a concrete platform barely big enough to hold them—there wasn't a hidden stash of emergency blankets.

Olivia was shivering now. Hypothermia.

As further proof that perhaps he was not quite mentally alert himself, he found himself reaching into his nonexistent jacket for his phone to look up the treatment for hypothermia.

What did he know about hypothermia . . . ?

Absolutely fucking nothing. Why would he?

I must know something.

Warm up the victim.

Oh, yes, helpful indeed, as if he hadn't already been trying to do that. He had to go for help. But if he left Olivia unconscious, she could roll off the platform. Or wake, confused, and stumble off in the dark.

He had to rouse her first. So he shook her. Talked to her. Talked *sternly* to her. When his voice snapped with frustration, she tensed, her face screwing up, as if she was, on some level, aware.

Talking gently made her shift toward him, bringing her further out of whatever subterranean mental world trapped her. The best response, though, came when he touched her hands or her face, bare skin to his. Her lips would part then, in a soft sigh, and while it would be somewhat flattering to think his touch earned such a response, he realized it was the *heat* she sought.

He reached under her jacket, as circumspectly as he could, and laid his hands on her bare stomach. Olivia sighed and pushed against the source of the heat.

Careful, Gabriel. Be very careful.

He silenced the voice with a growl of annoyance. She was unconscious, nearly drowned, and his mind was certainly not going to slide *that* way.

He gingerly removed her wet jacket. That left her wearing only her bra, but he avoided looking at her torso. He draped the jacket across her legs and then rubbed her bare arms, being careful of the slice in her arm. She wriggled toward him again, as if she could feel his body heat, like a fire just out of reach. He stripped off his shirt and put it around her shoulders. Then he lay down on his side.

Careful, Gabriel . . .

He pushed the voice away. He was not a fifteen-year-old boy with a half-naked girl. Olivia was shivering, possibly sliding into hypothermia. He lay down beside her and rubbed her arms, keeping her just close enough for the heat of his body to warm her. Which was a fine plan, except that the moment she felt his body heat, she moved toward it, and then she was snuggled against his chest, her arms pulled in for warmth, her head tucked under his chin, her face pressed against him.

That felt . . . Gabriel couldn't even process how it felt. Except good. So good, Olivia snuggled against him, her breath warm against his collarbone, his face in her hair, smelling her, holding her.

Just until she stops shivering. I need to get her warm. As soon as she stops shivering, I'll move away.

And then she did stop shivering, but she stayed pressed against him, and when he removed one hand, tentatively and reluctantly, from her back, she tensed, and he laid it back against her skin to feel her relax and snuggle deeper, sighing softly.

I'll let her get a little warmer. Maybe then she'll wake up. In the meantime, I'll think of what to do when she does wake up.

Again, a fine plan. Except he did not think of the next step. Thoughts fluttered through his brain where they usually raced. It was like a slow, drowsy waking. *I'm warm. I'm safe. I'm happy. Just let me stay here for a few more minutes, and then I'll get to work.*

He buried his face against Olivia's hair, tightened his arms around her, closed his eyes, and relaxed. Just for a moment. Just a moment.

It might have been more than a moment. But he did snap out of it. No, he pushed himself out of it, mentally kicking and screaming, lifting his head and loosening his arms and saying, "Olivia?" She tried to get closer, and he had to grit his teeth to resist letting her.

She's unconscious. She needs help. Focus on her. Get her awake. Get her help.

"Olivia?"

He pulled back a little more, took her chin in his hand, and tilted her face to his.

"Olivia?"

He rubbed her back with his free hand, his grip on her chin tightening.

"Olivia? Can you hear—?"

Her eyes snapped open, wide with surprise, and he tensed, waiting for her to shake her head in confusion and pull away from him. But she looked up into his eyes and smiled and said, "Gabriel."

And then she kissed him.

He would later replay that moment—more times than it needed to be replayed—telling himself he had to revisit it to be sure he hadn't taken advantage of her confusion. He had not. She kissed him. There was no doubt of that. There was also, he would admit, no doubt that he kissed her back without even a split second of hesitation.

There wasn't even a *thought* of hesitation. Nor a thought of whether he *should* kiss her. It was like seeing her fall from the bridge and leaping after her. She started, and he followed, and there was no other choice, because that kiss . . .

That kiss . . .

If there was a part of sex that Gabriel could happily do without, it was kissing. The rest was about satisfying biological urges, much the same as eating or sleeping, and therefore it could be handled in the same way he ate or slept—dispassionately and perfunctorily, getting it out of the way. Kissing was different. It served no purpose other than intimacy and therefore, to him . . . No. Simply no. Fortunately, he'd discovered that if one picked the right partner, kissing was not required.

That did, however, lead to a problem. One he had never considered until he'd experienced another first for him: *wanting* to kiss someone. On the beach, with Olivia, too much wine drunk, hearing her laugh, watching her in the moonlight, and thinking, unbidden, that he wanted to kiss her. He hadn't, of course. That would be a violation of trust, an unwanted trespass. He had thought it, though, and then, upon thinking it, he'd felt a surge of panic, as he'd realized that if it did somehow happen . . . ? Well, the problem with avoiding kissing? He was almost certainly not very good at it.

But now she kissed him, and he kissed her back, and it was like hearing about ice cream and thinking it sounded revolting, and perhaps getting a taste or two of some cheap ice milk and agreeing it *was* revolting, and then tasting the real thing and realizing this was not what you'd imagined at all, not what you'd tasted before, that even to give it the same name seemed a sacrilege. Because that kiss . . .

That kiss was a blazing fire in an ice storm. It was a clear running stream in a desert. And yet it wasn't quite that. It was finding something that you didn't know you wanted, didn't know you needed, and then suddenly it was there, and you couldn't believe you hadn't been looking for it all along.

Gabriel had spent his life knowing exactly what he wanted. Pursuing his goals with single-minded determination. And then along came Olivia. She'd stopped him in his tracks, and he'd circled tentatively, questioning, unsure, thinking that maybe this was something he wanted but the urge was too foreign to be taken at face value. Perhaps he was wrong, misinterpreting, confusing a need for companionship for a need for more. And then she kissed him, and he knew he wasn't wrong. He was not wrong at all.

What he wanted to do most at that moment was seize it. Immerse himself in that kiss because that's what it demanded— no thought, just feeling. And for the first few minutes, he was able to give it exactly that. But then he felt the spark of an emotion never properly developed, never truly part of his admittedly flat emotional landscape until recently. Until Olivia. The emotion he liked, perhaps, least of all.

Guilt.

It was not guilt at kissing another man's lover. Gabriel could fathom such a response in only the most abstract way. A lover was not property. If Olivia chose to kiss him, that was her business. Perhaps, though, he should feel some guilt at the betrayal of someone who was—yes, admit it—a friend. For now, though, he really didn't give a damn about Ricky. No, the guilt was for the niggling and growing acknowledgment that Olivia *did* give a damn about Ricky. That Olivia was not the sort of woman who'd kiss a man when she'd made a commitment to another. That if Olivia had not pulled away by now, then Olivia was not truly present, not truly awake, not truly and mindfully kissing him.

No, that's not true. She opened her eyes. She looked at me. She said my name. Goddamn it, she said my name. Not Ricky. Not Gwynn. She knows exactly who she is kissing.

Was he sure?

Yes.

Then he shouldn't mind checking.

Gabriel had witnessed children's tantrums. In school. In shopping malls. In restaurants. A child howling at the universe because it did not give him what he wanted. Gabriel had never, even as a child, thrown such a tantrum, because he had not lived a life where he could presume the universe was in any way inclined to give him what he wanted. That wasn't how life worked. But now he felt like those children, stomping his feet and clenching his fists and raging at the unfairness of it all.

She said my name. Mine, mine, mine.

And how would he feel later, if he discovered he'd been mistaken? What if, instead, she'd had too much to drink? If she'd been drugged? If she kissed him then, would he claim she said his name and that was enough?

No. He would not.

He could do many things to many people, but that was one offense he had never been remotely guilty of. However uncomfortable the act of seduction, however much he wished to get what he needed and disappear into the night, he had never even been tempted to walk into a bar and choose someone too inebriated to make a conscious decision to leave with him. If he wouldn't do that to a stranger, he certainly wouldn't do it to Olivia.

He pulled back then, cupping her face and holding it away from his own.

Her eyes opened.

"Gabriel," she said, and smiled.

There. See? *See?*

The child in him pointed in glee. That "proof" was enough, wasn't it? He wished it was. But the adult in him looked into her eyes and saw that they weren't quite focused, felt the awareness, in the pit of his stomach, that she wasn't quite there.

"Olivia?"

She closed her eyes and pushed her hands into his hair, trying to pull him back to her.

"Olivia? I need to ask you something."

She wriggled in his grip, frustrated that she couldn't get back to him.

"Olivia? Can you open your eyes?"

She did not.

"Olivia? Do you know where you are? Do you know what's happened?"

No answer. She started shivering and whispered, "Cold, so cold." Her hands fell from his hair, and she pulled them between their bodies, shivering against him, and when he released her face, she pushed her head under his chin, finding warmth there and snuggling back into his arms.

"Cold," she said.

"I know."

"Gabriel," she sighed, and nuzzled against him.

"I know," he said. And *that* he did have—the knowledge that wherever Olivia was, whatever she was imagining, it was with him. Not mistaking him for Ricky. Not mistaking him for Gwynn. She might not realize where she was or what had happened, but she knew she was with him, contentedly curled up in his arms, and that was, for now, enough.

"Ma-til-da!"

A voice shouted, somewhere deep in Gabriel's brain. No, not just a voice. Arawn. Gwynn stirred, annoyed, and felt Matilda curled up against him, his face buried in her hair, the summer sun beating down on them, lying in the meadow's long grass.

"Ma-til-da! Gwynn!"

Go away. Just go away.

You have to get up now. Before he finds you. Before he sees you like this.

Gwynn tossed in half sleep, knowing the voice was right, that they had to get up, couldn't let Arawn see them together.

And there was more, too. Something else . . . Something had happened . . . Water? Why was he thinking of—

"O-liv-i-a! Ga-bri-el!"

Gabriel started awake, and pushed up on one forearm,

blinking against the darkness. Why was it dark? There'd been sunshine only a moment . . .

He squeezed his eyes shut, and the thought evaporated, leaving him even more confused. He was lying on cold concrete, but warmth pressed against him, so familiar and . . .

He looked down to see Olivia in his arms. A bridge. A fall. Olivia, not breathing. Olivia, breathing. Olivia, shivering. Olivia, kissing . . .

Oh.

He didn't move away then. Didn't feel any inclination to move away, just pulled her tighter to him, telling himself it was still cold, which it was. He shook off the last threads of sleep. He hadn't meant to doze off. He *shouldn't* have dozed off. Olivia might be breathing and warm, but she was still unconscious, and to simply drift off to sleep while she needed help was unconscionable. He pushed up again.

I need to . . .

Thought was still slow in coming. Damnably slow, like swimming through molasses.

"Ga-bri-el! O-liv-i-a!"

Ricky? That did have him pushing away from Olivia, the guilt that had failed to come earlier now surging. Well, if not quite surging, at least prickling enough for him to move back an inch or so.

Focus, damn it. Focus.

Ricky. He'd heard Ricky. Why would he . . .?

Because Gabriel had texted Ricky, before he went to meet Olivia. Just a quick note to say where they were, and Olivia should be done in an hour and would call him then. What Gabriel had *really* been doing was covering their backs, just in case.

"In here!" Gabriel shouted, as loud as he could, and while Olivia started, she still didn't wake. Goddamn it, why didn't she wake?

"Ricky! We're in here!"

His voice echoed through the tunnel. Echoed . . . and stayed trapped there.

He set Olivia down and moved her against the wall, as far from the edge as possible. Then he slid off the side and swam, stopping every dozen strokes to shout. He was about ten feet from the entrance when he heard, "Gabriel?"

"Here! The tunnel!" He covered the last part of the distance, dove, and came up to see figures on the shore, about fifty feet down, shining searchlights on the water.

"Here!" he shouted, waving one arm, and a figure turned and the light hit him, and Gabriel exhaled in relief.

GRACE AND UNDERSTANDING

Ricky rode in the back of the ambulance. Gabriel needed to be treated for hypothermia, and the paramedics had quickly realized it would be easier to do so if Ricky was there. He'd distracted Gabriel by explaining how he'd found them.

How much of the story did Gabriel process? Not much, Ricky suspected, but he didn't tell him to shut the fuck up—or, in Gabriel-speak, give a curt "That's enough." Which proved that the paramedics were right: hypothermia slowed mental processes.

As Ricky talked, the paramedics worked on Olivia. Every few minutes Gabriel would rouse from his stupor and demand to know why she wasn't regaining consciousness, and that was when *Ricky* would have liked to tell *him* to shut up, because he didn't need the reminder.

All that ended when, in the course of treating Liv, the paramedic discovered a thin knife wound, like a stiletto stab, on her right side, between her ribs. The ambulance ride wasn't nearly as calm after that.

"She fell in the river," Gabriel snarled at the desk clerk. "From a bridge. No, wondrously, she does not have her wallet with her. Meaning she does not have identification or proof of health insurance."

It was not as if the hospital was actually refusing Liv

treatment. The clerk had simply asked for the information, and hesitated when told why it could not be provided. That hesitation had been enough, though, considering that Gabriel was already in a frothing temper over the paramedics' slowness in discovering Olivia's stab wound. A temper which Ricky knew was fueled by the fact that Gabriel himself hadn't realized she'd been stabbed.

"Her name is Olivia Taylor-Jones," Ricky said, as calmly as he could. "Her family owns the Mills & Jones department store. She can definitely cover her bills. If you need proof of her identity, just google her name."

The clerk still hesitated. Ricky resisted the urge to snap at her. Liv had been taken in already and was being assessed. This was merely a formality.

Gabriel snapped cards onto the counter from his soaked wallet. "Visa and American Express Platinum. A hundred-thousand-dollar limit on each, both currently empty because I use this." He waved his debit card. "If you can point me to an ATM, I can secure you a down payment and those"—he pointed at the credit cards—"are yours to keep. Does that resolve the issue?"

The full force of those ice-ray blue eyes locked on the hapless clerk, and she froze, her mouth opening and closing.

"Take the cards," Ricky said, pushing them into her hand. "We'll come back for them later." Then, to Gabriel, his voice lowering, "Let's go find Liv."

Locating the correct floor would have been easier if the desk clerk had been more useful, but Ricky had always known how to get people to do what he wanted—the right smile, the right tone, the right words. He'd always presumed he inherited that from his father. It turned out he was partly right—it was a gift they'd *both* inherited with their Cŵn Annwn blood. He hadn't yet told his father about that. He wasn't sure where to start.

They found the room where Liv was being assessed, and Ricky obtained a promise for an update ASAP, which he got from a harried doctor minutes later.

When the doctor left, Gabriel reached for his inside jacket pocket to pull out his phone or ever-present pad of paper. The coat he was actually wearing contained neither. It was Ricky's leather jacket. Under it, the borrowed T-shirt was about two sizes too small, stretching tight across Gabriel's chest. For trousers, he had a pair of jeans from Wallace's saddlebags. Between the biker jacket, jeans, tight T, and dark stubble, Ricky understood why the desk clerk had been so flustered. She'd probably already alerted the banks to their obviously stolen credit cards.

When Gabriel patted his pockets, scowling, two nurses scuttled out of the way. Ricky jogged to catch up with them and ask a favor. Then he returned and handed Gabriel a sheet of paper and a pen.

Gabriel nodded curtly and began jotting notes. When he reached into his jacket again, he didn't even have time to scowl before Ricky held out his own phone. This time Ricky got a grunt of thanks, and Gabriel went to work, fingers flying as he searched the words on his list—terms the doctor had used to describe Liv's condition.

"Can I have that back?" Ricky asked when Gabriel finished and tucked the phone away.

Gabriel started, as if from his thoughts, grunted something semi-apologetic, and returned the phone.

Ricky cleared his throat. "May I borrow your list, too? I remember most of it, but . . ."

Gabriel glanced over. It took a moment for his eyes to focus, and when they did, he frowned. "Yes, of course," he said. "You want to know, too . . . Of course."

"Let's go sit down. You still seem a little out of it."

He got a frosty, "I'm fine, thank you," for that.

"Well, I'm going over there to sit," Ricky said.

They sat, and Gabriel explained what he'd found, filling in what they'd gotten from the doctor.

When he got to the part about the stab wound, his voice sharpened with anger.

"You couldn't have known," Ricky said.

"I should have."

"You thought her attacker only pushed her. You didn't see the blade. Then it was dark, and the blood had washed away."

"I was careless."

"And nothing I can say will help, will it?"

"No."

"So stop trying?"

"Yes." Then, grudgingly, "Please."

Ricky shook his head and they lapsed into a silent vigil, both watching the room where Liv lay, out of their reach, beyond their care.

It was 8 a.m. on Wednesday. Almost thirty hours since Liv had been rushed to the hospital. Twenty-four since they'd been allowed into her room. Ricky had checked in on her at seven and then went out to get breakfast for himself and Gabriel. Liv had not regained consciousness. Gabriel had not left her side. Which meant Ricky had spent the night in his apartment, because there was only one bedside chair.

Did he resent that, just a little? Yes, he did. But it was only a little, and ultimately as pointless as . . . well, as trying to kick Gabriel out of her life. Worse than pointless. Dangerous.

When Ricky first made his play for Liv, he'd made sure Gabriel wasn't interested in her and then told himself he believed Gabriel's denials. But that was bullshit. He could tell there'd been more growing between them. Ricky was not an idiot. Nor, however, was he stupidly noble or generous. He wanted Liv, and Liv wanted him, and Gabriel wasn't stepping up to the plate, so . . . batter out.

Except it wasn't that simple, a fact he hadn't acknowledged until he got the Gwynn–Matilda–Arawn story. But even that only came as confirmation of what he'd suspected: that he didn't have Liv to himself. That he couldn't have her to himself. That, maybe most importantly, he *shouldn't*. Because that way lay misery and tragedy and endless grief for all of them.

Grace had asked if Ricky knew Arawn's mistake. He did. It was exactly that: Arawn thought he could have Matilda to himself.

It was easy to blame Gwynn for what happened. Gwynn broke their pledge, and he made Matilda keep their betrothal secret and persuaded her that Arawn would be happy for them. Gwynn was, indeed, at fault for that betrayal. But when Arawn learned the truth, did he realize Matilda loved Gwynn and back off? Hell, no. His sin, then, was as grave as Gwynn's, his betrayal of Matilda as deep.

Arawn tried to force Matilda to love him. If she came to him the night before her wedding, she'd lose Gwynn and have no choice but to be Arawn's. Ricky fervently hoped that if Matilda had lived, she'd have told the asshole where to stick his so-called love and walked out of his life forever. Liv certainly would.

Ricky would not make the same mistake. He knew he couldn't have Liv to himself, and railing against that would be like blaming a tree for blocking his path. It was there first. He saw it there. He chose to take that particular route. Deal with it.

Ricky loved Liv, and she loved him back, and whatever happened, that's what he didn't want to lose. Her love. Their bond. He just happened to be enjoying the rest while he could get it. Because he knew that one day, hopefully not too soon, he wouldn't be getting it, and he hoped to hell he handled that the same way he'd handled ceding his hospital bedside spot to Gabriel: with understanding and dignity.

"Breakfast," he said as he walked in, bag raised in one hand, coffee tray in the other.

If Gabriel had slept in the last thirty hours, there was no sign of it. Yesterday Ricky had brought clean clothes from Gabriel's apartment, but he still wore the borrowed jeans and T-shirt.

Ricky reached over and cleared away the late-night snack he'd left—chips, a candy bar, a coffee, and a can of Coke. There was a bite taken from the bar and a few sips from the coffee. Ricky tossed them and set out a fresh coffee, juice box, muffin, apple, yogurt, and foil-wrapped breakfast burrito. The variety, as with the snack, wasn't because Gabriel had eclectic food tastes but because he seemed to have no tastes at all. In the four years Ricky had known Gabriel, he'd seen him served coffee with every variation of fixings and watched him drink it without reaction. If asked, he'd say, "Black," but Ricky hadn't decided if that was because he preferred it black or if it was just the most efficient way to make it.

Ricky set out the breakfast and then stood there, watching, as Gabriel sat with his gaze fixed on Liv's sleeping form. Ricky picked up the coffee and put it in Gabriel's hand. He got a head shake for that, but Gabriel did take a sip. Then Ricky replaced it with the juice. Now came that cool glance that said, *You are beginning to annoy me.*

"Drink," Ricky said. "At the risk of nagging, you don't want the first thing she sees to be you . . . passed out from low blood sugar."

The look chilled. "I'm not trying to be the first thing—"

"I know."

"I'm here so I may explain what happened."

"Confess, you mean. And you can stop giving me that look, unless you're trying to cool down your coffee, because it doesn't work on me."

Gabriel's eyes narrowed.

"Nope," Ricky said. "Keep trying, though. You might be able to scare off the rest of the nurses."

A snort that, from Gabriel, was a laugh, and he settled back into his chair.

"You're allowed to use the shower in here," Ricky said. "Apropos of nothing."

Gabriel looked at him.

"Since it's a private room, you can use it," Ricky said. "In fact, the staff were very eager for me to tell you that."

Gabriel returned to watching Liv. Ricky sighed and held out a bag from the pharmacy downstairs. Gabriel glanced in and grunted.

"Yes, deodorant. Again, apropos of nothing."

Gabriel took the bag, rose, and headed into the bathroom. Two minutes later he returned, having washed up, run his hands through his hair, and presumably used the deodorant, which he tossed aside. He then took the apple, chomped half of it in one bite, and arched a brow at Ricky.

"Yes, I'm happy. I'll stop nagging. Sit. Scowl. Just try to be in a slightly better mood when she wakes up."

Gabriel grunted. Ricky didn't add *and she will wake up.* The doctors all said this was only temporary, as her body healed itself. Gabriel seemed to accept that. He was here for the same reason Liv had spent the night in a police station when Gabriel had been arrested for James's murder. Because that's where they wanted to be. Where they needed to be.

As Ricky looked at Gabriel watching Liv, he knew that as much as he himself loved her, it wasn't like this, couldn't be like this. Hell, he wasn't even sure what *this* was. He only knew he couldn't touch it, and sure as hell couldn't duplicate it.

Gabriel finished the apple. Then he reached for the juice, and when he didn't find it, hand stretching out blindly, he turned. That's when Liv moved. Just her fingers uncurling, as if stretching.

Ricky started forward. Then he stopped.

"Hmm?" Gabriel said as he turned back to Liv, juice in hand.

"I . . ." Ricky swallowed. *Grace and understanding, remember?* "Shit, you know what I forgot? I was going to grab something for Liv. I'll be back. You need anything?"

Gabriel shook his head. Ricky started for the door. At a noise from Gabriel, he turned. Gabriel gestured at the juice.

"Thank you."

Ricky's gaze went to Liv, her fingers twitching again, and he forced a smile. "No problem," he said, and hurried from the room.

CHAPTER FIFTEEN

I fell from the bridge, landed in the river, and heard laughter ringing out above me. I pushed through the surface into a sun-dappled day, trees casting shadows on the crystal water. I looked around to see more trees and a distant meadow.

"If you stay there, don't expect to stay afloat, Mati," a voice called from far above, and I craned my neck to see a dark-haired boy crouched on a tree branch. A blond boy sat beside him, legs dangling, both of them grinning down at me.

"You have been warned," the blond boy—Gwynn—called, just as Arawn jumped. He hit the water beside me, the force of his cannonball dragging me back under, sputtering, as they laughed. Another splash, before I could surface, and hands grabbed my arm, pulling me up.

"Not going to let me drown?" I said.

Gwynn smiled. "Never."

"Olivia!" The voice seemed to come from far away, and as I turned, the sky darkened, the trees on the shore morphing into fog-shrouded buildings. I saw a face in front of mine, blurred through the murky water. A woman's face, her long blond hair fanning around her, blue eyes wide with horror. She reached for me and I saw, not a hand, but a hoof, the feathered hair like seaweed.

I yanked back with a scream, water filling my mouth.

Hands grabbed me again and pulled me up to the surface, and I saw sunlight and smelled trees and heard birds chirping. I looked to see Arawn and Gwynn, each holding me by one arm, their faces drawn with worry.

"I—I saw—" I began.

Then the kelpie surfaced, but this one had long, flowing red hair, like a mane. She rose, frowning, and the boys laughed.

"Did you scare Mati?" Arawn said.

"I did not mean to," the kelpie said. She put out her hands, fingers now. "Come and swim, Matilda. I will show you wonders below."

I froze, remembering the kelpies from my vision at Villa Tuscana, dragging a young woman to her death. When the kelpie tried to take my hand, I jerked back.

Arawn laughed. "Someone's been listening to stories again."

"They aren't stories if they're true," Gwynn said.

"All stories have truth," Arawn said. "If you look hard enough."

"I'd not hurt you, Matilda," the kelpie said. "You are one of us. Come. I'll show you magic."

She closed her eyes and transformed into a roan horse with a dark red mane. Arawn climbed on her back and held out a hand for me. I looked at Gwynn. He sighed, put his leg over the horse's back, and patted the spot between them. I got on and the kelpie dove through the clear water, impossibly deep, then through a dark hole, and we came up again in a cave glistening with crystals.

The scene faded and I felt a blast of cold only to wake again in the cave, lying on a ledge at the side, curled up with Gwynn, both of us almost a decade older. It was the same cavern, though. Our secret place, and he was pulling me against him, his lips going to mine, and then—

"Olivia!"

I blinked, and I was cold, so cold. I was out of the pond, lying on stone, hearing the echo of water sloshing against rock. There was warmth here, too, like a blazing fire on a winter's day, and I squirmed to get closer to it, and then the warmth became hands, hot against my icy skin, and that felt so amazingly good. My eyes opened and I looked up into pale blue eyes, and I smiled as I said, "Gabriel."

That fae cavern had turned dark and cold, but we were out of the water and safe, and snuggled up together. A small part of me snorted and said, "Seriously? Um, no. Not happening." But that's what dreams are for—to weave reality and fantasy and memory and stitch together something you can't hope for in waking life. To fulfill that little part of you that wants something so bad.

As long as I was stitching together a perfect fantasy scene with Gabriel, I figured I might as well make it worthwhile. So I kissed him.

I remembered my first vision of Gwynn and Matilda. And that kiss . . . Damn, that kiss. Magical and perfect, in a way one would only ever imagine a kiss from a fairy prince to be, even someone who had never, in her entire life, entertained such a frivolous fantasy. But it had been a kiss to remember, a kiss I couldn't pry out of my mind, as hard as I tried. Now, this kiss, with Gabriel? It knocked that one—and every other one I'd ever had—clear out of my memory, as if this was the only one that counted. And it was.

I began falling through endless memories, not of Gwynn or Gabriel, but of kelpies and lamiae and other fae, unrecognizable, the visions starting pleasant and turning dark, until I had no idea what I was seeing. Something was chasing me, and I ran as fast as I could, as if from Death itself. Then in the distance I heard a soft laugh, followed by a grunt, both as familiar as actual voices: Ricky and Gabriel. I stopped running and turned toward the sounds. Ricky's voice floated over.

"Sit. Scowl. Just try to be in a slightly better mood when she wakes up."

There! I changed direction, and it was like running downhill through a tunnel, the end blazing a lighted welcome, voices still flitting out, guiding me until . . .

My eyelids fluttered open. I was staring at . . . white.

A clatter sounded beside me. A hand gripped mine, the touch as familiar as that grunt, and I turned as he leaned over, and I smiled and said, "Gabriel."

Gabriel took me through the events of the night before. No, *two* nights before. It was now Wednesday morning. I'd lost Tuesday entirely. I also lost about half of his narrative, as I kept mentally fading and needing to ask him to repeat himself, which he did, with astonishing patience.

"A flood tunnel?" I said.

"Yes, and I don't know why it was open. Clearly such things should be sealed, because if you'd continued down it, who knows where you'd have ended up."

"But I didn't." I smiled at him. "You saved me."

He ducked the smile. "The platform saved you. Or whatever it was."

"So, we were in something like a cave? Lying on rock?"

"Concrete."

"Right, but it would have felt like . . ." The dream rippled back. Gabriel and I in the cavern, lying on the ledge and . . . My cheeks heated.

"Olivia?"

I shook it off. Obviously I'd been aware enough of my surroundings that the memories of Gwynn and the cavern had merged with Gabriel and the tunnel, and since Gwynn and Matilda used that as their secret make-out spot, I'd done some mental editing myself.

Another shake, and I looked at Gabriel and . . . "What are you *wearing*?" I said with a sudden laugh.

"You've been unconscious for a while," said a voice from the doorway. "Gabriel joined the Saints. He's even got the jacket right there."

Ricky pointed to his jacket, on the back of the bedside chair.

"Put it on," I said to Gabriel. "This I have to see."

"I'm afraid that would violate club rules," Gabriel said. "Ricky only lent it to me under extreme circumstances, to alleviate my hypothermia."

"Oh, I won't tell anyone," Ricky said. "Go on. Humor her. She's had a near-death experience. She deserves a treat."

When Gabriel ignored us both, Ricky leaned in and whispered, "Don't worry. I may have photographic evidence."

"What?" Gabriel said.

I pulled Ricky into a quick kiss. He added a second to my forehead before setting a mocha on my tray.

"Wow," I said, taking it. "Now that's timing."

He shrugged. "I had a hunch you'd wake up soon."

As I lifted the cup to my lips, he took it and replaced it with a glass of water.

"Better start with this," he said.

"Tease."

"Drink all the water. Slowly. Then you can have the mocha. But if the nurses come by?" He jerked his thumb at Gabriel. "*He* brought you coffee."

I propped up the pillows on the bed, shifted over, and patted a spot for him to take.

He perched on the edge, giving me plenty of room. "So where in the story are we?"

"The rescue," Gabriel said.

"Ah, good. Keep going, then. This is your part."

"I mean the part where you rescued us."

"*Found* you. The rescue was the bring-Liv-back-from-the-dead part. Which is totally yours."

"Back from the dead?" I said, rising.

"He's being dramatic," Gabriel said. "It was CPR."

"I stopped *breathing*?"

"Oh, he skipped that part, did he?" Ricky said. "The doc will tell her everything, Gabriel, so you might as well fess up. The whole story. Leave nothing out."

Gabriel went still. An odd look crossed his face, and he shifted, his gaze escaping to my pillows, which he fussed with, grumbling that I needed to keep my head supported.

"He saved your life," Ricky continued. "He just doesn't want to admit that, because it totally blows his tough-guy rep. Fine, then. He brought you back to life. Meanwhile, I . . ."

Ricky finished telling the story. Then he detailed my injuries. When he got to the stab wound, Gabriel said, "That is my fault."

"Uh, no," I said. "Pretty sure you didn't stab me."

"He means he's taking responsibility for the fact he didn't realize you'd been stabbed and therefore didn't tend to it right away. Which, as the doctors have pointed out, wouldn't have made a difference." Ricky mock-lowered his voice. "He's not quite himself yet. I'd take full advantage and ask for a raise."

When Gabriel gave him a look, Ricky said to me, "It's the hypothermia. The paramedics said it causes mental confusion and poor decision making. Luckily for both of you, he only had the confusion."

Gabriel shifted back and sipped his coffee. I opened my mouth and then paused. A thought had slipped through the periphery of my mind. Something important.

Speaking of mental confusion . . .

"Aunika!" I said. "The last we saw . . ."

"I'd love to tell you she's all right," Ricky said. "But honestly, I don't know. I went by the center yesterday, and I managed to get a girl who works there to talk to me."

"Was she about twenty? Dark hair? Sleeve tattoos?"

"That's her. She finally admitted she hasn't seen Aunika since Monday. Aunika did text her, though, saying she was fine and needed a couple of days off."

"That text could have been sent by her captors."

"Yeah. I'm still working on getting her home address. That girl sure as hell wasn't giving it to me."

I fell silent, chasing another thought, and then said, "Over the drop-in center. She said her apartment is on the second floor."

"Good," he said. "We'll check that as soon as you're up to it. In the meantime, just tell me what legwork you need done. I can do the online stuff, too, but I did bring your laptop. It's over there with a bag of clothing."

"Laptop. I left that in . . . Shit! My car!"

"It's at Gabriel's office, along with his."

Gabriel looked taken aback. "Thank you. I didn't even consider that."

"I know. Mental confusion, right? It's handled. As is . . ." He took two cell phones from his pocket. "Your boss bought you a new phone, Liv."

Gabriel frowned at him.

Ricky held up two credit cards. "I fetched these from the front desk. There's a charge on the Amex for both phones. I set it up with your provider by impersonating you."

"And me?" I asked.

"Yep, impersonated you, too."

I smiled and took the phone.

"You just need to download your backups," he said. "Please tell me you have backups."

"We do," I said. Then I pulled him into a hug. "Thank you."

"I knew you'd want to be up and running as soon as you could. Gabriel handled nurse duty; I did this. I also updated Rose on the situation and she went over to feed TC. Oh, and I know you lost your wallet in the river, so just make a list of what you need replaced and I'll make the calls before you get out."

"Before tonight?"

"You're not getting released today, Liv."

I made a noise that meant, *We'll see about that*, but just thanked and hugged him again for all he'd done.

CHAPTER SIXTEEN

Gabriel went home around ten to shower and shave. At noon he was back with lunch. One of the nurses smelled the food, and came in, as if to give us shit for it. Seeing Gabriel, she turned and walked out. Evidently, he'd made an impression.

After lunch, Ricky had a class. Gabriel and I were on our laptops, catching up on two lost days as we talked about Aunika and our next steps.

"Working?" said a voice from the doorway. "Didn't you just fall in a river?"

"No rest for the wicked," I said. "As you can see, we're very busy. Thanks for coming by, leave the flowers at the door . . . Oh, no. Wait. You didn't bring me flowers. You brought . . . a book? If it's from your library, I'm not really in any shape for literary visions."

Patrick walked over. "I know, which is why I brought you one that is pure entertainment."

"And while normally I'd say that's very sweet and actually quite considerate, I have the feeling . . ." I took the book from him and read the cover. "It's one of yours."

"How else can I guarantee it's any good?"

I snorted and set it aside. "The door is behind you."

"I came all the way to Chicago—*and* brought you a book—and you're kicking me out?"

"You came because you're wondering what happened

and want to find out before the other elders. If you came bearing a *useful* gift, we could negotiate. But a copy of your own book earns you this much: Gabriel and I were pushed off a bridge. We survived. We don't know who did it, but we intend to find out."

"I think a copy of my book is at least worth the true version. You were pushed; Gabriel jumped."

"What?" I looked over at Gabriel.

"He jumped after you, Liv." A satisfied smile spread across Patrick's face. "Did you expect anything less?"

"How would you know that?" Gabriel said, rising.

"I know you," Patrick said.

"Wait," I said. "So you *did* jump—"

Footsteps sounded outside the door, a shadow stretching in. Then a voice said, "Ms. Jones has reached the maximum number of visitors, sir."

A man's murmur, too low for me to identify. Before Gabriel made it halfway to the door, the nurse said, "Briefly, please. She really does need her rest."

"Of course. I appreciate your understanding."

Now I recognized the voice. Patrick tilted his head as if he did, too, but couldn't quite place it.

The newcomer walked in carrying flowers and a perfectly wrapped basket of fruit and chocolate. Then he saw Patrick and stopped.

"Ioan," Patrick said, walking toward him. "How long has it been?"

"Not nearly long enough."

Patrick lowered his voice. "Everyone says that. You'll need to do better if you want to insult me." He took the flowers and basket. "Thank you so much. Liv will appreciate these. It's too bad you can't stay, but we have a lovely parting gift for you." He handed Ioan the book. "It's a ripper."

Ioan looked down. "Is this . . . your book?"

"One of them. It's signed to Liv, but you can scratch that out and write in your name. Oh, and if you can leave a five-star review on Goodreads, I'd appreciate it."

Ioan set the book down. "I'm here to talk to Olivia. Alone, please." His gaze flicked to Gabriel. "If you would take your *epil*—"

I coughed. Patrick said, "No, my book stays. Epilogue and all. So do I."

Behind Gabriel's back, I shook my head for Ioan. *Epil* is Welsh for offspring, and the word the fae use to refer to their sons and daughters. Luckily, while I may have used the term in front of Gabriel, he hadn't been paying enough attention to recognize it now.

"Liv was just about to tell me about her river plunge," Patrick continued. "If you want to hear it, you may stay."

"One, I wasn't about to tell you anything," I said. "Two, as the patient here, I think I get to decide who stays and who goes. Yes, you may both stay. Yes, I will tell the story . . . on the condition that you'll help me figure out what the hell is going on, regardless of our agreement."

"However," Gabriel interjected, "any lifting of the terms is temporary, confined to this discussion only, and does not in any way relieve either party of their contractual obligations going forward."

"Would you like that in writing, Gabriel?" Ioan said.

"Preferably, yes. But in this instance, I believe you and Patrick can act as our witnesses to each other's agreement, given that you are unlikely to collude in disavowing that agreement."

Ioan gave a dismissive wave and moved forward, as if getting closer to my bedside, while effectively putting Gabriel at his back. When my lips tightened, he wisely shifted to the side.

I told Ioan and Patrick the story. When I finished, I said, "The obvious issue here is that there's a young—apparently human—woman who works with lamaie. And she knows enough to set up fae-detection traps."

"*Mhacasamhail*," Patrick said.

Ioan shook his head. "There's no such thing as *mhacasamhail*."

"No such thing as fairies, either."

"Don't I wish," Ioan muttered.

"Not unless you're into self-annihilation."

"The Cŵn Annwn are not—"

"Are, too."

"My God," I said. "How old are you two?"

"I'm older," Patrick said. "Cŵn Annwn don't live nearly as long as other fae. That's because—"

Ioan cleared his throat, cutting him off.

"Oh, come on," Patrick said. "Let me tell her. The rules of the agreement *are* temporarily suspended."

Gabriel shook his head. "That opens the door to retaliation, and we have a case to focus on."

Patrick sighed. "Oh, sure, be reasonable about it."

"He must get that from his mother's side," Ioan said.

I shot him a warning look and said to Patrick, "Tell me more about *mha* . . .*"

"*Mhacasamhail*. It's Gaelic, meaning counterpart or equal, which is not exactly accurate, but it's the term that was chosen for these families."

"And if they're going to pick a term, why not go with the toughest one to pronounce?" I said. "Do I even want to know how it's spelled?"

"Probably not. The Americans go by *samhail*. Typical immigration. Come to America and simplify your name because we wouldn't want anyone to strain themselves linguistically."

"Uh-huh," I said. "So modern samhail—"

"—are a fairy tale," Ioan grumbled. "In the most literal sense of the term."

"You may state your case for that when Patrick's done."

Patrick chuckled. "Liv knows when she has the upper hand, and she's not afraid to use it. Must get that from *her* mother's side."

"Enough," I said. "Seriously, you two. I feel like I'm trying to plan a wedding with rival mothers-in-law. Patrick, focus. The samhail."

Patrick explained that they used the word for counterpart to recognize an equal relationship. A symbiotic one. An entire bloodline of the samhail would bond to a specific type of fae and provide any assistance those fae needed when interacting with the human world. In return, the fae would use their powers to enrich the samhail's lives.

"You may confirm that in my library when you get home," he said. "I can also tell you Ioan's side. He'll say the samhail *were* real but have long since died out. Whether he actually believes that is another story."

Ioan bristled. "The Cŵn Annwn do not lie."

"I know, it's one of your many failings."

"Stop," I said. "Ioan, is he right? The part about the samhail, at least?"

"He is. I will admit that we have had sporadic reports of them. Very sporadic, though, and unproven. I suspect they are humans who know about the fae and assist them but are not samhail."

"But the lamiae would only accept the girl's help if there's a familial bond," Patrick said. "One allowing them to trust her. I know of no other group who match that description. Do you?"

Ioan hesitated, then shook his head.

"Then I propose that we tell Liv about the samhail," Patrick said. "On the understanding this young woman may or may not be one of them. Agreed?"

I nodded.

"Excellent. Ioan, the floor is yours. Then Liv may get further information from my library."

Ioan snorted. "Nice try, bòcan. I'm not telling *you* what the Cŵn Annwn know about samhail."

Patrick sighed and turned to me. "I'll amend my proposal to this: Ioan and I will conclude our visit and allow you to rest, and when you're released, we'll provide you with what you need, separately, on the understanding it won't be shared. Now, Ioan, let's see if we can walk to the parking garage together without bloodshed."

Ioan nodded and said his goodbyes. I thanked him for the flowers and the basket. When Patrick cleared his throat, I ignored him.

"Tell Ricky I said hello," Ioan said before he started out.

"Oh, that's right," Patrick said. "Where is the boy?"

"He had classes," I said.

Patrick's lips twitched. "You don't have classes, do you, Gabriel? Of course not. Because *you* are an adult." He looked at Ioan. "A grown member of society, with a respectable job and a legal source of income."

"From what I hear, I wouldn't call *all* of it legal."

"Good God," I muttered. "Just go. Both of you."

CHAPTER SEVENTEEN

Ricky had said that hypothermia causes mental confusion. I was sure I'd be using that as an excuse for any less-than-brilliant choices over the next month, but one sign that I was still suffering from some lingering effects is the fact that I endured that day in the hospital with minimal complaint.

To say I hate hospitals is an understatement. It had always seemed a bizarre and groundless fear for a healthy kid. Then I discovered I'd been born with spina bifida—the condition my mother's murders had cured. I'm sure I spent a lot of time in hospitals over the first two years of my life, and I'm sure little of it was pleasant.

Knowing the cause of a phobia does not resolve it, though. At first, waking in the hospital, I'd had a general sense of anxiety. Even that ebbed and flowed as I talked to Gabriel and Ricky, then Patrick and Ioan. As the day wore on and the meds wore off, the more anxious I got, until the nurse came to check on me and I mentioned the possibility of a discharge before nightfall. She left, laughing.

Gabriel watched her go, and then got to his feet. "I'll fix this."

"No," I said. "She's right. I'm in no shape to look after myself."

"I can do that."

"You've done enough. *More* than enough. I'll spend another night and—"

146

"You don't want to be here," he said as he walked to the door.

And that was the sum of the argument. I didn't want to be in the hospital, so he would make sure I wasn't, even if it meant taking care of me himself.

He jumped into the river to save me.

I still struggled to understand that. Patrick had said it, and Gabriel hadn't argued, which meant it was true.

You fell off the bridge. So I fixed that.

I wanted to acknowledge what Gabriel had done, if it's possible to truly thank someone for saving your life. But at worst, he'd find some excuse to leave until I got over all that emotional nonsense. At best, he'd remind me of the times I'd risked my life for him, and I didn't want that, either, because it made this a repayment of debt. He didn't stand on that bridge and make a conscious decision to erase an obligation by jumping in after me. If he had, he certainly wouldn't have ducked the subject when Patrick brought it up.

Gabriel returned to tell me I'd been discharged. I had to sign something acknowledging that I was leaving against the doctor's orders, but otherwise I was free to go.

I was thrilled. Someone else was not.

"You are leaving *against* doctor's orders," Ricky said when I called to tell him. "Do you get that?"

"Of course—"

"No, I don't think you do, Liv. You want out. Badly. I understand that. But you nearly drowned. You suffered from hypothermia and a concussion. You didn't wake up for thirty hours. You can't walk out of the hospital on day one."

"Technically, it's day two."

As soon as I said that, I regretted it. He was seriously concerned for me, and I was making jokes.

"I—" I began.

"I get it," he said. "Gabriel gives you what you want, and I have to play the heavy, the guy who—" He inhaled sharply. "No, I'm not going to . . . Hell, yes. Yes, I am, because I'm pissed, Liv. Gabriel is being irresponsible. He's giving you what you want because you want it, and that's all that matters."

I'll fix this for you.

"You're right," I said. "I'm sorry. We shouldn't make you be the grown-up."

"You don't—"

"Yes, sometimes we do," I said as Gabriel walked back in. "I'll stay another night, and get some rest."

"As long as you're in that place, you *can't* rest." He exhaled a loud sigh. "Fuck. I don't know. Are you staying in the city or going home?"

"We hadn't . . ."

"You hadn't planned that far." Another sigh. "Can we do that, then? I know you'd be more comfortable in Cainsville, but I'd like you closer to a hospital. You're welcome to stay at my place. I'm supposed to do some work with my dad tonight, but I can either skip that or Gabriel can watch you until I get back."

Gabriel gestured for me to hand over the phone. If he can overhear a conversation, he doesn't see the point in pretending otherwise.

"I do have a plan," he said. "Whatever Ricky might think."

"I never said he didn't," Ricky said.

"Hash it out with him," I said, passed the phone over, and thumped back on the pillows.

Two hours later, I was heading to Gabriel's condo. His plan included a nurse drop-in visit Thursday morning and a more thorough visit from Dr. Webster in Cainsville on Friday.

When we got up to his apartment, he declared it a work-free night. We'd do something fun. How about . . . ? Cue two minutes of awkward silence.

"I have this," I said, waving Patrick's book.

"I said *fun*. If you'd like a novel, I have some that I suspect are more to your taste."

"I thought you didn't read fiction?"

"If you'd like quiet time, that's perfectly understandable." He went into his room, fetched pillows, and returned to the sofa. "But I thought we could do something together."

"Sure."

"Perhaps . . ." Ten seconds. Then, "You like movies. We'll watch one of those."

"Uh . . ." My gaze swept the screen-free condo. "On what?"

"Oh. Yes. Of course." He looked around. "Maybe on your laptop."

"How about cards?" I said. "You've gotta be able to play, considering you put yourself through college running an illegal gambling ring."

"Allegedly."

"Um, no. You confirmed that, remember?"

His lips twitched in the barest smile. "Ah, right. I certainly can play. However, you may also recall that I'm rather gifted at—"

"Cheating?"

"I was going to say sleight of hand."

"Same thing."

"Allegedly."

I smiled. "Well, I'm not going to wager. We will, however, need cards. Do you have a deck?"

"No, but I can acquire one far more easily than I can acquire a television."

"Mmm, I don't know. I bet one of your neighbors has a lovely big-screen TV you could lift faster than you could go out and buy a deck of cards."

His eyes glinted. "I thought you weren't wagering tonight."

I laughed. "Tempting, but we'd better stick to cards."

"Then make yourself comfortable. I'll be back shortly."

CHAPTER EIGHTEEN

That night, I dreamed that Gabriel found us something fun to do together. And it wasn't cards.

I woke from the dream, stretching in bed, pillows against me, face buried in them, inhaling the smell of him, drowsy and happy and—

Oh, shit.

I jumped up, pushing the pillow away and gasping for breath, struggling to clear the images from my mind because . . . Shit, shit, *shit*.

It was one thing to stay overnight at a guy's house. It was another to sleep in his bed. And it was another still when you could smell him in that bed, as if he was lying right beside you.

Shit, shit, *shit*.

I flicked on the bedside light. I still picked up the faint scent of him, tugging along the image of Gabriel himself, in bed and—

He'd wanted to change the sheets earlier, but I'd said not to bother. Insisted on it, actually. Maybe because I didn't *want* those sheets changed. I'd remembered other nights, the faint smell of him coming through the fresh pillowcase.

I had to change the sheets. At least that should keep me from having any unwelcome dreams. But doing that in the middle of the night? At best, it would suggest my head injury might be serious. At worst, it would be downright rude, implying the sheets stunk.

I glanced at the bedside table. Gabriel had picked up ginger ale because that's what I'd had in the hospital. I splashed the sheet with sticky soda.

Off with the soiled sheets. Now to find a new set.

A peek in the bedroom closet showed clothing. The en suite bathroom didn't have a closet. I'd seen one in the main bath, so I tiptoed through the living room and inside, closing the door all but a crack before turning on the light.

I opened the bathroom closet. Toiletries. Towels. A folded duvet cover, which suggested there were sheets in here somewhere. The shelves ran deep, and I tugged out the duvet cover and what looked like unused pillow shams—yeah, really couldn't imagine Gabriel using pillow shams. There was something behind them. A box. I peeked in and . . .

It looked like cans. I pulled one out. I didn't stop to consider whether I should—it was cans, not hidden client files.

I was holding a can of beef stew.

I reached into the box and felt around. More cans. Okay, well, that wasn't what I'd expected, but it was none of my business. I backed out and . . .

And Gabriel was standing right there. Still dressed from the day before, in trousers and a half-buttoned shirt.

"Hey, sorry," I said. "I spilled pop on the sheets and was looking for clean ones and—"

I lifted my hands in a shrug and realized I was still holding the stew. He looked at it. He looked at me. I put the can back so fast it clanged against the others, and I shoved the duvet and shams back in.

"I'm sorry," I said. "Really sorry. I wasn't snooping. That's why I didn't close the door and . . . And I guess I should have asked, but I didn't want to wake you, and I figured this was the obvious place, and I saw the duvet and there was something behind it and . . ."

And I'm babbling. Desperately babbling in hopes you'll get that look off your face.

Except it wasn't a look. That was the problem. His face was blank, and that emptiness wasn't a lack of emotion or reaction— it was a ten-foot-thick wall of ice.

I closed the closet door. "If you can just direct me to the sheets. Or get them. Right, that's better. You get them, and I'll put them on, and you can go back to bed. I'm sorry for disturbing you. Really sorry—"

He turned and walked out. I hesitated. Then I followed him into the bedroom. He was opening the dresser's bottom drawer and removing sheets.

I forced a strained laugh. "I would never have looked there. Thanks. I really didn't want to be looking at all. I just thought I'd check the bathroom closet and then I'd have given up." I had my hands out for the sheets, but he walked past me and started unfolding them on the bed.

"I can do that," I said.

No response.

I picked up the discarded sheets. "Where can I put these? You send it out, right? Is there someplace . . ."

He started making the bed. I folded the soiled sheets as well as I could, babbling the whole time.

Just going to put these here, right over here, and did I mention how sorry I am for snooping, except I wasn't really snooping, because I'd never do that.

"I'm going to take the sofa," I said. "I'm so sorry about this. I guess the sheets weren't that wet. I should have just left them."

He picked up a pillow and changed the case.

"I *am* sorry," I said. "You know I don't pry. I *hope* you know that. I'll . . . I'll be on the sofa, and I'll see you in the morning."

I got halfway to the door. Then, "Wait."

I turned. He had his back to me, kneeling in front of the bedside table, and I thought I'd misheard, but I paused anyway. He reached under the top shelf of the table. There was a ripping sound. He folded a length of duct tape and set it on the table. Then he turned with a gun in his hand.

I started in surprise. Yes, I suppose having a pissed-off guy pull out a gun was cause for shock. But the surprise was simply seeing him with a weapon.

He set the gun on the bed. Then he reached between the mattress and box spring, pulled out a knife, and put it beside the gun. Money came next, taped under the bed, an envelope of hundreds, which he dumped onto the sheet. He walked to the closet, dug into the back, and took out a case of Coke.

When he walked wordlessly past me and out the door, I looked at those things on the bed, that odd collection of items he'd kept stashed away. The gun I understood, for home security. Gun plus a knife? Options. The money made sense. The case of Coke, though? I stared at that and I thought of the stew in the bathroom closet and then . . .

Then I understood.

As he walked back in, carrying the carton of stew, I said, "Oh."

He stopped short, still no expression but his jaw tensing as he said, "Oh?"

I opened my mouth to say that I got it, that I understood. Then I realized how presumptuous that sounded. And how much worse this could get if I was wrong, and it seemed I was trying to analyze him.

So instead I said, "When I was in first grade, my teacher went on mat leave and we had a substitute for two months."

That got a lifting of the brows and an expression that could best be summed up as *Huh?* I moved to the bed and lowered myself beside the weapons and money.

"She was a real bitch," I said. "She'd retired a few years before. I'm guessing she needed extra cash and resented that, so she took it out on the kids. She had this rule that you couldn't use the bathroom except at recess and lunch. I didn't think much about it until one day I had to go bad. Really bad. My stomach started cramping and, well, I'll spare you the details. Let's just say I had an accident. Then I had to sit there while it seeped . . . Yep, skipping the details. The point is that by the time I could get up, everyone knew exactly what had happened. For weeks, they called me a baby. One of the boys brought me a diaper and . . ." I stopped and looked over at him. "As childhood traumas go, I know that's really lame. Compared to— Well, compared to most kids. But I had a damned near perfect childhood. Other kids liked me well enough, and I'd never been picked on, and for me this *was* traumatic. All I could think was that the whole thing could have been avoided if I'd had clean underwear in my backpack."

His brows lifted again.

"Yes, I know. That makes no sense. Clean underwear wouldn't have fixed anything. But it was like . . . it was like I needed to feel I could control the situation. To make sure that it never happened again. Which I could do by keeping clean underwear in my backpack. I don't even want to admit how many years I did that. It was about feeling that, if I had those, I'd never have to endure a trauma like that again. I was prepared."

I looked at the weapons and food and money, and I winced. "And that is the worst analogy ever. I'm sorry. I was trying . . . I wanted . . . Obviously, me and my clean underwear story isn't anything close to . . ." I pressed my palms to my eyes and got up. "I'm sorry. I'm tired and babbling. I just wanted . . ."

"To tell me you understood."

"Which I don't, obviously. I can't, and to even pretend I can is presumptuous."

He shook his head. "It's not."

"It is, and I'm sorry. Whatever reason you have for keeping this around is your business, and if you want to explain, then I'm happy to listen, but I won't analyze and pretend I get it."

"Tell me what you think it is," he said.

"I don't want to—"

"If you're wrong, that's fine." He looked at me. "But I don't believe you are."

I took a deep breath and turned to the items on the bed. "Weapons, money, food, drink . . . It's survival stuff. Like what people stash away in case of a natural disaster or a nuclear bomb or, hell, a zombie apocalypse. It makes them feel the same way I did, carrying around clean underwear. Like they're in control and prepared. Except you aren't worried about the end of the world. For you, it really is about survival. You lived for years where all this"—I waved at the items—"was a matter of life and death, and I'm sure there were times when you didn't have it, not nearly enough of it, and now you do and . . ."

I took another deep breath. "It's like my underwear times a hundred, because, let's face it, my childhood trauma isn't exactly traumatic. Yours—" I swallowed, biting back any observation that might make him uncomfortable. "I don't know how you did it, Gabriel. I don't know how you got from there to here"—I motioned at the room—"because I can't even fathom what it takes to accomplish that, and if having a case of Coke and a gun under your bed helps you feel like you'll never end up there again, then it's a small, small thing, because if it was me, I'd need a whole lot more than an envelope of money to give me what I needed to put my past behind me and move forward."

He nodded and said, "Yes." That's all he said. *Yes.* Then he picked up the case of stew and returned to the bathroom. When he came back with a roll of duct tape, I helped return the rest to where it went, and he didn't try to stop me. Didn't say a word, either, but that horrible, dead silence from earlier had passed, and this was . . .

I won't say it was comfortable. I could feel his lingering discomfort, pulling the room down, the mood somber. But it was relaxed enough for us to get everything back in place. Then I said, "Do you have ice cream?"

He looked over.

"I'm going to guess that's a no," I said. "And also, 'Why the hell are you asking about ice cream at four in the morning?'"

I won't say he smiled—or even that his lips moved—but his eyes warmed.

"That day with the underwear fiasco," I said, "my dad took me out for ice cream. I kind of feel like ice cream."

Totally untrue. I hadn't told my parents about the "great underwear incident" until a week later, when my dad finally convinced me to confess what was wrong. He'd gone to the school first. Then he took me to Six Flags, knowing the speed and thrill of the rides was the best thing to clear my mind and get me back on my feet. But I wanted to help Gabriel find his balance, and ice cream seemed a perfectly reasonable way to do it.

"I know there's a twenty-four-hour shop down the road," I said. "Can we walk over?"

"I believe I can do better than ice cream from a convenience shop," he said, the faintest smile breaking through.

"At four in the morning?"

"Let's see."

CHAPTER NINETEEN

Gabriel did not know where to find an open ice-cream parlor at 4 a.m. He did, however, know where to find all-night restaurants, not surprising given the hours he kept. One of those was a takeout diner. I got a milkshake. Gabriel said, "The same," and when the waitress asked which flavor, he frowned at the list, as if annoyed that options existed. "Whatever she had," settled the matter efficiently.

We went to sit, only to notice a couple of men watching us and whispering. That was less common these days—I'm getting to be old news—but normally, when it happened, Gabriel ignored it. Tonight, the look he gave the men suggested that if they said a word, he'd have a few to say back.

"How about outside?" I said. "There's a park a few doors down, and it's not too cold."

We sat in the park until the first hint of sun touched the horizon. It wasn't exactly a warm night, and the milkshakes didn't make it any warmer, but once we got talking, neither of us seemed to notice. We talked about the lamiae case and Aunika Madole—hashing it out because that's what we did, talked and bounced ideas around and segued along any path vaguely related to the topic at hand.

When I slurped the melted last of my shake, he said, "Good?"

I nodded.

"Even if it wasn't ice cream like your father got you?"

"He . . . didn't actually get me ice cream. Not that time."

"I know."

I laughed softly. "I'm that bad a liar?"

"No, you're a decent liar. Not on my level, of course, but perfectly adequate. I could not, however, imagine you telling your father that story and him resolving it by taking you for ice cream. At least, not until he'd resolved the core issue. He went to the school, I presume."

"Got the substitute teacher fired."

"Good."

"I feel a little bad about that."

"No, you don't."

I smiled. "Okay, you're right. I don't." I took his empty cup and stood. "How was the milkshake?"

"Excellent. I believe the last time I had one, I was five. The elders would buy them for me when I ran errands."

"They stopped when you were five?"

"No, I was five when I realized the shakes were, essentially, empty calories, and I could ask for something more nutritionally substantial." He leaned back on the bench. "Until I was eight and asked for money in lieu."

I laughed as I took away the trash, but the laugh was for his benefit, and as soon as my back was to him, I was no longer smiling. I was thinking of a five-year-old boy, telling the elders he'd prefer something more nutritious than milkshakes. I imagined them smiling and humoring him and, yes, kids go through those phases, when they learn that something isn't good for them and resolve to make better choices. But if a five-year-old voluntarily rejects sweets to eat healthy and then starts asking for the money instead, at some point you have to realize something is wrong. Seriously wrong. Like maybe he's asking because he damned well needs the decent food he's not getting at home. The elders should have figured out—

Behind me, pavement scraped underfoot. I turned to see Gabriel rising.

"Olivia?" he said, his voice perfectly calm, his gaze fixed on a stand of trees. "Your purse?"

I threw the trash into the bin with one hand and pulled my gun from my purse with the other. My attention—like his—never left those trees. Then Gabriel's swung to a brick pavilion. He started toward it at a slow lope. I covered him, breaking into a jog when he disappeared around the wall.

At a thump and a gasp, I was running, ignoring the pain shooting through my side. I saw Gabriel swing at a dark figure. Movement flickered behind him, but before I could call a warning, he'd knocked his target aside and was turning to the new threat. By the time I arrived, he had the second assailant pinned to the pavilion wall. The first was still on the ground, struggling for breath and holding his stomach.

The man on the ground wobbled to his feet. Gabriel let him. Then, without releasing his grip on the other assailant, he clocked the first guy, dropping him again.

The figure pinned to the wall was the man from Monday night, the one who'd pursued Aunika and me.

"If you have your switchblade, you might want to use it on that one." Gabriel nodded toward the man on the ground. "Preferably in his right side."

"He's the one who stabbed me?"

"Yes."

"You can't intimidate me, Walsh," the man said, rubbing his jaw.

"Intimidation suggests no intention of follow-through. I'd be quite happy to see Olivia stab you in retaliation. In fact, if I thought she'd do it, I'd insist. However, barring that . . ." Gabriel turned as the man rose again, and then kicked him in the gut so hard the man howled as he fell back.

"You—you bastard. I think you broke something."

"The correct term would be 'ruptured.' I'd strongly suggest you seek medical attention when you leave." He turned to the man he had pinned to the wall. "Who hired you?"

"Hired us? No one—"

"You are a gun for hire. Or muscle for hire, given that you don't actually seem to have a gun. Which is odd, suggesting that's a stipulation by the man who hired you. Who is also, presumably, the one who tried to stop your colleague here from attacking Olivia."

"I don't know what—"

"Let me go slower, then. You are hired muscle. A mercenary, to use the proper term. Former military, judging by that tattoo and your bearing. You've slipped a little in your grooming and your mannerisms, which tells me you've been out of the service for a while yet still try to maintain the lifestyle to project a military image for your clients. Ergo, mercenary."

"Who the fuck are you? Sherlock Holmes?"

Gabriel's lips twitched at that. He nodded to me, letting the actual detective take over.

"As for the gun stipulation," I said. "You're clearly more accustomed to using weapons than brute force, given how easily you were both rousted. That suggests the absence of a gun isn't your choice. Which also suggests you weren't hired to hurt Aunika. Just scare her. That goes for anyone else you encounter in executing those duties. Like me. You seemed to think Aunika knew why you were after her. But when she asked, you wouldn't tell her. What was the point of that?"

"You're the clever one. I'm sure you have an answer."

"*You* don't know why you're targeting her. Men like you don't need reasons. Even if your boss told you, I don't think you're bright enough to remember it."

"I'm sure my IQ is higher than yours, blondie. I don't want details for security reasons. The less we know, the better. The client told us that Madole knows exactly what's going on. She's just playing dumb. We're supposed to scare her until she breaks and does what the client wants."

"Which is?"

He fixed me with cool gray eyes. "That's not our concern."

"And your client thinks I'm connected? Is that why you're following me?"

The guy on the ground—clearly feeling left out of this confessional moment—said, "No, he wanted us to make sure you're okay."

His partner shot him a shut-the-fuck-up look, but his partner was tired of playing stoic paramilitary dude and continued. "We followed you from the hospital, but we couldn't get good-enough photographs. That's what he wants: pictures to prove you're up and around, no harm done."

"Shut—" the other man began . . . and Gabriel hit him. A punch to the jaw as effortless and casual as if he'd reached up to scratch his nose.

"You needed pictures of Ms. Taylor-Jones as proof she was not seriously injured," Gabriel said to the man on the ground. "You may tell your employer that she *was* injured—seriously—and when I find him, he will pay for that. Preferably through a civil suit, but other methods may be substituted as needed. Now, your client asked for proof that she survived her ordeal. Specifically her?"

"You, too, though he was more concerned with her."

Gabriel nodded, processing. "Do you have anything to add?"

"No."

"All right. Before I release you, I'd like the name of your client."

The man against the wall managed to laugh, wincing from his injured jaw. "Address, e-mail, and social security number, too?"

"Some method of contact would be appreciated."

"God, you're a piece of work, Walsh. That arrogance might work in a courtroom, but in the real world, people don't just give you whatever you want—"

"True." Gabriel pinned the guy, forearm at his throat, silencing him, as I began searching his pockets. "But I do like to give them the option. It's only reasonable."

I found a cell phone and a knife tucked in his shoe. I took both. That's when the guy on the ground decided rather belatedly to make a run for it. Gabriel tossed mercenary #1 aside and caught #2 by the back of the jacket. The guy didn't bother waiting for me to pat him down. He handed me a phone and a knife while his partner cursed him out. I still did the pat-down, and found only a set of car keys. We released the men, and I watched them struggle to pull their dignity back in place as they strode away.

CHAPTER TWENTY

We sat in the car, on a hill near the city limits, and watched the sun rise. It was Gabriel's idea. Even if he cannot quite fathom the appeal of watching something that occurs—without fail—every day, he knew that it'd been a ritual with my father and brought back good memories. So he got me a mocha and brought me here.

I went through the phones we'd confiscated. Texted instructions confirmed the two guys were hired help and that their mission had indeed been to provide proof that I was alive and well. Which was a little weird, and made Gabriel and me both wonder if the client knew who I was—not Olivia Taylor-Jones or Eden Larsen, but Matilda, prized by the Tylwyth Teg and the Cŵn Annwn, both of whom were not pleased I'd nearly died.

I was going through those when my phone buzzed. Incoming voice mails. A whole bunch of them.

"Seems the new phone is taking its time releasing my messages," I said as I flipped to the inbox. "I have three from Ricky. One—oh, shit. Pamela got my number, and I totally forgot to tell you."

Dismay crossed his face, disappearing under an impassive mask. I knew it was difficult for him to talk about her, as much as he pretended otherwise. This was the woman who'd had him framed for murder.

"She called right before I met up with Aunika Monday

night. She found out about Ricky somehow. That he's in trouble. She says she has information that can help him."

"I'll speak to her."

"Absolutely not. She's just manipulating me, and I'm not even going to listen to her messages." I scrolled down the list. "Despite the fact she left six of them. How the hell is she doing that? When she called, I didn't get the penitentiary warning."

"She's borrowed or stolen a phone. It happens. However, it might be wise for me to contact her and tell her you're all right, given that your accident made the paper."

"Right," I muttered. "Shit."

"I ought to get a message to both Pamela and Todd, assuring them you are well."

"Can you tell Todd to call me? So I can let him know myself that I'm fine. And have Lydia handle Pamela. I really don't want you having contact with her."

That flash of dismay again. He saw avoiding Pamela as weakness. He cleared his throat and said, "We need to talk. I . . ." Another throat clearing, then he looked out the car window to see the sun was finally up and said, with some relief, "You wanted to see Ms. Madole's apartment. We'll do that now."

Gabriel picked the building's rear-door lock. We made sure no one was inside, and then hunted for the apartment access. I found it easily enough—a set of stairs behind what seemed like a closet door.

"This is more likely to have a security system," Gabriel said.

He picked the lock. As he pulled back, his bare wrist touched the metal, and he jumped as a red welt rose on his wrist.

"It's electrified," he said. "I don't believe I've ever encountered that."

"Mmm, maybe not." I took off my glove and touched the knob with the back of my knuckle. Then said, "Try again. Carefully."

He did, and his lips curved in an unspoken curse as he got another jolt.

"Cold-forged iron," I said. "I feel it as a weird tingling, but it affects you more since you're at least half—" I caught myself. "I mean, fae runs strongly in the Walsh side."

"I can't imagine I have more fae blood than you."

"Todd's line is Cŵn Annwn. It's different," I said quickly. "The point is that cold-forged iron affects you. So once we're inside, avoid anything metal."

He slipped inside to check for alarms. After a few moments he returned and said, "It's disarmed."

"That was fast," I said, joining him.

"I mean it was already disarmed. Aunika must not have come back after that night."

I didn't like the sound of that but told myself that her pursuer hadn't wanted her harmed. After our plunge off the bridge, she probably wisely decided to hole up and stay safe, which didn't include making a trip back for her toothbrush.

Aunika's apartment looked like a generic hotel suite—basic and cheaply furnished. It was the decorations that turned it into a home, yet they weren't so much decorations as keepsakes. Homemade knickknacks. Faded greeting cards. *Thank you Aunika, for making a difference.*

Photos of girls covered the walls. Portraits, like the ones downstairs, plus a stack of photographs on an end table. These were the stories she wanted to remember. Memories of girls who grew up. Girls who weren't the lamiae, who had a future if they could get their lives on track.

I looked for girls in snakeskin belts. Dark-haired girls with ancient eyes. I didn't see them until I went into her bedroom, where I found a collage on the wall. They were smiling here, caught off guard and tossing Aunika a genuine smile—girlish and innocent.

I took pictures of that wall. Intrusive, yes, but putting faces to the local lamiae would help.

When I heard a beep in the front room, I went in to see Gabriel standing over an answering machine.

"Hey, Aunika," a male voice said. "Wow, you really do have an answering machine. Very old-school. But I guess you have to, if you don't carry a cell phone." A nervous laugh. "Anyway, it's Rob. From last week? I know things didn't go too well, but I'd like a, uh, second chance. I promise I won't talk about my ex. Okay? Call me back?"

The next message was from a neighbor complaining about two men who were asking after Aunika and could Aunika please tell her friends not to pester her neighbors?

"Those 'friends' were stalkers, lady," I said.

The next message was an appointment reminder. The next was a returned call from a service company. And then,

"Hey, Ani. It's Erin. I opened up today, which isn't a problem. But you aren't answering your door or your cell, so I'm getting a little freaked. Can you call me back?"

"That's the girl who works downstairs with her," I said. "And apparently Aunika does have a cell phone. She just doesn't give the number on first dates."

Another couple of non-important calls followed. Then, "Ani?" A girl's voice paused and then gave a low chuckle. "Answering machine, right? I remember those. It's Melanie. Where are you? Erin says you're taking time off, but I can't reach you on your cell, and we were supposed to meet up for coffee, and it's not like you to forget. You know how to get in touch with me. Just let us know you're okay, all right?"

The next one was the same girl. "Ani? I'm getting worried now. It's been three days. The others are freaking out. After Lucy and Rina and Steph, well, they're really freaking out. Please tell us you didn't go after this guy yourself. Get back to me. I've got a number you can use." She rattled it off and I jotted it down.

———

The number provided by the lamia—Melanie—was answered by a guy who grunted that he'd take a message. Gabriel dropped me off at the office, where the nurse met me for a checkup while he headed to meet a client. Gabriel's admin assistant—Lydia—and I were chatting when my phone blipped with an incoming text from Pamela.

I was about to erase the message. Then I stopped, seeing the words.

Ciro Halloran. Lucy Madole. Lamiae. Ricky.

Another came in.

I can help you.

I slid off Lydia's desk. "I need to talk to Pamela. If Gabriel comes back early, can you give me a head start before you tell him?"

"Enough time so he can't catch up and stop you?"

"Please. Pamela's being a pain in the ass, and I don't want him dealing with her. I'll shut her down myself."

I arrived at the prison and was putting my phone in the glove compartment when it started to ring with Gabriel's tone. I hit Ignore, murmured an apology, tucked it away, and hurried off.

CHAPTER TWENTY-ONE

I was ready to do battle with Pamela. Ready for that wide I'm-so-happy-to-see-you smile that lights up her face and makes me feel guilty for cutting her out of my life. Ready for the I-just-want-to-protect-you-Eden bullshit that led to a good man's death.

But for the first time, my mother walked into the visiting room with her head high, no hint of a smile on her face. No smiles for the guard, either. No whispered words of thanks for the escort, whom she dismissed with a flick of her fingers.

"Eden," Pamela said. "You got my message."

"I did."

"You're well?" Her gaze surveyed me. It was a thorough assessment, but a cool one, as if ensuring one's prize mare hadn't been injured. "Gabriel left me a message detailing all of your injuries and your prognosis and your release from the hospital." A humorless smile. "I would thank him for being so considerate, if it didn't come with a warning to stop contacting you. Screw him."

This was my mother. My real mother. Looking in her eyes right now, I could finally reconcile the woman before me with the one who'd murdered four people.

"What do you want, Pamela?" I asked. "You're offering me information. Therefore you want something. Quid pro quo. It's the Tylwyth Teg way."

That icy composure cracked at the edges. My mother hates the fae, even if we both share their blood.

"I want to renew contact," she said. "With you."

My laugh came harsh. "Bullshit. I see through you now, Pamela. Don't play the doting mother—"

"You don't see me at all, Eden. And yes, I will call you that. You are Eden to me. You are Eden to your father, even if he is more circumspect. I *am* the doting mother. I'm simply not the kind of doting mother you're comfortable with—the one who bakes cookies and sings you to sleep. Look to your father for that sort of love. Look to me for protection."

"All right. Since we seem to be putting our cards on the table, let me lay out mine. Don't ever use that word with me again."

"Mother?"

"Protection. We both know where your maternal protection led, and I'm sick of hearing how everything is for my own good. Move on."

Her lips curved and that ice thawed, just a little. "Good girl. Consider the matter set aside. Yes, I do want something. I want a place in your life, and if I need to bribe you to get it, then that's what I'll do."

"You said you have information on the lamiae murders. From where?"

"The same place I get many special treats these days, Eden. I've always had benefactors. In the past, the Cŵn Annwn looked after me. That was the deal—if we were convicted, they would make prison easier for me and your father."

"So this information comes from the Cŵn Annwn?"

"No, they have made sure I am safe in here and never need to worry about anything as trivial as my commissary fund. But it's not as if they visit me or seek my favor by offering useful information."

"Which someone now is."

"Several someones."

"Starting with Tristan."

"Yes. And after his disappearance, my stock soared in value. I am the mother of the new Matilda. I paid the price of my freedom to cure her from a crippling condition. Then I enlisted Tristan and, ultimately, left him to take the fall for crimes we conspired to commit. I bested one of their own. And they fall over themselves to praise me for that as a sign of my power, my strength. I have met monsters in here, but there are none that compare to the average fae."

"Yet you use them to your advantage."

"I do. I just never forget what they are. They court my favor now, in hopes I'll use my influence with you."

"Influence for what?"

"Everything. To convince you to side with one or the other. To side with neither. To betray one. To take them under your wing and give them sanctuary in Cainsville. To champion their cause and invoke the fury of the Cŵn Annwn on their behalf. There is much you can do for fae."

"So that's the price: you give me information, and I grant them favors."

"No, I promise them nothing. I would never see you obliged to the fae, Eden."

"Okay, so this information . . ."

"Ciro Halloran's common-law wife was murdered two months ago," she said. "My sources tell me he is now killing lamiae. Two so far. I trust you know that much."

"I do."

"His wife, Lucy Madole, came from a family of *mhacasamhail*. That's Gaelic for 'counterpart.'"

"Families with ties to the fae. Generations-long reciprocal relationships."

Pamela sniffed. "Generations-long slavery. But yes, the Madole family are samhail. So is the Halloran family."

"Ciro's?"

She smiled. "Good. I've added new information to your investigation. Yes, the Hallorans are also samhail. That's how Lucy met Ciro. It is also why he's been able to avoid death by the hounds of the Cŵn Annwn."

"It also means he *knows* he isn't killing random street kids."

"Yes."

"Do you know *why* he's killing them?"

She shook her head. "My contacts only see what's happening. But take a closer look at the murders. They aren't random stabbings."

"I know the killings themselves seem ritualistic. Is there more?"

"My contacts don't know. The bodies haven't been found. That's common with fae. After death, the glamour breaks."

"On to Ricky, then," I said. "What do you know about his connection to this?"

"That he's been framed for Halloran's disappearance. Framed poorly."

I had to bite my tongue not to comment on that.

"I'm still worried," I said.

"Of course you are. Ricky is a good man. The Cŵn Annwn are not fae. They have principles. Like your father. I'm trying to get more on this problem with Ricky. Right now, I know only that he was accused. Getting a reason is my priority, Eden, because I know it's yours."

So she would keep digging, but to hear what she found, I had to visit her. I agreed to that.

As I rose to leave, she said, "Before you go, I'd like to thank you for letting Gabriel take my case."

I took a moment to assimilate that. Then I said calmly, "You were doing so well. I really thought we were making progress. But when it comes to Gabriel, you cannot resist."

"He didn't tell you?"

"You know he didn't or you wouldn't have brought it up."

"So I should have kept that from you? Let you go on thinking you can trust him?"

"I can trust him. Yes, in the past he's done things that hurt me because they benefited him financially. But that isn't the reason here, is it?"

"Of course it is. He'll be well compensated—"

"There is not enough money in the world to make him represent you again. This is about exonerating Todd. I want my father out. To give me that, Gabriel's willing to represent the woman who tried to put him in jail for life."

"And he made that decision without consulting you."

"He had to. Even if it means hurting Todd's chances, I could never have let Gabriel do it. So he's taken that choice out of my hands, and maybe it makes me a coward and a hypocrite, but I appreciate what he's done."

"You appreciate him betraying your trust."

"Yep. And I appreciate you telling me, because it gives me the perfect excuse to say *screw off, Mom*."

I got to my feet. The guard started forward, but Pamela's hand shot up to stop her.

"All right, Eden. You win that one. You're right. I cannot overlook an opportunity to drive a wedge between you and Gabriel. You're going to need to allow me that one weakness. However, you have my word that I won't hurt him to do it."

"You're in jail. You can't *physically* hurt him yourself. Nice loophole. Try again, Pamela."

I walked back to the table. Sat. Folded my hands on it. Waited. It took at least two full minutes before she said, "I will do nothing that could lead to him being physically harmed. I will do nothing that could lead to him being incarcerated or otherwise forcibly removed from your life. If I ever do, you have the right to never see me again."

"Still a loophole, should you decide that getting rid of him is worth it."

Her jaw tensed, just a little, but she said, "Fine. You have my unequivocal word. I will do nothing to see him physically harmed or forcibly removed from your life."

"Good." I rose again. "I'm still going to penalize you for that foul, though. If you have more information on Ricky, I will come see you. However, you need to contact me through Gabriel."

"And trust he'll actually tell you?"

"He will."

CHAPTER TWENTY-TWO

Gabriel was waiting in the hall. Not standing there impatiently. Not checking his e-mail. Not jotting notes on a scrap of paper. Just standing, his attention fixed on the visiting room door. When I walked out, his gaze shot to my face. I kept my expression impassive as I said, "Is there something you wanted to tell me?"

It was, I will admit, a cruel jab, given that I'd just told Pamela I was fine with what Gabriel had done. But if I walked out of that room and said, "It's okay. I understand," that would give him an excuse the next time.

His only reaction was a cheek tic and the slightest shift of his gaze. For Gabriel, though, that was as sure a sign of shame and guilt as if he'd dropped to his knees.

"I should have told you."

"*When* should you have told me? At what point, exactly?"

A glimpse of something almost like panic, as his mind whirred to come up with the right answer. He knew the one I wanted, and while Gabriel Walsh had no problem telling people what they wanted to hear—truth be damned—I was different.

"It's not a test, Gabriel," I said. "Put it this way—when do you think I'd want you to tell me?"

"Before I first spoke to her."

"And when do *you* think you should have told me?"

"Immediately after she agreed."

I laughed. The sound startled him, as he looked at me in confusion. I rose up on my tiptoes and brushed my lips across his cheek. "You passed."

Now he really did stare at me, as if suspecting I'd been passed an illegal narcotic during my brief prison sojourn.

"Sorry," I said. "I'm sure you'd rather have had a handshake, but I couldn't resist. You'll survive."

I pointed toward the exit, and we started out. We got through the doors. Then I said, "Waiting for the other shoe to drop?"

"Yes."

I smiled. "Okay, I think you should have told me right away. I can hardly say that I'm *glad* you went behind my back, can I? In future, just tell me, okay? Then do whatever you think is best. But I understand why you skipped that this time, and so I accept your apology."

"I haven't apologized yet."

"Mmm, right. Do you want to do that? Or just pretend you did?"

"I made a conscious decision to do what I thought was right, knowing that you would likely disagree. I'm sorry if you thought it was the wrong decision."

"That's kinda like an apology. Sure, I'll take it. Now, do you have dinner plans?"

"Do I ever?"

"You do now."

Our early dinner turned into a late one, lingering over the meal and then dessert and then coffee. We talked about his strategy for Pamela and Todd. We talked about what Pamela had told me. We talked about Aunika and Ciro and the lamiae and what we'd do next. And we talked. Mostly, we just talked.

I'd had a bit too much wine to fetch my car, so Gabriel drove me to Ricky's. If I needed a lift in the morning, just call. No, scratch that—he'd pick me up at eight.

When I opened Ricky's door and saw him dozing on the couch, textbook open on his chest, I watched him and thought how lucky I was. I stood there, grinning like an idiot, the wine still singing through my veins. Then I crept forward until I was right beside him and—

Ricky grabbed my arm and pulled me down onto him in a kiss.

"Gotcha," he said.

"That was supposed to be my line."

"You're too slow."

He tugged me on top of him and pushed the book to the floor with a thump. Then he kissed me, a sweet and deep kiss that seemed to ignite that lingering wine, sending it roaring to my head, making me light-headed and giddy and happy. Indescribably happy. When he ended the kiss, he caught my chin and lifted my face over his, looking up at me.

"Yes, I may have over-imbibed on the cabernet."

He chuckled, a delicious throaty chuckle, as intoxicating as the wine. He stroked his thumb over my cheek and said, "You look happy," and I thought I caught a note of wistfulness in his voice and I pulled up a little, worried, but his smile held no hint of that, and his next kiss was even better than the first. A kiss that had me stretching out against him, pressing against him, as he entwined his fingers in my hair. No quick shedding of clothing. No hands moving anywhere other than hair and hips. Just a kiss. A wonderful kiss.

When it broke, he took my face in his hands again, fingers stroking both sides of it, eyes looking up into mine as he smiled and said, "I'm glad to see you happy again, Liv."

"Um, pretty sure I've been happy for about six months now, ever since a certain guy convinced me to go out with him."

He smiled. "You've been happy. Just not like this. Not for a while. It's good to see." He kissed me again, briefer now, slower and sweeter.

When I pulled back, I said, "You could make me happier," and his smile grew to a grin.

"Could I?" he said. "And how would I do that?"

"You want details?"

"Painstaking detail. Explicit instructions. I'd hate to get it wrong."

I stretched over to lean down to his ear and told him.

CHAPTER TWENTY-THREE

That night, I dreamed of Arawn. I've never done that. I've caught snatches of him in visions, yes. Seen him while I'd been drowning, yes. But when I dream, it's Ricky I see. Now it was Arawn.

We were riding together, sharing a horse. I sat behind him, holding on tight as he spurred the stallion ever faster, whipping through the forest so fast my heart was in my throat and I was sure every leap was going to see me unseated, my brains dashed against a tree. And I loved it. I loved that pounding adrenaline, that delicious fear, and he knew it, and I loved that most of all—that this ride was for me. For us.

The ride seemed to last forever, the horse moving preternaturally fast. I heard the hounds in the forest. I could see only glimpses of red eyes, but I knew they were there and I smiled. His hounds. Keeping him safe.

He took me so far that I no longer even knew where I was. Then there was a hill, and the coal-black stallion raced up the steep face as if it was flat ground. At the top, I looked around and sucked in breath.

"By the gods," I whispered.

Arawn turned to me, and I saw his face for the first time since the vision began. He was a young man, not yet out of his teens. Wild dark hair. Wild dark eyes. A grin so big and so dazzling that I stared, transfixed, before yanking my gaze to the sight that had transfixed me only a moment ago.

Standing stones topped the hill. Ancient, weathered, moss-covered stones. They glowed as the moonlight shone on them, bright as the midday sun. I slid off the horse and ran between the stones, running my hands over them, feeling their power as I raced from one to the next, greedily touching each. Then I stopped and looked up at the moon, and I laughed. I laughed with pure joy, pure glee, and when I lowered my gaze, it fell on him. Arawn. Standing in front of me, smiling.

"You're happy?" he said.

"I am incredibly happy," I said, grinning up at him. "Thank you."

"That smile is all the thanks I need." He stepped closer and lowered his voice. "I want you to be happy, Mati. That's all I want."

I smiled, and he moved closer still. His hand went to my chin, and he lifted my face to his. I saw him there, the handsome face of a boy I loved. And yet it lasted only a blink before I saw another face. A fair-haired boy with blue eyes I could lose myself in. Blue eyes I *had* lost myself in, and it didn't matter if Gwynn had given no sign he felt the same. I told myself I should take this, take Arawn's kiss, be happy with that, because I did love him. He leaned in for that kiss and . . . I dipped my head. Ducking away. He hesitated. Then his lips brushed my forehead and he pulled me into a tight embrace.

"Whatever makes you happy, Mati," he said, and there was a wistfulness that pulled me out of the dream, just a little, reminding me of Ricky.

Arawn kissed my forehead again. "Friends?"

I kissed his chin. "Best friends."

"No matter what?"

I hugged him tightly. "No matter what."

"Why aren't you paying attention?" a plaintive voice asked behind me. I turned from Arawn to see the lamia who'd spoken to me in the vision, that night I'd seen one of their deaths.

"We die, and you play with Arawn and Gwynn. You laugh and you flirt and you fuck, and we die, and you care not at all."

I was back to myself, standing alone on that hill, the girl in front of me.

"Actually, I'm pretty sure what I'm doing right now is sleeping," I said. "Which I'm going to need to get back on the case." *Oh, and sorry I missed a couple of days there. Being unconscious in the hospital. After falling off a bridge while on that case that I'm* not *investigating, apparently.*

"Do you have anything to help my investigation?" I asked.

She said nothing, just fixed that reproachful gaze on me.

"Can I ask you questions?"

"You need to pay attention, Mallt-y-Nos. Pay attention to us. To what's happening to us."

"No, actually, she does not," said another voice. I turned to see a man. Tall, golden hair, bright blue eyes. It was the eyes I knew. Otherwise, he was so much older than I'd seen him before, his face lined, those blue eyes exhausted.

"Gwynn," I whispered.

I looked down at my hands again, expecting to see Matilda's, but they were still mine.

"Pay the lamiae no mind," he said. "You have more important things to focus on."

"He's right." Another voice. To my left. I looked, and it was Arawn, just as old, his dark beard shot with gray, eyes as tired, as if he had lived longer than he cared to. His lips quirked in a smile, a hint of the boy I knew. "Yes, occasionally he *is* right. It's rare, I know."

Gwynn rolled his eyes. Arawn stepped toward me. "Ignore them, Mati. Ignore the lamiae. As cruel as that might sound. They are but a symptom of the disease. Cure the disease, and you help them. Decide your future, and you help them."

"Choose, you mean." I glanced from Arawn to Gwynn.

Arawn gave me that same tired but affectionate smile. "Not that choice. That one is decided. It always has been. We were just too selfish to see it. Too selfish and afraid."

"I meant choose Tylwyth Teg or Cŵn Annwn."

"Ah, did you now?" Arawn's lips twitched. "Yes, there is that choice, but it isn't so simple, as I think you've begun to realize, which is why you're avoiding the issue altogether. You tell them you're taking a bit of time to get your thoughts straight. Really, you're postponing and procrastinating."

"Nothing will change by waiting," Gwynn said. "The answer will not come in a dream or a vision. The longer you delay, more problems will arise." He waved at the lamia, frozen as if she was a statue. "To solve those problems, address the core issue."

"Not while girls are dying," I said.

"They aren't girls."

When I tensed, Arawn said, "He doesn't mean it like that."

"Yes, I do," Gwynn said. "They are *not* girls. It doesn't mean they deserve to die, but they aren't innocent children in need of protection."

"No?" I said, meeting his gaze.

"No, Matilda. They're not. The sooner you remember that, the easier this will be."

"I'm not Matilda."

His lips curved, the smile so faint that I couldn't help but see Gabriel in it. "You are our Matilda, as much as we are the men you know now and as much as we are the boys you remember."

"That makes no sense," I snapped.

He met my gaze. "Doesn't it? I am the Gwynn in Matilda's memories. *Your* memories. Whatever is left of me is there, in your world, in your Gabriel, just as whatever is left of our Mati stands before us. As much as you don't want to hear that."

"I—"

"You don't want to hear it because you want to be your own person. You want Gabriel and Ricky to be their own persons. Which you are. Which they are."

"You're only confusing her," Arawn said. "You do realize that, don't you?" His hand went to my arm. "He's right in this, though, Liv. We want you to forget the lamiae. Yet we know you will not. Matilda would not, and so you would not. Just take care. Please." He leaned and kissed my forehead again. "Now it's time for you to wake up."

CHAPTER TWENTY-FOUR

I bolted upright in bed and looked around. Ricky rose beside me.

"Liv?" he croaked.

"I . . ." I peered around the dark and silent room. "I was having a dream. I think it was . . ." I rubbed my eyes and shook my head.

He reached up and tugged the blind, letting moonlight slide across the bed.

"A vision?" he asked.

"I . . . I don't know. Arawn was there."

A twist of a smile, one that mirrored Arawn's so well I shivered. "Was he being a jerk?"

No. Arawn was never a jerk in my visions. Not Arawn nor Gwynn. Not even in that terrible last one, when they'd forced Matilda to choose. Not jerks. Just young men, a little arrogant, a little frightened, a little angry, both struggling to hold on to her, only to both lose her.

"We were riding and . . ." I shook my head. "Never mind. Details aren't important."

He tugged me down as he stretched out on his back. "I'd like to hear them."

I hesitated. Then I told him everything I remembered, from the thunder of the horse's hooves to the baying of the hounds. This is the dilemma, the contradiction we cannot resolve. We do not want to be them. Yet we are fascinated by them, because every detail tugs at a buried memory. It's like smelling balloons and getting a flash of a forgotten birthday party, and as I talked, Ricky pulled me against him, both of us sharing those tugs of memory.

I told him the rest, too, about the lamiae and the older Arawn and Gwynn.

"Well, that's bullshit," he said.

"Telling me to ignore the lamiae?"

"No, that's just pointless, which they seemed to realize. The bullshit is that lamia saying you aren't paying attention to their deaths. You almost *died* working their case."

"Maybe it's my subconscious then? Making me feel like I'm not working hard enough?"

"I'd buy that. I also get where Arawn and Gwynn are coming from—whether they were visions or subconscious manifestations. The lamiae aren't your responsibility. And, no, I'm not telling you to stop investigating. But maybe . . ."

"Holding the Tylwyth Teg and the Cŵn Annwn to my timetable isn't helping anyone. I'm pushing them off because I don't want to deal with it."

"You were giving yourself mental space. Which you needed. If two more months helps, then screw the dreams. They might very well just be your subconscious, expecting too much of yourself. As usual."

"Hmm."

He slid his hands under my arms and pulled me onto him.

"You do," he said. "You have a very high set of personal expectations. It's not necessarily a bad thing . . . except when you beat yourself up for not meeting them."

He kissed me before I could answer, a slow and wonderful kiss, his hands sliding up my back, warming my chilled skin, and I lifted my hands to his hair, wrapping my fingers in it and kissing him back and—

My phone rang. Ricky let out a growl, and I chuckled.

"It's no one on my ring-tone list," I said. "Therefore I can safely ignore it."

I kissed him again, but before I closed my eyes, his gaze shifted toward my phone on the nightstand. I sighed and pulled back.

"You want me to answer?" I said.

"I think that the fact an unknown number is calling at three in the morning might not be something to ignore."

I reached for the phone, but he beat me to it, picking it up and saying, "May I? If it's nothing, I'd like to give them proper hell."

I smiled. "Go for it."

He answered with a grunted, "Hello," devoid of his usual charm. He held the phone far enough from his ear for me to hear.

"Wh-who is this?" a young female voice asked.

"Ricky Gallagher."

"Arawn," the voice breathed, exhaling the name, and Ricky stiffened.

"It's Ricky," he said.

"I-I know. Sorry. Is Mat—Eden there?"

He said nothing.

"Olivia," the voice said quickly. "She goes by Olivia now. I'm sorry. I'm just—I need to speak to her. Please. I know it's late—early—but I really need—"

"Who is this?"

"I-I'm a friend—a client of Aunika. One of her girls. From the clinic."

"If you know who I am, then you don't need to beat around the bush. Liv has spent two days in the hospital because of Aunika and her 'girls,' and she's recovering with some much-needed sleep."

"Lamiae," the girl blurted. "I'm one of the lamiae. I'm sorry. I'm just . . . I'm not accustomed to—"

"Get to the point."

Every time he was curt with the girl, I had to resist reaching for the phone. Gwynn was right—I may know they're fae, but I see teen girls, and right now I heard a lost girl in trouble.

"They call me Melanie," she said.

"What matters to me is that it's three in the morning, and if you so desperately need to speak to Liv, you'll tell me what it's about before I hang up."

"Something's wrong at the clinic. There's—"

"Why are you there at this hour?"

"Looking for Aunika. One of the others saw a light after midnight. We thought Aunika might be back. But I can't get in. There's cold iron blocking the doors."

"Isn't there always?"

"Not the main doors. She just puts it on her office and her apartment because there are fae who'd like to hurt her."

"Why?"

A soft hiss of frustration, reminding me what Melanie really was. "I'll answer all your questions later, Arawn. Right now, something's wrong. I can't get past the doors and I . . . I smell blood."

"All right. Thank you for the information."

"Wait! You're not—she's not coming?"

"Whatever happened in there will wait until a decent hour."

"But—"

"If you were so concerned about Aunika, maybe you should have returned the message Liv left for you this morning."

"I—"

"If you want to speak to Liv, wait at the clinic. She'll show. Eventually."

He hung up, handed me the phone, and rolled out of bed. He didn't ask if we were actually going to wait until morning. He didn't need to.

"You make a very good hard-ass," I said. "You know that."

"I don't get nearly enough practice, so I take advantage of every opportunity. Long-term job training."

I smiled and grabbed my jeans as he tossed them my way.

CHAPTER TWENTY-FIVE

Ricky stopped at the end of the clinic block and let the bike idle, as if he was surveying the playing field. Which he was, but this was also an unspoken opportunity for me to pick up any omens that shouted, "Thou shalt not proceed."

I took off my helmet and looked around. It was a crisp October night. The full moon hung low in a star-filled sky.

Perfect night for a hunt.

I smiled as the thought came unbidden. Sadly, that wasn't why we were out here. I was about to put my helmet on when I caught a flicker of movement to my left. I turned sharply. Ricky followed my gaze, squinting with his visor raised, but all I saw was shadowed darkness.

I tilted my head to listen. The idle of the Harley made that impossible. Ricky turned off the engine without any sign from me.

We both looked into the silent night. Then his chin shot up, and he turned. I followed his gaze but saw nothing.

"I thought I heard . . ." He frowned and then said, "A horse whinny. I thought I heard a horse whinny."

Perfect night for a hunt.

But the Cŵn Annwn couldn't ride here. There wasn't a forest for miles. Ricky stayed tense, his sharp gaze cutting through the night, and when I leaned in to kiss the back of his neck, my lips brushed goose bumps.

"What's wrong?" I whispered.

He said nothing. Just kept looking. Then I heard him inhale, and I caught the faintest whiff of horse.

With his gaze still on our surroundings, he reached back, took my hand, and moved it to my pocket. I pulled out the boar's tusk. He felt it in my hand and nodded.

"But if it's the Huntsmen . . ." I whispered. The tusk was *from* the Cŵn Annwn, to protect us against everything *else*.

"It's . . . wrong," he said, still searching the street and the surrounding buildings.

"Not Cŵn Annwn?"

"I . . . I don't know. It's just wrong." He rolled his shoulders. "Sorry. I'm—"

"No, stay with that." I tugged his own tusk from his pocket and pressed it into his hand. "Follow your gut. Always."

He nodded, started the bike, and rolled it slowly down the street. I kept my helmet off and continued searching the shadows. He stopped a few doors from the drop-in center, turned into a gap between the buildings, and killed the engine.

I hopped from the bike while he kept it steady. Helmet off, he scanned the street. Then he nodded, as if satisfied that whatever he'd sensed was gone. There was no one in sight. No one even peeked out from behind a window blind at the very distinct sound of a Harley rolling along their street.

We were about to cross the road when I noticed that flicker again, dark movement in the shadows. This time, I spotted a large shape hunkered down behind a parked car. I tapped Ricky's elbow, but he was already turning that way.

As I reached for my gun, his hand closed on mine, and he shook his head. He took a slow step toward the shadow. It moved, and the moonlight glinted off dark red eyes.

"A hound?" I whispered.

That couldn't be right. Hounds didn't cower. As Ricky walked toward the car, the dark shape shrunk back, and I thought for sure he was mistaken.

I tucked the tusk into my pocket and palmed my switch-blade instead. Ricky didn't seem to hear me even as I jogged up, gravel crunching. But then he lifted his fingers, holding me back as he continued until we were close enough to see black fur.

The beast lay flattened against the pavement, as if thinking itself safely hidden there. I lifted my switchblade and flicked on the penlight.

It was definitely a hound. And yet not like any hound I'd seen. Its fur was matted. One eye was glazed white. One ear a stump. A leg crooked, as if broken and not allowed to heal properly. The worst, though, was the look in its eyes: absolute terror.

"No," Ricky whispered. "How . . . ? Who . . . ?" He dropped to one knee on the sidewalk and lowered his hand to the ground. "Come here."

The hound backed up.

"It's all right," he said.

The hound stopped. It lifted its eyes to Ricky, and the hope in them was heartbreaking to see.

"Who would do this?" Ricky whispered. "Who would dare . . . ?" He shook his head and crooned, "Come here. It's all right."

I turned off the penlight. The hound started at the click but then crept forward, still belly to the ground, gaze fixed on Ricky's face.

"That's it," Ricky said. "Come on."

The hound crawled closer, good ear pricking forward. Then a car skidded around the corner, tires squealing, music blaring, and the hound wheeled and took off running.

"No!" Ricky shouted. "Come back—"

He ran a few loping paces after the beast, but it disappeared down a side road.

"Fuck," he said, shooting a glower at the car as it sped past. "What the hell happened to that hound? Who would do that?"

Rage pulsed from him, his eyes glowing with it. Rage and indignation, that one of his hounds could be so mistreated. Yes, *his* hounds. Arawn's hounds. That's what he felt—the fury of Arawn for his beasts.

"Go after it," I said. "It was coming to you. It knows you."

He shook off the idea. "No, it was just—"

"It knows you, Ricky," I said. "At the very least, it recognizes your blood. Go after it, and I'll take care of this."

"You got a mysterious call in the middle of the night," he said, already crossing the road, headed for the drop-in center. "From a freaked-out girl. Remember what happened the last time?"

"She's not a girl."

"Yep, which only makes her more dangerous. The hound can wait. I'll talk to Ioan. See how the hell something like that can happen."

He was pissed off enough that he nearly strode through the front door. It was only when I caught the back of his Saints jacket that he halted.

"Fuck," he muttered. "Sorry. Have you got—?"

"Gun out, switchblade and tusk in pocket."

He nodded and took out his blade.

"We should circle the building," I said as he reached for the knob. "See if the lamia is around."

"Right. Sorry. Distracted."

"I know, so fall in behind and watch my back."

I added a "please," but he was already moving behind me. We conducted a full circle of the building. There was no sign of Melanie or anyone else.

"Before we go in," Ricky said, "text Gabriel, presuming you haven't already."

"I don't want to bother him."

"When he came after you the first time you were here, he texted me so someone knew where you both were. We should do the same."

"I'll leave a message at the office—"

"He didn't ignore your cry for help when you were trapped, Liv. He ignored what he thought was just you trying to get in touch after your fight. He won't do *that* again, either."

"I know. I—"

"You don't want to be proven wrong. You'd rather tell yourself he'll never repeat that mistake, cross your fingers, and hope you never have to test the theory."

"It's not like that."

"It's exactly like that, and I don't blame you one bit. If you want me to text, I will, but we need to keep him in the loop." He lowered his voice. "You've already tested him, Liv. You fell off a bridge."

"I know."

"Then you also know that jumping after you was a conscious choice, not a mistake he regrets. Text him. Please."

I sent the message and let Ricky take the lead as we headed for the back door.

CHAPTER TWENTY-SIX

The door was unlocked. As Ricky held it open, I leaned through to find the cold-forged iron Melanie had mentioned. As soon as I did, I felt that weirdly burning cold. When I shone my penlight around the door frame, the beam reflected off a glaze of iron shavings, encircling the entire frame. I touched them and felt the icy burn.

"Thou shalt not proceed," I murmured.

"Innovative," Ricky said. "It looks like they spray-glued a layer of the stuff. You said Gabriel feels it?"

"It burns him. I'm guessing for a full-blooded fae it would be like leaping through a ring of fire." I set the knife down, took out my phone and texted a warning to Gabriel, on the off chance he needed to come after us.

I picked up the knife again and shone the light on the door frame, as Ricky ran his hand up and down it.

"Nothing?" I said.

"Just a tingle."

As soon as we stepped from the back hall, I smelled blood. Ricky did, too, and we followed it into the main room. The first thing I saw was the portrait of the lamia who'd died in my vision. Blood spattered and streaked the glass. It spattered and streaked the walls, too, and when we peered in, squinting against the darkness—

I fell back as moonlight lit a figure in the middle of the room.

Ricky caught my arm. He held me there a second and then whispered, "You can stay here."

An offer. Not an order or even a request, and he only nodded when I shook my head.

Ricky barely spared a glance for the figure as he checked through the two open doors and closed them. Only once he was sure no one could surprise us did he turn to that figure. He let out a deep sigh, muttering, "Fuck."

It was Erin—the young woman who worked with Aunika. She'd been bound to a chair and tortured. I'll say no more about that, only that the room was flecked with blood and I suspected she hadn't had the answers her killer wanted.

As Ricky crouched in front of Erin's body, my phone rang. It was on vibrate, but in the silence, even that was loud enough to make me jump.

"Gabriel," I said.

I told him what we'd found.

"Should we notify the police?" I asked.

"Not if you don't have to."

That's what I'd figured. Considering the sheer number of dead bodies that turned up in my wake, I needed to avoid being associated with one whenever possible. Especially when I didn't have a valid reason for being here at four in the morning.

Gabriel had me run through what we'd done so far, to determine how likely it was that we'd ever be tied to this crime. Then he said, "Exit the way you came in. Wheel the motorcycle. Don't start the engine until you're at least a block away. Have Ricky remove his Saints jacket until you're a few miles from the scene. Then ask him to drive here. I want to discuss this with both of you."

"Sure. We'll—"

Sirens sounded in the distance. Gabriel must have heard them and said to me, "I'm sure they're going elsewhere, given the neighborhood. But ask Ricky to check out a front window—"

"He's already there."

"Good. If you don't see lights, leave through the back immediately. But make sure before you step onto the street."

"Look both ways and don't walk in front of any police cars?"

The flash of lights filled the room.

"They've turned the corner, heading this way," Ricky said, striding back to me. "We need to go, just in case—"

Brakes screeched as we jogged into the back room.

"Shit!" Ricky said.

"Gabriel? They're coming here. Do we—? No, wait. There's a secret passage."

Ricky looked back at me. "What?"

"That's how Aunika and I got out. Gabriel—?"

"Do that," he said.

"I'm going to lose you as soon as we go underground, so this is goodbye. We'll call as soon as we can. Hopefully not from the police station."

Ricky was as impressed by the escape hatch and subterranean passage as I'd been.

"We need one of these under the clubhouse," he whispered.

"You can dig a tunnel, but you aren't going to get the ambiance of a proper nineteenth-century version."

"We'll decorate."

I smiled and, we strained to listen to what was happening overhead. It only took a few minutes before someone banged on the front door hard enough to shake the ladder. Then a shout of "Police!" The door opened with a crash and boots stomped in, and I squeezed my eyes shut, trying not to fall into memories of my parents' arrest.

"It's okay," Ricky whispered, his arms going around me. "Look at me."

I opened my eyes, and his face was right over mine.

"Just focus on me. Deep breaths."

I wanted to say I was okay, but his arms tightened around me. I took a minute to recover and stepped back with a thank-you.

Ricky reached for my switchblade and pushed the off button for the light. "Just for a minute, okay?"

We didn't want cops seeing light coming from a closet. Ricky found my hand in the dark again, entwining his fingers with mine while we listened.

The police found Erin. They called for assistance and began searching the building. Ricky flicked on my light just long enough to see our surroundings. Then he moved my free hand to hang on to his jacket while he led us deeper into the tunnels. My night vision is pretty good. His is better—another gift of his stronger Cŵn Annwn blood.

Once we were partway down the next tunnel, he turned on my light and held it out to me.

"You want it back?" he whispered.

"No, keep it," I said.

He shone the beam around. "Wow. If we weren't running from the cops, I'd totally want to go exploring down here."

I chuckled. "That's what I thought last time I was fleeing through here. It's fascinating, isn't it? All this, abandoned, and—" I stopped short, my head swinging to the left.

"You hear something?" he whispered.

"No, sorry, just . . . I'd totally forgotten what happened the last time I was down here."

"Hypothermia, remember? The doctors said you might have black spots. Was it a vision?"

I nodded. "There were lamiae, they'd been held captive . . ."

I'd promised to see to their remains. I had to make sure I did that.

I continued, "The point for now is that the last time I was down here, I had visions."

"Got it. Which means this time . . ." He took my hand.

"Hold tight. If you see anything move, tell me. Don't wait to be sure it's not just a rat."

"There are rats?"

"Underground? Near the river? Nah."

I managed a soft laugh. "Right. Okay then, let's press on."

We couldn't hear anything overhead. Which didn't mean the police were gone—they'd be there for hours. We had to find our own way out. That would be much easier if I could recall anything about the layout of this place.

We continued down one passage after another.

"Starting to feel like we should have brought bread-crumbs," Ricky said.

"Wouldn't help. The rats would eat them."

He chuckled and pushed open a door. It got partway open and stopped. He looked down. "What the—?"

The room strobed. I heard soft sobs. The rattle of chains. A man lay on the floor, his body decomposing. Another body lay near—

"—and wrong room, apparently."

A yank on my arm, hard enough to make me stumble, and I found myself back in the corridor with Ricky, his fingers wrapped tight around my arm as he shut the door he'd been opening.

"Wrong room," he repeated.

"Yep." I glanced down. "Was there a . . . ?"

"Skeletonized body blocking the door? Unfortunately." He looked around. "Okay, so let's back up, away from the vision-inducing hell-room and—"

"Wait!" I said. "This way. There's a window right around the corner. That's where Gabriel found me."

I led him through a doorway to see a figure coming through the broken window. I gripped his arm. "I'm seeing—"

"It's not a vision," he whispered. "Unless we're sharing it." He tugged me back along the passage. "You said Gabriel came through there?"

I shook my head. "He couldn't fit, so that can't be him."

He turned off the light and we stood there, listening. Footsteps whispered across the floor. Then Ricky pulled me toward a doorway. We slipped in and waited.

As I listened, I picked up breathing. Fast, deep breathing, like someone trying not to panic. Three careful, light footfalls.

"Don't take another step."

I jumped at the voice—an unmistakable baritone.

"There is a gun trained on you," Gabriel said. "You will raise your hands and take two steps back toward me."

"I'm—" It was a girl's voice.

"I do not care. You will step back or you will be shot, and it may not kill you, but I suspect a bullet doesn't need to be cold-forged iron to be rather uncomfortable."

We slid from our hiding spots. I took the lead now, my gun in hand. I peeked around the corner to see Gabriel crouched at the window. Moonlight flooded through. He caught my eye and nodded.

"Turn my way," he said to the lamia.

She did. Then she said, "Hey, you don't have a—"

"I said there was a gun trained on you. I did not say I was holding it."

"That'd be me," I said.

She looked over her shoulder. "Mat—Olivia." She went still. Then she turned sharply to Gabriel. "Gwynn," she whispered. "I didn't recognize you at first."

"Possibly because my name is Gabriel," he said dryly.

"I-I'm sorry. I meant no disrespect." She glanced quickly at us, nodding for Ricky, but then turned back to Gabriel and stared. "Th-thank you. For coming. To help us. We appreciate it."

"*They* came for you," Gabriel said. "I came for *them*."

"We need to get out of here," she said. "Before the police join this party."

"Which is, I believe, why Olivia and Ricky are crawling around in those tunnels," Gabriel said.

"Yes, my—sir," the lamia said. "I just meant . . . I'm sorry. I'm flustered." She stopped suddenly. "The police. That means there's a body, right? It—it's not . . . Aunika?"

"Erin," I said. "She's—"

"I know her. We . . . we were on the streets together a few years ago." She closed her eyes and looked sick. Then she asked, "Was it quick?"

"Seemed so," I lied.

She nodded, her gaze down as she chewed her lip. I took my first good look at her. She appeared as a girl of maybe seventeen. Dark hair in a ponytail. No makeup on an olive-skinned face that wouldn't have been out of place on a Grecian urn, with big dark eyes and a somber expression. Her outfit, though, was classic twenty-first-century teen: hoodie, jeans, and sneakers.

Ricky spoke up. "Considering the police are upstairs, and they conveniently arrived after we were summoned here by you, you're going to follow us and answer some questions. Hopefully, with responses we like."

"Y-you think I called the police on you?"

I'd say that the shock on her face proved she hadn't, but I reminded myself of what Gwynn had said. Remember these were fae. I could not take their expressions at, well, face value.

"If I framed their Mallt-y-Dos, the Cainsville fae would stomp me *and* all my sisters," she said, "just to make a point."

"You said you couldn't get into the center," I said. "But we just caught you using the secret route."

"Which is blocked by cold iron at the door to Aunika's office. I can't use it to get up there."

That was true. Of course, it raised the question . . . "If Aunika is so intent on helping the lamiae, why is she block-ing her office and apartment?"

"Can I answer later? Please? The police—"

"—are otherwise occupied," Gabriel said. "The longer we're down here, the easier it'll be for us to leave, allowing the first responders to clear the scene. Now you will answer Olivia's questions or you will not contact us again."

Melanie cast a sidelong look at Gabriel and finally said, "We don't ever need to go into her office. The iron protects her against *other* fae. It's a place to retreat if she's threatened, a precaution all samhail take, warding their private quarters. In her apartment, it's just the doorknob. We can get in if she lets us. As for why I was entering this way, I knew Mat—Olivia and Ricky were inside and I wanted to help them. I hoped I could do that without crossing her office threshold."

"You weren't exactly rushing to our aid," I said.

"We know the tunnel exists, and we've used it in emergencies, but we avoid it when we can. Things happened here. To our sisters. A long time ago." She wrapped her arms around herself. "I can still feel it. I hear them. Crying and—" She broke off and rubbed her arms.

That was why she wanted out of here so fast.

"We'll go," I said.

"I need to make a stop once we're out," Melanie said. "My sister is waiting."

"I'm sure she can take care of herself."

"No," Melanie said. "Actually, she can't."

CHAPTER TWENTY-SEVEN

Melanie led us nearly a half mile along the wharfs until we came to an empty building. As she tugged open a heavy door, I took out my gun.

"Pepper?" she called. "It's me. I brought company." She glanced over at us. "I'm hoping she recognizes you, but if she spooks, I'll have to go after her." She turned back to the dark room. "Hey, Pep? Come on out. I—"

A girl appeared in the circle of my penlight beam. It was the one from my visions—the one who'd chided me to help the lamiae. Yet it wasn't. The girl in my visions had been younger than Melanie, smaller, too, with straight dark hair and a solemn face. All that matched this girl. But her expression wasn't merely solemn. It was empty. And her eyes . . . She had a snake's eyes, greenish yellow and slitted. She stared at us, unblinking. That empty gaze moved from me to Ricky. Then it landed on Gabriel.

Something flashed in those eyes. Life. Thought. Emotion. Enough to say someone lived behind the serpent's gaze.

She walked toward Gabriel, and I could see him holding himself still, wary. She reached to touch his arm, and as he tensed, I caught her hand.

"Pepper, right?" I said.

Her skin was ice-cold and rough, like scales, though I saw only skin. As my fingers touched hers, she let out a sigh, almost a hiss of satisfaction, and her fingers wrapped around mine, her other hand reaching for my bare wrist. I started to pull away, but Melanie said, "Don't! She won't hurt you. It's just . . . You're warm. She can't regulate her body temperature."

Pepper laid both hands on my skin, her eyes slitting as she shuddered. I motioned for Ricky to take my gun. Then I clasped Pepper's hands to warm them, and she melted against me.

"Pepper," Melanie said, taking her shoulder. "We'll get you warmed up. She doesn't want that."

"It's okay," I said, and awkwardly embraced the girl. As Pepper huddled against me, her one sleeve pushed up and I saw scales. I rubbed my finger over them.

"What's wrong with her?" I asked.

"Her glamour's broken." Melanie hesitated, and her voice cracked. "*She's* broken."

I rubbed Pepper's shoulders, and she snuggled closer, her body warming as she absorbed my heat.

"What happened to her?" I asked.

"There was a man. A client. She'd been seeing him for a while, and he seemed fine, but I guess he was . . . what do they call it? Grooming her? He invited her to his place for a night. Promised her a lot of money. Only it wasn't just him, and it wasn't just a night. We didn't find her for a week, and by then . . . Lamiae can handle a lot. We're used to it. But sometimes . . ." She walked over and hugged Pepper. "Sometimes even we break."

Melanie backed up, hands going into her hoodie pockets. "Aunika helps with her. We—the others and I—we feed her. We'd never expect her to . . . She couldn't . . . Not after that. We can feed her our energy. It's not enough to fix her, though. Nothing's enough." Melanie exhaled. "Anyway, that's Pep. She'd never hurt anyone. But she can *be* hurt. Easily. With this psycho hunting us, Aunika was trying to figure out a safe place for Pepper. Where he can't find her, and where we won't have to worry about her so we can focus on protecting ourselves until someone catches this guy. That's what you're doing, right? Trying to catch him?"

"Let's get her someplace warm," Ricky said, his first words since we arrived. "Do you guys eat?" He looked at Pepper. "Or I guess public places are out of the question, with those eyes."

"She has contacts. Aunika got them." Melanie squeezed Pepper's shoulder. "Hey, Pep. Can you put in your contacts? We're going someplace warm. Get you some soup, maybe."

Pepper's empty eyes lighted as she dipped her chin in a nod. Then she hurried to a backpack in the corner and riffled through it.

"She doesn't talk, but she understands," Melanie said. "Aunika says she's like a five-year-old. She can follow instructions. She just doesn't always want to." She forced a smile. "Right, Pep?"

The girl was putting in contacts. When she straightened, her eyes were unnaturally dark but close enough to normal.

"Okay, Pepper," I said. "We're going to take you in a special car where even the seats heat up. Does that sound good?"

Her enthusiastic nod said it sounded very good. I mouthed, "Sorry," to Gabriel—in case having lamiae in his Jag wasn't quite what he had in mind—but he only waved for us to head out.

It was past dawn. Breakfast time. I offered to find a place that would still serve soup if that's what Pepper wanted, but Melanie said she'd be fine with anything hot. We stopped at a diner. Pepper got a steaming bowl of oatmeal and a large hot chocolate, and settled into the corner of the booth, blissfully warming her insides as we talked to Melanie.

The first big question was, how'd she know who we were?

"Rina told me about you before she died."

"Rina—that's one of the victims, right?"

Melanie ate a mouthful of oatmeal before replying. From the bliss in her eyes as she ate, hot food didn't help just Pepper.

"She's one of the two girls who died. We call them girls. Or sisters. It's about assimilating. That's what Aunika's mom said. Use the human words so we fit in better. Talk like teenagers so we fit in better. Anyway, the two girls who died were Rina and Steph. We use human names, too. Like most assimilated fae. But I guess you knew that."

A long drink of her coffee. Then she continued. "You met Rina and Steph. Or they met you. You wouldn't have known what they were. It was months ago, back when that stuff about your parents came out."

"The girls outside the apartment. I was trying to find a place to stay, and I saw them by the street, and then in an alley, where they were threatening . . ." I trailed off, not wanting to speak ill of the dead.

"Threatening a bogart," Melanie said. "Rina told me. It was a territorial issue, and those two could be . . ." She shrugged. "Some of us are more aggressive with other fae. Rina and Steph would rattle their cages, which is what you saw. When Steph died—she was the first one killed—Rina came to me. The two of them stuck together. They were *theegateers*—from the same family—like me and Pepper. They kept apart from the rest of us. But then Steph died, and Rina wanted me to get Aunika to contact you."

"Me?"

"She knew who you were, after it all came out a few months ago. Other fae were talking, and she realized you were the one who'd caught them with the bogart. She wanted your help."

"Because I'm an investigator?"

"No, because you're Matilda. Rina thought you could intercede on our behalf with the Cainsville fae to get their help stopping the killer. Which I know you can't," Melanie added quickly. "So I put her off by saying I'd think about it. Then she disappeared, and we discovered she was dead. Before I could decide what to do, Aunika disappeared, and I heard you'd been to see her. When you left that message for me, I looked you up and learned that you're a private investigator. I'd been trying to decide whether to phone you back about Aunika and the murders, to see if that's what you'd been talking to her about."

"It was," I said. "The Cŵn Annwn asked me to look into the deaths." Which wasn't completely true, but I didn't want to admit I'd seen it in a vision.

Melanie looked surprised. "Why are the Cŵn Annwn involved?"

"Because it's the murder of fae," Ricky said. "That's what they do, right?"

"Yes. Sorry. I just . . . I didn't think they'd bother with us."

I asked what she knew about the murders. Even less than we did, it seemed. She had no idea the killer was Ciro Halloran. As for Lucy Madole . . .

"I don't know what Lucy was doing when she was killed. It's near our territory, where we hunt." She flushed. "I mean, where we work. One of our sisters thought Lucy might have been lured there by someone pretending to be us. Another wondered if she was mistaken for one of us. She's lighter-skinned than Aunika and looks young for her age. But now Aunika's missing, and there's no way the killer could make that mistake twice. And there's Erin . . ." Her gaze lifted to mine. "They're looking for us, aren't they? Going after anyone who can lead them to us."

"Did Erin know what you were? You said you knew her from the streets."

"We did. She was Aunika's first big success. She didn't know what we are, though. We'd discussed it—me and Aunika. There's only so long we could keep coming around before Erin would wonder why none of us got any older."

"Could Aunika have already told her?"

Melanie shook her head. "She'd have warned us. But if Lucy's dead and Aunika's missing and now Erin's dead . . . They're the three humans who knew us best. The killer must have thought they knew where to find us. We went underground after he killed Rina and Steph. We're being careful. We stopped working, but we can't do that for long. Some of the girls are already getting weak. No matter what I say, they're going to feed, and once they venture out, he'll be waiting."

"Is there someplace you can go?" Ricky asked. "Someplace safe?"

"There's no *safe* for us. He's found our haunts in the city, and we need to be around people. The only true sanctuary for us is the one we cannot enter: Cainsville."

"Cainsville?" I said.

"I tried to get Pepper in there after her attack. I pleaded through an intermediary for temporary sanctuary until she was stronger. The elders refused."

"On what grounds?"

"The only grounds that matter. Who we are. What we are."

"Lamiae? That's enough to deny you sanctuary?"

She gave a bitter laugh. "They don't need a reason to deny us. It's *their* sanctuary. They don't allow foreign fae. I hoped they'd make an exception. I was willing to repay them, of course, but they wouldn't even meet with me."

"I know you're Greek, and Cainsville is primarily Tylwyth Teg, which is Welsh. Those from the British Isles are the ones identified as fae in human folklore. Lamiae are not. Yet you *are* fae."

"That depends on who you ask. The Cainsville elders say that if I was true fae, I'd be immolated if I stepped through Aunika's warded door. I wouldn't. I'd still be burned, though. I am fae."

"Evolution from a common source," Ricky said. "Evolution, however, alters the genetic structure. A fae from Greece or from Russia won't have the same genetic makeup as one from the British Isles. Celtic fae are the ones with the deathly allergy to cold-forged iron."

"Which doesn't mean non-Celtic fae are inferior," I said. "Only that they don't have the same genetic makeup. But since Celtic fae are the defining type in folklore, they see themselves as the superior subtype."

Melanie smiled. "Exactly. Thank you. In the old country, we consider ourselves fae. It was only when we immigrated to the new world—where Celtic fae had already settled—that we were . . ." She struggled for a word.

"Reclassified. Okay, so Cainsville is for Tylwyth Teg. Which explains why the place is so damned white. As for the rest of you, if you didn't build your own secret towns three hundred years ago, that's not their fault. The fact that you weren't *here* early enough to settle a town? Also not their problem."

"That sums it up nicely."

"But you still need a place to stay, and if Cainsville wouldn't let Pepper in, even with her condition, they won't let you in. How many are we talking about, anyway?"

"There are three more I'm looking after and another one I'm trying to find shelter for, but she's . . . stubborn."

"We need to figure out what to do with you guys. Find a safe place. I'll work on that."

"Stopping the killer would do that," Gabriel said.

I nodded. "You're right, of course. Catch the killer and the problem is solved." I snuck a look at Pepper, who was gawping at Gabriel like he was the second coming. The lost and broken child. Catching a killer wouldn't solve her problem.

I pulled my gaze away and said, "Gabriel? Can you drive them wherever they need to go? Ricky and I have an appointment." We had to talk to Ioan about the hound. I knew that would be important to Ricky.

Gabriel took out his phone and texted me . . . making it obvious to all that he was conveying a message he didn't want them to hear.

Cainsville?

I texted back. *Ioan. I'll explain later. But yes, then Cainsville. With you, if that's okay.*

He read my message, and I waited for a nod. But he kept his gaze on that text, his frown growing.

Then he texted back, *You want to ask for sanctuary for them in Cainsville. That puts you in a precarious position.*

I replied, *Discuss first?*

He exhaled, relieved that he didn't need to fight me on this. Which told me exactly how deep the schism between us had become, our relationship fractured to the point where he could not rely on me to seek his counsel.

"Text me later," I said. "We'll meet up."

CHAPTER TWENTY-EIGHT

Ioan ushered us into his office, told his assistant to hold all calls, and shut the door.

"I want to know more about the hounds," Ricky said before we were even seated.

Ioan stopped partway to his desk. He glanced at me. Then at Ricky. And he struggled. God, how he struggled. I couldn't ask questions about the Cŵn Annwn without violating our agreement. Ricky could. While Ioan could— and should—refuse to answer, this was what he'd been waiting for—Ricky taking an interest in his ancestry and his future.

"The hounds . . ." Ioan said carefully.

"I saw an abused hound in Chicago, and I want to understand how the hell that happens."

Outrage simmered behind Ricky's eyes, and seeing that, Ioan lost the battle. Neither Ricky's interest nor outrage was feigned. Ioan looked on Ricky, saw Arawn, and could deny him nothing.

"Ask," he said.

"Are they corporeal?" Ricky said. "Mortal?"

"The answer to both isn't as simple as it might seem. They are mortal in the same way the Cŵn Annwn are. They can and will die. But not as easily or as quickly as other canines. They are as corporeal as we are. Yet they can make themselves unseen."

"Same as you can," I said. Then, "Sorry. For the purpose of our agreement, we'll stick to the hounds."

"As you have seen both the hounds do it and me do it, I will give you that. We cannot disappear. But we can make ourselves almost invisible to the human eye. There are still signs, if you know where to look."

"Are the hounds your equivalent of dogs?" Ricky said. "Fae animals, not shape-shifters."

"You mean are they sentient fae in animal form? No. In that, they are indeed the equivalent of a dog, as our loyal companions and our helpers. Unlike your dogs, they can be given detailed instructions."

"Such as finding us and watching what we're doing and then reporting back," I said. "You can communicate with them?"

"We can communicate *through* them. See through their eyes. When you spot a hound, it is the Cŵn Annwn watching over you."

"Spying on us."

"If we wanted spies, we'd stick with the ravens."

True. The hounds weren't exactly inconspicuous.

"You say they're companions and working canines," Ricky said. "So where do they stay when they aren't 'on the job'? A kennel? A house? With a specific Huntsman? A handler?"

"They're more autonomous and intelligent than dogs. They choose where they stay, usually with one of us, sometimes at the stables."

"There are stables?" I said. "So the horses are corporeal— Sorry. Beyond the scope of the current questioning."

He smiled indulgently. "Yes, the horses are—like the dogs and us—mostly corporeal. They have stables, although—" Another smile. "Now *I'm* sorry. I should restrict myself to the questions asked."

Ricky said, "If the hounds are autonomous, does that mean you can't account for their whereabouts at all times?"

"We can summon them. Which we do, either for tasks or for hunts. You're asking because you say you saw one that seemed abused."

"Not *seemed*. It very clearly was."

"That isn't possible. It may have been another type of fae creature or glamour."

"I know my— I know *the* hounds."

"It was definitely a hound," I said. "It responded to Ricky."

"Perhaps it was only dirty? Bedraggled? They may be fae, but they are still canines. A swim in the river and a roll in the mud can be their idea of an entertaining evening."

I detailed the hound's injuries. "*Old* injuries," I clarified. "Long healed. But the way it acted was worse. It hid from us. Cowered. Ricky managed to coax it out, and then a car came roaring around the corner and it took off like a shot. Exactly the way an abused dog would act."

"But that's not— No hound would— We've never lost one. *Ever*. A few have perished in the line of duty, but we've looked after their remains. Our lineage has been here for three hundred years, and we have *never* lost a hound."

"Then it's not yours."

He looked at me.

"You aren't the only Cŵn Annwn in existence, right? Therefore, this is someone else's."

"That's not possible. If a hound disappears, the Cŵn Annwn search to the ends of the earth to find it. That is our vow. We have their loyalty because they have ours. They protect us because we protect them. Always."

"For you. Your particular tribe, group, whatever. While you might hope other Huntsmen remain equally dedicated to the old ways, there's no guarantee of that, is there?"

"No, you don't understand. We are bound . . ." He trailed off.

"Fine," I said. "You can't get into details because it violates our agreement."

"That's not why I stopped, Olivia. I will say only that it isn't possible for a pack of Cŵn Annwn to abandon their hounds. However, an individual Huntsman may leave the pack."

"And take a hound with him?"

"Technically, no. The pack wouldn't allow it. A hound may bond to one Huntsman—they usually do, like your dogs—but they belong to the pack. Both the Cŵn Annwn pack and the hound pack."

"So this one's fellow hounds might have ripped it up like that when it left."

He shuddered. "Never. But if a hound was badly injured, it could lose its connection to the pack—its psychic bond."

"Broken," I said, thinking of Pepper.

"Yes, fae can be broken psychologically, much like humans and other animals can be. If a Huntsman separated from his pack and wanted a hound, he would be able to take one like that."

"If he applied the right pressure, he could force it to do his bidding rather than return to its pack. It would be damaged but still useful."

"Any Huntsman who would do such a thing—" Ioan spat the words, before biting them off. "He does not deserve to be a Huntsman."

"Which he isn't," Ricky said. "If he's left his pack."

Ioan nodded. "Yes," he said. "He is not."

"So we seem to have a lone Cŵn Annwn near Cainsville," I said. "And his hound showed up in Chicago at the site of a murder."

Ioan frowned. "Another lamia murder?"

"No, but it's connected."

"What happens to Cŵn Annwn when they leave their pack?" Ricky asked. "Do they keep doing the same thing as independents? Tracking crimes against fae?"

"Rogue Cŵn Annwn are extremely rare. Yes, they could keep pursuing justice. Or they could take another path."

"Like torturing and murdering a human to gain information on missing fae?"

"Absolutely not. A Cŵn Annwn who strayed that far from our goals and our purpose would be hunted himself. Subject to the same punishment as any of our prey, because he would *be* no better than them."

"But we're talking about a guy who obviously hasn't formed a loving, companionable bond with his hound. If you're going to treat an animal that way, it's not a huge leap to torturing humans."

Ioan went quiet. Then he said, carefully, "I cannot imagine that any Huntsman could torture a human or a fae. But nor could I imagine one would mistreat a hound. So the answer, then, as much as I hate to give it, is that I don't know what you have here. But you can be assured we're going to find out."

I was heading to Cainsville with Gabriel. As we turned onto the highway, he said, "I would like to speak to you about this plan, requesting Cainsville as a refuge for the lamiae."

"That was the idea, right? That we'd discuss it. Anytime you disagree with me, I expect you to say so. You've never had a problem with that before."

He said nothing, just zoomed into the fast lane, bearing down on the car ahead of him.

I twisted to look at him. "I rely on you for advice, Gabriel. You know that, right? I need someone to tell me when I'm full of shit. When I'm about to do something stupid. That's you."

"All right. Then I believe you're about to do something that is unwise."

"By asking the elders to give sanctuary to the lamiae? You think it'll put me in their debt." I shook my head. "They owe me, Gabriel. The balance is clearly weighed on my side."

"Where it should stay. You will be asking them for a favor. That is not free."

"It shouldn't be a favor," I said. "Melanie and Pepper may not *really* be street kids, but they are vulnerable. I'm not asking the elders to throw open the doors to all lamiae. I'm asking them to take in a small group, just until we solve these murders."

"Then let Melanie plead their case to the elders. Agree to arrange that meeting. Do not otherwise intercede on their behalf."

Silence ticked past. Then he said, "This is why I was reluctant to bring it up, Olivia. I know how it looks. You want to help vulnerable fae. In saying you shouldn't, I appear cold and heartless."

"I never said—"

"It is cold. It is heartless. And it is exactly the advice I will give, because my concern is for you. I do not want to see you invoke favors from the Tylwyth Teg on behalf of strangers. I do not even particularly want to see you putting yourself in danger on behalf of strangers. But I understand that you cannot stand idly by when you feel you have the power to help. I will help you solve these murders, and I will accompany you to speak to the elders. But I'm going to ask you to be careful, Olivia." He turned to me. "Be very, very careful what you give up to help these girls."

I remembered Gwynn and Arawn counseling me to forget the lamiae, while saying they knew I would not. I could not. It was what kept me human. Yet Gabriel wasn't really telling me to forget the lamiae. Just don't go falling off bridges for them. Don't go putting myself in the elders' debt for them.

"Will you keep me from doing anything stupid?" I asked finally.

"*Unwise.* Not stupid."

I smiled for him. "Okay, will you keep me from doing anything unwise?"

"I will."

CHAPTER TWENTY-NINE

"They're going to give you the house," Gabriel said.

Gabriel and I were sitting in the garden behind the Carew place. That's where the elders wanted to hold our meeting. They'd be here shortly. Until then, I was poking around the garden, tugging vines from statuary, saying, "Oooh, a dryad. And a baby griffin." Gabriel sat on the bench, watching me, saying nothing until . . .

"They're going to give you the house."

I glanced over. "Hmm?"

"Why do you think they asked you to meet them here?"

I straightened. "It's a reminder of my roots. Yet another way for them to tell me I belong in Cainsville." I sat beside him on the bench. "Should I fight that?"

"Not if you agree."

"I could argue, just to be contrary, but they know it's bullshit. I moved back to Cainsville because this is where I want to be. For now it's home. If I don't do what they want and they kick me out . . ." I shrugged. "It'll hurt, but I'm not going to choose their side just to stay."

"They won't force you out. No matter what you decide. They'll want to retain some influence over you, and in return, if you choose to make Cainsville your permanent home, it will be. Which is why they're going to give you this house."

"That would be quite the bribe."

"Perhaps 'give' is the wrong word. They would do so, if necessary, but you have your trust fund coming due shortly and accepting the house as a gift puts you too far in their debt. So they will make you a very reasonable offer."

When I didn't reply, he said, "It's what you want, isn't it? This?"

I looked around, imagining what I'd do with the gardens, with the house, how I'd make it mine, this magical perfect place.

Six months ago, I'd been living in my family home. Now I was on my own, having started a career I'd never imagined, living a life I'd never imagined, and considering buying a house, putting down roots in a town where I already had deep ones. Embracing this new life. Making it mine. Was I ready for that?

After a minute of silence, he said, "What's that one?"

I followed his finger and could see the barest sliver of gray through a thick tangle of undergrowth. I hunkered down and began pulling back a branch, but he said, "Careful," just as a thorn pricked my finger.

"Wild roses," he said as he came up beside me.

"Not cranky gargoyle babies?"

I got a quarter smile for that. "No, not this time." He crouched beside me and reached to untangle the rosebush from whatever statuary it hid, working carefully so as not to break the branch, saying, "Now the trick is to pull it like . . ." As I watched him, the scene hitched, and I was crouching in a meadow, beside a rabbit hole, Gwynn beside me, no more than ten or eleven, whispering, "Now the trick is to wait very quietly, until they think the coast is clear and . . ." A baby rabbit popped its head out and Gwynn scooped it up as Matilda laughed, and he held it out for her.

The scene faded, and Gabriel was tugging back the last of the branches. "There. Now let's see what . . ." He glanced over at me and frowned. "Olivia?"

I could feel the trickle of a tear on my cheek. I wiped it away and smiled. "Just the thorn. It startled me." I inched up beside him, being careful not to get too close and make him jump away. "Oh, it's . . ." I stopped. "I have no idea what it is."

"It's certainly odd. Let me clear away the rest of this."

The statue looked like a tiny man, somewhere between a dwarf and a gnome, exceedingly ugly, wearing a helmet and carrying a lantern.

"Is it . . . a tommy knocker?" I said.

"Close," said a voice behind us. "It's a *coblynau*."

I turned so abruptly I tottered. Gabriel put his hand to my back to steady me. Ida walked into the garden, followed by Walter and Veronica, and Gabriel's lips tightened, as if he was annoyed at the interruption.

"We'll wait inside," Veronica said. "You can finish exploring the garden."

"No, it's fine," Gabriel said curtly as we rose. He led me toward the house, his hand still against my back. Then he glanced back at the garden, and his voice softened a little as he said to Veronica, "You said a *coblynau*?"

"Yes. A Welsh version of the tommy knocker. In folklore, if miners are kind and feed them, they'll help by tapping at particularly rich areas. In truth, they were originally mountain-dwelling fae. Now they live urban lives, like most. They are hardworking, generally kind-hearted. If you are good to them, they will be good to you in return. That's true of most fae, but *coblynau* are more inclined to see goodness and return it. They are not particularly given to tricks."

"Are there any in Cainsville?" I asked.

She smiled. "Perhaps," she said, and her eyes glinted in a way that made me say, "Wait, are you—?" but she was already through the back door.

We followed her. The house was quiet and still, as it was whenever I visited. It had been empty for years and even thinking of that made me ache, just a little. I could feel the history here. My history. For such a beautiful old house to sit empty . . .

I could feel Ida's keen gaze on me. When we walked into the front parlor, I tried not to gape at the frieze of magpies. My great-great-grandmother had put them there. Like me, she'd been able to read omens.

I remembered what the little girl from my visions said about the house: *It was built for you, long before you were born.*

"We'd like to offer you the house, Olivia," Ida said.

Gabriel snorted, and she looked over, then said, "I'm sure that comes as no surprise."

"Not at all," he said. "I'm simply impressed by the speed with which you got to it."

"I believe in being forthright," she said.

"Ah, trying a new tack."

"Sarcasm does not become you, Gabriel."

Veronica cleared her throat. "We've earned his sarcasm, Ida." She turned to me. "We believe living here would both strengthen your powers and ease their negative effects."

Gabriel cleared his throat. "You say that, knowing—"

"Knowing you're concerned about those negative effects. Yes. That may seem like an obvious ploy, but I strongly believe Liv would do better in this house. To test that, I suggest she live here for a while and see if it helps."

"That was not what we discussed," Ida said.

Veronica smiled sweetly at her. "I'm improvising. As is my right."

Ida glanced at Walter, who pretended not to notice.

"I'm not really looking to buy a house," I said. "I'm only in my apartment about half the time anyway. What would I do with a place this size?"

Even as I thought it, my mind threw up answers. I'd turn one of the bedrooms into an office and leave another as a guest room, for when Gabriel needed a place to crash. I'd put exercise equipment in the basement—I didn't get to the gym nearly often enough lately. I'd redo the kitchen and maybe ask Rose to teach me to bake. I'd add a solarium, where I could curl up with a book and a mocha and—

Stop. Just stop.

"Think of it as an investment," Walter said. "You could flip it. That's the term, isn't it? Fix it up and then, if you no longer wish to stay, sell it for a profit."

"Sell it to whom?" I laughed. "I know how real estate works in this town. Newcomers have to pass a screening committee. I'm guessing that's because the preference is for those with fae blood, presumably Tylwyth Teg. You need to let in some outsiders, but to keep the town under control, you tightly regulate admission. That's why this house has stood empty for so long."

"No, it's stood empty because we were saving it for you."

"You'd sell it to us," Ida cut in. "That's how it works. We buy it, as recompense for the inconvenience of our town policies. We purchased this one for three hundred thousand, which was the fair market value. Given that it has stood empty for years, repairs will be necessary, and so we're taking that into consideration and offering it for two-fifty."

I could hear my dad whispering that it was a steal but of course I should try to bargain down to two-twenty-five. I had to smile at that. It was good to hear his voice. I worried sometimes that with Todd in my life, my dad would fade away to silence.

"That's very fair," I said. "But right now, I have about two grand in the bank."

"We're well aware that your trust comes due in a month," Ida said.

Veronica nodded. "If you chose to live here as a test, you wouldn't even need to decide until you have the money in the bank."

Ida's look warned Veronica to stop this nonsense about a trial run.

"I'll think about it," I said.

"Why don't you do as Veronica suggests," Walter said. "Move in for a while. I can have some of the young men fetch your furniture from Grace's, and you could be in by nightfall."

"Considering that Grace owns all the furniture in my apartment, I don't think she'd appreciate that."

"Then we'll find you some."

"I think I'll take it a little slower. But thanks. Now, the reason I asked to speak to you . . ."

I told them about the lamiae. When I finished, I braced for a crafty look from Ida, as she tried to figure out how best to use this "request" to their advantage. Instead, she simply said, "No."

"What?"

"No, they may not stay here. Cainsville isn't their home."

"They're being *hunted*—"

"Fae have always been hunted. Those of us with foresight built towns like this, to protect ourselves and our descendants. Others cannot merely dance about, enjoying their freedom, until they need sanctuary, and then take advantage of our hard work."

"They aren't asking to move in permanently."

"But they'd hope to. That's where this is leading."

"Then set limits."

"Allowing them inside Cainsville cracks open a door that must remain shut. This town is for us, Olivia. For us, for you, for Gabriel. I realize that sounds cruel, but we built our fortress. They built nothing. They must live with the consequences."

"Or die with the consequences."

"Yes." She met my gaze. "If you can stop their killer, then they will stop dying and they will owe you. That is the proper way to handle this. It reflects well on you to help them. It does not reflect well on you to become indebted to us doing so."

"I had no intention of incurring any debt to bring them here. I was simply asking you to hear their request."

"The answer is no. I hate to refuse you, Olivia, but here I must. The lamiae may not come to Cainsville."

"Under no conditions?" Gabriel said. When she looked at him, he said, "I'm not offering to incur any debt myself. I am attempting to negotiate a settlement because this situation impedes our ability to pursue this case. I want these fae in a safe situation so they will not seek protection from us."

Ida's eyes narrowed. "It isn't enough that Olivia is helping find their killer? They now expect her to protect them?"

"They expect no such thing. Yet they obviously hope for it . . . and not from Olivia."

Walter looked at Gabriel and said, "Oh."

"Yes, *oh*. While this Matilda situation most obviously affects Olivia, fae have discovered that I am . . ."

"King of the Faeries?" I offered helpfully.

I got a sidelong glower for that.

"Sorry," I said. "But as much as you might hate that particular title, the point is valid. Fae like the lamiae have no idea exactly what it means to be Gwynn ap Nudd. They only know that he's the legendary king of the Tylwyth Teg."

"And therefore, they have certain expectations," Gabriel said. "I would like to disillusion them. However, at this moment, I'm rather busy solving these murders. While I do not want the lamiae to think they can call on my favor, it seems in the best interests of all to shunt them off to temporary safety. I propose that those affected be allowed to come to Cainsville for a maximum of one week. In return, they will be placed under any restrictions the elders impose. They will also, naturally, owe the Cainsville Tylwyth Teg."

"What could we possibly want from lamiae?" Ida said.

"Anything. They will also owe me, for negotiating this arrangement. That is *me*, not Olivia. It is less likely local fae will mistake *me* for a soft touch, and in future I will make it clear I am no benevolent . . ." He struggled for a word. "Figurehead."

"That seems reasonable," Walter said. When Ida turned on him, he said, "Gabriel has a valid point. He and Olivia should be free to investigate, in case these murders are a sign of anything greater."

Ida sniffed. "They aren't."

"But your consort also has a point," Veronica said. "Let Liv and Gabriel sort this mess while we give the lamiae a place to stay, under very strict conditions and as an exception rather than a precedent."

Ida turned to us. "I disagree. But as this is a democratically run town"—her tone implied deep regret at that—"and two of the elders support your suggestion, we must take it before the others. You will have your answer before nightfall."

CHAPTER THIRTY

I got my checkup at the doctor's, and then we swung by the diner to pick up a late lunch and a scone for Grace. When I got to my apartment building, though, there was no sign of her. I went inside and looked around.

"I'm sure she hasn't gone far," Gabriel said.

"Oh, I'm not trying to find her. I'm just making sure she isn't around to catch me checking in here . . ." I walked to apartment 1B. I'd mentioned to Gabriel what Ricky had glimpsed when he opened the door. Now I glanced over my shoulder, to be sure he wasn't going to stop me. Silly question. He was right behind me.

I took one last look around. Then I reached for the knob, turned it, and—

"Locked," I said.

He took out his picks and two seconds later I heard the click. I sighed. "I need *so* much more practice at that."

A faint smile. "I also have a natural talent, don't forget." He turned the knob. The door cracked open and—

"May I help you?" Grace said from behind us.

Gabriel had the door shut and the pick hidden before we turned.

"I, uh, thought I heard something in there," I said. "We were knocking to be sure everything was all right."

Grace peered up at me. "You're fae, child. Surely you can lie better than that."

"Ricky had an odd experience opening this door while searching for TC," Gabriel said. "In light of everything Olivia has gone through, that concerned me. I was breaking in to investigate."

"Much better. The best lies contain a generous dose of truth." She turned back to Gabriel. "The answer is no, and if I ever catch you picking the lock on one of my apartments, I will curse you with boils, Gabriel Walsh."

"Bogarts have no ability to invoke curses."

"Fine, if I catch you doing it again, I'll be very unhappy. And you don't want to make me unhappy." She shook her head. "You're no better than children, either of you. Sneaking about, playing detective, solving murders, jumping off bridges. You do realize it's entirely the wrong time of year for swimming, I hope."

"Our mistake," I said.

"Go on and open the door, then," she said. "Just this once."

I looked to be sure she was serious. Then I reached out and turned the handle. It opened. I pushed and—

The door opened into an apartment filled with dust motes.

"Oh, I'm sorry," she said as I stepped inside and looked around. "Were you expecting something else?"

I glowered at her. She only said, "When you agree to hear the elders out, all the doors of Cainsville will be open to you, Miss Olivia. Including the ones you'd rather stayed shut." She snatched the scone bag from my hand and thumped toward the front door. "Close that when you're done. You wouldn't want to catch a chill."

The elders agreed to the terms Gabriel had suggested. One week maximum, during which the lamiae would stay with Veronica and a few others. They would be introduced in town as exchange students from Greece.

We were driving back to Chicago to get the girls when Ricky texted.

Still on for a hunt tonight?

"Shit," I whispered.

"Ricky?"

"Mmm, yeah. We—"

"You're supposed to go looking for that hound again to see if it can lead you to our rogue Huntsman."

"Which we'll have to postpone."

"Absolutely not. It is connected to the case, and the case is our priority. You will meet with Ricky and find the hound. I will escort the lamiae to Cainsville. Melanie said only four of them are ready to go tonight."

I shook my head. "You go with Ricky. Avoid the king-adoration."

"That is primarily Pepper, and given her condition, I can hardly fault her for that. As for the others, I would appreciate it if you might take them aside and advise them that we have names and any other designation is . . . not complimentary."

I looked over at him and thought of Gwynn. Of the boy with the rabbit, and the boy in the swimming hole, and the young man in the cave. A good boy. A good man. One who'd made a critical mistake.

I remembered the little girl telling me I judged them too harshly, that they—all three of them—were young and made youthful mistakes. There was more to them than those terrible mistakes. A lifetime more.

We did judge too harshly. I had to figure out how to tell Gabriel that, if he would listen. To tell him that my memories of Gwynn—like Gwynn himself—were golden and bright, all up until the end, and even then, in his grief, he redeemed himself.

"I'll speak to the lamiae," I said.

Tonight we hunted a hound. Yes, the fact it had been at the drop-in center when Erin was murdered suggested a link between its "owner" and the lamiae killings. Yet a stronger reason drove Ricky onto the streets that night.

Someone had broken his hound. Someone would pay for that.

As for how Ricky would find a semi-spectral hound in a city of three million people . . . Well, that might take a bit of magic. Our hope was that the hound retained enough of its severed psychic bond that Ricky could find it again. Not so much magic, then, as faith.

As we rode, Ricky left his helmet off, which is perfectly legal in Illinois—he just wears one because he's more interested in protecting that brain of his than in looking the part of the badass biker. He did, however, ask me to leave mine on.

Ricky rolled up and down the streets of the neighborhoods where the lamiae lived and hunted. He wore his Saints jacket, which meant we got our share of shouts and taunts from the local wildlife. Ricky ignored them until we'd been out for two hours without a trace of the hound, and a car veered into our path and forced us to stop.

"Hey, cracker," a guy shouted from the passenger window. "You lost?"

"Yeah, Hardly Davidson," another called from the backseat. "Redneck country is thataway. You come down here, we might decide that's a mighty fine bike you're riding. And a mighty fine bitch on the back of it."

The guys in the car laughed. Ricky just idled there, the *put-a-put-a-put* of the bike engine filling the night. The laughter trailed off into awkward silence.

"Hey," one yelled. "You hear us, blondie?"

Ricky said nothing.

"You deaf? Or just dumb?"

"He's definitely dumb," one said. "Dumbass cracker. You waiting for your posse, cracker? We'll hear them long before they show up. Which means we can kick your ass long before they show up."

Ricky turned to me. I lifted my visor. His eyes glittered with frustration over not finding the hound. He wasn't spoiling for a fight. That *is* another side of Arawn, but there was none of that tonight—just a glimmer that said he wanted to work off his frustration.

"Go ahead," I mouthed.

He put his hand on my knee, telling me to hang on tight. I leaned into his back and wrapped my arms around him. Feet planted, he began wheeling the bike backward.

"You running away, boy?" one called.

Ricky just kept backing up the bike. Two guys leaned out the window.

"You think you can reverse all the way outta our neighborhood? Is that some dumbass cracker code about not turning your back? If you keep going, we'll—"

Ricky stopped the bike. He laid one hand on my leg and tapped it with his fingers, counting down. Three, two . . .

The bike shot forward. The guys yelled something. One leapt out of the car, as if we were going to ram it. Ricky leaned down nearly flat against the bike, with me holding on for dear life, feeling the rush of the wind, the delicious, incredible rush, my eyes squeezed shut and then—

And then Ricky sat up, fast enough that I was glad I was holding him tight. The front end of the bike popped right onto the trunk of that big old Cadillac, and then we were airborne, shooting over the car. And I laughed. I couldn't help it. It was terrifying and exhilarating and absolutely mad, and I hugged Ricky tight and I laughed.

The bike landed with a jolt. Ricky hit the throttle and we were gone, zooming along the empty streets at impossible speeds, and it was like I was back in that vision, behind Arawn on the horse, holding tight and laughing with sheer joy.

He veered down a dark side street about a mile away and then turned into an even darker alley. His hand went to my leg, squeezing it, his fingers trembling as he turned back and mouthed, "You okay?"

I grinned at him. Just grinned and then tugged off my helmet, hopped off the bike, grabbed him by the shirt-front, and pulled him into a kiss. And God, that was a kiss, his frustration over the failed hunt for the hound mingling with the thrill of the jump and the triumph of his fuck-you escape.

A breathtaking, mind-blowing kiss, and when it ended, I was sitting in front of him on the bike, no idea how I even got there. I kept kissing him, hands in his hair, straddling him as I leaned back onto the bike. I slid my fingers to his crotch, rock-hard, and murmured, "Yes?"

"Fuck, yes," he said, his breath ragged.

I managed to get out of my jeans more easily than I'd have thought possible on a bike. Then he bent to kiss me again and that kiss, that kiss . . .

It was like being in the forest after the hunt, the smell of loam and pine needles, the smell of night and sweat and the hunt, those times when I'd swear I heard the hounds and the horses as he kissed me, as he pushed into me, hungry from the chase. This time, though? This time I wasn't lying on the ground, and when I closed my eyes I didn't feel the thrum of the idling bike under me. I felt as if I was still on the horse in that vision, except it wasn't Arawn with me—it was Ricky, stretched out over me, pushing into me, and God, oh God . . .

Fuck, yes, indeed.

I said that aloud, when we finished, and Ricky gave a ragged laugh, burying his face against my neck, saying, "Yeah . . ." He straightened, and then turned off the bike with another chuckle, saying, "Guess I should shut that off next time."

"Mmm, definitely not."

I reached up and pulled him down into a kiss, and we

stayed there, locked together, until I realized it might not be the most comfortable position for him.

"Sorry," I murmured. "Probably getting a little tired of holding up the bike, huh?"

"What bike?" he said, and kissed me again as I laughed.

A couple of minutes later, we were off the bike and on the blanket from his saddlebags, lying half naked in a grungy alley.

"If you close your eyes," he said, "you can imagine that faint eau de garbage is actually a nearby swamp. I *did* catch a whiff of something decomposing. Just need a big pile of deer shit nearby and we'd be right at home."

"You say the sweetest things." I craned my neck and looked up at the sky. "I think that's a star up there. Or is it a plane?"

"A star. Blinking and moving fast. They do that in the city."

He pulled me against him, and I snuggled in, the heat of his body perfect against the chill night air. I closed my eyes, and when he kissed me I could smell the forest, see it, feel it and hear it all around me, and then I was there, not just imagining it but lying in a forest glen. I could feel the warmth of him still on my skin, but he was gone. I didn't jump up. I just stretched out on my stomach, toes brushing the grass.

A whine floated over on the breeze. I lifted my head and squinted. Another whine came. Then a sigh. A deep, shuddering canine sigh.

The hound.

I rose and hurried to the edge of the clearing. I could hear the hound, sighing and shuffling, as if moving about. I jogged toward the sound and spotted it near a cabin. The hound guarded the door, and while I could see no sign that it was bound in any way, it *felt* bound, as it looked into the forest as if longing to run. It was a perfect fall night and yet the hound couldn't enjoy it, and I felt the grief and the frustration and the sadness of that as it paced and then, with a sigh, lay down in front of the cabin door.

When I started forward, the hound lifted its head and peered into the darkness. Its red-brown eyes glimmered as it searched, as if sensing me but seeing nothing. Then it stood and whined and tried to come to me but stopped short and gave a growl, ears pricked forward, seeing me and . . .

No, not seeing *me*. Not sensing *me*.

"Forest," Ricky whispered, and I was back in the alley, Ricky pulling from the kiss, saying, "The hound is in the forest. Guarding a cabin. You . . ." He grinned and pulled me into a tight hug. "You found it. Thank you."

"Um, you . . . saw . . . what I was . . .?"

He grinned again as he rose. "Forest. Cabin. Hound. That *is* what you were seeing, right?"

"Yes, but how . . .?"

"No idea. Hound radar plus omen vision, I guess. We should have skipped the riding around and gone straight to bike sex."

"I'm pretty sure it wasn't the bike sex that did it."

"Of course it was. Anytime we need to figure something out, we'll start with bike sex. If that doesn't work, we'll keep trying until it does."

I laughed as I pulled on my jeans. "As for a location, though, all I got was forest."

"I know where to go."

CHAPTER THIRTY-ONE

We were about a half hour south of the city, long off the highway, on roads I'd never seen before until, finally, Ricky brought the bike to a stop at the side. I could see forest across a moonlit field. He tilted his head, considering, and then squeezed my thigh, telling me to hang on, before he turned the bike into the field, rolling slowly over the rough ground. When we reached the edge of the forest, he idled there and I tugged off my helmet. I could feel tension strumming from him as he looked into the woods.

"Wrong place?" I said.

"No, just wrong."

As I leaned against his back and looked into the woods, I felt what he must. Uneasy. Unwelcome. This wasn't like other forests—no sense of invitation, of adventure, of voices whispering in the dark for us to come play. I looked at this stretch of woods and I felt that ancient sense of the forest as alien territory. Dangerous territory. The dark unknown.

As I shivered, I tumbled into a vision. A cabin. Not the one from my hound vision. This was a home in the forest, the door bolted shut, the shutters battened tight. I was inside, fumbling with a lantern, desperate to ignite it as a girl's voice whispered, "Something's out there," and I could feel that, beyond those closed shutters. Something out there, something in the night. That primal fear of what the dark brought, what the forest brought, when the sun dropped.

I snapped back to reality with a shudder, still feeling the terror of our ancestors, shut in for the night, praying for morning, knowing that beyond their door lurked danger, that unshakable fear that would, even today, make children beg their parents to check under the bed, look in the closet, please don't turn out all the lights.

I rubbed my arms, reminding myself that I had a gun and a switchblade, and I was no peasant cowering in the dark. I knew what was out there. I'd faced it. Overcome it. And yet . . . well, logic and confidence only gets you so far against those primal whispers.

A dog started crying. Not the hound. Just a dog.

Ricky murmured, "Bad omen?"

"Yep. Better late than never." I was twisting to look around when I spotted a raven gliding silently across the moonlit field. It swooped toward us, as if to fly into the woods. Then it veered sharply and instead came to rest in a dead tree twenty paces from the forest's edge. It hunkered down, feathers ruffling, head pulled between its shoulders.

"Uh, yeah . . ." I said. "Let's see . . . Overwhelming sense of foreboding. Omen of impending danger. Freaked-out Cŵn Annwn raven. Do you get the feeling—?"

"That this is definitely the place?"

"I was thinking more along the lines that the universe is sticking a big Do Not Enter sign outside that forest."

"That, too."

"So . . ." I waved at the forest. "Shall we?"

He smiled and slid off the bike, and we walked into the woods, hand in hand, like Hansel and Gretel. When I mentioned that to Ricky, he said, "You think there'll be candy?"

I took out my boar's tusk. When I touched it, I thought I'd accidentally grabbed my gun instead. The tusk was as cold as metal. I held it out for Ricky to touch and he said, "Weird." Then he checked his own and confirmed it was the same. "So that's a sign they're working *extra* well, right?" he said.

We shared a smile. In our guts, we both knew it meant the opposite. Our handy-dandy fae-evil-repelling boar tusks had shut down, as if their power couldn't penetrate these woods.

At a loud croak, I looked over my shoulder and saw the raven launch from the tree and fly back toward the road.

"Abandoning us already, huh," I murmured. "If the mortals are too stupid to heed flashing danger signs, screw them."

I turned toward the forest. It was unnaturally dark, the moonlight seeming not to penetrate the tree canopy. When I looked up, I could see gaps in that canopy, but not a single star glinted in the blackness beyond.

"Second thoughts?" Ricky asked.

"Never."

The woods were larger than they seemed from the road, and we walked at least a mile, Ricky moving sure-footed and straight, his gaze fixed on something only he could see. Then I caught the sound from my vision—the whine of the hound. Not boredom and frustration now, but anticipation. Ricky's hand squeezed mine.

"Before we get there," I murmured, "what exactly do we expect to find in that cabin?"

"Presumably his master."

"So do we split up? You take the front and I slip around the back?"

"I'd *really* rather not split up here, even for a second."

"Okay, so we stick—"

I stumbled. I didn't feel any obstacle or dip in my path. I just stumbled. Ricky's hand tightened, his grip pulling me up. Then his hand disappeared and I staggered forward and when I caught my balance and turned . . .

I was alone in the forest.

THE HOUNDS OF HELL

"Liv?" Ricky spun around, but even as he did, he knew he wouldn't see her.

"Liv!" he shouted again. Yeah, that wasn't smart, yelling so close to his quarry's den, but what mattered was that she was gone and this forest was wrong, unnatural and wrong, and he'd brought her in here. Fuck the signs. Fuck the omens. Fuck the fact that the raven wouldn't cross the threshold and their damned tusks were cold weights in their pockets. They had their weapons, and they had each other, and that was enough.

It's never enough. It never was.

Ricky squeezed his eyes shut as if he could block Arawn's voice.

You did this. So cocky. So confident. You dragged her into this place knowing—feeling—the danger.

Which was bullshit, of course. No one *dragged* Liv anywhere. But that didn't mean Ricky failed to accept responsibility. He would never be Arawn, blaming Gwynn for centuries until he'd finally faced the truth—that he'd been equally responsible for Matilda's death.

Ricky had sensed the danger here, and they came in anyway. He hadn't told her exactly how this forest made him feel. Had not been clear enough, and that was where his failure lay: in believing he could simply hold her hand and keep her safe.

"God-fucking-damn it," he cursed. Then he yelled again, "O-liv-i-a!"

"Lose someone?" a voice whispered through the trees, and Ricky's hackles rose.

He didn't need to see the figure to know it was a Huntsman. And yet not a Huntsman, no more than this forest was truly a forest or the hound truly a hound. The hound and the forest were tainted, warped, by no fault of their own. The taint came from the voice that oozed through the trees like an oil slick, black and unnatural, corrupting everything it touched.

"Show yourself," Ricky called, and the voice laughed.

"Arawn, I presume? Yet another pretender to the throne. And such a child, too. A swaggering, grinning child, clutching his switchblade and telling himself he's a man. Telling himself he's Lord of the Cŵn Annwn."

"Pretty damned sure I never claimed any such thing. But I did come on behalf of the Cŵn Annwn. To take back something you stole."

"Your girl?"

Ricky snorted. "Hardly."

"Oh ho, so the girl doesn't matter? Perhaps you are the true Arawn after all—finally man enough to stop playing silly romantic games, chasing a girl he'll never have."

"You have something of ours. A hound."

"Yours? No, the hound is mine. A broken and useless beast that I found and saved. But let's test exactly how little you care for your Matilda. You may choose which I return: her or the hound."

"You misunderstood. When I laughed, it wasn't because I don't care for Liv. It's because you didn't steal her. If you'd managed that, you wouldn't have time to come mock me— she's a bit of a handful. Something has separated us, but you have nothing to do with it, and as much as I'd love to tromp through this forest, shouting, I won't find her until it's time. I trust she can look after herself until I do."

"Are you certain?" The voice slid around him now. "Very certain?"

"Yep. Sorry. And the weird-ass spooky-voice thing really isn't going to work. Why don't you just come out where I can see you and talk?"

"I have nothing to say to you, little Arawn."

"Then you won't mind if go collect my hound."

A shadow cut in front of him as he turned, formless, the very trees seeming to shift and slide as it moved.

"It is not *your* hound, boy."

"Wanna bet? Bring it here and we'll see who it chooses."

A laugh resounded through the trees. "You *are* an arrogant child, aren't you?"

"Confident, not arrogant. There's a difference."

"Ricky!" It was Liv, deep in the forest. He turned to track the sound.

"Your borrowed lover calls," the voice said.

"Liv!" he shouted.

"You say you are not concerned, but that bellow gives you away. Does she wander from you often, boy? I bet she does. Wanders from your side to his, comes back when she wants something from you."

"Yep, she comes back when she wants to be *with* me. Which is all that matters. Now, if you'll excuse me . . ."

He turned in the direction he'd heard Liv, because as brash and bold as he might act, the man was right—he was more concerned than he let on. He could hear the hound whining, but it had waited all this time, and it would understand if it had to wait a little longer.

He broke into a jog, yelling for Liv as the voice chuckled behind him.

"Ricky!" she called.

"Here! Coming!"

"Damn it," she said, her voice carrying in the night. "We've really got to figure out how to stop separating like this."

"Agreed."

"You know what we need more of?"

"Bike sex?"

She laughed, and he knew that wasn't some random snippet of conversation shouted across a forest—she was making sure it was really him.

"Run, little Arawn," the voice whispered. "Run after her while you still can."

Ricky shot his middle finger over his shoulder and picked up his pace. A shape leapt in front of him, darkness against darkness, pulsing there. He veered, as if it was no more than a stump in his path, but when the shadow dove for him, he was ready, blade slashing. He could still see nothing, but the knife met resistance and there was a sharp intake of breath.

"Guess my puny weapon can do some damage after all, huh? Even if you don't have the guts to uncloak yourself."

Ricky saw the blow coming. No fist. Not even a shape. Just darkness flying at him, but he'd been in enough fights to recognize the sense of movement alone, and he wheeled out of its path, shouting, "Liv? Be careful! I've found our rogue Huntsman."

"Kinda figured that's who you were talking to," she yelled back. "You two keep exchanging semi-witty banter and I'll have no problem finding you."

"I think he'd rather exchange semi-useless blows."

The next one came from his right, and Ricky wasn't quite fast enough to duck. That was, of course, the danger of being a smart-ass. You can enrage an opponent into wild blows, but one of those blows is bound to hit. This one struck him in the jaw and—

Holy fuck.

He'd say it felt like a sledgehammer, but there was no pain, just . . . explosion, and then—

Terror. Overwhelming terror, like something had reached into his brain and released every nightmare, the shock of that doubling him over, breath stopping, heart stopping, everything stopping, that blackness swallowing him and—

God-fucking-damn it, no. Just no. Get a fucking grip.

He gave himself a mental smack upside the head. He would not go down. He would not let this bastard put him down. He was better than that. Stronger than that.

He was Arawn.

Or at least he could fake it long enough to smack himself back into shape.

"You find this funny, boy?"

Ricky realized he was laughing. Doubled over, barely able to breathe, but wasting what little breath he did have laughing at himself. Because sometimes, that's all you could do. You make a fucking stupid mistake, and you could only call yourself an idiot and then snap back before you screwed up again.

He heard Liv in the forest, trying to sneak toward them, and when he looked, the rogue Huntsman's shadow had taken shape. Still black as night, no features to be seen, but the form of a cloaked man turning in Liv's direction.

Ricky ran at the figure. He jumped at its back and hit solid flesh and thought *Yes!* and then his hands started to pass through it, to pass into absolute cold, that ice running up his arms, pitch black enveloping his arms—

Running.

He was running so fast every breath was a dagger through his lungs, but the terror—that crushing terror— kept his legs moving as pain ripped through them, ripped through his entire body.

Bless me, Father, for I have sinned . . .

Prayers raced through his head, the words expelled on each exhalation, words Ricky didn't know, prayers he didn't know. Another man's prayers, coming in desperation, a ward against a fear for which there was no ward, a hope against a fate for which there was no hope.

A vision? A memory? *Someone's* memory. Not the Huntsman's, but from him, a straight shot of terror, sending Ricky tumbling into some stranger's body, in some long-ago place. He tried to hold on to that, tell himself this wasn't real, but all he could think, all he could feel, was whatever this poor man was thinking, feeling . . .

The hounds, dear Lord, the hounds, he could hear their baying growing ever more distant, and in the beginning that had given him hope, until he'd discovered that the farther away they sounded, the closer they actually were, and when he glanced over his shoulder—

Do not look! Do not look!

He looked anyway, and he saw fire. The fires of hell on his tail, giant hounds whose eyes blazed, giant black steeds who breathed flames, whose fetlocks and manes burned with it. And the riders. He could see the riders now. Faceless cloaked men with red eyes. Eyes that burned hellfire and promised damnation.

No more than I deserve.

Bless me, Father, for I have sinned.

Hail Mary, full of grace.

No grace, no blessing, no escape, no mercy for him, because he'd shown none. Shown none to those women he'd taken and toyed with, and this was the price, yes, this was the price.

No one told me it was the price!

The world had lied. It told him that if he was caught, the most he'd suffer was a lifetime in prison, and with it would come fame, glorious fame, his face in every newspaper.

But there was no fame. No face on a newspaper. No name in a headline. He would die, his deeds unnoticed, his body torn apart in the forest, corpse left to rot and feed wild creatures and hungry earth, because this is what she'd promised him. The last woman. The one whose skin had shimmered when he'd sliced her open. The one who'd spouted madness when he captured her, who'd promised him this ignoble end.

The hounds will come. The Huntsmen will come. You will burn.

No more than he deserved, and he knew it now, as he ran.

Is that not enough? That I know it? I confess. I confess! Bless me, Father, for I have sinned.

Hail Mary, full of grace.

Isn't that how it worked? Confess and ye shall be saved. Repent and ye shall be forgiven.

He heard the woman's tinkling laughter as he ran. She'd laughed as he'd sliced into her, promised that no matter what he did to her, his death would be a thousand times worse.

He stumbled then. Felt his foot slide out. Felt his brain scream, *No!* Heard it rip from his lungs. *No! I repent! I repent!* and the woman's laughter rang out like a trumpet at his ear.

The trumpet of the archangel, on the Day of Judgment, calling him home to heaven.

"Oh, no," her voice whispered in his ear. "This *is* Judgment Day, but heaven is not where you're going, Michael O'Grady."

He felt the body strike his. A massive furred body, knocking him off his feet, onto his back, and then he saw it, the hound, the giant hound, its eyes blazing fire, jaws opening, fangs slashing down—

Ricky Gallagher. I'm Ricky Gallagher!

Through the wild and swirling vision, Ricky found himself and shouted the words in his head, and he snapped back so fast he felt himself hit the ground, flat on his back, the *oomph* of the blow exhaled on a single breath.

He blinked hard, pulling back the scattered piece of his psyche, forcing the last remnants of the vision away and—

He felt something moving over him. Something on his

chest. He tried to jerk upright, but it shoved him back down and all he could see above him was darkness and then . . .

Eyes. Blazing red eyes. A massive paw on his chest. A huge shadowy head taking form above his. The head of a hound.

No, damn it. I'm Ricky Gallagher. I'm—

"I don't know if you can understand me, hound," a voice said. "But if you lower those teeth another inch, I'm putting a bullet through your skull."

"Liv," he said, her name coming out as a croak, his throat as tight and dry as if he *had* been the one shouting prayers and protests.

She moved into his field of vision, her gun pointed at the hound. "You okay? Well, other than being pinned under a giant hound?"

He managed a laugh. "Other than that, yeah. Where—?"

The hound snarled, as if to say, *Hey, asshole, did you forget I'm here?* and he saw that it was *the* hound. The injured one. The broken one.

It was and it was not, because when he looked into those fiery eyes, blazing with hate, he didn't need to ask where the Huntsman had gone.

"I see you," he whispered.

The hound snarled. Those massive jaws opened, and Liv leapt forward, covering the last few feet between them.

"Don't you dare, hound," she said, a snarl in her own voice, and when the hound ignored her, she was right there, the gun barrel at the back of the beast's skull.

"No!" Ricky said.

"I won't unless I have to. But if those fangs get any closer—"

The beast lowered its head an inch. Taunting her. Testing her. And her finger tightened on the trigger.

"No!" Ricky said again. "It's not the hound. It's him—the Huntsman. He's possessed it."

"And I'm sorry," she said slowly. "But that doesn't matter. That can't matter."

The hound's lips curled, and Ricky swore he heard the Huntsman's laughter. Rage rippled through him.

You bastard. You twisted son of a bitch. The hound served you well, no matter how much it hated you, and this is how you repay it. As a pawn in a game. A lesson to me.

Ricky looked into the hound's eyes and his knee shot up, catching it in the gut. As that knee made contact, his hands shot around the beast's throat, but the blow surprised the beast for only a second and it wrested its head free, and they rolled, him grappling for a hold, the hound slashing at him, and then the beast convulsing as a blow rocked it, and Ricky glanced over to see Liv falling back, her leg still raised from a kick.

The hound slashed and snapped at him. Liv cursed as she tried to intervene. Ricky managed to land a blow under the hound's muzzle, and its head jerked up, and he grabbed fur in both hands, fists of fur, holding its head aloft as it fought and snapped, the beast stronger than him, so fucking much stronger. He tried to knee it in the gut again, but the angle was wrong. It fought wildly against his hands, and out of the corner of his eye he saw Liv lining up her shot. He yanked the beast's head down—*toward* him—and the surprise of that startled the hound enough for Ricky to lock gazes with it and shout, "Mine!"

This is mine. My hound, you son of a bitch, and I'm taking it back.

Darkness swirled, wild darkness, and when Ricky opened his eyes, he was looking down at himself, unconscious on the ground.

"Ricky!"

He stumbled back fast. He saw Liv raise the gun.

"What did you do to Ricky?" she said, that gun pointed at him.

I'm the hound. Shit, I'm inside the hound.

He glanced down at his feet . . . which were now giant black paws.

There, sorted? Now get the fuck away from your body before she shoots.

He kept backing away, staggering and sliding, his limbs moving awkwardly as he scrambled. Liv advanced on him, gun still raised, fury burning in her eyes. He whined and lowered his head.

Damn it, Gallagher, figure this out before—

But she didn't shoot. She just gave him one glower before dropping beside his body, her gaze still on the hound, her trembling fingers going to his body's neck, her eyelids fluttering in relief as she picked up a pulse. Then she looked at him, the hound, her eyes meeting his. Her head tilted, nose scrunching, as if seeing something she couldn't quite decipher. Her eyes widened and her lips opened, and before she could get the words out, darkness swirled, and when he opened his eyes again, he was lying on the forest floor, staring up at Liv crouched over him as the hound teetered and collapsed.

CHAPTER THIRTY-TWO

Ricky's hazel eyes looked up into mine. I put my arm under his shoulders and helped him sit.

"Were you just . . .?" I began.

"Possessing a huge fae hound?" he said. "I have no idea. At this point, I'm starting to think someone sprinkled acid on my pizza and I'm passed out on a sidewalk somewhere."

"We ate the same pizza," I said. "Which may be the explanation."

He chuckled and rubbed his eyes. "Yeah. If that's what visions are like, I don't know how you do it, Liv. I'm here, and then I'm not, and then I'm someone else, and then I'm some*thing* else, and holy fuck."

He got to his feet, still wobbly as I helped him up.

"I remember when I turned eighteen," he said. "My dad took me to the cabin, and he brought out a bunch of shit. Product. You know. He said if I was curious, that's how I was going to do it. Try it there, with him to watch me. Get it over with."

"Did you?"

He shook his head. "I wasn't curious. I'd smoked pot when I was a kid. It made me feel just kind of . . . flat. Relaxed. Mellow. Not really my thing. Now?" He rubbed his temples. "I feel like my brain exploded . . . and not in a good way."

"Sorry," I said.

"I'm the dumbass who had to see what was in the forest—" Ricky wheeled, gaze flying to the hound, still lying on its side. "Shit!" he murmured as he ran and crouched beside it. "Okay, it's breathing. And . . ." He looked around. "The Huntsman?"

I shook my head. "No idea. Last I saw, he was over there"—I pointed—"when you jumped him. Then you blacked out and before I could even get to you, the hound barreled out of the forest and pounced."

"He possessed it."

"And then you did, and while I'd love to think that means the Huntsman got his psychic ass kicked, that's probably too much to hope for." I looked around, my gun raised. "If there's any way of waking the pooch, I'm going to suggest we get it out of—" I stopped. "No. There's someone in the cabin."

"What?"

"When you disappeared, I found the cabin, with the hound guarding the door. Then I heard you and the Huntsman taunting each other in the forest."

"Which means the hound wasn't guarding *him*."

"And whoever it was guarding isn't being guarded anymore. You stay with the hound. I'll—"

"No."

"I won't go inside, I'll just see what's—"

"No, Liv," he said, walking back to me. "Maybe we can't control when we get separated, but we're sure as hell not compounding the issue by *voluntarily* separating. The hound . . ." He trailed off, then came back firm. "The hound will be fine."

I glanced at him, his jaw set, gaze resolutely turned away from the fallen beast. Determined to walk away and tell himself it would be fine while every fiber screamed for him not to abandon his hound. I knew which side would win. The one he'd already chosen. Because that was how we remained ourselves. Olivia, not Matilda. Ricky, not Arawn. Make the choices from our heads, not from our hearts.

But it's the heart that matters, isn't it? That's what we really are. Not Arawn with his hound. *Ricky* with his hound.

"Let's wake it up," I said, walking back to the beast.

"No, we need to—"

"We can spare a few minutes. Get it up and moving. It's not hurt—just unconscious."

Of course, I had no way of knowing that for certain, but I pushed the fear aside and lowered myself next to the beast. Ricky did the same, and he shook it, talking to it, and after a moment I realized this would be easier for him if I didn't hear what he said, so I made the excuse that I should walk around, check for the Huntsman.

"Not out of sight, okay?" he said.

I nodded and walked and listened to him coaxing the hound, as if he was trying to bring its spirit back. He promised it everything he could promise and nothing that he couldn't. It felt like eavesdropping. This was the side he'd grown up learning to keep to himself. The gentler side. The *softer* side, he'd say, with that disparaging twist he used for the word because that's the one he'd heard whispered among the Saints, the worry that Ricky was "a little soft." He could find his edge, but *this* was the Ricky I knew, the guy who worried about a hound, who'll whisper to it and coax it back, while asking me not to leave his sight. Consideration. Caring. Which is no weakness at all.

When he exhaled in relief, I turned to see the hound lifting its head. Ricky rubbed it around the ears, then he got to his feet and said, "It's fine. We should go check the cabin." Because that was Ricky, too. The side that cared and worried never interfered with whatever needed doing.

"Can it follow us?" I asked. "That would be better."

I moved slowly toward the hound, ready for it to flinch.

It only watched me. When I drew up alongside Ricky, it snorted and laid its head on the ground.

"If it can follow, it will," Ricky said. "But it's safe here." He surveyed the forest. "The woods are different now. Lighter."

The forest did feel more itself. Still unnaturally dark, but I could make out faint stars overhead.

"The Huntsman's gone," I said.

"For now."

"You showed him."

Ricky smiled. "Nah, he's just regrouping."

"Which still means you were more than he bargained for."

Ricky shrugged and was starting to speak when running footsteps sounded. He took off at a lope.

"So I guess the hound wasn't protecting someone," he said as I caught up. "It was holding someone captive. I shouldn't have waited to wake—"

"That was my call," I said. "I didn't want the Huntsman zapping back into it and coming after you again."

He glanced over, telling me he knew that wasn't why I'd insisted he rouse the beast.

"It's not like our quarry is sneaking off into that good night," I said, waving in the direction of the crashing.

He grabbed my hand and squeezed. "Thank you."

"Pretty sure I haven't done anything."

"Yeah, you have. You always do. Fuck, I love you."

"So . . . hunt?"

He laughed and smacked my ass with one hand. "Yes, my lady. No more inconveniently timed spontaneous displays of affection. On to your hunt."

CHAPTER THIRTY-THREE

We flanked the captive, and ran alongside him until
we reached the perfect spot, where the trees thinned
to my left. Then Ricky veered and barreled through
a pile of dead leaves, startling our target, making him
swerve toward open ground.

When the man entered that semi-clearing, he glanced
over his shoulder, saw Ricky, and then turned back to find
me right in front of him. He pulled up short, his arms windmilling and—

It was Ciro Halloran.

"Who are you?" he said.

"Turn around," Ricky said.

As Ciro did, I circled him in case he went after Ricky.

Ciro's forehead wrinkled. "Do I know you?"

Ricky walked farther into the moonlight. "Is that better?"

Ciro's expression said it wasn't.

"You don't know him?" I said.

Ciro shook his head slowly, his gaze fixed on Ricky.

"His photos were found in your condo," I said.
"Surveillance photos you'd taken."

"Surveillance photos?"

"He's Rick Gallagher," I said, watching for any glimmer
of recognition in his eyes. "Of the Satan's Saints."

"Satan's . . .?"

"You sent him a letter."

"E-mail, you mean? I didn't. If someone used my address—"

"And you don't know me, either."

He took a better look at me, and that's when I got a glimmer of recognition, though the spark didn't ignite.

"Olivia Taylor-Jones," I said. "Also known as Eden Larsen."

"Eden . . ." He stared at me. "You're . . ."

"Daughter of serial killers. Well, at least you read the papers."

"No, I mean you're . . ." He swallowed. "Right. The papers. That's where I've seen you."

"Which isn't what you were going to say at all," Ricky said, advancing slowly. "I'll ask you to finish that sentence."

"I didn't—"

"I'll *insist* you finish that sentence."

Ciro's mouth worked. I got a better look at him then, this killer of fae. He wasn't tall, maybe only an inch or so over my five-eight. Narrow face, thin build, hands at his sides, clenching into fists and then quickly unclenching, as if realizing the nervous gesture could be taken for an aggressive one.

As Ricky moved closer, Ciro seemed to fight the urge to run. His posture was downright submissive, gaze lowered, chin tucked down, like a little boy in the schoolyard, watching the bully bear down on him and fighting not to flinch.

"Here are a few more words for you," I said. "Cŵn Annwn. Tylwyth Teg."

His gaze shot to me. "You . . . you know? It's true, then?" He blanched. "No, tell me it's not true. Tell me I didn't lose my opportunity . . ." He swayed, as if his knees were about to give way. "No, no, please. It's not true. He lied. He must have lied. Otherwise . . . Lucy. Oh God, Lucy."

"What's not true?" Ricky said. "Something about Olivia?"

"Your parents," Ciro said, talking to me. "The Cŵn Annwn fixed you because of what your parents did. Their crimes."

I glanced at Ricky. His lips tightened, and he said, "Tell us what you heard."

"That she—Eden—was sick. Dying. The Cŵn Annwn made her parents a deal. If they committed murders the Cŵn Annwn could not, they would be repaid with their daughter's life. And they were. She—you—Eden died before all the lives were taken, but with the sacrifices, they were able to bring you back from the afterlife. The Cŵn Annwn returned you. That was the deal."

"I didn't . . ." I trailed off as the pieces clunked into place. "Lucy. He promised you Lucy."

Ciro's eyes closed and he swayed, face paling. "I didn't have faith. I thought he was lying. When he first came to me, I was angry. So damned angry. I blamed them, and it all seemed easy."

"You blamed the lamiae for Lucy's death."

"That's the only reason she'd go to that neighborhood. For them. Her family . . . My family . . ."

"They're samhail," I said. "We know."

"My family broke away from the pact. They didn't see the point in it. The Hallorans kept some contact with fae, and they'd help for adequate compensation. Fae don't have the power they once did. We've learned so much as humans that petty fae magics and healing are all but useless. At least, that's what my family believed. To the Madoles, though, it was an ancient obligation, and they still wanted to help."

"By setting up a drop-in center for the lamiae."

He nodded. "That was their mother's mission. Then Aunika's. But Lucy . . . Lucy wanted more. She couldn't break away completely, though. She still cared. That was the part I hated. If the lamiae needed her, she went, any time of the day or night. I said they didn't appreciate it. They treated her help like it was their due, resented her for not giving as much as Aunika did. Ungrateful little—" He bit the word off, his voice snapping with old anger.

"So Lucy went to help the lamiae and she was killed, and you blamed them."

"I was crazy with grief, so when he said that the lamiae actually *killed* her . . ."

"What?"

He squeezed his eyes shut and shook his head. "I was out of my mind, and I hated—*hated*—them so much. He said the lamiae murdered Lucy, that they summoned her there, pretending they were hurt, and then demanded money, claiming she owed them for abandoning her duty. When she threatened to tell Aunika, they killed her. The Huntsman couldn't touch the lamiae because Lucy isn't fae, so he came to me. He said that if I killed four lamiae, I'd get Lucy back, just like your parents got you back."

"And that was the same Huntsman who was holding you captive?"

"He wasn't holding—Not at first . . ." Ciro ran his hands through his hair. "I failed. God, I failed, and now I won't get her back—"

"I never died," I said.

"The Cŵn Annwn can't resurrect the dead," Ricky said.

"How do you know that?" Ciro said, meeting Ricky's gaze with a look that was belligerence and fear and hope, because he still wanted to think it was possible, that he could somehow get Lucy back, but he also wanted to believe it *wasn't* possible, that he hadn't lost an honest chance.

"How do you know?" he repeated.

Ricky met his gaze and said, "I just do."

"Whatever that Huntsman told you?" I said. "He's full of shit."

"I . . ." Ciro swallowed. "I suspected that. After the—" He closed his eyes again and rocked on his heels. "After what I did. After I stopped being so angry. After I had a long talk with Ani."

"Aunika?" I said, trying to keep the worry out of my voice. "What did you tell her?"

"Nothing. I mean, I said I thought the lamiae called Lucy out that night. We talked, and I started to think I'd made a mistake. So I told the Huntsman I thought *he'd* made a mistake. He said that was fine, I could stop. Next thing I know, the Cŵn Annwn were after me, and I needed to get to safety."

"The Cŵn Annwn were after you? You saw them?"

"It's mostly what I heard. Hooves. A hound baying. I caught a glimpse of it, but only a glimpse."

"*It,*" I said. "You saw one hound. Heard what could have been *one* set of hoofbeats."

"I guess so."

That's what I'd seen in my vision. Like Ciro, I'd presumed it'd been the whole pack of Cŵn Annwn. But it'd only been one hound and one rider. The rogue Huntsman and the wounded *cŵn*.

"Then the Huntsman offered you sanctuary here. To escape the Hunt."

"Right. Then I overheard him on the phone after he thought I fell asleep. He was talking to some guy he'd sent after Aunika. Apparently, someone had been hurt. When I heard that, I freaked out, and he said Ani was fine, just fine, and I'd misunderstood and he'd been saying someone *else* went after her, and his friends were trying to stop it. But I knew then it was a lie, that Ani was right and the lamiae would never have hurt Lucy. I didn't dare accuse him of lying, so I've been trying to sneak out, but the hound . . ." He looked around quickly. "Where's the hound?"

"Close by," Ricky said. "It's mine now. Answer our questions and you'll be fine. But you really don't want to run."

As if on cue, a hound bayed, loud enough that Ciro wasn't the only one jumping. I spun, and then realized it wasn't Ricky's hound.

"The Cŵn Annwn," Ricky said. "They must be stuck outside the forest. Like the ravens."

"Wh-what?" Ciro said. "You said the *real* . . .?"

"Did that guy honestly seem like Cŵn Annwn to you?" I said. "I know you said your family doesn't follow the old ways, but I think you'd at least know your fae lore. They hunt in packs, right?" I waved at the baying. "*That* is a pack. What you dealt with was a rogue Cŵn Annwn."

"No, that *thing* is an abomination," Ricky said. "He told this guy to *murder* fae—"

"That's why they're here, isn't it?" Ciro said, still turned toward the sound. "The real Huntsmen. I killed fae. I'm theirs now."

"We'll handle this," Ricky said. "You—"

"Handle it how?" Ciro said. "I *murdered* fae. Killed them horribly, and for what?" His voice rose. "Lucy's not coming back. She's *never* coming back."

"We'll speak to the Cŵn—" I began.

"You can't reason with the Hunt. I have no excuse."

"Just calm down and we'll call them." I took out my cell.

Ciro started to laugh, his voice rising hysterically. "Call them? On your cell phone. Of course. Because you have their number. The cell phone number of the Cŵn Annwn."

"Calm down," Ricky said. "They're not going to—"

A growl cut him off. We turned to see the hound—the broken cŵn—on the edge of the clearing, its gaze fixed on Ciro. When I looked over, the forest tilted for a moment, and I was in a ruined building, watching Ciro crouched over the body of a lamia. Watching him dip his hands into her blood. Watching her, dead eyes wide with terror, her glow fading as her spirit passed. Seeing that, I felt the hound's rage, one that echoed what Ciro had said—that there was no excuse, that he had murdered those fae girls and he should pay.

"No."

The word came quietly, calmly, but it jolted me out of the vision, and I saw Ricky, his gaze on the hound as he said, "Not this one."

The growl died in the hound's throat as it raised its gaze to him, ears drooping, head bowing in submission.

Ricky walked over and rubbed behind the hound's ruined ear, murmuring, "None of that," and it slowly, carefully, straightened, its gaze on him, waiting for a raised hand or other sign that it had misinterpreted. Finally, it pulled itself up straight, submission evaporating, and it watched Ciro, its gaze saying he still deserved death, but it would wait. For now, it would wait.

I turned to Ciro. "Okay, we're going to get you out of here. We'll—"

"No," he said, looking toward the baying hounds. He drew himself up straight and waved toward the unseen Hunt. "Isn't that what I deserve?"

"Just—"

"Lucy's gone. She's not coming back." He looked at the hound. "And you can take me to her, can't you?"

Ciro flew at Ricky. The hound crouched for attack, but Ricky said, "No!" and dodged Ciro's clumsy charge, grabbing him by the jacket as the hound stood there, hackles raised, snarling.

"Yeah, sorry," Ricky said. "That's not going to work."

Ciro threw himself in the other direction, breaking Ricky's hold. He ran. And the hound went after him.

Ricky shouted, "No!" and lunged, but they were already out of his reach. Out of his reach and running my way.

Ciro veered at the last moment, and I caught one glimpse of his face, horror mixed with resolve. He tore past, and I went after him, and I could hear the hound on my heels and the pound of Ricky's boots as he shouted, "No! Damn it, no!" and then "Liv! Get out of the—"

The hound leapt. I felt it knock me aside, and heard the

click of its fangs and I thought for one second those fangs were for me, that it was too consumed with its mission to realize it had the wrong person and I was going to—

Ciro screamed. My arms went up to ward off the hound, but it was already past me, taking down Ciro, who screamed again just as I heard another shout, a deep boom from the forest.

"Olivia!"

I threw myself on the beast, saying, "No!" even as Ricky shouted for the hound to stop, get the fuck off Ciro, don't you dare—

The hound's head slashed down. That's all I saw. That massive head go down. And then blood. Blood arcing everywhere. Blood spurting, the smell of it, the taste of it as it hit my open mouth. Someone hit my side. Tackled me, pushing me off the hound, arms pulling me up, fingers going to my face, swiping away the blood, a panicked voice saying my name. I looked up into pale blue eyes, clouded with worry.

"Is she hurt?" Ricky skidded up beside us, and Gabriel shot him a look.

"Not mine," I managed to say, the shock still thick. "Blood. Not mine. It's—Ciro!"

I scrambled up, pushing Gabriel aside. Or trying to, because he grabbed me back and let Ricky race past to the hound.

"Goddamn it!" Ricky said. "God-fucking-damn it!" and I knew Ciro was dead. Of course he was dead. That was the hound's job, and when Ciro bolted, nothing could hold it back. Ricky still cursed, and I knew he was cursing himself, his failure, but the hound whined and backed off Ciro's body, head lowered.

Ricky reached for the hound, and it tried to duck again, to avoid a blow, but Ricky only rubbed it behind the ears, murmuring, "It's okay. Just . . . damn it."

"Sit," Gabriel said to me.

I lowered myself to the ground, and he surveyed my blood-covered face. Then he pulled out his shirttail and started to rip the cloth and Ricky said, "No, here," and tugged at his shirt, but Gabriel said, "I've got this," and gave him another of those hard looks. Ricky ducked it, not unlike the hound, murmuring, "I'm sorry."

"No," I said. "Whatever happened out here, it was both of us."

Gabriel said, "I know," and the look he turned on me was softer, but I still saw the reproach there, that edge that said we'd done something reckless and foolhardy. Worse, we'd done it without him there to help.

Gabriel tore a strip from his shirt and used it to clean my face. I glanced over at Ciro, lying on the ground, his throat torn out, and I felt . . . I didn't know what I felt. Well, yes, I did. I just didn't like it.

"He killed them," I said as Gabriel cleaned my face. "The lamiae. He was told they murdered Lucy and that killing them would bring her back." Another glance Ciro's way. "Whatever the excuse, he still murdered them."

"I know," he murmured. "He had a choice."

I nodded. When he worked at a spot on my temple, I leaned against his hand, just briefly, and he rubbed his thumb across my cheek instead, the touch equally brief, but equally meaningful.

"Like Pamela," Ricky said, his voice low, as if not wanting to interrupt.

I glanced to see him crouched beside the hound, one hand on it, his gaze on me, and I nodded, because that's exactly what had been swirling through my brain since Ciro first told us of the deal he'd made with the Huntsman. Ricky understood that. I've had people in my life whom I felt a deep bond with, but it was never like this. I look at these men, and I feel that connection, the sense that they get me in a way I'd always presumed no one could.

"Like Pamela," I murmured, as Gabriel's critical eye declared my face clean of blood spray and I started to rise. "Which raises a hundred questions, all of which Ciro's not going to be able to answer."

"I don't think he ever could," Ricky said. "He was just another human pawn in a fae game."

"We need to figure out this rogue Huntsman's particular game. I'm guessing he killed Lucy and set it all in motion. The question is why. But first: we have a dead body."

"I believe they can take care of that," Gabriel said, and before I could ask, I caught the thunder of horses. The hound heard it too and leapt up, quivering in anticipation. Then it went still and gave a convulsing shudder and turned sharply, ready to flee.

Ricky caught it, his hands wrapping in its fur as he said, "Uh-uh." Then he turned to me. "Can you guys . . .?"

"Head them off before they scare the hound away?"

"Yeah, thanks."

CHAPTER THIRTY-FOUR

Gabriel and I caught up with Ioan and his Cŵn Annwn. They weren't in actual Hunt mode—just regular guys in jeans, boots, and jackets, astride horses. Not unlike the Saints, really. All they needed were patches on their jackets.

They'd managed to breach the forest, which was the best proof that the rogue Huntsman was gone, his power fading as he fled and his hound shifted allegiance to a new master.

Ioan acknowledged Gabriel's presence with a nod, curt but not rude, and I said that everything was under control. Then I asked if he'd walk with me, leaving the horses and the others behind.

"We have the hound," I said. "But if you go tearing over there, we won't have it for long. It's already spooked."

Ioan was off his horse without a word. I explained what had happened as we walked. When I finished, Ioan said, "You're right. We cannot bring back the dead, nor could we facilitate such a deal with any power that could. To resurrect the *immediately* dead, within moments of their passing? Perhaps, if death came from something reversible, such as heart failure. But to return someone who has been in her grave for months? It speaks to his grief that he even believed such a thing was possible."

"People will believe anything when they're in pain."

He dipped his chin. "And this impostor took advantage of that. I will not even call him Cŵn Annwn."

"That's what Ricky said, too."

Ioan smiled. "Of course he did. Our ways have always been there, in his head and in his heart, and he can pull on that as easily as he can recall the alphabet. Proof he is not another imitation of Arawn."

He looked at Gabriel as if to make a point. *Ricky* was the real deal.

"You never told us how exactly you got here," I said to Gabriel. "My text only mentioned we were heading into a forest south of the city."

"I looked around and saw the bike and the riders."

"In the entire south-of-Chicago region, you just happened to glance across a dark field and see guys on black horses?"

His brow furrowed as he wondered why I was bringing this up. Then he caught Ioan's look, the flashed annoyance of a doting grandfather bragging about his boy's field pass only to watch his competition score a touchdown. Gabriel gave me a look, as if to say that my efforts were too awkward by far.

Ioan cleared his throat. "So the hound trusts Ricky?"

"It does," I said. "It couldn't seem to help going after Ciro when he ran."

"That instinct is compulsory, no matter how damaged the creature might be."

"Ciro knew that. Which is why he ran. Death by fae hound."

"Hmm." Ioan tugged my elbow, steering me around a rabbit hole without even seeming to glance at the ground. "About the hound. Ricky should take it. It obviously trusts him and—"

"No."

"It would be easier, particularly for the hound. If the beast has overcome a learned fear of Cŵn Annwn to trust Ricky, that speaks to an incredible bond, and its rehabilitation would be best facilitated—"

"Ricky lives part-time with his dad, part-time in a student apartment, and part-time at my Cainsville apartment. Two of those places are not hound-friendly. He drives a Harley. Also not hound-friendly. He goes to college and works for a motorcycle club. His *life* is not hound-friendly. If you suggest the *cûn* needs him, he'll feel guilty, and he doesn't deserve to feel guilty. Worse, he'll feel pressured. You don't want him to feel pressured." I turned to Gabriel. "Hey, did I mention that Ida wants to give you a house in Cainsville? She says it's time for you to move in."

"What?"

I turned to Ioan and waved my hand at Gabriel. "See that expression? It's the same look of horror you'll get if you mention Ricky taking the hound. Like offering an engagement ring on a first date."

Ioan rolled his eyes at my dramatics, but after a moment he said, "We will care for the hound, but it may require help from Ricky."

"Which he will give. Just . . . for your own sake, take it slow."

I'd hoped, when Ioan saw the hound, he'd be able to mind-meld or whatever and get its story. But the link had been truly severed. He suspected it had suffered some trauma and the lone Huntsman took advantage of that.

"*He* did not do this," Ioan said as he examined the hound's long-healed injuries. "The hound would never have stayed with him if he did. Something happened to this poor beast. She was orphaned from her pack. He took her, and he did not treat her well, but . . ."

He hunkered back on his heels, rubbing the beast's ears. She—the hound was apparently female—kept giving him sidelong looks, uncertain, not ready to commit to eye contact.

"The damage he did seems disrespect rather than abuse," he said. "A hound is our companion, not our slave."

"And he enslaved this one," I said. "He treated her as a dog, which damaged her further."

Ioan nodded, rose, and turned to Ricky. "I would like you to help us bring her to my house. I'll keep her there. The pack alpha stays with me, and she'll be comfortable with him."

"Wouldn't she be *more* comfortable with a hound lower in the hierarchy?" I asked.

"The alpha would never mistreat her, and the hound will take comfort in his attention. Once Brenin accepts her, the other hounds will." He paused and couldn't help looking at Ricky and saying, "Unless you have a better idea . . ."

"Nope. I'll do what I can, but I'm definitely not in the market for a hound."

I had to bite my cheek at that.

Ricky turned to me. "The Cŵn Annwn will take care of Ciro's body. I'm handling the hound. You have to get rid of those clothes. And you and Gabriel need to talk about what Ciro said. I'll catch up once the hound is situated."

"Actually," Ioan said, "Liv should accompany you. The hound obviously trusts her as well."

"No," Ricky said. "She should go with Gabriel."

Ioan's lips tightened, but Ricky only walked over and gave me a hug before we left.

CHAPTER THIRTY-FIVE

W e stopped at Ricky's place. I kept extra clothes there, so Gabriel had me shower and change and then he disposed of what I'd been wearing.

An hour later, we were in Gabriel's apartment. He poured us both a Scotch and we settled on the sofa, which we'd moved in front of the window.

"You should leave it here," I said. "I know an interior designer would have a fit . . ."

"Yes, that was my concern. That I'd horrify all the interior designers I invite up here."

I smiled and tucked my feet up under me as I sat sideways on the sofa. He attempted to get comfortable, which for Gabriel meant facing forward and slouching an entire quarter of an inch.

"You need a bigger couch."

"I don't believe they come much bigger. Not if they'll fit through my door."

"Get one with two recliners. Then we can sit and stretch out and . . . talk to the window. Huh. I don't suppose they come with the recliners on an angle, so we can partially face each other while still looking out the window."

"I believe they would call that two separate recliners. Which can be placed at any angle you desire."

I made a face. "I want a sofa."

"I will refrain from pointing out that it's actually my apartment."

"Oh, I know, how about one of those big circular ones? It's very seventies, but it looks comfortable. And if I doze off, you can just leave me there."

"I already do that. On this couch."

"Which *isn't* uncomfortable."

"There's also the floor."

I slid down to it. "Not bad."

"I meant for sleeping."

I pulled down two pillows, arranged them on the floor, and settled in. Gabriel gave a deep sigh, and lowered himself beside me.

"Okay, this works," I said. "Now what you need is a fireplace."

He laughed. A deep laugh that echoed through the room, and it was wonderful to hear, and I curled up, feeling the warmth of it, like hot cocoa on a cold day.

"Right there." I pointed in front of us. "But it has to be really low to the floor, so it doesn't interfere with the view. Nothing can interfere with the view."

"Of course."

"And just think, I haven't even *started* drinking yet."

He smiled at me, a smile as real as his laugh. His unabashed I-forgot-I'm-not-supposed-to-do-this smile, the one I usually only got after he'd had a glass of wine, the one that fades his eyes to the warmest blue imaginable. Winning that smile is like acing my SATs and running a marathon all in the same day.

I sipped my Scotch, and he did the same, and we sat, staring out the window and drinking, letting the night settle on us, until the alcohol worked its way into my system, tugging my mood down just enough that I said, "I shouldn't be joking around tonight, should I?"

"Hmm?"

"After what happened. With Ciro. I shouldn't joke and goof off."

"If you're feeling bad about not feeling bad *enough*, I do believe you're talking to the wrong person."

"What do you fee—?" I cut myself off sharply and put my glass down with a click against the hardwood. "Sorry. That was rude. I'll blame the booze and apologize."

"No need. It is, I realize, considered a nonintrusive question from a friend." He eased back against the sofa, long legs stretching, and then looked my way, his head reclining against the cushions, eyes bright. "I understand concepts even if I don't embrace them."

I nodded and sipped my drink.

"As for any concern over your reaction to Ciro Halloran's death, it is, I believe, invalid. I would say 'ludicrous,' but I suspect *that* would be rude."

"You just said it."

"With a somewhat sincere disclaimer attached. The point is that I know you worry about your lack of altruism. Which is ridiculous. You're not investigating the lamiae murders for personal profit. You aren't concerned about the disappearance of Aunika Madole because she owes you money. You didn't try to save Ciro Halloran from the hound because there was a reward in it. As for trying to save him at all, I would like to think it was a spontaneous impulse and that you would not have put yourself in danger for him if you'd considered the matter. But that is, in part, a projection of my own feelings—I don't want to see you take risks for strangers."

"But it's true, too," I said. "If I'd thought it through, given what he'd done . . . I might not have."

"Good. That's what I want to hear. However, it's not entirely true, because in the moment that you took to decide whether to give chase, you would have realized you wanted him alive for questioning and taken the risk for *that* reason.

If you really *did* only want to save Ciro out of the goodness of your heart? I could not comprehend that."

He took another, longer drink and then said, "You asked what I feel. The answer is nothing. That is, I hurry to qualify, on this particular topic. The face that I present is not a false face, but I am capable of emotion."

"I know."

He nodded, not looking over. "The truth is that, in the matter of the lamiae, when I said that I wanted to get them into Cainsville so they'd be out of our way, that wasn't me putting a logical slant on the matter. That *is* me. It's what I feel. Or do not feel, as the case may be."

Another sip of the Scotch, his gaze still on the window. "People wonder how I represent the clients I do. Do I not feel empathy for the victims and their families? No, I don't. I *think* about them, though. I think that their loss is a tragedy, and I think of how their lives were affected, and I think that what happened to them was unfair. But the world does not promise fair, and if my client is indeed guilty, then let the court decide that. Perhaps the greater sin is that I realize I feel nothing for strangers, and I still do not care."

I was formulating an answer, desperately searching for the right words, when he downed the rest of his glass in a single gulp, shut his eyes for a moment, and then opened them and said, still facing forward, "Does that bother you?"

"Hmm?"

He looked my way, yet not directly at me. "Does it bother you that I cannot look at those lamiae and take pity?"

"I have spent enough time with you, Gabriel, to understand what you are and what you aren't, and if I had a problem with that, you'd know it."

It seemed an honest and positive answer, but his gaze slid away, and he lifted the empty glass to his lips, and when he realized it was empty and I said, "More?" he shook his head, but there was a hesitation there.

"I'm having more," I said, and poured myself a finger and took the bottle over to him, and he didn't hesitate to lift his glass.

When I sat again, he said, "My lack of caring doesn't apply to you. I hope you understand that."

"I know." I pulled my knees up as I turned to face him. "For me, it's a stretch to feel what others do naturally. Like with Ciro. I wanted to stop the hound from killing him, but then I was back here, joking around, and I had to stop and think, 'Oh, right, I watched a guy die tonight.' So I do understand, and I'm sorry if that wasn't clear."

"It was." He sipped at his drink. "But you said you understand what I am not. You accept it." His gaze lifted to mine. "You don't need to accept it." He lowered the glass. "I don't mean the lack of altruism. That won't change. But there are other things you don't have to accept. You don't need to apologize for asking me how I felt earlier. You don't need to avoid displaying emotional pain around me. Yes, I am uncomfortable with that. Yes, when you do it, I have the urge to run, as fast as I can. But not because I don't *want* to help. Because I don't know how." His eyes widened, and he murmured a rare curse. "And with that, I have definitely had too much to drink. I'm sorry. I don't—"

"It's okay."

"I just—"

"Gabriel?" I leaned toward him. "It's okay. I know you don't like to admit anything like that." I lowered my voice to a mock whisper. "But it's not inappropriate, and I promise I won't hold it against you."

He hesitated. Then he snorted a laugh. "Yes. Sorry." He sipped the Scotch. "What I'm saying is that I know sometimes you feel you're walking on eggshells with me. I've made you feel that way. But that is my inexperience with a relationship that is neither familial nor business in nature. I make mistakes." Another quick drink. "I've made a lot of mistakes, and I just want to say that you can expect better. I am past the point where I'm going to bolt and slam the door behind me." He glanced around. "Which is good, considering it's my apartment."

"Mmm, no. If you bolt, I get the condo. That's the deal."

A faint smile. "Is it?"

"Yep. You need stakes. Run away from me and you lose your apartment."

He glanced my way. "I don't need stakes to stop me from doing that. Losing you would be—" He stopped, horror filling his eyes, and he drained the rest of the glass as fast as he could.

"The floor is not comfortable."

"What?" he said, looking up sharply.

"I'm changing the subject before you really do bolt. Because, as much as I love your apartment, I'd rather keep you." I lifted my glass. "And thus ends our drunken sentimental exchange. So, the floor . . ."

" . . . is uncomfortable, and I would agree. I would also agree that I require comfortable permanent seating to take full advantage of the window view. Which I did intend to buy. I never got as far as walking into a furniture store. Once I was moved in, new furniture seemed . . ."

"Frivolous?"

"Exactly."

"I would point out that, given that no one actually comes here, the only person to judge you for such frivolity is yourself, but I know that's the opinion that counts. We will get you proper window-side seating."

His lips twitched in a smile. "And a fireplace?"

"Yes." I turned toward him. "On that topic, since I've passed the slightly drunk stage—and since you've given me permission to push—I'm going to ask a personal question."

"God forbid," he said, and then gave me a smile, as warm and relaxed as his earlier one.

"It's about fireplaces. Namely, the one in your office. Have you ever used it?"

"*That's* personal?"

"Sometimes, with you, I think 'Would you like fries with that?' is too personal."

He leaned back against the sofa, getting comfortable again. "To be honest, I've always found that question rather insulting. If I wanted fries, I would order them. The answer, by the way, is no. I do not—ever—want fries with that."

"Good to know."

"As for the fireplace, the answer is again no. I have never used it, and not because I don't want to. It's like window seating. I intended to take advantage of it and haven't."

"Was the office what you wanted, then? Or did you just get a good deal on it?"

Another twitch of the lips. "Had you asked me that six months ago, I'd have said I got a good deal. Which I did. Also, the proximity to the county jail is a distinct advantage. And that is what I told myself when I first leased it. But the truth?"

He eased down further, stretched out. "The truth is that the style reminded me of Rose's house, and there was comfort there. It also reminded me of the house I told you about, the one I dreamed of owning someday. I was, therefore, pre-inclined to appreciate a building of that era. And yet . . ." His lips pursed. "I walked into that office, and it was like something out of a novel, and somewhere in my head there was an image of what a lawyer's office should look like. I wanted that office, as I've wanted few things in my life. Although I did lease it at a very good price, given that the basement was being used as a meth lab."

"What?"

"I never told you that part?"

"Um, no. But you will now, right?"

"The man who originally owned the building was a

former client who . . . *allegedly* ran a meth lab out of the basement. I used the main floor for my office on the condition I'd never come in past nightfall or before dawn and would provide free legal advice. After two years of this, if I wished to purchase the building, I could, at a very reasonable price, so he could relocate without the undue attention that might come with a normal resale."

"You *own* the building?"

"Did I not mention that?"

"You mention nothing, Gabriel. Ever. Okay, forget owning the whole damned building. Tell me about the meth-lab dude."

"He actually made an excellent landlord. All went perfectly fine until the day . . ."

CHAPTER THIRTY-SIX

I woke smelling something and leapt up swinging. Gabriel didn't miss a beat, just pulled the coffee out of striking range and waited patiently while I rubbed my eyes.

"You are sleeping on my floor," he said. "I would have moved you, but I fell asleep myself. And yes, the floor is terribly uncomfortable. But . . . coffee?"

He held it out again, and I sputtered a laugh.

"No comment on the fact that I nearly punched you?" I said.

"I would expect no less. Which is why I remained out of range."

"So I couldn't get you back for the first night you slept at my apartment. When I made the mistake of waking you and got clocked."

"We both have excellent reflexes."

"Or it's a sign that we're both paranoid and need to lead much less dangerous lives."

He shook his head and handed me my coffee.

"You have time to drink that and dress," he said. "Before Ricky picks you up for breakfast."

I grabbed my phone. "Did I miss—?"

"No, I contacted him this morning and told him to come."

"You *told* him to take me to breakfast?"

"We have a full day, and I know you'll want to see each other. I have a few things to do at the office, but I'd like you there by eleven so we can leave for Cainsville."

"Cainsville?"

"You'll want to see how Melanie and Pepper's first night went. Also, you wanted to speak to Patrick about Cŵn Annwn deals. And we should go talk to Pamela, but I would suggest we have more data before we take that step."

He walked into the kitchen and returned with a bottle of aspirin. "If you require it. I did wake with a slight headache from the alcohol."

I smiled and took the bottle.

Ricky had club duties that afternoon, so he dropped me at the office. After lunch, Gabriel and I headed to Cainsville. We visited the lamiae first, making sure that they were settled in.

Gabriel took us the long way to Patrick's because he allegedly wanted to show me a hidden gargoyle. Instead, he only led me near one and then told me to find it. When I couldn't, he said, "It's the wrong time of year," and I slugged him for that.

"So it can only be seen during a certain season?" I asked.

"One night, actually. Winter solstice."

"How the hell did you find it?"

His brows shot up. "Who says I did?"

"You found them all. Veronica told me." I paused, and then pushed on. "That means there's one more than when you found them. Your gargoyle."

I waited for him to tense, but his eyes stayed that same soft and mellow blue as the corners of his mouth twitched. "Perhaps."

"So where is it?"

"Do you really think I'd tell you?"

"Do I get a prize if I find it?"

"Perhaps." He pointed up at the town hall bell tower. "As for this one, that's where you'll see it on solstice night."

"In the bell tower? Like the Hunchback of Notre Dame?"

"Exactly what I said."

"And you just randomly found it?"

"Not entirely," he said as we resumed walking. "We are allowed hints for the last gargoyle. I said I didn't want them. Patrick gave me one anyway, in a roundabout way. He asked if I was coming for winter solstice. The most important day of the year for Cainsville. But an even more important night for gargoyle hunting."

"Ah, and you got the hint?"

"I did."

"Clever boy."

He smiled, and we continued on. So it was a good walk. Very good. Why, then, as we approached Patrick's house, did my breathing pick up, a pit of panic forming in my gut? Because talking about Patrick helping Gabriel find the gargoyle reminded me that I was keeping a secret from him. And the last time I'd done that had nearly cost me Gabriel's friendship.

"Dare I offer you refreshments?" Patrick asked as we sat on his sofa.

Gabriel said no for both of us. Patrick might insist that the old stories about fae food and drink don't apply to us, but we didn't take any chances.

"Gabriel says you have questions, Liv. Admittedly, I might hope that someday you'll visit for the pleasure of my company . . ."

"Then you would suspect we had an agenda," Gabriel said. "You would not appreciate the subterfuge. Also, a visit for merely social reasons would bore you as much as it would me."

Patrick said, "True . . ." He added something else, but I didn't catch it, because having Gabriel point out a similarity between them, however innocuous, was like a hammer blow to the spike already driving into my conscience.

"So . . . questions?" Patrick said.

Gabriel motioned for me to go ahead, but I shook my

head and murmured that he could start, and I got a searching look for that.

"Is everything all right?" Gabriel asked, his voice low.

I nodded.

"Oh, something is definitely not all right," Patrick said.
"You've barely said a word since you got here, and Gabriel
is practically bouncy."

Gabriel turned a cool gaze on him. "I am hardly—"

"You're as close to bouncy as I've ever seen you. You
didn't eat enchanted fortune cookies, did you?" When
Gabriel frowned, Patrick said, "*Freaky Friday*? Body
switch?" He sighed. "It's a sad day when the three-hundred-
year-old bòcan makes pop culture references that the thirty-
year-old humans don't get."

"You're three hundred?" I said.

"There. Got your attention. Even in your lowest mood,
your curiosity will get the better of you. Three hundred . . . give or take a few decades. After a while, one stops
counting. Are you back with us, then, Olivia? Leaving the
brooding to Gabriel?"

"Brooding and bouncing," Gabriel murmured. "I'm not
sure which is worse."

"The bouncing is adorable," Patrick said. "It'll keep
people on their toes, wondering what you're up to. The pro-
verbial cat with the canary."

I cut in. "We've made significant progress solving the
lamiae murders. Which we haven't shared with the elders."

"That's why I like you, Liv. You know how to play the
game. Very refreshing. So, in return for questions answered,
I get the scoop on the murders. Which don't interest me
personally, but the fact that you confide in me is currency."

"Even if I only confide in you because you're useful?"

"You aren't supposed to admit that."

"Honesty, remember? But because your ego is so delicate,
here's a boost for you. You were right; Ioan was wrong."

"Naturally." Patrick leaned back in his chair. "What was I right about this time?"

"The samhail. They still exist. Which I confirmed because the guy who killed the lamiae—Ciro Halloran—also comes from a samhail family. Unlike the Madoles, his family has mostly retired from the biz. They didn't feel they were getting enough out of it."

"As a pragmatist and a realist, I must admit he is correct. Our skills did not hold their value well. Take the leprechauns, for example."

"There are leprechauns?"

"Irish fae known for making trouble. Related to bòcan, but with far more press, which we are very happy to let them have. They've gotten a little bitter about theirs. If you ever meet one, be sure to offer him some Lucky Charms. They *love* that."

"Do they grant wishes? That's the lore, right? Three wishes if you catch one?"

"Sadly, no."

"Pot of gold?"

"One gold coin. Which in past times meant you could feed a family of twelve for a year. These days? What's an ounce of gold? A few hundred dollars?"

"Sixteen hundred," Gabriel said. "It's doubled in the past four years and quadrupled in the last twenty." When I looked his way, he shrugged and said, "I have investments."

"Well, consider me behind the times, then," Patrick said. "Perhaps I should go round up a few leprechauns myself."

"Your point," I said, "is that the value of a single gold coin has dropped drastically over time. Which is an example of how the value of the fae and samhail relationship has fallen. Those who remain in it do so out of obligation and charity."

Patrick made a face. "Unfortunately, yes. Which is a hard blow for fae, and the reason most no longer avail themselves of samhail services."

"Those who do still accept the help are like the lamiae. Where need outweighs pride. Similar to those in the human world who accept charity. And maybe also those who consider it their due."

"Correct. Rumor has it that a few fae subtypes have virtually enslaved samhail families, insisting that they continue aiding them or they will reap punishment instead of benefits. An interesting side note, but unconnected to the current case."

"Unconnected to lamiae, you mean," I said.

"Yes. Their only negative power is the draining of energy during intercourse. Which most men would not find such a terrible fate, but given that the lamiae require variety—to avoid draining a particular victim—sexual slavery would be rather counterproductive." He paused. "Though it might make an interesting story. Not quite my usual fare, but there is a market for—"

"And we'll stop there," I said. "Moving on to deals with Cŵn Annwn. Ciro apparently had one. That was his motivation for killing lamiae."

Patrick went still. When he spoke, it was with care. "I am not fond of the Cŵn Annwn, Liv, but as someone who considers himself well versed in both lore and fact, there is nothing in my understanding of the Hunt to suggest . . ." He trailed off, and I could see him struggling, the troublemaking bòcan and the scholar.

"It wasn't actually the Cŵn Annwn," I said. "Not officially, at least."

He nodded in obvious relief at not having to defend the other team. Then he said, "Officially?"

"It's a rogue Cŵn Annwn. We're still trying to get his story. Apparently, he told Ciro that the lamiae murdered his wife, but if he killed four of them, he could bring her back. He invoked my parents' case, saying I'd died of my illness and the Cŵn Annwn brought me back."

"The Cŵn Annwn *personally* had nothing to do with—"

"Yes, I know. They invoked some higher power, which is neither god nor demon, and let's not even go there again, because my head is still spinning from the last conversation."

"Because there's too much mortal blood in you. It constricts your imagination."

"Or, possibly, you just aren't very good at explaining things."

"I can't explain what your mind cannot—"

Gabriel cleared his throat.

"Back on subject," I said. "This rogue Huntsman twisted my parents' case, and lied about the lamiae killing Lucy—Ciro's wife. He convinced Ciro to murder lamiae in a ritualistic way, presumably because my mother also used a ritual, though we now know she was only copying the first deaths. Also, Ciro had no clue who Ricky was, which proves that part was a setup. This rogue made it look as if Ricky was involved in Lucy's death, but it wasn't exactly a bang-up framing job."

"Just enough to get Ricky involved," Patrick mused. "To get your attention. All of you."

"Maybe? The point is that we have all these connections, but they aren't fitting together. Cŵn Annwn, my parents, rituals, Ricky, deals . . . They all link to one or another, but there's no through line. Feel free to tell me it's a failure of my puny human imagination and you have the solution."

"I'll think about it."

"Thank you. In the meantime, I know enough about the samhail for now, so instead I want to cash in my research chit and look up Cŵn Annwn bargains."

"You have a chit?"

"You said I was free to use your books to research samhail. Instead, I want to know more about Cŵn Annwn deals. How do people get them? What kind do they offer? *Why* do they offer them?"

"Bargains with Cŵn Annwn are rare, but not unheard

of. When you came to me about your parents' deal, I did some preliminary research, which you didn't end up needing. It does make for entertaining reading, though."

"Not if you're the subject of one of those deals."

"Which you can't really regret, under the circumstances."

"Um, mother turned murderer? Father in jail twenty years for crimes he didn't commit? Yeah, I can regret it."

"Despite the fact your adopted family gave you every advantage? Love plus money? It doesn't get better than that."

"My birth parents might disagree. And if they hadn't done the deal? I wouldn't be Matilda, which would have saved me a whole lotta grief."

"Grief, perhaps. Excitement, definitely. Your life, Liv, will be nothing if not interesting. *To live is the rarest thing in the world. Most people exist, that is all.* Also, there is no guarantee that a disability would have lessened the interest in you as Matilda." He turned to Gabriel. "*You* recognize the sacrifice her parents made to provide her with the life she has. Imperfect but wondrous."

"And dangerous," Gabriel said. "I could live without that part."

"Without that, her life would not be nearly as much fun for her. Cŵn Annwn live for the adrenaline rush. We all do, in our way."

"Which takes us back on topic," I said. "Cŵn Annwn and deals."

He waved at the bookshelf. "I suppose you'd like that route. It gets the adrenaline racing more than dry explanation." He glanced at Gabriel. "Liv prefers a life fully lived. Fully experienced. That's the lesson she's teaching you, and I'm glad to see you're such an apt pupil." When Gabriel gave him a look of complete incomprehension, Patrick only sighed and waved his hand. "As long as you take the lessons to heart, you don't need to recite them. Do I dare ask if *you* want to read one of my books?"

"What?" Gabriel's composure and formality fell away in almost comical surprise.

"That would be a no," Patrick said. "Liv dives in. You still need to test the waters. Ah well, it's a start."

Patrick handed me a book that was newer than most on the shelf. I've done enough work with Victorian original texts to recognize the binding style. It was a cloth cover, embossed in gold, simpler than many of the books I've worked with, with only a Celtic moon on the front.

It felt oddly light for the size. When I opened the cover, I saw why. Entire sheaves of pages were missing and others were burned, as if someone had set fire to the book.

"It's in rough shape," Patrick said. "That's the problem with handwritten texts. I can't just run out and replace it. That is one of a kind."

I flipped through it. The pages that had been removed had been done so surgically. Even on some undamaged ones, entire paragraphs had been blacked out.

"Redacted material?" I said.

"Apparently."

I lifted the book to examine it more closely. "It was intentionally mutilated, then."

"So it seems. My theory is that the owners really would have liked to destroy it before it got into the wrong hands, but they couldn't quite bring themselves to obliterate decades of work. The fire damage suggests one owner even got so far as to toss it into the fire before changing his mind."

"Dark, arcane knowledge?" I said. "Unfit for the hands of fae or mortal?"

Patrick chuckled. "I wish. No, the contents are much more prosaic."

Before he could continue, I began skimming, picking up what Welsh I knew. Two words, repeated many times, made it very clear what this was.

"It's a history of the Cŵn Annwn," I said.

"Yes."

Patrick sat beside me, nudging Gabriel away, which was rather like nudging a stone block. He got a cool look for his efforts and, with a sigh, Patrick pulled up the ottoman and perched on it instead. Then he reached over and flipped through pages while the book lay on my lap.

"It appears that around the turn of the last century a Huntsman decided to compile a history of their kind. This is his life's work. You'll see it's all in a single hand, the ink changing and . . ." He turned to the back, where at least twenty pages were blank. "Continued right up until his death."

"Why the mutilation?" I said.

"Fae consider themselves a secretive lot, but . . ." He waved at his library. "Obviously that doesn't apply to our books. It's arrogance, really. We presume we can write what we like, and if any mortal finds it, he'll think it a work of fiction. The Cŵn Annwn are far more careful. The thought that someone outside their community would find such a book . . ." He gave a mock shudder.

"So a Huntsman wrote it, and his pack found it after his death. They cut out and redacted the most sensitive information but couldn't bring themselves to destroy his life's efforts. Dare I ask how you got hold of it?"

He smiled. "You can ask. I won't tell. And I would very much prefer that Ioan didn't discover I have it."

"Of course not. Once he got it, I'd never see it again."

"Smart girl. All right, then, the information is a bit fragmented, particularly the parts on deals." He turned to near the back of the book, where a section had been almost entirely redacted.

"Uh-huh," I said. "I'm surprised they didn't just cut this out completely."

"Mmm, I can understand their reluctance. In matters of business—as in law—it is helpful to be able to refer to a precedent. For our purposes, it's good that they left the pages in, because while the words are covered, they still exist. You'll notice jumps and jolts, but you should be able to get the general picture. You'll want to start here . . ."

He pointed partway down the page. I began to read, translating the general gist of the text that remained.

The offering of deals is a difficult business. It allows the Cŵn Annwn to pursue justice in cases where they otherwise could not, and as has been previously explained, it is the pursuit of justice that drives us. Quite literally. It feeds a hunger that is never quite satiated. The actual pursuit—the chase—only takes the edge from that hunger. To see justice done temporarily stills that relentless drive. While exacting justice ourselves is best, we can take pleasure in the victory of others.

The danger, obviously, is the temptation to offer such deals as often as we can. Yet to do that, perversely, would nullify the effect. It speaks to the dual nature of our basic drives. We want justice, and we want it to be righteous. To accept deals for substandard reasons means we would also choose substandard victims— those where the righteousness of the punishment is questionable. We risk falling victim to our drives, a danger that faces anyone who vehemently pursues justice. At what point are we taking lives for our own pleasure rather than fulfilling our contract with the universe? Such a thought is abhorrent to the Cŵn Annwn and, therefore, we offer deals very selectively.

The concept behind any deal is the sacrifice of life, which allows us to channel those powers we cannot name. Lifeblood must soak the earth. Again, the idea is repellent to us, but if the deal is offered in such a way that it also fulfills our need for justice, then we can righteously act as mediators in the transaction.

The rest of the paragraph had been redacted. The next one
started . . .

> *The earliest example I was able to find—which is*
> *almost certainly not the very earliest—was a case in*
> *the old country . . .*

At last, the ink swam and I braced myself for it to open, and
when it did, I tumbled through into a forest.

CHAPTER THIRTY-SEVEN

A man crouched by a well-worn path. His clothing suggested a Celtic clansman, but my knowledge of such things is pretty much limited to movies and novels.

As he crouched there, breathing hard, I picked up the thunder of hooves. Then the bay of hounds, so loud the man stumbled back, and he grabbed a tree trunk, as if needing to hold tight to keep from running for his life. His breath came ragged and loud, his face a pale mask of panic. Fire blazed through the trees, the baying of the hounds softer, the pounding of hooves hard enough to shake the earth. A man raced past, tearing down the path like the hounds of hell were on his heels. Which they were.

The man himself wore armor—a helmet and leather breastplate. He had a sword in hand, but he didn't stop to use it. As he tore past us, the hounds pursued, and I swore sparks flew as their paws struck the earth. They passed, and the man beside me threw himself toward the path, using the tree as leverage to launch himself there.

That's when I saw the Hunt. The true Hunt. Black steeds bore down on us, red-eyed and fire-maned. Dark-cloaked men rode on their backs. Or I must presume they were men—their hoods were drawn up and all I could see were red glinting eyes.

The clansman dropped to the path and covered his head and shouted, "Mercy, lords of the Otherworld. Mercy!"

The soldier long past us shrieked and the hounds snarled, and I knew from that sound that they'd caught their prey. The horses whinnied, and the riders reined them in.

The scene stuttered, like a film caught in the projector. And I glimpsed a house, a modern house, so briefly that I could tell nothing more about it. A house and a voice, and then I was back in the forest, shaking my head and remembering what Patrick said, that there might be fits and starts from the book's mutilation. When I looked up, the front rider had brought his steed to the cowering man.

"You are not our prey tonight," he said, his voice a sonorous boom from the depths of that hood. I was pretty sure he—like the cowering man—didn't speak modern English, but as usual, that's what I heard. "Go home, and tell no one of what you have seen, lest the Hunt come for you next."

"I-I wish to speak to you. I have waited for you."

"You interrupt our hunt *intentionally?*"

"I beg pardon, my lord. It was the only way to gain your attention, and the hounds have taken their prey, so I hope the imposition is not too grievous."

"You hope wrongly. I can tell you come from a family of cunning men, which explains how you know of us, and perhaps you think that excuses you, but that knowledge is the very reason why you *have* no excuse. You have impeded—"

"And I will pay the price, whatever it may be. But I beseech you, my lords, to hear me out. My wife has been taken by the Romans. She is forced to serve in their kitchens, and from what I have heard . . ." He swallowed. "That is not all she is forced to do."

The Huntsman shifted on his horse, the beast dancing in place as he let out a sound not unlike a hound's growl. "The Romans are a plague on this soil." He gestured to where the hounds snarled in the distance. "We took one of their damned soldiers tonight. He'd come upon a dryad in the woods, and when she could not escape, he took his time with her and has now paid. This is still our land."

"Yes, my lords. Yet as long as the Romans remain, we are subject to their tyranny. Freeing my wife would be difficult enough, but if she escapes, she brings down the wrath of the eagles on our heads. I need another solution. A magical one."

"To free your wife in such a way that her captors do not realize she's gone," the Huntsman mused. "Presumably also freeing others from your village, which will require more than simple fae compulsion. An interesting proposition."

"In return, I will do whatever you ask of me."

There was a silence so long the man began to plead, but the Huntsman raised his hand. "Would you murder Romans?"

"Gladly."

"Murder them in a way that you might find repulsive? There was a tribal camp a half day's ride from here. A dozen women and children forced to flee their homeland. While their men were away, four Romans struck. They raped, and they slaughtered, and there is nothing we can do about it, no victim having fae blood. We would like the perpetrators killed in a way that will teach others that the women and children of this land are not their playthings."

"Yes, my lords. I will do as you . . ."

The scene flickered again. I was in a bedroom, looking out from behind bars. The bars of a crib. I remembered the cribs in the abandoned asylum, but this was a child's bedroom, sparking some deep memory—

"Got a deal for you," a man's voice said.

I shot back through time, landing this time in a tavern thick with smoke and stinking of fish and cheap whiskey and unwashed bodies. Three men sat at a corner table. They were not dressed finely, but they were clean and well groomed, and they held themselves apart with an air of fastidiousness, like travelers who've wandered into the wrong part of town in search of a drink. A few men circled, as if thinking they might be easy marks, but cold looks from the trio sent them scuttling off. All except this one, who stood beside their table.

"I have a deal for the Huntsmen," the man said.

The oldest of the three lifted cool green eyes to the man. "And you think this is the way to bring it to us?"

"I thought it better than accosting you in an alley."

"We would prefer not to be accosted at all. Particularly when we are enjoying our ale. And hunting."

The man cast a careful glance around the bar.

"Ah, yes," the Huntsman murmured. "Perhaps that would explain why you found us here. Did you think we would frequent such an establishment by choice?"

"I do not question the ways of the fair folk."

The Huntsman's lip curled. "We are not fair folk. Now, before you insult us further, may I suggest you wait outside until we are done our ale and our other business, and then we may speak to you."

The man pulled out the fourth chair and sat. "No need. I'll be quick about it. My family used to be *mhacasamhail*. We no longer follow the ways. Too little profit in it."

"The vocation of the *mhacasamhail* is not about profit, no more than that of the Cŵn Annwn. It is mutual service and—"

"I think there's a better alliance to be made. With you and your lot. I have heard that you will offer deals. We hunt the men that you cannot, send their blighted souls to purgatory, and you pay well for the deed."

"Pay?"

"Usually in favors, but I don't want favors. Twenty guineas a head. You provide the names; I'll do the rest. No need to tell me what they done to deserve it." He winked. "I trust you."

"Twenty guineas a head." The Huntsman looked at his brethren. "Is that the value of a human life these days?"

"It's negotiable," the man said.

The Huntsman turned on him, slowly. "No, John Miller, it is not negotiable. Human life cannot be weighed in pence and shillings, and any man who thinks it can has obviously done such work before."

"N-no, course not. I'm just offering—"

"I see blood on your hands, John Miller. On your hands and in your eyes. An employer who dared complain when you stole from him. A prostitute who dared expect the money you promised her. And . . ." He leaned over, peering into the man's eyes. "Your brother? No, tell me that's not true. You murdered your brother over an inheritance barely larger than the price you just quoted for the life of a stranger?"

The man pushed back from the table. "No. I-I've never killed anyone."

"Oh, but you have." The Huntsman rose to his feet, the other two rising with him. "I think you'd best leave now, John Miller. I think you'd best run fast and run far, and stay out of the woods at night, and remember that if the moon has fallen and you hear the baying of hounds . . ." He leaned over, hands planted on the table. "They may be coming for you."

Again, the scene shorted out, and I was back in that crib, trying to get out of it. I'd crawled into a corner and was pushing up as best I could. My legs didn't work, but they never had, so I didn't miss the use of them. I'd devised a way to escape the crib, getting into exactly the right position on my folded legs and then using my arms to heave myself up. It took effort, but I was determined. I could hear Mommy in the front room talking to a man, and I was deeply vexed at the thought that we had visitors and I wasn't there to be coddled and cooed over.

I managed to get over the railing. Then came the tough part—the tumble to the floor. From experience, I knew there were two ways to do it. If I wanted Daddy to come

running, I'd fall onto the carpet with a thump. If I wanted
a silent escape, I'd fall onto the pile of stuffed toys. That's
what I did now, squeezing my eyes shut and bracing for the
blow. It hurt. I didn't care. Such was the price of freedom.

I tugged myself from the pile of toys. My arms were
strong enough that I could drag my body with ease. My
bedroom door wasn't shut. It was never shut, not completely. I pulled it open and then wriggle-crawled through.

The voices in the next room came clearer now.

"Four people," Mommy was saying.

"Yes." The man's voice was calm, soothing. "That is the
amount of sacrifice required to invoke the cure you're looking for. The Tysons murdered that young couple, which
means in killing them, as a couple, it will appear a continu-
ation of the pattern. You'll then need to follow their pattern, including the marks and the mutilations. Can your
husband manage that?"

"It won't be a problem."

"Nor will it be easy."

"I'm not looking for easy. I'm looking for a cure. You want
four killers dead, and I don't have a problem doing that."

A pause, and I continued dragging myself, hearing their
voices but not processing what they were saying. Grown-up
talk. Unless it was about me, it wasn't important.

"You do understand the implications," the man said. "If
you are caught—"

"We won't be."

"But if you are, we cannot set you free. We can make
your life in prison simpler. We can ensure you have money
for appeals. Nothing more."

"Understood."

Another pause, and I managed to get myself almost to
the living room before the man said, "I really would like to
speak to your husband."

"I'm handling this."

"He's committed to the course, though?"

"He is. We both are. Now the rituals . . . the real ones."

"Yes, simple acts you must conduct before the deaths to ensure the sacrifices are recognized. You can purchase the ingredients in any New Age shop. You'll want to keep those hidden, though."

"Why? If they can be bought legally, presumably for Wiccans or whatever . . ."

"Keep them hidden, Pamela. Preferably outside the house."

"Yes, yes. Now back to—"

I'd pulled myself into the living room. Now I saw Mommy on the sofa and let out a squeal. She stopped mid-sentence and turned, her eyes widening.

"Eden!"

She flew from the sofa and snatched me up.

The man chuckled. "She's quite the little explorer, isn't she?" He reached to rub my back, and I closed my eyes, enjoying the attention, but Mommy pulled me away, stepping back and saying, "*This* is why I didn't want to meet here."

"How old is she now? Eighteen months?"

"I don't care. She shouldn't hear—"

"She's too young to understand, Pamela."

"*I don't care.*" Mommy hugged me tight, and I could feel her trembling. "We meet away from the house. Away from her. Is that understood?"

"As you like." The man reached and rubbed the back of my head. "You had to see what was going on, didn't you, Eden? Curious, resourceful, and determined. It will serve you well, child."

"I'd like you to leave."

"I'm no threat to your daughter, Pamela. The opposite, I should say, as I think you well know."

"We'll see when this is done. For now—"

"I'm going." One last stroke on the back of my head. "Be well, little Eden."

I snapped back into the present, hard enough that I must have toppled, because Gabriel grabbed me and before I was fully back, I was stretched out on the sofa.

Gabriel's hand went to my forehead with his typical bed-side manner, which meant more of a smack than a gentle fever check. His fingers were cool against my skin and stayed there at least twenty seconds.

"I'm fine," I said. "Not that you asked."

"Because you'd tell me that with a fever of a hundred and five."

I shifted into a sitting position. "Am I feverish?"

"Your temperature is elevated."

"But not by much. Meaning I really am fine." I started to get to my feet, but a wave of light-headedness pushed me back down.

"Would you like to rediagnose?" Gabriel said.

"Just give me a minute."

I rubbed my temples and then told them about the two cases I'd witnessed, which was guaranteed to distract Gabriel from his hovering.

"In other words," I said, "no really new information, but it confirms what we've been told. Deals can be offered, for more than curing illness, it seems. But there are strict lim-itations. The Cŵn Annwn aren't in the market for hired killers. They have their own code of ethics, and they must abide by it. They try to do the right thing."

Patrick rolled his eyes but said nothing.

"Is that all?" Gabriel asked, as if knowing the answer already.

"No, another vision kept intruding. Except this one didn't come from the book." I told them what else I'd seen.

"A scene that you witnessed," Patrick said. "But didn't understand at the time."

"Apparently. It does confirm, though, that Pamela did it and the Cŵn Annwn honestly believed my father participated. It also explained the witchcraft supplies. The Huntsman warned her not to keep them around. She thought he was being silly. Which he was not, in light of what happened."

"And . . ." Gabriel said after a moment.

"There's no *and*. That's all I saw." Which was true, but there was more to it. I kept thinking about Pamela, how she'd acted, what she'd said. I wanted so much for her to be a monster. To believe she was a sociopath hiding behind the mask of a fiercely devoted wife and mother. That made it easy to reject her completely and utterly, which is what I needed, because I couldn't reconcile it otherwise. She'd arranged the murder of James. She'd tried to frame Gabriel. That was all that should matter.

I felt Patrick's assessing gaze on me, handed him back the book, and said, "Thank you."

"Does it help you solve your little mystery?" he asked.

"I don't know," I said, a more honest answer than I'd usually give, my brain still muddled from the visions.

I got up, Gabriel rising with me.

"I'll take one of your books," I said.

When his brows lifted, I said, "Not these," with a wave at the library. "One of the ones you wrote."

"And you might even read it?"

"Don't push your luck."

"Oh, you'll try it out of curiosity, even if you're only taking the book to make me feel better. That's an odd way of going about it, don't you think? A book from the author ought to be the gift, not the act of accepting it. However, the fact that you're actually asking is a step in the right direction, telling me I'm inching toward the realm of valuable ally."

"Is there a book coming at the end of this speech?"

He led me into another room, a storage area with shelves of his own work. He took one off the shelf.

"Do you like sex?" he asked.

Gabriel cleared his throat behind me.

"I mean in books."

"In general, I'm fine with it. Do I want to read a sex scene knowing you wrote it? No."

"You're missing out. Bòcan are naturally gifted lovers. We have an endless well of creativity."

Gabriel's throat clearing now had a bit of growl attached. "I will warn that the direction of this conversation is ill-advised. Olivia will not appreciate your attempts at flirtation."

"And neither will you?"

"You aren't flirting with me."

Patrick laughed. "I do believe you just made a joke, Gabriel. Liv's influence is, indeed, delightful to see. But no, I'm not flirting with her. That would be wrong. Many shades of wrong. I was merely telling her it's a gift that bòcan possess and share with their offspring—"

"Stop," I said, skewering him with a look that Gabriel couldn't see. "Give me one without sex. Please."

"Does this mean I can't count on you to beta-read my sex-slave-lamiae story?"

I made a move to leave.

"Fine," Patrick said. "Take this. It's one of my gothics. The seventies were, sadly, not the time to include sex scenes of any satisfying nature. When the lights go out, you can imagine the hero and heroine are lying in bed, fully clothed, making shadow puppets on the wall. However, if you want to know what I was imagining them doing—"

"No, I do not," I said, taking the book. "Thank you, Patrick. And goodbye."

"Wait, don't you want that signed?"

"Only if it'll get me more on eBay."

CHAPTER THIRTY-EIGHT

Rose had invited us to dinner, which we'd accepted. Gabriel suggested I go over early and take tea with her while he ran errands. I texted to be sure that was okay with Rose. It was.

As I walked in, I held out Patrick's novel. "Book?"

"*Embrace the Shadows*?" Rose said.

"Sounds hokey, I know. Believe me, I have no intention of actually reading this crap."

"It's actually quite good."

I looked at her as we walked into the parlor. "You've, uh, read it?"

"I like crap."

My cheeks heated. "I didn't mean— I'm more a mystery buff, but I've read my share of romances, too. Mostly historical, including a few gothics. The crap comment was directed at the author."

"Patrice Rhys? As I said, she's actually very good. I read most of her work as a teen. She stopped writing in the late seventies."

"Umm, no, actually he hasn't." I sat in a chair across her desk.

"He?" She paused and glanced toward the door. "Gabriel said you were at Patrick's. That's . . .?"

"Yep."

She sighed. "Wonderful. Now I'll have to decide whether to tell him I enjoyed his work and risk inflating his ego."

"You'll get free books if you tell him, and his new series apparently has lots of sex."

"Which is why, despite knowing he writes *those*, I've never tried them. I have no issue with the concept. Done right, it can get you through many a cold night. But knowing who wrote those scenes . . ."

"Yep. Kinda what I said."

She headed for the kitchen. "If he's also Patrice Rhys, though, I might have to check them out now. I'll just skip the sex."

I stopped on my way to the desk and walked to a table bearing a bottle and a pair of very old socks with the toes cut out.

"Okay," I called. "I'm not sure about the bottle, but these socks are definitely new."

"They are," she called back. "Both belonged to Daniel Dunglas Home."

"Oh, I know this one. Mr. Sludge the Medium. *Now, don't, sir! Don't expose me! Just this once! This was the first and only time, I'll swear.*"

"You know your Browning."

"I'd be a poor Victorian lit major if I didn't."

Admittedly, Home's connection to Conan Doyle was what made me remember it. He was one of the writer's favorite spiritualists. Browning had not been nearly so impressed, as the poem suggested. It seems Home materialized a blob of flesh that he said was Browning's son who died in infancy. Not having had a son die in infancy, Browning called foul, reached over, and discovered the fleshy blob was Home's foot. He'd wear shoes he could easily take off and then socks with the toes cut out so he could ring bells and tug clothing under the table.

I picked up the tiny bottle. "But this bottle . . ."

"Open it," she called from the kitchen, her words barely audible over a clatter of dishes.

I did. The inside glowed. Phosphorus, to make glowing, ghostly hands. I smiled and took my seat as Rose came in with the tea and cookies.

"I want to do a reading for you. And don't give me that look, Liv. I know you don't like glimpses into your future."

"You've said the cards only reveal the consequences of the path I'm on, so I can change it, but I still don't like . . ." I shifted in my seat. "Isn't it tempting? To keep peeking?"

"I don't see *my* future."

"But it could be tempting for someone like me. Every time there's a fork in the road, come to you to see which prong I should take."

A faint smile, not unlike her great-nephew's. "You have a hard-enough time asking the advice of a friend before choosing a path. You certainly aren't going to get hooked on consulting the cards. But yes, people do. I recognize the addicts, and I fleece them only as much as they can afford to be fleeced, while teaching them a valuable lesson."

"Good of you."

"I think so. Now, the cards?"

"There's a point to this, isn't there? You didn't just randomly decide you want to foretell my fortune."

She took a cookie, her voice casual as she said, "I had a premonition."

"What was it?"

"That I should read the cards for you."

I sighed and shook my head.

"I'm not dissembling, Olivia. I had a premonition that bothered me. I don't wish to say more until I've done the reading."

"All right. Tell me my future, Rosalyn Razvan. When will I be rich and happy?"

She closed her eyes. "I predict you will come into great wealth in approximately three weeks. Roughly . . . wait . . . I see a number. Is it . . . ? Yes, five million."

"With interest," I said. "I'm told there has been interest. Okay, I walked into that one."

"As for happy . . . The pursuit of happiness may be written into our Declaration of Independence, but that only means our founding fathers were hopelessly sentimental. You don't pursue happiness. You pursue everything you need to have a fulfilled life, and then, if you achieve it, you'll be happy some of the time. The rest of the time, you'll be content. One can't sustain happiness forever."

When I looked skeptical, she said, "Do those cookies make you happy?" as I reached for another one.

I took another bite. "Yep."

"Imagine if you ate nothing else. What would happen?"

"I'd get fat. But I'd be very happy."

"No. After two days of nothing but chocolate chip cookies, you'd be sick of them. Even having them every day would dull the effect. The trick is to eat them just often enough that you still savor them. Too much of anything reduces the overall effect of happiness and satisfaction."

"Not everything."

"That includes sex, which is what you're thinking even if you believe you're being coy. How would you like it ten times a day, every day?"

"Ouch."

"I rest my case. My point is that the cards can't tell you how to be happy, because it varies for every person. You *are* happy, in the sense of mostly ranging between content and truly happy, and that range is the goal. Onto the cards, then . . ." She took a deck from her desk. It looked like an Italian version, hand-painted and gorgeous antiques.

"Can we use the Victorian tarot?" I asked.

A small nod, as if she'd only been testing me. Tarot cards from the Victorian era are actually rare. Many modern versions are done in a Victorian style, because the era brought with it the mystique of spiritualism, but tarot reading was uncommon in that period. These cards, though, were the real deal.

When I said so, she nodded. "Gabriel got them for me when he was young. As a solstice gift."

I'd seen these cards many times, and she'd never mentioned where they came from. In that, she was also like her nephew, keeping her past and her personal self under lock and key, but in a way that you never realized how little you knew until she opened that box and let one scrap escape, a sign that you were moving from acquaintance to friend.

"That's some gift," I said. "Must have been expensive."

"Oh, I'm sure it was. He even earned part of the money through perfectly legal means."

When I laughed, she said, "He was very quick to tell me that he took on errands to raise money for gifts. Note that he never said *all* the money."

"It was important for you to know that he'd worked for it. Not that picking pockets isn't work, but that your gifts were special. He put both thought and effort into them."

She fingered the cards, her gaze distant. "Yes, I suppose so. I always thought he didn't want me to think poorly of him, but in our family, light fingers are a skill to be admired. It was the additional effort that mattered to him."

A long sip of her tea, as if to wash away any sentimentality, and then she laid the cards out for me. I knew the drill and took one.

"That was fast," she said. "Not surprising for someone with a touch of the sight herself."

It was the Queen of Swords, which Rose says is my card. I looked it up once, and got as far as seeing that one of the meanings, under the reversed format, included the word "bitchy." The card today, though, was right side up. The next one I drew was the King of Pentacles. Gabriel's card. Then the King of Wands.

"Are you sure you can't just *see* them?" Rose asked.

"If I could, I made a mistake there. Ricky is the Page of Wands, right? That's what I got before."

"Page evolving into King. Apparently, evolving rapidly."

Which he was, moving into his role with the Cŵn Annwn, showing his strength and his leadership with the rogue Huntsman and with the broken hound.

"Now," I said to the cards. "Tell me something I don't know. Gabriel, Ricky and I will . . ."

I turned over a card showing a thief making off with an armload of swords.

"The Seven of Swords," Rose said. "It signifies secrecy and selfishness, doing something for yourself at the expense of others. Possibly hurting others in the process. It suggests someone will—"

"Betray me." My gaze slid to the King of Pentacles card.

"We're asking the cards about an event concerning you and Ricky and Gabriel. Yes, there will be a betrayal. Most likely *to* you as a group, rather than between you."

I nodded, but must have looked unconvinced, because she said, "I know Gabriel has—"

"Can we just continue? Please." I turned over another card before she could answer. The Hermit, reversed.

"Signifies isolation and darkness." She tapped her fingers against it. "It can mean an overabundance of introspection, but the sense I get is darkness. A dark and empty place."

"Gabriel, Ricky, me, dark place, betrayal . . ." I exhaled a little in relief. "Okay, no offense, Rose, but I think your precognition is running on a delay. That happened about four months ago."

"Yes, there was a betrayal, but it did not *lead* to you being in that dark place. Connected in time, rather than circumstance."

I turned over two more cards, which didn't add anything to the mix.

"Gabriel, Ricky, me, dark place, betrayal," I said again. "That's all I'm getting, isn't it?"

"That's what I saw in my premonition. The three of you, both together and divided. In a dark place. And . . ." She shook her head. "And that's all." She began collecting the cards.

"No, it's not. What else did you see?"

She said nothing until I prodded again, and then only, "Shadows, violence, anger, a struggle . . ."

"A struggle?" I prodded.

"A struggle against a violent impulse. Someone who desperately does not want to do something and yet the impulse . . ." She knocked the deck against the desktop, straightening them. "The impulse isn't strong enough to come to anything. But it's dangerous nonetheless."

"Can I get anything more concrete?"

She looked at me. "My nephew is involved. I would not hold back if I knew more."

"So beware dark places, dark impulses, and betrayals. That last one can't really be avoided, though. Unless I'm the one doing the betraying."

"Which I cannot imagine."

I wrapped my fingers around my teacup. "But I am, aren't I? Betraying Gabriel."

Her blue eyes bored into mine. "You have done nothing to Gabriel, Olivia. Nothing except good. Whatever choices you've made, they were because he offered no other option, and because you are free to pursue your own happiness rather than wait for something that may never come, because someone is too damned dense . . ."

She trailed off as I looked up at her.

"And that's not what you meant at all," she said, leaning back. "Which is a relief. Also rather awkward. This betrayal you were referring to, then . . ."

"Patrick."

She refilled her tea and mine. "Not telling Gabriel that Patrick is his father."

"Like I didn't tell Gabriel that he's Gwynn. Apparently, I haven't learned my lesson."

She gave me a hard look. "I'd hope you realize it's not the same. But now that things are going well with Gabriel, you're anxiously scanning the ground for any obstacle you could trip over."

"I—"

"You hate that. You hate fretting and worrying. You think, if it's a solid relationship, it should be smooth sailing. Like it is with Ricky."

"I don't—"

"Ricky is easy. He demands nothing of you. Expects nothing of you. You see eye to eye on most things and when you don't, you accommodate each other, effortlessly. Smooth sailing. Gabriel, on the other hand, is a wild ride through stormy waters, both exhilarating and exhausting."

"Yes." That was all I said, all I could say. *Yes.*

"I wish I could tell you it'll get better. But Gabriel will never be Ricky. I would also rather he didn't find out about Patrick. The problem, though, is that he will eventually, and it's better coming from someone who cares about him."

I sipped my tea. "Ioan almost let it slip. Patrick makes sly comments, and I'm sure he's always done that because it amuses him, but now *I* react when he does. Gabriel is going to figure it out. It apparently wasn't exactly a well-kept secret. It just wasn't important at the time. *He* wasn't important."

Rose was quiet for a minute. Then she said, "I could tell him, but I really think it's better coming from you. He's not going to run, Liv. At least, not far and not for long. You know that now. As hard as it was the last time, it was only Gabriel retreating temporarily."

"Behind his wall."

"Yes."

"Which I can climb, but I'm never going to knock down."

"Yes. I'm sorry."

"No, I know that. I've always known—"

The front door opened. Rose called, "Gabriel?"

"Do you need more time with Olivia?" he replied, his voice echoing from the hall.

She glanced at me. I shook my head, and she said, "No, come in and join her for tea while I start dinner."

CHAPTER THIRTY-NINE

Gabriel and I were in the kitchen, washing dishes while Rose met with a client. We'd almost finished when he said, "I have a question, one for which the answer may be obvious to most, but I am going to ask it anyway."

"Shoot."

"It's about gifts."

"Abilities, you mean?"

He set a plate in the drying rack. "No, presents. There are times when a gift may be considered a presumption. For example, giving someone a pet."

"Yeah, unless they ask for it, that's never a good idea."

He paused in washing another plate. "So if the giver is not certain that the gift will be well received, it shouldn't be offered, no matter how pure the intentions."

"Not if that gift requires paper training."

"A poor example, then. I mean a gift that is given with all good intentions, knowing there is a chance it will seem presumptuous. Perhaps if the recipient has already declined the gift, but the giver believes it is actually desired."

"You do realize you're talking in riddles, right? I need concrete, Gabriel. Is this something for Rose? Tell me what it is, and I'll give you my advice."

He washed all the cups before saying, "I'm not looking for advice. I'm looking for absolution in case I've made a grievous error." He folded the dishcloth and laid it aside.

"Enough of that. I'll show you, and if I have indeed made a mistake, understand that it was well-intentioned."

I saw where we seemed to be heading but said nothing, even as Gabriel paused to open the front gate of the Carew house.

"No, I'm not buying you a house," he said. "That would indeed be presumptive. Also unnecessary, given that your net wealth will outstrip my own in a few weeks. And yes," he said as he ushered me through, "I know you don't like to be reminded of your inheritance, because you feel you didn't earn the money. But it isn't as if you stole it."

"I think I'd feel as though stealing it *was* earning it in a way. Even if I probably shouldn't admit that."

"If you did, you would be admitting it to someone who would hardly judge you for the sentiment. You have earned this inheritance, though, by birth."

"Adoption."

He led me up the front walk. "You did not ask for the money. You do not expect the money. You will not use it to feed some bad habit. It will be re-invested, and you've made it quite clear you'll continue to work. Your inheritance will simply make life easier for you, and there is little to argue with about that. If you must, you can give some of it to charity."

"If I must?"

"I don't see the point, but I'm told that's a minority opinion."

"No, it's just a minority of people who admit to it. And to change the subject, ooh, we're actually going in the *front* door. This is new."

He made an uninterpretable noise in his throat. As he turned the knob, my gaze lingered on the knocker, a brass cuckoo's head. A good marriage omen. I'd seen it before, but only now did I see how detailed it was. Like the fence, it wasn't the sort of thing you pick up at your local home improvement store. It was only as he was prodding me through that I noticed a shiny new deadbolt.

"Did the elders . . .?" I began.

He brushed past me to turn off the security alarm.

"New locks *and* an alarm system?" I said.

"Yes. I . . ." He cleared his throat. "I took the liberty—"

"There's furniture," I said, moving into the living room.

"From the attic. Temporary furnishings. They are, as you can see, rather old."

I gave him a look. "It's antique, which you know very well, and after the drunken confession about your office, you can no longer play that card."

"Card?"

"The one that says you have no interest in such frivolities and whims as antique furniture. Did the elders bring all this . . .?" I turned to him. "No, it wasn't the elders, was it?"

"If you're suggesting I carried dusty furniture . . . Well, not much of it. The elders facilitated the hiring of locals." He cleared his throat. "I believe the property is an excellent investment opportunity. The elders owe you, and you ought to take advantage of that in a rising housing market. I am not, however, advising you to buy it immediately. The furniture and the security is to allow you to move in temporarily, as the elders suggested." He looked around. "I believe TC would appreciate the extra space."

I sputtered a laugh. "TC? You're *really* stretching for justifications with that one." I moved into the front parlor and sat on the sofa, which was remarkably comfortable for a boxy davenport. "I'm surprised you're encouraging me to move in."

"Because the house triggers visions? Not significantly more than other locations, and I have come to accept that the elders may be correct—that it could be helpful for you to work through the visions rather than avoid them. However, I would ask that you do not stay alone until we're certain it's safe. I can spend the night—there's a second bed. Or Ricky or Rose, once I have properly educated them on how to deal with your fevers."

"You've worked it all out."

He walked to the window and looked across the yard. "Last night, we talked about frivolities. I don't believe I'm the only one who avoids them. You wouldn't even drive the Maserati until your other vehicle was disabled."

"By persons unknown."

"The point, Olivia, is that all practical justifications aside, you want this house."

When I said nothing, he looked over and after a moment said, "You want it, yet you will not accept it." Before I could respond, he said, "Is it Ricky?"

"What?"

He walked to the corner of the Oriental carpet and bent to straighten it. "You have been together for months. I understand that, after a certain amount of time, it becomes impractical to continue moving from apartment to apartment, and cohabitation is a natural progression. Clearly, Ricky would not be comfortable living in Cainsville, nor would I advise it. His apartment is hardly suitable for two, and he is graduating this term and must give it up. If you had plans, then, to find a more permanent residence . . ."

"Move in together? No. That's not happening."

He glanced over. "Is there a problem?"

"No. We just don't plan to move in together. That would add pressure, and it's just . . . It's not what either of us wants. We take it as it comes and take it for what it is."

He frowned slightly, as if he didn't understand, and I suppose a lot of people wouldn't. If you're in love, you should want to live together and begin that trek toward a wedding and babies. I'd been on that road before, and I was happy to step off it and just enjoy what I had, while I had it.

"So the house is simply . . . too much?" he said finally.

"I'm worried about the message it sends to the elders, and I'm worried about getting too comfortable."

"That making Cainsville your home would influence your ultimate decision."

I nodded. "Otherwise, I'd take it in a heartbeat."

"Let's talk about that, then."

GIFT

As they walked up the stairs, Gabriel struggled to prepare his defense. Normally, that wouldn't be a problem. Even in a prison visiting room with his client in tears, Gabriel could pretend to listen while mentally composing his opening arguments. Now, though, he was distracted. By two things.

First, he had not, evidently, committed a grievous error in preparing the house for Olivia. He knew a comment on that would be forthcoming, once she'd settled distractions in her own mind, but it did not seem it would be negative. His goal was to show Olivia that he could be what she needed in a partner. In knowing that she wanted this house, he'd proven he understood her. In readying it for her, he'd proven—he hoped—that he could be considerate and anticipate her needs.

Second, the matter of Ricky. He hadn't considered that Ricky and Olivia might be moving toward cohabitation until she'd hesitated at the thought of moving in here. They'd been together for months. They spent most nights at one apartment or the other. Cohabitation was the next logical step. Followed by . . .

He tried not to consider the "followed by" part. He'd spent the last few months trying not to consider it. Yet Olivia had no intention of moving in with Ricky, much less anything else.

That gave him hope.

So why was his stomach tightening and twisting with every step up those stairs? Because hope was a dangerous thing. It said the failure would be his own fault alone.

He should be fine with that. That's how he lived his life: control all factors and thereby accept the blame for failure. But here? Yes, here, if he failed, he wanted to be able to say he'd had no chance of success—

"Bedroom?" Olivia asked, pulling him from his thoughts. They were at the top of the stairs, six closed doors surrounding them—four bedrooms, a bath, and the attic. "I'm guessing not that one?" She pointed at the rear corner room, with the triskelion.

"Definitely not."

"I wouldn't want to trigger visions stumbling to the bathroom at night."

He noticed she didn't add *if I do move in.*

He motioned to the front right door. "That appears to be the master bedroom."

She passed him, threw open the door, and said, "Oh my God," and ran inside, the door swinging behind her. By the time he opened it, she was in the middle of the room.

"The tower," she said. "Obviously, I knew there was a half tower . . . but wow."

There was indeed a half tower, extending up from the bay windows in the living room. In the master bedroom it formed a cupola, a semicircle of cushioned window seats with windows that reached to the ceiling, decorated with stained glass along the top.

"Reading seats," she said. "A table for my tea. Even pillows."

She scooped one up and surreptitiously sniffed it, as if checking for mildew.

"They're new," he said.

"The elders bought me pillows?"

He started to say yes, they must have. Because that was the safe answer. He was not a man who bought pillows. He was not a man who noticed that someone liked pillows. But if he was trying to show her a better side of himself, it did not behoove him to pretend the elders had bought Olivia pillows. Still, it was with no small amount of trepidation that he said, "I picked them up in the city earlier today."

"So you *weren't* working all morning?"

"No."

"They're perfect." She turned toward the huge sleigh bed, the wood gleaming.

"You'll want to replace the mattresses," he said. "But that set will do for now with new bedding."

"Which you also bought," she said, walking over and checking through the pile, still in the plastic. "Your taste is a whole lot better than mine."

"My budget is a whole lot higher than yours. Temporarily."

She looked around the room, the fading sun suffusing it with a warm glow. "Wow. Just wow. I'm going to keep saying that. In case you're wondering about the thank-you part, I'm waiting until after the tour, or I'm just going to keep saying that, too, and making you very uncomfortable."

Which was not untrue. His thanks came from her expression and the glow in her eyes.

"There are bookshelves in the attic," he said, "but I thought you might prefer them in whichever bedroom you choose as an office. I'd suggest the one with the triskelion. It has the best light."

She popped back into the hall and waved at the other front room. "That's your room, then?"

"The spare bedroom," he corrected.

"The only person who'd sleep in it is you. Unless I kick Ricky out of bed."

She laughed at that, suggesting the number of times that had happened—or was likely to happen—was zero. Regrettably.

Olivia zipped into the spare room. Gabriel followed, more slowly this time. He had considered taking another, perhaps the small, dark one beside it. The second front bedroom, while it lacked the half tower, was still big and airy, with oversized windows and stained glass. It seemed, yes, frivolous to put a bed in there.

He could tell himself he was selecting a guest room—not *his* room—and that's why he'd chosen the better one. But Olivia was right that no one else would use it, and he'd decided that if it seemed not to matter which he took, he might as well take what he wanted. Which should be easy. He spent his life taking what he wanted. Olivia was correct here, too, though, that there was a difference between buying his greystone office because it best suited his needs and buying it because he liked it. Practicality versus frivolity. Logic versus emotion.

"The other two rooms are unfurnished," he said. "There is furniture in the attic, if you decide to stay. The elders say it all comes with the house. I've put the table and chairs in the dining room and added basics to the kitchen—a set of dishes and cutlery, pots, a coffeemaker."

"Gotta have the coffeemaker."

"I thought so."

She turned to him. "All right, then, counselor. Convince me I won't be shooting myself in the foot if I move in temporarily."

He gave her his argument, namely that the elders understood the purchase of the house in no way indicated she was leaning in their direction, no more than living at Grace's did. It was the safest arrangement. It was also a balanced one. Cainsville provided Olivia with shelter, and her living there provided the town with greater access to her than the Cŵn Annwn had.

"Do you want it?" he asked as he finished.

"Yes, but—"

"Do you honestly believe that a house, however much you like it, would make you side with the Cainsville fae if you did not believe it was the right decision?"

"No." She took a deep breath. "I guess that answers my question."

"It does, and having decided, I suggest we put that coffeemaker to use and step into the garden."

"Which is going to need some serious elbow grease."

When he said nothing, she looked over at him. "No . . ."

He shrugged, and she hurried down the steps, through the house to the back window. What he heard then was not quite a girlish shriek, but very close to it.

"It's only cleared," he said as he walked up behind her. "It's too late for planting, but Rose said the garden ought to be put to bed properly."

She turned and gave him a wide grin, a bouncing-on-toes, little-girl-at-Christmas grin. Then she put out her arms and said, "Can I? Just say no if—"

"You can."

She threw her arms around his neck and hugged him, fairly strumming with excitement, and he thought, *I did it.* Also *Top that, Ricky,* and yes, he did feel a twinge of guilt, but it was a very small twinge, and really only because it was not quite sportsmanlike to compete against someone who didn't realize there was a competition.

But Gabriel hadn't gotten where he was by being sportsmanlike. And he did respect Ricky enough that he would never try to seduce Olivia away in any more overt way. Which wasn't, to be honest, a moral choice so much as the admission that, there, he would probably fail. But there was some degree of—if not morality—personal respect, the same quality that knotted his stomach when he thought about the river tunnel and the kiss. He did feel guilty about that. He really did . . . even if that guilt took a while to arrive, following well after other emotions that accompanied those particular memories.

"Sorry," Olivia said. "I'll stop hugging you now."

You don't have to, he thought, but in the time it took for him to realize he could have said that, at least with a smile, she'd already backed off and the moment had passed, which was probably best. For now.

"Okay, so coffee . . ." She turned slowly, as if in a semi-daze, still glowing with excitement. "Is that—? That's not a coffeemaker, Gabriel."

"It makes cappuccinos as well, which I'm told can be used for mochas."

"That's . . . You didn't need to . . ."

He tensed. Here he'd crossed the line. Here it was too much. Too extravagant.

He'd wanted to say, in the most unmistakable way, *I hear you*. That he paid attention. That changing the locks and having furniture brought down was the least she needed. The bedding and towels and dishes took it a step further, but were still basics, as a host might provide for a guest. The rest was where he really said what he wanted to say. *I know you'll want that cupola for a reading room and you'll want pillows. I know you'll want to sit out in the garden while you can, without fretting that you should be clearing it for winter. I know you'd like a mocha when you sit outside or up in your reading nook. I know all this. I know you.*

But the coffee machine went a step too far. It was not merely an act of consideration. It was a gift that, while easily covered by a trip to the bank machine, was more than one friend ought to give another, and now, seeing it and thinking of all the rest, she seemed to realize that.

"First you save my life," she said. "Now this. Racking up your side of the tally, huh? I owe you big-time now."

His insides chilled. "You owe me nothing, Olivia. I was merely preparing the house for your possible arrival."

She flushed. "Right. Sorry. There's a bill. Of course. I knew that."

More chilling, settling in the pit of his stomach. "No, this is a gift. I would hardly purchase items for you, without your consent, and expect you to repay me."

She reddened more, stammering out an apology.

For God's sake, Gabriel, stop being an ass. Get your back down and apologize.

She'd been smiling when she said she owed him. Teasing him, in a way that wasn't entirely teasing because she wasn't entirely sure. That was how relationships worked with him. Take nothing and owe nothing. Keep the balance firmly in his favor.

When he got snippy and said he was only preparing the house, she'd presumed he meant he expected her to pay, and had flushed in embarrassment at her mistake. Could he blame her for that? Before she'd come to work for him, he'd charged her for his time, a bill to be paid when her trust came in. Of course she would think he might have only been showing consideration in buying the items, to also be repaid.

"I'm sorry," he said.

"No, I—"

"I overreacted, and I was unclear regarding the nature of the gesture. It is a gift. I appreciate everything you've done." He knew he should say more, but here he struggled. *I appreciate the work you've done for me, at the firm?* True, but that said he'd done this for her as an employee. *I appreciate your friendship.* Also true, but when he opened his mouth to say that, the words wouldn't come out. They were still too damning an admission.

Damning an admission? That she was a friend? That he valued her friendship? There were greeting cards for that, for God's sake, and he couldn't even say the words? How the hell did he ever expect to say *more?*

Sweat beaded on his forehead.

I feel as if I've taken huge leaps, and I haven't even caught up to where a normal person would start. Ricky would have been able to say he valued her friendship after a few coffee dates.

Say something. Say anything. Goddamn it, just—

"I appreciate everything," he blurted. "That's what I'm saying. I know I'm not always the easiest person. I know I've made things difficult for you. I know you've . . . you've . . ." *Words, Gabriel. Words.* "You've stuck by me regardless of my mistakes. And I . . . I appreciate that."

She hugged him again. No asking for permission this time, but it was a quick hug, too brief for him to complain if he'd wanted, which he certainly did not. Brief and fierce, and then she stood there, looking . . .

Not looking the way she had five minutes ago. Not glowing and bouncing. Not at all.

"I . . . I have to tell you something," she said.

His heart slammed against his ribs, and he had to struggle for breath. Which was ridiculous. Overreacting. But he couldn't help it. He saw that look on her face, and he knew, whatever she had to say, it was bad and it involved him, and he would not be happy about it. That's what her expression said. All the possibilities ricocheted through his head, all the things that could give her that look.

I'm sorry, Gabriel, but . . .

Ricky doesn't want me hanging out with you so much.

I can't work for you anymore.

I'm pregnant.

Admittedly, they all seemed unlikely, particularly the last, but he had considered them, at one time or another. It was like preparing to defend a client in court—what was the worst the opposing side would say and how would he counter it? These were the three possibilities he'd agonized over the most. The last was not in itself an issue, but rather he feared it would push Olivia and Ricky together in a way that closed any opportunity for him.

"Gabriel?"

"Go on," he said.

She crossed her arms and rubbed them. "I'm sorry. It's . . . it's something I probably should have told you before. I just . . ." She looked up, not quite meeting his gaze. "With the Gwynn thing, I was afraid you'd react badly."

"Which I did."

"This isn't the same. It's not how you'll react. It's . . . it's how you'll feel."

"It's about me, then."

She nodded.

"Just me?"

Another nod.

He tried not to exhale in relief, and looked across the kitchen. "Would you like a coffee? I believe there are ingredients for a mocha in the refrigerator—Veronica said she'd pick them up at the shop. There are cookies, too. From Rose."

Olivia stared at him, and he replayed his words, searching for some way they could be misconstrued.

"It may be late for coffee," he said. "But I believe Veronica also bought decaffeinated."

"I . . . have something important to tell you, Gabriel."

"Yes, and I thought we'd take coffee and go outside to discuss it."

"It's *really* important."

He could see that. However, as it only concerned him, he couldn't imagine it was nearly as monumental as she seemed to think. But he supposed, if she was upset, she might not want coffee.

"All right," he said. "What is it?"

"It's about . . ."

She took a deep breath. He waved her into the next room. "Let's sit."

She nodded and followed him to the living room. They sat and . . . nothing. She perched on the edge of the sofa, hands in her lap.

"I don't know how to tell you this," she said.

"Go on," he said, trying not to sound impatient, while well aware that night was falling, which meant it would soon be too chilly to sit outside. He remembered taking a meeting in a client's garden once, and she'd had a wood-burning stove out there. He would suggest that for Olivia, to extend the use of her garden.

It took a moment to realize Olivia was talking again, and given the apparent gravity of the situation, he should listen.

"—because I don't want you to find out another way, like what happened with Tristan and Gwynn. Others know—fae, that is, and Cŵn Annwn—and they're going to tell you at some point."

"All right." It would probably be rude to stop her while he turned on the coffee machine to warm up. He should have done that before they left the kitchen.

"It's . . . it's about your . . ."

He had to resist the urge to tell her to just blurt it out.

"Your father . . ." she said. "Did your mother ever hint at who . . .?"

"No."

"Okay, well, I know who . . . I know who he is."

"All right."

She looked at him as if he might not have heard right. Clearly his reaction was not what she'd expected. Discovering her own parentage had been life-changing. Devastating, at least in the beginning, and even now she dealt with the ramifications daily. Yet he'd never wasted a moment wondering about the identity of his father. Rose had broached the subject once—did it bother him, not knowing? His honest reply had been no.

As long as the man didn't actually expect contact with Gabriel, he supposed it would be helpful to fill in his missing medical history, but otherwise he had no interest. Unless his father would want money. In that case he'd rather not know. However, *knowing* would in no way obligate him to help.

"Gabriel?"

"Go on."

"I said I know who your father is."

He softened his voice. "I realize you consider this momentous news, Olivia. But to me? It is merely filling in a blank that I never cared was empty."

She exhaled. "Okay. But . . . it's . . . it's not just some random guy your mother slept with. I mean, it is, but . . ."

"I know him?"

She nodded, her gaze fixed on him. He quickly compiled the evidence.

"Patrick," he said finally.

Olivia went still. "You knew?"

He shook his head. "Given what you've said, that simply seemed the most obvious answer. I'll presume I'm correct, then. It would explain why Seanna became so upset when I had contact with him as a child."

"She forbade you to speak to him. Not surprising, given she'd have been barely eighteen when he seduced her."

"Knowing Seanna, I rather doubt that's exactly how it happened."

"But she was so young."

"Seanna was never young, Olivia. If you think a teenage pregnancy sent her life into a downward spiral, I can assure you, that isn't what happened. Rose says the drugs came much earlier. I was a minor inconvenience rather than a life-changing event."

"I'm sorry."

He gave her a brief smile. "There's no need to be."

"I still am. I'm sorry for what you went through with her, and I'm sorry Patrick did nothing about it. That's why I didn't want to tell you. To let you know your father had been there when . . ."

"Ah. Is that why you've been angry with him?"

"Of course," she said, as if the answer was obvious. He'd noticed her relationship with Patrick had changed a few months ago. She'd seemed fine with him, and then she wasn't.

"He's fae," Gabriel said softly. "I don't think we can expect him to take a normal parental role."

"I don't care. He should have done something."

Her voice was fierce, and if this was secondhand outrage he was getting now, he could only imagine what Patrick must have gotten. The full brunt of her fury. For him.

I love her.

That was hardly a revelation. If he didn't, he wouldn't take the risk of trying to further their relationship. Yet he had never said the words even in his mind, because even there they blew a cannonball through a fortress he'd spent a lifetime erecting. To care about someone was quite enough, and even that was difficult to admit. Only a few minutes ago, he'd been unable to say he valued her friendship.

To say he loved her was like teetering on the edge of a pit, every fiber in him wanting to scramble back from the edge, saying *no, no, no.* To love her meant that if he didn't win her, if he never got a chance to prove . . .

His breath seized at the thought, and that pit seemed to rear up, ready to swallow him whole.

Now you know how I felt.

He flinched at Gwynn's voice, and then everything in him truly did rebel, scrambling away as fast as it could. Whatever he felt, it would never lead there. Never, ever—

"Gabriel?"

He snapped back to see Olivia watching him, her face drawn with worry. He found the barest smile for her. "Sorry. I was just . . . processing. I appreciate that you were concerned. That . . ."

He cleared his throat and forced the words out as fast as he could. "That means a lot to me. But my own feelings on the matter . . . ? Patrick is fae. He made some effort, and while it would not come near your standard for proper parenting, it exceeds my own experience." He said the last with a tiny smile, but the flash of pain on her face made him wish he hadn't gone there.

She loves me, too, in her way.

"Coffee?" he said.

She smiled. "Yes, I'm finally done, and we may have coffee."

CHAPTER FORTY

We took our coffees into the garden, where we sat on the bench and drank, and Gabriel mentioned the possibility of a backyard stove or fire pit, and we discussed that—types I'd seen at garden parties, and which would work best here.

"Then you *will* buy one?" he said.

"As soon as you use the fireplace at the office."

"Would you settle for a fire in my wastebasket?"

I mock-glowered at him. "No. Get yours going, and I'll buy more comfortable seating, too." I shifted and made a face. "Soon. Please."

We sipped our coffees and talked about lawn furniture. There was still part of me that worried he was in shock about Patrick. He'd handled the revelation as if I'd been telling him the weather forecast, and really, it wasn't as if he planned to be out of doors anyway.

When Gabriel's phone rang, I recognized the ring tone, having set it up myself. "The office? It's Saturday night"

"Lydia planned to work this evening in return for a half day off next week." He answered the phone, and I heard uncharacteristic rapid-fire speech from the other end.

Gabriel glanced at me and hit a button. "Olivia's here. I'm putting you on speaker."

"—don't need to put me on speaker, Gabriel," Lydia said. "You need to get over here. Now."

I rose, but Gabriel held out a hand, stopping me.

"You said there's a girl—"

"—in your office. Completely panicked and refusing to speak to anyone except you or someone named Gwynn."

I took the phone and started for the gate. "It's me. We're on our way, but we're in Cainsville and the car is a half mile away. Can you put her on the phone? Tell her it's Olivia, and Gabriel is right here."

"I would, but she's out cold."

"What?"

"I think it's drugs. She was talking about someone named Gwynn and seemed to get him confused with Gabriel. She mentioned you, but she said she really needed Gabriel. Then she was speaking in another language. Then back to English, about hounds and pepper, and it made absolutely no sense, Liv. I couldn't even get her to calm down enough to let me phone Gabriel until she passed out."

"We'll be there as soon as we can."

We found the lamia on the chaise lounge in Gabriel's office. Lydia apologized for that, but it was the only horizontal surface.

"You should go," I said to Lydia. "We've got this."

She shook her head. "I can—"

"You've done enough," Gabriel said. "We appreciate you staying with her."

"You know what this is about, then," she said.

When Gabriel didn't answer, I said, "Yes, we do."

"And it would be better if I left?"

"Yes, it would."

I walked her to her desk, where she got her jacket and laptop bag. "Thank you. For handling this."

She busied herself putting on her jacket. "I know things have changed, Liv. Not just because you're here, and Gabriel no longer practically lives in this office. Which is wonderful to see, but . . ." She looked at me. "I'm not demanding to know more, but I think it would help if I did."

"Gabriel doesn't want—"

"He's always been very careful to keep me out of anything that could land me in a jail cell." She smiled. "He'd hate the bother of replacing me. I understand he thinks it's unsafe for me to know more, but I'm asking."

At a noise from Gabriel's office, I turned.

"Go on," she said. "Just consider it. Please."

I said goodbye and hurried back to the office, where Gabriel had taken off his jacket and pulled a chair over to the chaise lounge. He sat there, watching the lamia, making no move to wake her.

The girl looked about sixteen with curly black hair, a thin face, and a thin body. No makeup. Dressed in a battered leather jacket, jeans, and combat boots. Not hunting, then. Just being a regular girl—regular fae.

I shook her gently, but she didn't move. When I pressed my fingers to her neck, I could feel a pulse. *Barely* feel a pulse.

"She's hurt," I said. "I don't see an injury, but help me get her out of this jacket."

He did, and at first I still saw nothing. Then, when I started turning away, I caught a splash of red on her white T-shirt. I looked back and it vanished.

"Olivia?" Gabriel said.

His expression told me he hadn't seen what I did. "I'm going to pull up her shirt."

He turned away. I tugged up her tee, but saw only unblemished skin and a beige bra. Then I caught it again: the blood. I stayed at that angle, looking out of the corner of my eye. The girl's torso flickered, and stab wounds appeared on her chest, blood everywhere. When I looked back, her glamour rippled, as if she was growing too weak to sustain it, blood and scales glistening on her skin.

"Gabriel?"

"Hmm?"

"Look at her out of the corner of your eye." When he hesitated, I said, "She's wearing a bra. Please look."

He turned, just enough to do as I asked. Then he blinked, and that small reaction told me I wasn't imagining things.

"She's been attacked," I said, dropping to my knees beside the girl. "She's using a glamour to hide it." I took the girl's shoulder and shook harder, trying to rouse her, and then said, "I'll get a cold cloth."

When I came back, the girl's eyelids were quivering, as she looked up at Gabriel, his hand on her forehead. She whispered, "Gwynn," and he pulled back quickly, but I hurried up beside him, took his hand, and put it back on her forehead, saying, "Please," and he tensed but nodded and crouched there awkwardly, his hand on her again.

"Gwynn," she said.

"Y . . . yes," he managed.

"And your name?" I asked, moving beside her and hunkering down. I reached for her hand, and she didn't hesitate to take mine, her skin cool.

"Not—not important," she managed. "But you're—you're Matilda. You glow. So pretty." Tears glistened in her eyes. "So lucky. So blessed."

Not sure about that, but I said, "You've been stabbed. Tell us what we can do."

"N-nothing. Dying."

"No," I said. "Let me get—"

"A first aid kit?" Her lips twitched. "An ambulance? Not for me. Just . . . just listen."

"Anything," I said.

Her eyes flickered open and shut, as if she'd used all her energy, and then she whispered, "Attacked. Not . . . not . . . wasn't . . ."

"It wasn't like the others? Not the same person?"

Her eyes glistened again. "Don't understand."

"Okay, sorry. Explain again."

"Not you. Me." Each word came slow, labored. "She . . . she wanted to help. Always wanted to help. Don't understand."

"She? Help?" I thought fast. "Aunika? Did Aunika do this to you?"

The lamia mumbled something unintelligible.

Gabriel leaned down over her, his face as close to her as he could get, though he seemed to grit his teeth to do it. "Did Aunika attack you?" he asked.

She opened her eyes, looked at him, smiled, and said, "Gwynn." Then her eyelids fluttered and she whispered, "Tell Toby . . ." Her eyes closed, and I gripped her hand tighter, leaning in—

Darkness. Light, darkness, light. Then darkness again. A hiss, not of anger, but of contented sleep. A warm body pressed to mine. Wrapping my arms around it and trying to get closer. A chuckle. A hand on my thigh, wonderfully warm hands. A voice, a young man's, saying, "Love you, too, Dami," and another hissing sigh, rippling through me. One eye open. Moonlight through a window. Cheap curtains. A mattress on the floor. A boy curled against me, and I was sighing and thinking, *This is the best. I don't deserve it. But I'll take it.* And I caught a glimpse in a broken mirror, and I saw the lamia, curled up with a young man in his late teens.

This is the best.

The best moment.

The best memory.

The scene flickered, and I was in an alley. I heard a noise and I stiffened and stifled a hiss. My eyes adjusted to the dark. I let them slit to snake form, but as soon as I did, I felt the cold of night. I opened my mouth, tongue darting out, sampling the air, catching a familiar scent before I shifted back to human, warming again.

"Stop hiding in shadow," I said. "Let's get this over with. Toby will be home soon."

"And you want to have dinner for him?" A sneering laugh in a female voice. "Do you like playing house with human boys, Damara?"

"This one? Yes. Very much. Skip the mockery, and tell me what you want. If you're offering to get me into Cainsville, the answer is no. I'm happy here. I'm safe here."

"No, actually, you're not."

A figure swooped from the darkness and I felt pain, incredible pain. Then I was lying on the pavement, and a voice whispered in my ear, "I'm supposed to do more, but I think that's enough. Sleep well, little Damara."

The vision ended, and I snapped back. I was on the floor. Well, mostly—Gabriel was propping me up, his fingers biting into my upper arms, anxious eyes over mine. I braced, expecting to be dropped, but he kept me there, holding me as he said, "I didn't try to bring you back. I thought whatever you were seeing was important. Or that it would be, to you."

I nodded, saying, "It was." His fingers went to my forehead and he exhaled softly.

"Barely warm."

"It was a quick one." I pulled up and looked at the lamia, dead on the chaise lounge. "Her name was Damara. There was a boy. Human. Toby. That's who . . ."

I trailed off, seeing Gabriel's expression of barely concealed impatience, and I gave a small, wry smile. I might hear that story and grieve for the girl who'd found a boy, found the best part of a very long and not very happy life, the girl who'd pulled forth that memory to comfort her as she died. Gabriel heard it and thought, *Yes, yes, let's get to the important part.*

"She knew her killer. It was a girl or a woman. Someone who knew what she was."

"Aunika?"

"It didn't sound like her voice or anyone I recognized. Damara was summoned to meet her attacker. She thought it was about moving to Cainsville. That was the entire conversation. She didn't see her killer. It was dark and the attack came from nowhere and— No, wait. Her killer said she was supposed to do more, but she decided that was enough."

"Complete the ritual."

I nodded. "In my first vision, the lamia was . . . sliced open. This killer skipped that, which is how Damara survived to get here. She played dead."

But now she *was* dead, her glamour faded but not gone, leaving a girl covered in scales, a girl with a half-dozen stab wounds in her chest, a girl who'd used the last of her energy, not to get home for a final moment with her lover, but to cover her injuries with a glamour and get here to speak to us. Only we were too far away, and when we arrived, she only had energy left for those few final clues.

"We need to . . ."

I gazed at the body. *We need to what? What do we do with a dead fae girl?*

"I-I'll call Veronica," I said.

CHAPTER FORTY-ONE

"She will fade," Veronica said after I explained. "If you leave her where she is, the glamour will dissolve and eventually so will she."

"Which is why the other lamiae victims weren't found." I thought of the bodies in the tunnel. I still needed to move them. As for why they hadn't faded, I'd ask about that, too, later.

"I would presume she doesn't look nearly as human now?" Veronica said.

I glanced over. I'd put my jacket over her, but could see her features changing, becoming more serpentine.

"No," I said. "She doesn't."

"That will last only an hour or so before she's gone."

"Where does she go? I mean, her spirit. To the afterlife?"

Silence.

"Sorry," I said. "I'm not trying to break our agreement. I'm just a little . . . shaken up."

"We don't go anywhere, Olivia," she said softly. "That is one part of the human lore that's true, which is why I hesitated. I thought you knew."

"You don't go . . ."

"We have no afterlife. We aren't mortal."

"But you're not *immortal*."

"Not invulnerable, but most of us can live until we are killed or until we no longer wish to live."

"Oh." I looked at Damara. I thought of a girl whose best moment in life—her most treasured moment—was cuddling up with a boy and feeling loved. That was all she got. All she'd ever get.

"Is there . . . Is there anything I can . . ." I glanced at Damara. "No, I guess if she doesn't go anywhere, there isn't anything more I can do."

"There is, but you do not need to feel obligated—"

"What is it?"

"Take her someplace wild before she fades. Forest, meadow, even a farmer's field or a park in the city. We don't pass into another life, but there is something left, an energy, some small awareness, and if she's in a natural place, that remains."

"We'll do that."

We took Damara to Jackson Park. It was past midnight now, and Gabriel was able to find a spot to park, if not quite legally, and we carried her covered body inside the grounds. Damara hadn't reverted any further. This was her true form—human and serpent combined.

By the time we got her there, she was already fading. We found a spot and stayed until she was gone, and Gabriel managed, with some difficulty I suspect, not to check his messages until we were back at the car.

I slept at Gabriel's. It wasn't too late to go back to Cainsville, but I didn't want to spend my first night in the Carew house feeling like this, and if I stayed at my apartment, I'd only think of the house, of a magical evening gone so horribly wrong.

Come morning, we did go to Cainsville. We got there early, and we walked Melanie and Pepper to the diner, knowing it'd be almost empty. Veronica went with us, and a few of the elders showed up, and I could say they went to eavesdrop, but they seemed to be there as protection, taking tables around us, so we could speak in private.

We could, of course, have spoken even more privately at Veronica's house, but I remembered how much Pepper had liked her hot breakfast, and I thought that might cushion the news. She seemed a little better in Cainsville. Melanie claimed she'd spoken yesterday, and I hated to hurt her now. But they had to know.

I told Melanie and Pepper what had happened.

Pepper let out a whimper and said, in a breathy voice, "Damara?"

"I'm sorry," I said.

Another whimper, and she caught Melanie's arm. "Toby."

"I know." Melanie turned to us. "Damara had a . . . relationship with a boy. A small-time hustler." She made a face, clearly disapproving. "That's why she wouldn't come to Cainsville—she didn't want to leave him. Anyway, the two of them used to take Pepper for hot cocoa."

"Dami," Pepper whispered, her gaze dropping.

Melanie squeezed her arm. "I know, *ee mikri mou*."

"Did this boy know what Damara was?" I asked.

"I don't know. It wasn't safe either way, but Damara was a stubborn . . ." She squeezed her eyes shut. "Damn it." Her voice cracked. "Stupid, stubborn—" She wiped the back of her hand across her eyes and put her arm around Pepper.

"She said goodbye to you, Pepper."

Pepper looked over, slowly, at me, frowning because the voice obviously hadn't sounded like mine. Then her gaze turned to Gabriel.

He cleared his throat. "Before she passed, she mentioned your name. She said goodbye."

Pepper stared at him like a god himself had spoken. Then she launched herself across the table, dishes clattering as she threw her arms around his neck. Gabriel's hands were already on her upper arms, ready to push her off. But he only looked at me, nostrils flaring, as if he was trapped in a headlock. I mouthed, "Three, two, one," and then, having given Pepper her moment, carefully removed her, with Melanie helping. Around us, the elders looked pleased. Very, very pleased.

"Gabriel's right," I said, even if it wasn't entirely true. "Damara said goodbye."

We settled back in, and I told Melanie the rest. When I finished, she stared at me. "Aunika? No, that's—that's not possible."

"I don't know that she's behind it, only that she's the only one who fits what Damara said—that it's a *she* who seemed to want to help the lamiae. And it was a she who killed Damara, but the voice wasn't Aunika's, which doesn't exonerate her, because the killer seemed to be acting on instructions from someone else. Possibly the rogue Cŵn Annwn."

"Wh-what?"

I updated her, carefully, leaving out Ciro's death.

"I . . . I don't understand," Melanie said.

"Which is exactly what Damara said," I murmured.

Melanie ran her hands through her hair. "It . . . it makes no sense. None of it."

"Damara's killer knew her. Knew she was a lamia, and knew some of you had retreated to Cainsville. Could the killer be another lamia?"

Melanie shook her head vehemently. "No. Never . . . I can't even imagine it."

Which might be what Damara meant when she said she couldn't understand. Why another lamia would murder her.

Later, I was lying in bed with Ricky, eating cold pizza and talking. The pizza was cold because, well, bed. Yes, it was the middle of the afternoon, but with our schedules, we took private time where we found it. He'd slept late after a Saturday night with the Saints, and I wanted to update him on the case, so I'd brought lunch to his place.

I started explaining at the beginning of yesterday evening. I didn't get far before Ricky stopped mid-bite and said, "Gabriel got you a house?"

"No, no. He—"

"I know—you'll buy it if that's what you decide. But he got the place ready for you. Bought all that stuff for you."

Ricky's gaze was averted, ostensibly fixed on the pizza as he pulled off another slice, but he didn't take it, just separated it.

"It was his way of saying thanks," I said. "And maybe apologizing for . . . the past."

He nodded, his gaze still on the pizza box as my gut twisted.

"I would insist on paying him back for the supplies," I said. "But that seems ungrateful."

"What?" He looked over, saw my expression, and pulled me to him. "Course you can't do that. You shouldn't. He was making amends and pushing you to take a step you weren't going to take yourself. Which is the best kind of gift. I just . . . I didn't expect that from him." A wry smile. "He's cutting into my gig—anticipating what you'll want."

Despite the smile, there was something in his gaze that made the knot in my stomach tighten.

"If it bothers you—" I began.

"If it bothered me, I'd take it up with him. It's good to see him paying more attention. Just . . . It's sooner than I . . ." He cleared his throat. "You should buy the house. He's right that it's a great investment. Live in it for a while, make sure there aren't any serious issues with the visions. You're not really an apartment dweller. You need roots. You need stability."

"You make me sound like a tree."

He chuckled. "You know flattering metaphors really aren't my thing. I'm just saying that a house is a good move for you."

Something wistful passed behind his eyes, and I felt a pang of alarm, but he pulled me to him, hands on my hips, mouth going to mine in a long, sweet kiss.

"That house makes you happy," he said. "I want you to be happy. Whatever it takes, because otherwise? Otherwise, it just doesn't work, and we'll both pay the price."

"I don't under—"

"Just trust me," he said, and rolled onto his back, pulling me on top of him.

CHAPTER FORTY-TWO

I told Ricky the rest of the story, about Damara's death. Something in it gave him an idea, which involved going to Ioan's house. He didn't tell the Cŵn Annwn leader we were coming, just pulled up at the gate. I swung off the bike, but before I could ring the buzzer, the gates opened, and I looked back to see Ioan pulling up behind us. He drove a Mercedes-Benz AMG, which looks like a damned ugly mini SUV best suited for grocery runs . . . and has over five hundred horses under the hood. All power. No show. I was impressed in spite of myself.

Ioan stopped just inside the gate and put down his window. Ricky opened his visor. "Just coming by to see the hound."

Ioan smiled. "She'll like that. Have you chosen a name?"

"I'd rather use her real one."

"I've been making inquiries, but as you know, we don't have much contact with other Cŵn Annwn. They're very unlikely to admit to having lost a hound. I'm hoping a third-party source may be able to supply rumors, but—"

"Slow and unreliable. I'm going to the source."

The Huntsman frowned. "If you mean the hound, while I still have hopes you can repair her psychic bond, that will likely take even longer than—"

"I may have a shortcut. Now . . ." He waved toward the house. "Onward?"

Ricky drove up the winding drive while Ioan looped around into the garage. As we waited at the door, Ioan walked up and took something from his pocket.

"This will make it easier," he said, and handed Ricky a set of keys and a gate opener.

When Ricky hesitated, Ioan said, "So you can check on the hound whenever you want."

Ricky took the keys and opener. It was, in a way, like me and the Carew house. This felt natural, and part of him longed to embrace it. He just knew—as I did—that every inch we moved in that direction made the fae and Cŵn Annwn a little too happy.

We went inside and paused in the front hall to take off our jackets.

"Will you stay for dinner?" Ioan said.

"Up to Liv." He glanced at me. "You're spending the night at the new house, right?" He turned back to Ioan before I could answer. "Liv is test-driving a house in Cainsville, for when her inheritance comes in. I think it's a good idea. Put down roots."

"I'm not sure Cainsville—" Ioan began.

"She was already living there. And the house has been in her family. It has . . . energy. The kind that'll help her get a handle on her powers. That's a good thing, right?"

He looked expectantly at Ioan, and I had to bite my cheek not to laugh. Rose's cards showed Ricky evolving from page to king, and I saw that here. He'd given Ioan a gift, in taking the keys and opener. Now he was righting that imbalance by telling him about my house. Keeping Ioan from thinking he'd gained too much ground.

"Liv will be careful," Ricky said. "The elders have promised to buy it back if she changes her mind." He gave Ioan that much, watching as the Cŵn Annwn leader nodded, relieved. And then . . . "She's staying there tonight, with Gabriel."

Ioan tensed. "Gabriel?"

"The house triggers her visions, and he can manage them. In the long run, it's better for her to have the visions so she can learn how to control them. But in the short term, they can be dangerous. I'll be asking him to stay with her." Ricky looked down the hall. "Is that the hound?"

When I strained, I caught the faintest whining. Then a tentative scratch at a door.

"She knows you're here," Ioan said.

"We'll go see her, then."

CHAPTER FORTY-THREE

As we approached the room, we could hear more quiet whines and tentative scratches. When Ricky pushed open the door, the hound backed away, her head lowered. Ricky dropped to one knee and rubbed her ears, crooning, and her tail banged against the floor loud enough to make the alpha hound—Brenin—look up from his spot on the sofa. He walked over and nudged the hound's haunches, telling her to stand straight. When she did, he grunted in satisfaction and then looked at me and waited.

Brenin's name means king, and he was not a beast one patted on the head or scratched behind the ears. Yet he did expect a token of recognition. I rubbed his neck, my fingers working through the thick, soft fur. Ricky did the same. Then Brenin snorted, as if to say, *Enough of that*, and left through a hatch. This was "his" room, complete with fireplace and furniture and that door hatch leading into the yard. Normally, the interior door would be open for him to wander the house, but the broken hound needed the sense of security that came with a more den-like environment.

"So you're going to ask the hound her name?" I said as we moved into the room.

"Nope, you are." He sat on the sofa. "Here's the reasoning. You can pick up visions from objects, like Patrick's books. And apparently from fae, like Damara. Yes, I know you'll say Patrick's books are made for that. With Damara, she may have actually passed you that vision. But you still have the receptors."

"Not for hounds."

"But I do. I channeled her. So my theory is that maybe together we can get more." He glanced over. "Don't argue."

"I wasn't."

"You were going to. You'd still do it, but only after a huge list of qualifications and warnings to cushion yourself against failure. Yes, I know there's a very good chance this won't work, and if it doesn't, that's no one's fault. Trial and error is the only way we'll figure out our abilities."

"How do you want to start?"

"I'm going to talk to her." He crouched in front of the hound, rubbing her ears and telling her what he planned to do. Whether she understood or not, the sound of his voice calmed her.

He lowered himself to the hardwood floor. The hound looked disconcerted at Ricky taking a lower position. When she rectified that by hunkering down, he tugged her closer. She stretched out, gingerly laying her head on his lap, tensed for the first sign of rejection. He put one hand on her head, and she settled in.

I took the spot on his other side, and he reached for my hand. Then he closed his eyes. After a few minutes of nothing but quiet breathing, Ricky let out a noise, like a whimper, and his body jerked. The sound of his breathing changed, syncopating with the hound's as she twitched, her eyes closed.

I tightened my grip on Ricky's hand, closed my own eyes, and focused.

It wasn't a sudden drop into visions. I focused on the sound of his breathing and the scent of the hound. Then I smelled forest and heard horses, the snort of *their* breathing and the clink of their bridles.

And then running. With the pack. The smell of our prey

filled my nostrils, the pound of paws rang in my ears, the joy of the Hunt sang through my veins as the moonlight lit our path. The joy of the Hunt and the pack and a perfect night.

Then tumbling. Sudden tumbling through darkness. Through memory. From the best to the worst. To pain. Agonizing pain, ripping me inside and out, and I fought to escape, to flee some dark force I couldn't see or hear, could only feel. I smelled blood. I heard yowls. My brothers and sisters. I had to save them, had to help them, but I couldn't even save myself, until finally I was thrown free, as if jettisoned from nightmare itself, cast into darkness.

I awoke on the ground. When I lifted my head, I saw the mangled bodies of three other hounds. Two pack brothers and a sister. Torn almost beyond recognition.

"Fwnion!" a voice called, and I went still, waiting to hear that voice resonating in my head, to feel the bond with my Huntsman. But there was nothing except his audible voice, calling my name.

I cowered against the ground as I looked at my dead pack mates. I'd failed them. I'd survived when they had not. I must have escaped through cowardice. I must not have fought hard enough. Or long enough. I'd surrendered, and this was my punishment: that I could hear my Huntsman's voice, but our bond was broken.

"Fwnion!" he shouted, desperation edging his voice, and I thought of him finding me here, with the corpses of my brothers and sister, and myself, broken and maimed but alive. Surviving when I ought to be dead. I did not want him to witness that. I did not want to cause him pain or shame. So I pushed to my paws, and I dragged my broken body into the forest.

The scene flipped, and I was in another forest, ripping apart a rabbit. An old rabbit, stinking of waste and death even before I caught it, because with my broken body, this was the best I could hope for. A hound of the Otherworld reduced to near scavenging. The shame of that made me want to stop eating, to just waste away and die myself, but when I'd tried, I'd fallen into delirium and woken with a belly full of deer found dead by a roadside. I could not even manage death without succumbing to cowardice.

"I have something better for you, *cûn*," a voice whispered through the forest.

I went still and lifted my head, sniffing. It was the only reliable sense I had left. My injuries seemed to have healed, but oddly my hearing had gotten worse as they did. My one eye no longer showed more than shapes. But I could smell, and I recognized this scent.

The Huntsman.

Not *my* Huntsman. I dreamed of mine. Dreams where he'd scoop me up, as he had when I was a puppy and he'd taken me for his own. Dreams of him nursing me back to health, as he had when I'd injured my leg in a hunt. Most of all, though, I dreamed of forgiveness, of his hand on my head and his voice saying, "It's all right, Fwnion. You're home."

But my Huntsman was long gone. I'd run so far I could never find my way back even if I wanted to. This one . . . this one had been tracking me for days. He was a loner, like myself. Tainted, like myself. I could smell that taint on him, and it made my hackles rise.

"There you are," he said. "I brought you proper food, *cûn*."

He emptied a bag of fresh meat. Then he hunkered down and said, "You're broken, aren't you? Broken and cast from your pack. What did you do to deserve such a beating?"

I growled, offended at the idea that my pack or my Huntsman would have done this to me.

"I can help," he said. "Some of those injuries haven't healed well. I can fix that, and I can give you shelter and food, and all I ask in return is that you do your job—the job of a hound."

I looked at him, at the madness roiling in his eyes.

Madness and something twisted and ugly, and I started backing away, growling.

"Or we can do this your way," he said, lunging, and a bag descended over my head.

The scene faded, replaced by flickering scenes, confusing scenes of hell and glimpses of something more, something better. The man healed my injuries as best he could. I walked easier. My hearing returned. Even my vision improved.

The Huntsman did as he promised. He provided care and shelter and food. But nothing more. No attention, no affection, and certainly no respect. I was like a dog to him. If I disobeyed, he punished me with a psychic pain that left me in agony. And so I learned to obey and eventually stopped trying to escape, because this was, I realized, what I deserved. *He* was what I deserved.

The flashing scenes slowed, and I was in his house. Indoors, which was rare. I had a run and a kennel in the back, like a common cur. But now he'd brought me in and given me clothing to sniff. A target, because without that psychic link, I was reduced to this, again like a dog. Sniff and find. Find and kill. Except . . . not this time.

"She isn't your usual prey," he said. "She hasn't done anything to deserve death."

My hackles rose, and I had to fight not to growl. Growling was rebellion. But this . . . this I could not do. He'd given me targets before, and I had looked into their eyes, and enough of my power remained that I could see their guilt. That allowed me to do my sacred duty and send them to the afterlife.

"You won't be killing her," he said. "Just find her and watch her. That's all they want. Surveillance."

I looked up into his eyes and knew he was lying. Not about killing her—he retained enough of his nature that, like me, he could not kill the innocent. Yet she would die at another's hands.

He gave me the clothing to sniff again and then a photo of a woman.

It was Lucy Madole.

The visions faded into another montage of scenes passing too quickly to make sense. When I surfaced, I still gripped Ricky's hand as he leaned against the couch, his eyes shut, lids flickering, still in the vision, his breathing matching the hound's. Then he gasped, his head jerking up, eyes opening.

He ran his free hand through his hair, saying, "Fuck. That . . . Fuck."

"What did you see?"

"Everything, I think. That wasn't like . . . Fuck."

"Are you okay?"

A wan smile. "Besides feeling like I was dropped a hit of LSD and plunged down the rabbit hole?"

I squeezed his hand and looked over at the hound, who seemed to be sleeping, her head on Ricky's leg. The door opened, and Ioan popped his head through. When I motioned him inside, he entered carrying an antipasto platter.

"And that is exactly what I need," Ricky said. "I feel like I just ran a marathon."

A flicker of confusion crossed Ioan's face, but he only said, "Good. Wine?" He glanced at Ricky. "Or would you prefer beer?" He made a face. "That was presumptuous, wasn't it?"

"Yeah, kinda," Ricky said. "Wine is good. I won't pretend I'm a connoisseur, though. I drink whatever Liv does."

Ioan gave me a few choices. When I picked one, he left and returned a few minutes later to find us still sitting on the floor.

Ricky laid his hand on the hound's head and that was all she needed to wake. She followed us into the next room. Brenin appeared as we were settling on a sofa and chair. He walked over, sniffing and nudging her. Then, satisfied, he lay by the fireplace.

"I suppose you want that turned on," Ioan said.

Brenin just looked at him. Ioan sighed and started the fire.

"We got a vision from her," I said.

That made Ioan stop and turn. "From the hound?"

"Her name is Fwnion." I looked at her and smiled. "It means mild or gentle."

"Fwnion," Ricky said to her, patting her head.

She whined and ducked away.

"Or maybe not . . ." Ricky looked at Ioan. "We got a sense of what happened. She fought something in a forest with three other hounds. They died. She blames herself. She thinks the psychic break is punishment. That's why she ran from her pack. I'm guessing her name brings up bad memories. Maybe we *should* try a new one."

I remembered the opening of the vision, how she'd felt on the Hunt. "How about Lloergan? It means moonlight or moonshine."

"Lloergan, then?" Ricky asked the hound. "A new name for a new life?"

She thumped her tail.

"A temporary new life, at least," Ricky said. "We should keep trying to find her original Huntsman."

Ioan pretended not to hear, but Ricky said, "It's only right. Put out the word to your contacts and see if we get a bite."

CHAPTER FORTY-FOUR

B ack to Cainsville after dinner. While waiting for Gabriel, I spent some quality time with TC, which amounted to feeding him and cleaning out his litter box while he watched. When I tried to pet him, he stalked off, and I threatened to replace him with a *cûn* puppy. He ignored me.

Gabriel arrived, and we walked to Veronica's. I told Melanie I'd like to speak to the other lamiae in Chicago, as part of the investigation. Just touch base, find out if they'd seen anything, heard rumors . . .

She said she'd talk to them, in a tone that warned me not to hold my breath. She knew full well I was looking for a killer among her sisters, and she was having none of it. Could I blame her? Not really. They were second-class fae and had suffered their share of witch hunts.

We returned to my apartment to grab my overnight bag and the cat. I worried a bit about how TC would react, given that he'd spent a few days locked in the Carew house basement. He zoomed in and made himself at home on the couch, as if nothing bad had ever happened to him there. Which makes him a lot like his human, who happily embraced the same house where she'd found a dead body in the attic.

"My office fireplace is cleaned," Gabriel said as we settled in the garden with mochas, cookies, and blankets. "I'll use it tomorrow."

"Then I'd better start looking for a garden one."

"That was the idea," he said as he tugged the blanket over his shoulders.

"Or we could just *not* sit in my empty garden when it's so damned cold."

He didn't even answer that, instead saying, "About the hound . . ." Which was the prompt I needed. I explained.

"So the Huntsman *was* connected to Lucy Madole's death," Gabriel said when I finished the story.

"Seems like it. He had Lloergan do surveillance, and the hound sensed Lucy would die at another's hand."

"Whoever he's working for had Lucy killed and then had him persuade Ciro to kill the lamiae. That person also set him on Aunika."

"Or has made it seem that way."

"Perhaps," Gabriel said. "False persecution to deflect attention and give Aunika what appears to be an alibi."

"As soon as I catch up with her, she's beset by mystery stalkers and then disappears . . . which allows her to continue carrying out her scheme. If I only had any idea what that scheme could be. Or what her motivation might be."

"You likely won't know all that until you find Aunika. We should rechannel our efforts in that direction. The Cŵn Annwn want to find the rogue Huntsman. See if Ricky can persuade them to locate Aunika instead."

"Right. Because leading us to her may lead them to him. Okay, then. We have a plan. I'll concentrate on that and stop chasing my tail trying to make connections with the rest."

After a few moments of silence, Gabriel said, "I will also speak to Melanie myself. I might be more persuasive."

"Persuade her as Gwynn."

He stiffened at the name.

"I saw him here in the garden," I said softly. "When I had the vision here last spring."

"Which explains the fever," Gabriel said. "Your brain's equivalent of an allergic reaction." He tried for a smile, but it faltered, and he busied himself drinking his mocha.

"It's not like that. When I see Gwynn, they're good memories. It's easy to paint Gwynn and Arawn as selfish and arrogant and thoughtless, and it's easy to paint Matilda as silly and weak. They were young and they got caught up in fear and jealousy and they made mistakes. Terrible, senseless mistakes."

"Can we discuss something else?"

"I just think you need to come to terms with Gwynn, or it's just going to get more and more uncomfortable."

"I will come to terms with it. In my own way."

"I wish I could show you—"

"No," he said, his voice harsh as he met my gaze. "If you are thinking you might be able to share a vision, as you did with Ricky, the answer is no. I'd like you to respect my wishes."

"I will. I'm sorry."

He was already on his feet, picking up the dishes with a clatter and headed for the house. "I have work to do. I'll be at the kitchen table."

So please find another place to be.

That was what he was telling me. It did not matter how far we came, the moment my toe crossed his invisible line, he was done with me.

"Fuck you, Gabriel," I said.

He turned. "I beg your pardon?"

"You heard me. Fuck you. I was only trying to help, and as soon as you said no, I backed down. Yet that wasn't enough. It's never enough. I've misbehaved, and so I lose the privilege of your company. You'll walk into that house—*my* house—and tell me where I can and cannot sit, because God forbid you should have to endure my presence when you're angry with me."

His gaze chilled. "I don't believe I said anything of the sort."

"No? Okay, then. Well, I have work, too. So we'll both sit at the dining room table."

He stood there a moment, and then said, "I think you should call Ricky and see if he can stay here with you tonight. I have things to do—"

"You are such a fucking coward, Gabriel."

Those eyes turned to ice. "Excuse me?"

"You don't even have the guts to say you don't want me around."

He glared at me, his jaw working.

"Come on," I said. "You can do it. *You're a pain in the ass, Olivia. You're a nag and you're a bitch, and I don't want to be around you. Go away.*"

"I never said—"

"Do you know what's worse than being a coward? Being a hypocrite."

"Are you calling me—?"

"You tell me you have my back. You fuss about my safety, make a big deal about protecting me. But the moment that's not convenient, Ricky can take over. You know what, Gabriel? I have an even better idea. Why don't you give me a ride back to Chicago so you can drop me off in a shitty neighborhood."

"You got out of the car—"

"I didn't realize where I was."

"Neither did I."

"I *waited* for you to come back."

"I didn't know exactly where you got out. Not until Ricky told me the next morning."

"Bullshit."

"I had other things on my mind, Olivia. All I registered was that you got out of the car."

"Which was such a relief that nothing else mattered."

Again his jaw worked, nothing coming out until he said, "I would never have intentionally left you there. No more than I'd actually let Ricky stay your first night here. I would have realized my error soon enough. I will ask you to spend the night at your apartment."

"No." I headed for the house.

"If you think that will force my hand and make me stay—"

I laughed. "*Make* you stay? Seriously? The moment you want to leave, you will, and there'll be no way to get you back until you decide you want to come back. You'll ignore my calls, my messages, my texts. You'll tell me not to come into work. You'll freeze me out again, and I can't put up with that. I just can't."

"So why do you?"

I stopped. Just stopped. It was like when he laughed at the thought we were friends.

Why do I put up with him? Why did I keep banging my head against this wall, knocking myself senseless trying to get through to him, and then raging and crying because I'd hurt myself.

Why did I put up with it?

Because I loved him. Because I was such a damn fool.

My eyes filled with tears, and I think that was the worst. As humiliating as if I'd said the words out loud.

Gabriel saw those tears and recoiled. And *that* was the worst.

This was the man I kept tying myself up in knots over? The man I couldn't quit even when I had a solid, stable, *amazing* relationship with Ricky? Instead, I wanted the guy who would shut me out if I crossed invisible boundaries? Who'd walk away if I challenged him on it? Think me a fool if I stayed? Think me weak if I cried?

I could tell myself I'd made my choice with Ricky and this with Gabriel was just friendship, but that was bullshit. A few signs of kindness from Gabriel, signs of consideration and caring, and I was right back, like Ricky's hound, desperate for scraps of attention, some hope that maybe, just maybe . . .

Maybe *what*? Even if I got him, what exactly did I get? A man who'd walk away at the first sign of trouble. Who'd slam the door and mock me if I followed. Who'd withdraw if I showed any sign of actual emotion.

I stumbled toward the house. I heard him call, "Olivia," and heard the first thump of his footsteps and I raced up the steps, eager to get inside, just get inside and bolt the door and collapse behind it and—

I tripped going up the stairs. I tripped, and Gabriel was right there, his hand going to my shoulder. In trying to duck his grip, I fell sideways, my head bashing the wrought-iron patio fence, and it wasn't enough to knock me unconscious, just to make the world dip and fade and spin as I fell to . . .

Rock. I tumbled heels over head off the embankment, my head striking rock as I fell, and when I came to, someone had me, a face over mine, a voice calling my name, hands gripping me, the voice sharp with worry. When my eyes fluttered open, he backed off fast, stammering an apology, explaining that I'd fallen—as if I wouldn't realize that. Even with pain shooting through my head, I had to smile at the thought that he needed an excuse to be caught holding me.

Typical Gwynn.

I started as I thought the name. Or the part that *was* me did, because even though I consciously recognized Gwynn's fair hair and face and voice, I saw and heard Gabriel, in his gestures, in his apology, perhaps not stammered, but the intent the same—to be certain I understood that there was a valid reason I was waking in his arms.

Gwynn awkwardly shifted me onto the grass, his hand lingering under my head.

"Can you move, Mati?" he asked.

What if I pretend I cannot? Might I get a few more moments of your care?

My lips quirked at the thought, as I brushed it off. Other girls might try that ploy. I would not, as tempting as it was.

"Well, that will teach me to watch where I'm going," I said.

"It was my fault for talking," he said.

"Yes," I said, mock-serious. "You really shouldn't do that."

I smiled at him but couldn't suppress a wince as I did, and he said, "Hold still. You've cut your lip."

He reached into the picnic basket, brought out the wine-skin, soaked the corner of a cloth, and reached to clean my lip. As he did, I watched him, so close and so intent on his task, and I thought, *I could kiss him.*

Kiss him and, yes, he might jump back like a cat with its tail on fire, but I had just struck my head and could not be held accountable for my actions. Of course, it might hurt, kissing with a split lip, but that was really the least of my concerns.

I'd seen signs lately, lingering looks, and then blushes when I caught him watching me, indications that a kiss might not be unwelcome. That I might win the prize I treasured above all others.

I closed my eyes and leaned forward and—

"*Cach!*" Gwynn said, which was not exactly the response a girl hopes for, and my eyes flew open to see him, staring up at the sky. When I followed his gaze, I saw how dark the clouds had gotten. Then lightning flashed and thunder rumbled, and Gwynn helped me to my feet. When my ankle buckled, he scooped me up without a word and started to run for a path winding up the cliff-side. The skies opened and rain fell—not in a pleasant shower, but sheets of driving rain.

"*Cach!*" he swore again, and I said, "Agreed," though the wind whipped my words away. I raised my voice to say, "Let me down, and I'll walk as best I can," and he pretended not to hear me and ran through the rain until we reached a cave in the cliffside. He bustled me in, and I realized it wasn't so much a cave as a shallow opening in the cliff, just big enough for us to hunker down and watch the rainstorm in relative dryness.

When I shivered, he leaned against me, and I took advantage of the excuse to settle against his side. He put his arm around my shoulder, gingerly, as if I might throw him off. I snuggled closer and may have exaggerated my shivering and chattered my teeth until his arm tightened around me.

"It is not the place for a picnic," he said. "But . . . wine?" He lifted the skin.

I chuckled. "Mmm, not sure I should take wine from you, my lord prince. How can I be sure you'll not use it to enchant me?"

He blushed at that, his fair skin turning ruby red, and I took a moment to enjoy that flush, that sign that his mind must have leapt to thoughts of love potions. Then I released him with, "I'll drink it if you promise it won't turn me into a frog," and he gave a sharp laugh and relaxed, his hand rubbing my shoulder.

"Are you sure?" he said. "This seems the perfect weather for a frog."

"True, but no."

He uncapped the wineskin and handed it to me. "What would you be, then, Mati, if I could indeed work such an enchantment? Temporarily, of course."

"A cat," I said without hesitation. "So the next time I tumble off a cliff, I'll land on my feet, not my face."

He laughed then, a glorious sound, and I nestled against him, handing back the wineskin and—

"This was a crazy idea," a young man said, in a tone that suggested by "crazy" he meant "good." Slang from a more modern era.

He continued, "It'll be a kick. I'm glad you suggested it."

"I've always wanted to try hunting," another young man replied. "You seemed the right person to teach me."

"I am indeed," said the first voice, the accompanying laugh a little boastful, a little arrogant.

I was in the forest, the voices floating over me. When I made my way toward them, I caught a glimpse of my own sneakers and the legs of my jeans. Back to myself, then, but still caught in some vision. I continued toward the voices.

"I really am glad you asked," the first said again. "I know you and I haven't always seen eye to eye, but you're Alice's friend. I get that."

A noise from the second young man, a grunt that could be agreement, and the first continued, "I mean it. You two have been pals since you were in diapers, and I've told her that's fine with me."

I finally reached them and peered through the trees to see that they were more boys than men. Maybe sixteen, seventeen. Dressed in hunting jackets and ankle-rolled jeans that put me in mind of the fifties. The boy in the lead was handsome—blond and burly in that captain-of-the-football-team way. The one behind was smaller, dark-haired, with a quiet intensity about him, and I knew, without another clue, who I was looking at. Another Arawn and another Gwynn.

I knew that, and yet . . .

These felt like relatives of Arawn and Gwynn, but distant. Very distant. I did not see Arawn and Gwynn in these two the way I saw them in Ricky and Gabriel. Another iteration, but a poor one, the connection weak.

"Did you hear me, Peter?" the blond boy—Arawn—said, glancing over his shoulder

The reply was a quiet, "Yes, I did."

"I said it's fine with me. You being pals with my girlfriend."

The blond boy clearly expected gratitude for his largesse, but Peter only nodded.

The blond boy's eyes narrowed. "I could tell her to stop seeing you. She'd have to. She's *my* girlfriend."

"I'd like to see you try, Carl," Peter said, his voice low.

Carl's face screwed up. "What's that?"

"I said that I'm glad you let her be my friend."

Carl turned back around, leading the way through the forest. "You're welcome. But I would like you to back off a little. Hanging out at school is fine, because I don't go to hers, but no more of this going for sodas in the evening and picnics on the weekend. That's for *boyfriends*." He glanced back. "Get it?"

Peter's voice cooled. "I have never made a move—"

"Course not, because you know you wouldn't get to first base. She's got me now. You don't stand a chance."

"Then you shouldn't be concerned." Peter's voice had gone ice-cold.

"I'm not." Carl resumed walking. "I'm just saying it looks bad, and other guys talk. I don't want that. You can be her school chum. That's it. You don't like that?" Carl waggled his rifle, his back still to Peter. "Remember what a good shot I am."

"Is that a threat?"

"Only if it needs to be, Petey," Carl said with a smirk in his voice. "But you know your place. And it's not with Alice." He glanced back. "Not *ever* with Alice. Remember that. As long as I'm around, she's mine. I'll never let her go."

"Yes, I know," Peter said.

"Good lad."

They continued walking. I could feel Peter seething as he watched Carl's back. They went another ten paces. Then Peter said, "Is that a deer?"

Carl stopped and surveyed the forest. "Where?"

"Up there, to the left."

Carl waved for Peter to stay where he was and crept forward, his footfalls silent. When he'd gone about five steps, Peter lifted his rifle and aimed it square at Carl's back.

"No!" I said, stumbling forward through the forest.

Peter pulled the trigger. The shot hit Carl between the shoulder blades and he flew face-first into the dirt. I heard a voice shout, "No!" but it wasn't mine, it was another, a familiar, deep voice, and I tumbled through into the garden, hitting the concrete of the patio, my cheek against the cool stone, hearing Gabriel shout, "No!"

SPOKES ON A WHEEL

abriel whiplashed back to the present. He could feel the cold patio beneath his hands. He could smell burning leaves in the air. He could hear Olivia saying his name. All that told him he was back, and yet his mind stayed trapped in the forest, the shot looping over and over.

Standing there, watching a boy he knew was supposed to be Gwynn—supposed to be *him*—shoot Arawn in the back. It sent him tumbling into memory, of being in the abandoned psychiatric hospital, when Ricky had been knocked out in the belfry. He'd been hanging there, wounded, as the voice in Gabriel's head whispered.

Look at him. He's barely hanging on. He's bleeding badly. It's a four-story drop. The fall would likely kill him, and if it didn't, he'd bleed out before help came. All you need to do is stay right where you are. Or better yet, walk away. No one knows you were up here.

Gabriel knew now it had been Tristan, trying to convince him to abandon Ricky. *Let him fall. Let him die.* But Gabriel could never shake that first impression. In his memory the voice was Gwynn. And Gwynn was him.

And what was worse, there had been—for one second that seemed in his memory to stretch to an eternity—a moment where he'd considered it.

Ricky gone. Olivia yours.

That guilt—that incredible guilt—was like nothing he'd

felt before. There had been a moment where he'd thought of Ricky dead and been glad of it. Now he'd seen it happen to another Gwynn, another Arawn. A Gwynn without his Matilda, unable to bear seeing her with *him*, convinced that if *he* was gone, the path would be clear. Opening that path with cold-blooded murder.

Gabriel dimly heard Olivia saying his name, felt her shaking him. But it was as if she called from another dimension, one he could not reach because he was trapped in that forest, seeing the boy shoot over and over, and thinking,

That could be me.

Yet there was also the beginning, when he'd first fallen into Olivia's vision, when he'd *been* Gwynn. Running to her after she fell, his heart pounding, the relief when he saw she was all right. In that moment, there was no barrier between Gabriel and Gwynn. It'd been him running to Olivia, because that was who he saw, who he heard, in Matilda's voice and her words and her smiles and her gestures. Olivia as Matilda, as much as he was Gwynn, feeling exactly as he felt when Olivia was hurt.

At that moment, he'd understood what Olivia meant. What she'd wanted to show him. That the figure he held in his head—the arrogant, thoughtless, obsessive bastard—was not the whole of Gwynn. Not even, perhaps, a significant part of Gwynn. Instead, he'd been a boy, deeply in love, unable even to think of the pact he'd made with Arawn, because if there was even a flicker of hope that Matilda might reciprocate his feelings, then he could no more remember his vow than he could remember to breathe when she turned that smile on him. Foolish, yes. Dangerous, certainly. But that was the power of hindsight. *Being* Gwynn, *feeling* what he felt, it was forgivable.

He'd cleaned the blood from her lip, and he'd run through the storm carrying her, and he'd huddled in that cave with her, and she'd teased him and they'd laughed, and it felt like some forgotten memory. Like something he'd shared with Olivia, but had slipped his mind, and now he had it back and he wouldn't push it away again. He'd put it back where it belonged, on a shelf in his memory, bright and shining, ready to be picked up whenever he wanted it. And he would thank Olivia for it. Thank her and apologize, because she was right. *This* was what he needed. An understanding that there was so much more to Gwynn than he'd realized.

And then came the other memory, of the other Gwynn, the boy in the forest. It took that pleasant memory and shattered it like glass against stone.

Forget the first Gwynn. The second is what counts. That's my future. That's what I'm capable of. The most unimaginable betrayal . . . not just of Ricky, but of Olivia.

"Gabriel, please. *Please.*"

It was the "please" that snapped him back, looking up at Olivia, then rising onto his elbows, realizing he was lying on the patio floor.

"Did you . . .?" She swallowed. "You saw it, didn't you? The visions."

"Yes." His voice came hollow, barely recognizable, as if still in that distant, lost place.

"I did not do anything to cause that," she said.

He struggled to focus on her voice against the pull of the vision, threatening to drag him back. When he didn't answer, her voice rose in panic. "I *didn't*. I wouldn't know how, and I'd never do that when you didn't want to see it."

"I know." He meant it, but with that hollow ring, his voice lacked conviction, and fresh panic sparked in her eyes.

"You have to believe me," she said. "I would never—"

"I *know*," he said, forcing himself to sit upright. "You fell, and I grabbed you, and that seemed to cause it."

He glanced up at the house. *You did it*, he thought, and felt rather foolish thinking it, but he knew that was the answer. The house gave Olivia the visions she needed, and he'd gotten them through her. Because, yes, he needed to see another side of Gwynn. But he also needed to see *that* side, the ugly and jealous side. To face it.

Face what? The possibility I could kill to win her? Not even to win her, because if I did that, I could never have her. Even if she came to me, I could not be with her, knowing what I'd done.

"That's not you," she blurted.

He looked at her.

"You saw Gwynn and then you saw the two boys, Carl and Peter, right?"

He tried not to flinch at the names. "Yes."

"Peter isn't you. It was different, wasn't it? With Gwynn, you *were* him, right? Seeing through his eyes."

He nodded.

"And Peter?"

"I was watching from the forest."

"Exactly. An actor in one and an audience in the other." She sat on the patio edge and twisted to face him. "It's like . . . spokes on a wheel. Gwynn is at the center. One spoke is you. Another is—or was—Peter. You and he aren't connected except through Gwynn. They're . . . variations on a theme. From the same initial source, like distant cousins of a common ancestor." She peered at him, face drawn, anxious. "Am I making any sense?"

"I'd rather not talk about it."

"But it might help. If we can work this out—"

"No." He said it sharper than he intended. But she didn't draw back. She sunk, as if defeated.

"I need to leave," he said.

"I know." And there was, in her voice, that same hollow note, not distance but resignation.

Goddamn it, say something. Don't run away. You don't need to have this conversation. Just don't run from her.

She'd called him a coward, running away whenever she

pulled him toward something he didn't like. It was not so much cowardice as ego, and not even so much protecting his ego as safeguarding the supports that kept it intact.

Success bolstered his ego. Doing what he was good at and avoiding failure in every possible way. He'd first realized that in high school, when he'd dropped out of geometry, not because he disliked it but because he wasn't good at it. Algebra came easily. Calculus was also fine. But there was something about geometry that he could not wrap his mind around. So he dropped the course.

The moment he discovered he did not have the knack for something, he stopped trying to do it. Empathy, friendship, dating, relationships in general. He embraced a challenge only if he knew he *could* succeed.

The hard truth of the matter was that Gabriel was spoiled. He got what he wanted, and did not want what he could not get.

"May I ask you a favor?" Olivia said. She continued without waiting for an answer. "Go to Rose's, please. I don't want you driving home, and I know you don't want me around, so just do that. Please."

She didn't look at him when she said it. It was not as if she was intentionally avoiding his gaze, but as though she simply couldn't be bothered facing him. Resignation dragged down her voice to a monotone, as if she were reading instructions from a card.

Just go, Gabriel. I'm done with you.

She was tired of him. Tired of tiptoeing around his moods. Tired of putting up with him.

Then why do you?

He'd asked her that because he wanted an answer. No, he wanted a declaration. Not of love but of *something*. Of friendship, of commitment, of caring.

He'd wanted her to say what he could not. He'd put the burden on her.

I'm not good at this, so I won't do it. You will.

Only she hadn't. Her face had crumpled and her eyes had filled with tears, and he'd pulled back sharply, trying to figure out what he'd done, what he'd said. It was only when she walked away that he realized she hadn't heard *Please tell me why you stay* but a sneering and sarcastic *Why do you stay, then?* Even if he hadn't said it that way, that's what she'd expected.

She rose. "Your jacket is inside. I know you keep your keys in the pocket. I'm taking them. If you insist on having them back, come and get them. But I'd really like you to stay at Rose's tonight."

Let Rose deal with you. I can't. Won't.

Could he blame her? No, not at all.

She got as far as the door, and then turned and said, her voice gentler, "If you want to talk, you know where I am." A pause, and a sadder, "I won't hold my breath," before she went inside.

Go talk to her. Just go talk to her. Or tell her you don't want to talk about it, and talk about something else. Or tell her you don't want to talk at all, and work beside her instead. Just stay with her. Show her you won't run. That you're making progress. That she can count on you.

He stared at that closed door for at least ten minutes. Then he walked away.

CHAPTER FORTY-FIVE

I called Rose right after I checked that Gabriel's keys were indeed in his jacket pocket. I told her I'd accidentally pulled him into a vision of another Gwynn, and it had been a bad one, and if he came over, he just needed a place to sleep. I didn't ask her not to question him or pressure him to talk. She knew better. I was the one who couldn't learn that particular lesson.

For the next hour, I did record searches on other cases. Busywork to keep my mind off what had happened. Resist the urge to call Rose and ask if he'd gotten there okay. Resist the urge to walk to her house on some pretense, in hopes of some sign that things between us were all right, that he just needed a little time.

When Rose called at midnight, I grabbed the phone before the second ring.

"He didn't come," she said.

I hurried to the front window. "His car's still here. Maybe he went to my apartment?"

"I checked. I gave him time to walk it off, but it's been too long for that."

"I'll find him and call you back."

I pocketed the phone and hurried to the back door. I was scooping up my shoes when I saw Gabriel in the garden, sitting on the ground, leaning back against the bench, blankets over his lap.

I tugged on my shoes and went out. I was sure he'd fallen asleep, but when I drew near, I could see his eyes were open. He just sat there, staring at the empty fishpond, hair tumbled over his forehead, not glancing up as I approached. Deeply lost in his thoughts.

I crouched beside him and said, "It's cold. Come inside," and he gave a start. Then he saw me, his gaze still unfocused. I waited for him to say no, he'd go to Rose's. Or that he wanted his keys back. But when I told him to come in again, he only rose and followed.

I woke the next morning to the smell of breakfast and found Gabriel in my kitchen, cooking eggs. I didn't say a word. Just walked in and sat at the table, and he poured me a coffee, and a minute later breakfast followed, my eggs done exactly as I liked them, toast made from Larry's rye bread and topped with Veronica's raspberry jam. Even my bacon was cooked exactly right.

Gabriel had asked why I stayed with him. Here was the answer: because he'd made me breakfast exactly as I liked it, and I didn't even know he could cook it.

This is why I stay. Because no matter how frustrated I get, no matter how much I feel like I'm banging my head against a wall, I know that I am making progress. The man I met five months ago would have walked away without a backward glance. This time, when he couldn't follow me inside, he'd settled in the garden instead. Then he cooked me breakfast as an apology.

"I hope you made some for yourself," I said as he refilled my coffee.

He looked at the stove, and I could see there was nothing on it, and that was the real sign of how much things had changed, that this wasn't even him making breakfast for *us*, just for me.

"I'm fine," he said.

"At least have toast and sit with me."

He put bread in the toaster, poured himself a coffee, and sat across from me. Then he cleared his throat. "Last night, when I asked why you put up with me—"

"It's okay," I said quickly.

"No, it's not. I wasn't being sarcastic. I just meant . . ." He struggled for words and settled on, "I didn't mean it the way you thought."

"Okay. So about this morning. We should—"

"I wanted to let you know . . ." he began, as if I hadn't spoken, but that's all he said. A few awkward moments of silence, then he repeated, "I want you to know . . ."

More silence.

"It's okay," I said.

"No, it's not. This is important. I want to say that . . . that . . ."

The toast popped up, and he scrambled after it, a drowning man spotting a life preserver.

"Thank you for breakfast," I said, as he silently buttered his toast at the counter.

He nodded and sliced it in two.

"Do you have any appointments today?" I asked, and there was another minute of quiet before he surrendered and said, "Yes, one at ten with a potential new client, and if you could be there, that would be helpful."

"Sure. I have a few things I want to chase down today . . ."

I spent the morning at the office with Gabriel doing "real" work. The kind that pays the bills. That afternoon, Ricky would be meeting with Ioan to persuade the Cŵn Annwn to hunt down Aunika. He didn't need me for that, so I'd pursue Aunika in my own way while Gabriel tackled more of the stuff that pays the bills.

When I'd exhausted my online work, I headed out to chase down leads. I'd made a list of people cross-referenced between Aunika's social media and cell records. As I drove to the first address, I called Melanie. We'd given her a cell phone, so she wouldn't feel overly isolated in Cainsville. We hadn't splurged on voice mail, though, so when she didn't answer, I called Veronica. I got her answering machine and left a message.

I was halfway to my first stop when Veronica called back.

"Melanie's in Chicago," Veronica said. "Have you tried her cell?"

"I have. When did she leave?"

"This morning. She wanted to speak to one other lamia and see if she'd talk to you in light of Damara's death. I drove her in, and she said they'd get a ride back with you or Gabriel."

"They?"

"She took Pepper, against my advice. She doesn't quite trust us yet."

I thanked Veronica, signed off, and called Melanie. Still no answer. I sent a text, saying I was glad she'd changed her mind about helping but really needed her to call me, or better yet, meet me at the office. Then I phoned to warn Gabriel, but he was in a meeting so I left a message with Lydia that if two teenaged girls showed up, I'd be there soon.

When I arrived back at the office, I found my parking spot occupied, presumably by Gabriel's client. I circled the block to the rear lot. There's a walkway through to the back door of the greystone, but no drivable shortcut. I was getting out of the car when I heard running footfalls and turned to see Melanie tearing toward me, her eyes wide, hair flying loose from her braid.

"Oh, thank you," she said, breathing hard. "Thank you for having that fancy car. The taxi driver dropped me off on the wrong street, and I thought I was totally lost, and then I saw your car and—"

"Slow down," I said. "Where's Pepper?"

"That's—that's why I ran—" she said, gasping for breath. "I didn't dare call. I couldn't. He's tracing my phone. He must be. He knew where we were going, and he took Pepper. He *has* Pepper, Liv."

"Who?"

"The Huntsman. The one you warned us about. He grabbed Pepper. He said she wants her."

"Who?"

"Aunika. Remember you said Damara told you it's about Pepper? She's right. It's all about Pepper."

"*What's* all about Pepper?"

"I have no idea. But Aunika has her, and she'll take her to the tunnels. She knows we don't like to go there. Come on."

"I need to get Gabriel."

"There's no time."

"He's right—"

"There's *no* time."

"Then I'm going to make time. I'm sorry, Melanie, but I'm not running off after Pepper without backup. Gabriel *and* Ricky are coming. I'm getting Gabriel now and calling Ricky—"

Melanie screamed. She grabbed my arm and wrenched, and I pulled away and twisted just in time to see the Huntsman swing out from behind a parked car. Melanie was already fleeing. I turned to follow, but he caught me, and as soon as he touched me, the pain was so sharp that I let out the first note of an agonized shriek. Then everything went dark.

CHAPTER FORTY-SIX

'd been kidnapped. My first thought on waking was, *Well, this is new.* With everything I'd gone through in the last five months, I had not been kidnapped before. Or, if I had, I couldn't recall it, and I'll blame that on my pounding head rather than the sheer volume of mishaps I've had.

Melanie had been right—I was exactly where she expected to find Pepper: in the tunnels under the drop-in center. I could tell by the smell alone, as I lay on damp earth that stunk of age and rot and mildew. I reached for my penlight, but given that it was attached to my switchblade, it came as no surprise to find it'd been taken from me, along with my gun and phone. I squeezed my eyes shut against the booming headache and struggled to focus. Bits and pieces of the day tumbled around in my brain, refusing to fall into place and tell me what was going on.

I remembered Melanie saying Pepper was gone, that she'd been brought here. By whom? An image of the rogue Huntsman answered.

Another image flickered. Gabriel. I'd been with . . . No, I'd been telling Melanie that I needed to *get* Gabriel. To bring him. Being smart, refusing to rush headlong into danger to save someone. And I'd be very proud of that, if the foresight hadn't come too late.

Oh, no, Gabriel. I don't need you along this afternoon. What's going to happen? That rogue Huntsman will show

*up in the parking lot in the middle of the day and knock me
out with his psychic powers? Ha-ha.*

I kept sifting through memories, like reading a book backward. Gabriel, Huntsman, Melanie, Pepper, Aunika . . . How
do they connect? What were we investigating?

The pieces fell into place, and when they did, it was as if
someone had blown apart my jigsaw puzzle and when I was
forced to reconstruct it, I saw an entirely different configuration. A different picture. A different solution. My brain
said, "That's not right," and started moving pieces back to
the answer I'd had before, but I stopped myself, put them in
their new configuration, and . . .

And yes. That solution worked as well as the last. Better,
even, because it contained the elusive element of motive.

I sat up, wincing as my stomach roiled along with my
aching head. I blinked and took a better look around. I was
in a tiny room, barely big enough for me to lie flat. No
windows. One wooden door. What looked like a candle
shoved into a crack near the roof. When I tried jumping to
retrieve it, all I got was hot wax dripping on my face.

I looked around again. Remnants of rotted barrel slats—
along with my visions from before—suggested the room
had once served for Prohibition storage. Other than those
bits of wood and the out-of-reach candle, it was empty.

I went to test the door only to find it wasn't secured at
all. Kidnapped and there's no lock on the door? Definitely
a trap.

I backed up and rooted around on the floor until I found
a barrel slat pointed enough to do some damage.

I returned to the door and eased it open. The first thing
I saw was another door. With my makeshift stake poised, I
opened my door wider and saw . . .

An empty room, exactly like the one I was still standing
in. Except, on a visual sweep, I realized it wasn't exactly the
same. On the floor lay a body. Melanie's body.

I stifled the urge to rush to her side and slid carefully through the door. Then I walked the few steps to the next door. It didn't budge, and when I looked through the crack, I could see a latch.

As I turned back to Melanie, I noticed metal embedded in the wall. Manacles, hanging on the ends of short chains. Leg irons rested on the floor below. I walked over and touched a manacle. My fingers tingled. Cold iron.

The room flickered. A man's voice said, "You don't like your bed, whore? Try these accommodations." Muffled scream as he snapped on cold-iron manacles. Another snap, the leg irons presumably following. The lamia kept trying to scream, as if from behind a gag. The man laughed and said, "I'll give you a day to wear yourself out. Then I'll bring you some company. There's a fancy man from the city who doesn't like our beds, either. He pays very well for this particular arrangement."

The man laughed, and the voices faded, and I fell back into the room, with Melanie at my feet. I crouched and checked her vital signs. She was breathing fine. When I squeezed her shoulder, she leapt up, eyes wild as she looked around the tiny room, saying, "No, please, no." Then she saw me and clutched my arm.

"We need to get Pepper," she said.

"The door's barred."

"No, you don't understand. We *need* to get Pepper."

"Because it's all about her. Everything is about her."

She blinked at my calm tone. "Are you all right, Liv?"

"Earlier, you said this was all about Pepper. You said Damara told us that. Except we didn't say that at all. Gabriel told Pepper that Damara said goodbye because it's what Pepper needed to hear, but the truth is that Damara only said Pepper's name."

Melanie's face screwed up. "Wh-what? All right. I got confused. But it is about her. Obviously. She's the one he took."

I hunkered down. "You're right. It's about Pepper. It's about her needing sanctuary and healing, and Cainsville refusing to provide it."

"What?"

"Cainsville wouldn't offer sanctuary, and Pepper was deteriorating. That's when you heard about me—the new Matilda, who used to work at women's shelters, who spearheaded fundraisers for girls on the street. Then there was Lucy, a samhail who refused to give the lamiae what you thought was your due. And Rina and Steph, two lamiae who'd been causing trouble with other fae. Put all those things together and a plan was hatched to get Pepper—and the rest of your sisterhood—into Cainsville. Through me."

"No! I would never—"

I grabbed her throat and pinned her to the floor.

"I'm bigger than you, Melanie. I'm stronger than you. Either you shut up and listen or I put you in those manacles and leg irons."

She hissed at that, her eyes slitting, glamour rippling.

"You hired the rogue Huntsman to help," I said. "He wouldn't kill, though. So you murdered Lucy yourself, maybe with the help of one of your sisters. You told yourself Lucy deserved it, for daring to want a life beyond service to the lamiae. Then the Huntsman made his fake deal with Ciro, and Rina and Steph died. And that, you hoped, would be enough to bring me running. You encouraged Aunika to get the police and the press involved, so I'd see the story. But without bodies, no one cared. To catch my attention, you had the Huntsman frame Ricky. You didn't dare take it too far. Ricky is the Cŵn Annwn's champion, and while your Huntsman must have delighted in tweaking them, he wouldn't risk bringing them to his doorstep. But having Ricky questioned was enough to bring the case to my attention."

I looked down at Melanie. She'd gone still, and it was only when she noticed I'd stopped talking that she reacted, her eyes going wide, head shaking vehemently. Too little, too late, and I squelched that part of me that hoped I'd been wrong, that *this* wasn't the betrayal Rose meant. But I'd known better. The pieces fit too well.

"You had the Huntsman menace Aunika, possibly to keep her from investigating. But it wasn't enough, so he captured her. You're keeping her, both to make sure she doesn't interfere and in case you need a scapegoat, because while she'd been a loyal samhail, as far as you're concerned she exists to serve you. Erin served you, too, and that didn't matter. When you needed to spur us to action, to convince us to help you get into Cainsville, you tortured and murdered her."

"No! I—" She stopped and clamped her mouth closed with a quick glance toward the manacles.

"Erin died. You got into Cainsville. But then somehow you found out Ciro was dead, which meant the elders might kick you out. So Damara died. Another expendable lamia, one who insisted on having a human boyfriend, meaning you could tell yourself she was a threat, like Rina and Steph. But the lamia you sent to do the job screwed up. She left her target alive, and you had no idea what Damara told us. Time to step up your game by having Pepper disappear. Bring me running and have the Huntsman take us both captive. What happens now? Oh, wait. Let me guess. Together we free Pepper and . . . Do I die in the process? No, if I die helping lamiae, the elders would never let you set foot in Cainsville again. Do we free Pepper? Kill the Huntsman and Aunika together? And then, bonded by this terrible experience, I convince the elders that the lamiae deserve permanent sanctuary in Cainsville?"

She said nothing.

"Oh, come on," I said. "Humor me, Melanie. How close am I? Eighty percent? Ninety?"

Her eyes narrowed. "This is a game to you, isn't it? Our *lives* are a game to you."

"No, I was the one who was trying to save them. You were the one ending them."

"I was protecting us. *All* of us. Rina and Steph were turning fae against us at the very time I was trying to persuade Cainsville we weren't a threat. Damara insisted on that human boyfriend even when I begged her to end it. If their deaths could get us into Cainsville? Could cure Pepper? Then yes, it was worth it, as hard as it was for me to kill my own sisters. They betrayed *us* first. And Erin? That was an accident. She caught me breaking into Aunika's apartment—getting things to make her comfortable. We fought, and Erin fell down the stairs, hit her head, and died. I decided to make use of the tragedy. The torture was done after her death."

"And Lucy?"

"She betrayed us, just like Ciro. Turned her back on her duty."

"*Duty*? It was a voluntary partnership, not indentured servitude. And she *was* helping you, in her way. You know that. You just needed her death to set your plan in motion, so you convinced yourself she deserved it. Now here's what you're going to do. You're going to call the Huntsman to let us out, and you're going to free Aunika, and you're going to let me take Pepper back to Cainsville, where I will make sure she's safe. And then you're going to run. Get your ass out of Illinois and never come back, or I'll set the Cŵn Annwn on your tail."

"Is that what I'm going to do, Olivia?"

"It is, because if you really give a shit about Pepper, you'll take the deal and—"

She twisted under me, my switchblade in her hand, and I realized she hadn't been cowed by my threats at all. She'd been faking it to see how much I knew.

On the bright side, the guy who'd given me that blade knew that the biggest danger of carrying one was that your attacker would use it against you. That meant hours of training, and I thanked Ricky when my arm instinctively flew up to block Melanie's. Then I grabbed her wrist, wrenched, and heard the satisfying clink of the blade hitting the floor. I dove for it. My fingers hit the handle . . . and the blade skidded through the open door into the other room. I scrambled up.

"Stop," Melanie said. "And turn around."

I did, and discovered that the knife wasn't the only thing she'd taken from me. My gun was pointed at my chest.

"You don't want to do that," I said.

"You think being Matilda keeps you safe? Killing Olivia Taylor-Jones will keep *me* safe, because you obviously didn't put all the pieces together until you woke up here, meaning Gwynn and Arawn have no idea what's going on."

"I promise—"

"You can promise nothing."

I dodged. She fired. I felt the bullet hit my side. She fired again but wide, and I ran at her and threw her into the wall, and the gun skittered across the floor. As I got to it, she grabbed me from behind, her hands going around my neck. Before I could throw her off, something jabbed the back of my shoulder. Her fangs, digging in, and I tried to wrench away, but it was as if someone knocked my knees out. They gave way, and I toppled to the floor.

TROUBLE MAGNET

Olivia's car was in the lot. And Olivia was not.

Gabriel had been in his client meeting when he'd gotten that feeling he'd come to know well. In the beginning, it had been a vague sense of unease coupled with thoughts of Olivia. At the time, "unease" had often accompanied thoughts of Olivia, and he'd paid little mind until he'd realized this particular sensation was always followed by the discovery that Olivia was in danger.

If there had been one positive outcome of the Gwynn reveal, it was that he'd been able to lay this particular issue to rest. Accepting that he was Gwynn's current representative, it made sense that he would have a deeper connection to Olivia. Now that vague anxiety deepened to a cold fist that gripped his gut and could not be dismissed as the result of too much coffee.

When it came during his client meeting, it had taken every bit of willpower—and the fact that this was a very wealthy client, with myriad and easily solved legal issues—to keep from walking out. Instead, he excused himself and went out to speak to Lydia, whereupon he received the message from Olivia.

That still gave Gabriel no excuse to run out on a very valuable client. He did, however, bring the meeting to a rapid conclusion. Now he was laying a hand on the hood of Olivia's car. Warm but not hot, meaning she'd arrived at the office not long after calling Lydia.

He phoned Olivia. No answer. He dialed Melanie's cell. There was no answer. Then he tried another number.

"Hey, what's up?" Ricky said in answer.

Gabriel told him, ending with, "Has she contacted you?"

"No." Keys jangled and a door slammed, as Ricky was already on the move. "If she's got her phone, I can find her. Let me look it up and I'll call you right back."

"Look up . . . ?"

"Uh, right. You remember how I got you and Liv new phones? This is probably a good time to mention that I put tracking devices in them."

"Excuse me?"

"Not like that." Ricky sighed. "See, this is the problem. I had them installed, and obviously I *meant* to tell you and show you how to use them, but then, with everything else, I forgot, and by the time I remembered . . . it was a little awkward."

"Telling us you were secretly tracking our phones?"

"Fuck, no. I haven't even turned on the damn app. But the longer I didn't mention it, the harder it was to say, 'Hey, Liv, I installed a GPS tracker in your phone . . . last week.'"

"And in mine."

"Mine, too. Look, I'm sorry. Dumbass move. But it's good that it's there now, right?"

Gabriel grumbled under his breath.

"Get in your car," Ricky said. "Head out. I'll call you back in five." He paused. "No, wait, you need a weapon."

"What?"

"Yeah, I know, you never carry one. Speaking of dumbass moves . . ."

"I do not require—"

"Liv is in trouble. Don't pull that shit. You have a gun at your office, right?"

The vision of Peter and Carl flashed, and Gabriel's stomach clenched. "No."

"Bullshit. Get the gun. Get in your car. By that time, I'll have an address for you."

CHAPTER FORTY-SEVEN

When I woke, something constricted my chest so tightly I could barely breathe. My shirt was unbuttoned, and underneath my bra was a tightly wound strip of cloth.

"You're lucky she's a lousy shot," a voice said. "Or you're just good at dodging bullets."

I knew that voice. Sadly, it wasn't the one I'd hoped for.

I turned to the Huntsman, who was leaning against the wall, arms crossed. He was nearly as big as Gabriel. Dressed in jeans and a leather jacket. Light brown hair and beard. Looking mid-thirties. That sense of wrongness he'd emanated in the forest was gone. Here, he looked and "felt" like an ordinary guy.

Yeah, an ordinary guy who tortured a hound and could knock me out with a psychic blow.

"I did not torture the hound," he said.

Right, also mind reading. I needed to keep my thoughts muddled.

"The hound was broken when she came to me," he said. "*They* broke her. Her pack. I healed her."

"It wasn't her pack," I said. "It was an encounter with some creature she didn't recognize. It killed her brothers and sister and left her maimed."

"How do you—?"

"She told me everything. You found her. You tried to

bribe her with food, and when that didn't work, you captured her."

"I healed her."

"You abused her."

"I never raised a hand—"

"You treated her like a dog."

"She's a *cŵn*. She serves—"

"You serve each other. That's how it works. At least with real Cŵn Annwn."

His face went taut, and he rocked forward as if he'd like to use that psychic TKO on me again. I wasn't bound, though, and the door was half open. This wasn't a hostage situation anymore. Or he wanted me to think it wasn't.

I gritted my teeth against the pain and rose to my feet.

"I rescued you," he said. "That lamia was going to kill you."

"How much?" I said.

"What?"

"How much are you charging for the rescue?" I looked at him. "That's how it works, right? You're a mercenary. A Huntsman for hire. Now that bank has run dry, so you're looking for a new source of income."

"It's not like that," he said, a gruffness in his voice that added, *Not exactly.*

"Which part? You *are* a mercenary, right?"

"I have to make a living," he said coldly. "My pack cast me out. Yes, I take money for the use of my skills, which do not involve murdering those who don't deserve death."

No, you just help others do it.

I managed to keep that thought hidden as he continued, "My deal with the lamia was not for money. She doesn't have enough for what she needed done. She paid in other currency."

"Please tell me it wasn't sex."

The look was almost a psychic blow in itself. "No. What they gave me is unimportant. I've terminated the contract because she tried to murder Matilda. I want nothing to do with madness like that. So I rescued you."

"Great. Thanks." I turned to the door. "Now, I need to—"

"—find Pepper before Melanie does. Yes. And the other one. The samhail."

"Aunika? She's down here?"

"They both are. But not where the lamia expects to find them. Once I have secured a promise of payment, I will tell you where they are. And give you these." He held up my gun and a penlight.

"What's the price?"

"A blood oath that you will return my hound."

"Hell, no."

"I don't think you understand the situation—"

"If I promise you the hound, you'll tell me where to find Pepper and Aunika, and you'll give me back my gun. Otherwise, I have to find them myself, unarmed."

"No, otherwise, I lock you—"

"Pointless. Gabriel or Ricky will come for me, so all that buys you is a head start. Here's my offer: I give you my oath to tell Ioan and his merry Huntsmen that you saved my life. They won't exactly thank you, but it'll give you a lot more time to run. In return, you do the same—you let me walk away. Personally, I'd prefer the deal where I don't give you shit, but being part fae, I understand the concept of a fair bargain."

"And I am Cŵn Annwn, which means I don't bargain."

"Um, isn't that exactly what you're—?"

"I'm demanding payment for services rendered."

"If you honestly think I'd return the hound so you can abuse—"

"I will treat her better. I'll give my blood oath on that. You obviously have some method of communicating with her, so you will explain the situation to her. She stays with me and obeys me, and I will treat her well."

"No."

He stepped toward me, his eyes glowing with that wild light. "She is mine. I rescued her. I've taken care of her."

I'd say she wasn't mine to give, but that implied I would otherwise, and there was no question of that. I'd been inside her head. Returning her to this monster would make me one.

The Huntsman snarled. "Monster? If you knew what they did to me, your precious Cŵn Annwn—"

"Love to hear it, but this isn't the time for backstory. You say Cŵn Annwn don't bargain. That's a lie. The fact I'm walking around proves it."

"That is a deal, not a—"

"Hair-splitting. You'll bargain, because you're fae, too, in your way. The hound is ours. Freedom is yours—and mine." I held out my arm. "You have my oath. Now take it in blood."

The Huntsman agreed to the deal. After I made the oath, I tried to wrangle my gun from him, but he was still pissed about the hound. I suspected I hadn't seen the last of him. For now, though, he was stepping off the playing field.

He did give me a parting gift: two minutes of deep and restful slumber. Yes, he knocked me out before he escaped, thankfully not with the head-splitting TKO. He'd touched the side of my head and I'd barely had time to say, "Wha—?" before I was on the floor, asleep.

When I jolted up, it seemed hours had passed, but a check of my watch showed it had been only minutes. The door was open, though, and he had left the penlight. I took it and made my way into the hall.

It wasn't long before I realized *why* he'd knocked me out . . . besides just being a jerk. He hadn't wanted me to see where he went. I wandered the tunnels for only a few minutes before I discovered Melanie had sealed the exits; I reached a metal door that I knew led back to the drop-in center, and it was bolted from the other side. So was the door that led to the room with the windows.

My goal, though, was finding Pepper and Aunika—I'd worry about locating an exit later. The problem was that the tunnels were, well, tunnels. They predated Prohibition, and I could only guess at their original use. Chicago has a rich history of putting stuff underground, despite the fact that we're on a lakefront and have several rivers running through the city.

As soon as I had an inkling of how big this place was, I stopped running down halls and randomly pushing open doors, and began handling it systematically, drawing a mental map in my mind and marking every door using a broken piece of brick.

I kept stopping and listening . . . and hearing nothing. What if Melanie had already gotten to them? What if she'd taken Pepper? Killed Aunika?

This wasn't a race. It was a hunt, and I had no scent to follow, and all I could do was proceed step by step and hope I wasn't too late, that if anything happened, I'd hear it.

I walked up to the next door and went to put my mark on it only to see an X already on the wood.

Damn it, this was an endless maze where every hall looked exactly the same. I could be walking in circles, lost in some alternate dimension, like in the psych hospital where all my logic and reasoning didn't do shit because this world wasn't logical or reasonable or—

Deep breath. Focus. This wasn't the psych hospital. I'd had flickers of visions when I opened doors in that one area— near the manacles and the room with the lamiae bodies. But they were flashes only, like I'd stepped over a trip wire.

I turned back the way I'd come, but the mental map in my head said I'd checked every passage. I'd looked everywhere.

Except behind the locked doors.

Therein lay the problem, didn't it? I'd encountered four bolted doors. Presumably, they would be exits, keeping me in. But still . . .

Damn it.

I took a deep breath and tried not to panic. Back up. Recheck and add a second X. It was all I could do.

I was heading down the next hall when I caught a noise inside a room. I eased the door open. Something darted across the dirt floor. Something furry and not nearly as small as I like my rodents. A wharf rat. I pulled the door shut, shuddered, and started to walk away. Then I stopped.

I backed up to that room, opened the door again, and looked in, expecting to see a rat-sized hole. But the walls looked solid. And there was no sign of the rat.

While ghost rats or disappearing fae ones were certainly a possibility, I wasn't jumping to that conclusion just yet. I walked into the room and started examining the walls. It didn't take long to find what I was looking for—a hatch on the side wall, set in a rough wooden-plank wall. It hung open an inch or so, not enough to be noticeable when I'd peeked through the door but enough for that rat to squeeze through.

I opened the hatch and peered into a narrow passage. I could see faint, flickering light at the end. I got down on my hands and knees, penlight between my teeth, and crawled into the passage.

The tunnel was about fifteen feet long. When I got to the middle of it, I had a mental image of someone slamming hatches on both ends, trapping me in—

Deep breaths. Which weren't easy to take when I had a metal tube between my teeth.

I continued on. As I neared the other side, I paused to listen. Silence answered. I crawled to the end and peeked out. An empty room with a partly open door on the other side. Wonderful—more rooms to search. The flickering light came through that door, though, which gave me hope I'd nearly reached my goal.

I pushed myself through . . . and a hand grabbed my hair, wrenching my head up, a blade pressing into my throat, Melanie's voice saying, "I think that's far enough, Olivia."

DÉJÀ VU

icky parked his bike beside the Jag. Gabriel was nowhere
to be seen, which meant he'd arrived at least five seconds
sooner and God forbid he should actually wait—not if
Liv was in danger. Ricky sighed softly, but it wasn't so much
annoyance as resignation and acceptance. This was how it was,
how it would always be, and he had as much chance of changing
it as he did of changing the course of the sun and the moon.

He broke into a jog and found Gabriel at the rear door,
attempting to open it without touching the metal. He'd
gripped it with his jacket but couldn't get the knob to turn,
scowling as the fabric slid. If they hadn't been in a bit of a
hurry, Ricky would have been tempted to take a picture. He
picked up the pace again and was about to say something
when Gabriel snatched his jacket off the knob and grabbed
it with his bare hand.

"Hey!" Ricky whispered loudly as he ran over.

Gabriel already had the door open . . . and had one burned
hand, which he tucked behind him as soon as he saw Ricky.

"Could you have waited two minutes?" Ricky said.
"Seriously? How about a text to see if I was close?"

Gabriel didn't even respond to that, just pushed open the
door and walked through as he tugged his jacket back on.

"Gun?" Ricky said.

Gabriel grunted something that Ricky was probably supposed to interpret as meaning yes, he had it. He knew

better, and as they stepped into the first open room, Ricky held out a nine-millimeter.

"Keep it," Gabriel said.

"Got one." Ricky waggled a second gun. Not his usual style— he preferred fists and a blade—but if Liv was in danger, that had warranted a stop at a nearby stash where the Saints stored some of their merchandise.

"I don't need—" Gabriel began.

Ricky slapped the nine-millimeter in his hand and said, "I'm not standing around arguing while Liv is in trouble."

Gabriel opened his mouth, then shut it and nodded.

Ricky led Gabriel to the hatch in Aunika's closet. At the bottom they discovered what seemed proof that they were in the right place: the door leading into the tunnels was barred from their side. Gabriel burning his hand in his rush to get inside also suggested this was the place. He'd found Liv before, as if guided by an internal beacon. Ricky could protest that he had that, too, but it wasn't the same. It just wasn't.

Before they set off into the tunnels, Ricky whispered, "I'm going to take it slow and quiet. Follow my lead."

Gabriel shook his head. "I'll lead. I—"

"You don't have my night vision. You don't have my stealth. Keep your gun out and stay behind me."

Gabriel stiffened at that, but Ricky ignored him and started moving, fingers over his flashlight beam to keep it low. He searched methodically . . . just like Liv obviously had. The moment he saw those Xs on the doors, he knew they were hers. When they found a room with manacles and leg irons, Gabriel marched over, ignoring Ricky's "Hold on." He grabbed the metal and, yep, once burned, twice *not* shy, at least if it was Gabriel in search of Olivia.

Ricky only sighed while Gabriel gave his reinjured hand a quick shake, as if the pain was a minor annoyance. There was blood on the wall, but Ricky could tell it was old. Gabriel had to check that, too, giving a grunt of satisfaction and then striding back into the hall. Ricky swung in front of him with "Uh-uh, fae in the rear, Cŵn Annwn in the lead."

They continued down the hall. After about five paces Ricky said, "Once we find Liv, I'm going to ask you to do something, Gabriel."

A grunt from behind.

"I understand she's your employee," Ricky said. "But I'd like you to restrict your relationship to that."

Silence for at least ten seconds. Then, "What?"

"I'm asking you—no, I'm *telling* you—to back off. With Liv."

"I have never—" The indignant reply stopped short, and Ricky felt his breath hitch.

Why can't you finish that sentence, Gabriel? What have you done?

Ricky pushed back the lick of jealousy. Nothing had happened between them. He trusted Liv too much for that. Even if there'd been a slip, her guilt would have made her confess. Unless . . .

"You've never what, Gabriel? Never made a move on her? Is that what you were trying to say?"

"This is not the time—"

"So you did." He resisted the urge to glance back. *Just keep moving. Play this out, but don't stop looking for Liv.* "Let me guess . . . she was caught up in a vision and mistook you for Gwynn."

"If you have anything to say to me, Ricky, you can say it later. We're trying to find Olivia, and carrying on a conversation—"

"I don't want you to see Liv socially anymore."

"I believe that is up to Olivia," Gabriel said, his voice ice.

"Nope, it's not. She loves me, and I can make her choose, and we both know who she'll pick. She's mine. Even if she wanted to leave? Too bad. I keep what's mine."

Ricky could feel waves of hate and cold rage rolling

against his back. He took three more steps and then said, "Are you going to shoot me, Gabriel?"

Silence. Then, "What?"

"You have a loaded gun at my back. Seems a little familiar, doesn't it?"

Gabriel said nothing, and Ricky continued fighting the urge to turn around.

"Liv told me about the vision. So I'm giving you a second chance."

"Second chance?"

"To kill me."

It'd been quiet before. Now the silence hung there, heavy, expanding, filling the corridor as Ricky stopped walking, his back still to Gabriel.

"Third chance, actually," Ricky said. "You had two in the psych hospital. First when I fell out of the belfry."

"I didn't. I *wouldn't*—"

"Then Tristan tried to make you do it. You didn't hesitate then—you wouldn't kill me for him. But the first time? Yeah, the first time, it took you a few extra seconds to decide to pull me up."

"I would *never*—"

"Right." Ricky turned around then. "You wouldn't. But that one moment where you considered it is driving you crazy. You can't forget that you imagined what it would be like. Kill me. Get me out of the way. Have Liv for yourself." Ricky lifted his hands over his head. "Go ahead and shoot."

Gabriel glowered at him. Then he bent, put the gun on the ground, straightened, and crossed his arms.

"So you won't kill me?" Ricky said.

"Never."

"Mmm, I wouldn't say *never*. If I lost my mind and threatened Liv, you'd kill me. I'd expect you to. But not for this. You would never kill me . . ." Ricky picked up the gun. "And I would never take her away from you."

Gabriel's eyes narrowed.

"Yeah," Ricky said. "I was just riling you up. Liv told me about the vision of those kids. The boys from the fifties. She was freaked out because she'd wanted you to see a good side of Gwynn, and instead you got that. I decided that you and I need to move past this. Prove that you aren't going to shoot me in the back or push me off a balcony. I'd say it's proving you aren't Gwynn, but that's bullshit. Gwynn wouldn't have killed Arawn. If he could have, that might have solved a whole lotta problems. But he wasn't that guy. Neither are you."

Ricky looked at Gabriel. "And yeah, you're probably thinking this really wasn't the time for this crap, but notice that I didn't stop moving until now. And I needed you distracted enough, worrying about Liv, not to question my acting. Now we need to find Liv. But before we do, I'm going to make you a promise, Gabriel, and I need you to make the same back. I will never interfere with your friendship with Liv. *Ever*. Now, your turn."

Gabriel's brow furrowed.

"Promise me that you'll never interfere with *my* friendship with Liv."

"With your relationship?"

"No, my *friendship*. Whatever happens with our *relationship*, you will not interfere with our *friendship*. I want your vow."

Gabriel gave it.

Ricky handed him back the gun. Then he took the cartridge from his pocket and passed it over.

"You'll need this," he said.

"The gun wasn't loaded?"

Ricky snorted and continued down the corridor. "I trust you, Gabriel. But I'm not crazy."

CHAPTER FORTY-EIGHT

The knife at my throat wasn't nearly as heart-stopping as it should have been. Okay, maybe my heart did skip a beat, but my body moved straight into survival mode, thanks again to Ricky's training. Also thanks to the fact that Melanie wasn't exactly skilled with a blade.

I grabbed her arm and wrenched it from my neck before she could do more than gasp. This time, though, she didn't release the knife. Her wrist flicked, the tip of the blade catching me. The bullet wound in my side blazed as I twisted, and blood from the knife slice welled up along my forearm, but I kept pulling her down, my other hand going to grab hers, both of us gripping the knife, her trying to slash, me madly struggling to break her hold in any way—

Bone snapped. Her wrist. She let out a howl of pain, and from somewhere through the next doorway I heard an answering cry. But we were already grappling on the floor, the knife knocked aside, the two of us locked in a hold, Melanie grabbing my hair with her good hand, me kneeing her as I gripped her broken wrist, squeezing until she yowled in pain and—

"Gods, Pepper," Melanie's voice said from some distant place. "Stop being such a baby. We all need to pull our weight."

I was standing in a room. Sunset glowed through the

window. Melanie was getting dressed for the hunt, wriggling into a miniskirt, while Pepper watched and nibbled at her lip.

"I don't like him," Pepper said. "I'm sorry, Mel. I can't. Not him. Can't I go with you? I like that better. It's easier."

"This isn't about what you like," Melanie snapped. "It's survival. When you come with me, I do the work and you get to share the reward. That's not fair."

"Can we go back to how we did it before? I'm good at picking pockets. I bring in more money than anyone else. I do more chores, too. That's fair, isn't it?"

Melanie turned, sighing, and put her arm around Pepper. "I know, *ee mikri mou*. That *is* fair. But after nearly getting shot in that drive-by last month, I realized if I'm gone, you need to be able to take care of yourself—to feed yourself. We'll still mostly do it the old way. You bring in the money and do extra chores, and you can share my feedings. But now and then, you need to feed yourself. Show me you can do it."

Pepper nodded, her gaze dropping. "Okay."

Melanie hugged her. "I'm only trying to protect you. You understand that, right, Pep?"

Another nod.

"This guy is a creep, but he's an easy mark. Let him take you to his cabin for the weekend, and you'll get plenty of food with little effort." She winked and nudged Pepper. "Believe me, very *little* effort. Five seconds and he's done. Now get yourself dolled up and I'll see you on Monday."

The vision broke, and I found myself under Melanie, my fingers still around her wrist, hers still in my hair, both of us frozen.

"You sent Pepper to that guy," I said. "The one who hurt her."

Melanie's eyes went wide as she realized what I'd seen. Then she snarled, "That was *my* memory! You stole—"

"You set her up."

"No! I sent her on an easy job. He'd never done anything like that before. I would *never* have let her go if I had *any* clue—"

"But you still blame yourself. That's what all this is about. You did this to her, and now you're determined to fix it, at any cost."

"Melanie! No!" It was Aunika's voice, and I glanced up to see her racing into the room with Pepper, a cut rope still dangling from one of Aunika's wrists.

Pepper saw us and her eyes rounded. She let out a howl and raced toward us, and I braced for her to attack me, but instead she grabbed the back of Melanie's shirt, pulling her off me.

Still blinded with rage, Melanie lashed out with her good hand. The blow caught Pepper in the knees and sent her toppling backward. Her head struck the wall with a dull *thwack*.

Melanie scrambled off me and raced to Pepper's side. She dropped beside her, grabbing her limp hand and saying, "No, baby. No. Please. I didn't mean . . . I never meant . . ."

She kept apologizing as I scooped up the blade. Aunika lowered herself beside Pepper, checked her vital signs, and said, "She's alive," and Melanie collapsed, sobbing.

The guys arrived a few minutes later. Well, Ricky did, Gabriel not fitting through that crawl passage. Ricky took one look at the situation and said, "Everything under control?" and as soon as I nodded, he hugged me and whispered, "Better run and tell the big guy you're okay, or he's going to squeeze into that tunnel and get stuck."

I kissed his cheek, and then took off to find Gabriel.

Melanie was banished. Banished from Cainsville. Banished from Chicago. The Cŵn Annwn agreed not to pursue her if she left the state altogether. Pepper would stay in Cainsville indefinitely and that was, for Melanie, both blessing and curse. She got what she'd wanted most . . . in the worst possible way.

Aunika returned to Chicago after a night in Cainsville and Dr. Webster making sure she was physically sound. Melanie had kept her healthy. Mentally, though? Her sister was dead, her brother-in-law was dead. Most of the lamiae she'd cared for were dead or exiled. If I could help her get back on track, I would, but this wasn't the time for her to plan a new life. First, she had to mourn the old one.

I'd refused to go to a hospital. That had not gone over well, but my reasoning was far more sound than "I don't like them." I'd been shot. I'd need to report that. If I was in serious condition, we'd have worked things out. But Ricky examined the wound and confirmed it was little more than a graze. Well, a gouge. A deep one. I was not in mortal or even serious danger, though, so they agreed I could be treated in Cainsville. We just didn't mention the gunshot part to Dr. Webster, and if she knew, she said nothing, just cleaned and plastered the gash and gave me painkillers.

The first night, I stayed at Rose's with both Gabriel and Ricky there, as if I needed three people to ensure I got my ass to a hospital if my situation deteriorated. Fortunately, it did not. I rested the next day. That night, I insisted on tending to the bodies in the tunnel, taking the lamiae to the forest and burying the boy in consecrated ground.

Afterward, Gabriel and I went to the Carew house, but without painkillers to keep me asleep I tossed and turned, plagued by memories and nightmares. When I woke with a nightmare-induced cry, Gabriel was in my room so fast you'd have thought I'd been shot again. I assured him I was fine—just startled by waking up in an unfamiliar place. I lay in bed long enough for him to fall back to sleep, then I slid out and crept down the stairs to the living room with a book.

I'd intended to grab a blanket and pillows from my room but forgot, and once I was down there, all I could do was collapse on the couch and stare out the window, book in hand. I'd been there a few minutes when I caught the squeak of bare feet on hardwood, and I looked up just as Gabriel was walking away, having apparently come to check on me and decided all was fine. Another minute later, though, he returned with a blanket and pillows, and I managed a smile for him.

"Thank you."

He nodded at the novel as he handed them to me. "You'll need light to read that. If you actually intend to. I certainly hope you don't feel obligated."

I glanced down to realize it was Patrick's book. "No, I'll try it. Which isn't to say I'll finish it, but I'll give it a go."

He motioned to the table lamp.

I shook my head and set the book aside. "Can't sleep, and I wanted to do something instead of just staring at my bedroom wall, but . . ." I shrugged.

"If it's the pain, you should take something. I know I'm not the only one who doesn't like relying on medication."

Another wry smile for him. "We're tougher than that, right?"

"No, simply more stubborn."

I laughed softly. "True." I looked over at him, his face cast in shadow. "I'll be fine if you want to sleep. But if you'd like to stay . . ."

I motioned at the other end of the sofa. He sat, and I moved my feet out of his way, but he lifted them and put them on his lap.

"If it's not the pain, is it the house? Or the case?" he asked.

"Of every murder we've investigated, I hate this solution the most. I mean, obviously, finding out Pamela was an accomplice to James's death *hurt* the most. But I understood it. This one . . ."

"You don't understand?"

"I do and I don't, and it keeps going around and around in my head, like a conundrum I need to solve, and I just can't."

"If you're at all concerned that Melanie wasn't responsible—"

"No, she was. The problem is how I *feel* about it. What she did. What Ciro did. Terrible things because they loved someone. Melanie to protect Pepper and ease her suffering. Ciro to get Lucy back and ease his own suffering. There was guilt there, too, in both. Melanie blamed herself for sending Pepper on that job. Ciro blamed himself for not getting Lucy farther away from the lamiae. I *hate* what they did. I want to write them off the same way I did Edgar Chandler and Macy Shaw and Tristan. Cold-blooded killers." I glanced at him. "You're right, you know."

"About what?"

"Motive. You said it wasn't important. It shouldn't be. Judge them for what they did, not why they did it. I know that isn't what you meant, but motive it muddles everything, and I want cut-and-dried. I want . . ."

"Monsters."

I twisted to look at him. "Yes, damn it. I want monsters."

Several long minutes of silence passed. Then he said, softly, "This isn't really about Melanie and Ciro. It's about Pamela."

I didn't respond. Couldn't.

"It would be easier if she were a monster," he said. "It would be even easier if she killed four monsters to cure you and could therefore be absolved. But there's James."

I nodded, my eyes filling with tears. "Whatever James did to me, he did it under compulsion, and he was never an actual threat. And there's you, too. What she tried to do to you."

He straightened. "Disregard that. It was a poor effort, and I survived it unscathed."

"No, Gabriel. I cannot *disregard* that. You may—I will not. Ever."

"She thought she was protecting you. And I believe the other cases feed into another, unspoken, aspect of it—that she blames herself. As Melanie and Ciro did. She bore a child, knowing her blood came with risks. That led to you having spina bifida. Then you were in danger from James and from me because of everything that's happened since you discovered she's your mother. That does not excuse what she did. But it is not as simple as 'Pamela Larsen is a monster.'"

I went quiet, a distant clock ticking. "I don't know how to reconcile that," I said, my voice barely above a whisper. "I want to put her out of my life. I know I said I was fine with you handling her case, and logically I am, but emotionally . . ." I shook my head. "There's a reason I haven't done one single minute of work on it."

Silence. Then, in that same soft tone, "If I refuse to represent Pamela . . ."

"The chances of freeing my father plummet. I won't have that. I can't. I need to accept that setting my father free might also free Pamela."

"Yes." That's all he said. All that could be said.

"Can we talk about that?" I said. "Just talk. I know that's not really your thing—"

"I'm here, Olivia. For anything you need."

When I still hesitated, he put out his hand. I took it, and he tugged me to sit beside him, so I could lean back against his shoulder.

"Talk to me," he said.

And I did.

CHAPTER FORTY-NINE

A week later, I was back where it all began: in the clubhouse with Ricky. No business to attend to, just hanging out, playing darts and poker, drinking and having a good time. We stayed until it cleared out. Then we took off for the backwoods, one of the last times we'd get the chance before winter set in.

A hunt, a chase and sex, wonderful and wild sex. Afterward, I discovered this was no spontaneous trip. Ricky had left a care package out there—a blanket, sleeping bag, champagne, and an assortment of snacks ranging from strawberries to chocolate.

"What are we celebrating?" I asked as I sipped my champagne.

"Us."

Which was as good a cause as any, and we drank and ate and talked, and capped off the evening making love under the stars. It was as perfect a night as I could imagine, and when I woke the next morning, snuggled into his arms, he said, "I love you. You know that, right?" and there was something in his voice . . .

I looked up at him. "I love you, too," I said carefully.

"I mean it," he said. "This is like nothing I've ever had before. Like nothing I thought I would have."

I nodded, still feeling a buzz of uncertainty, that tone in his voice . . .

He shifted and tugged me on top, so I was looking down at him. "I thought I had it good before. Everything going according to plan. That was good. It was comfortable. And I was perfectly content. Happy, even. Then you came along and shot those plans out the door, shot that *life* out the door, and it's like skidding on the bike, when you know you haven't lost control yet but you're right there, on the edge, and it's fucking incredible and . . ." He exhaled. "Shit, I really suck at metaphors."

I managed a chuckle, relaxing a little.

"What I'm trying to say, Liv, is that you upended my life, and spun it one-eighty, and it's the best damn thing that ever happened to me. It's like being on the bike, roaring along, thinking it's the best damn thing, and then you go over that hill or into that slide and you think, fuck, no, *this* is riding. With you? With all the crazy shit that comes with you? *This* is living. It slapped me awake and showed me what can be." He paused. "Am I explaining that right?"

I kissed his nose. "You're explaining it perfectly. I had it good in my old life, too. I really did. Moving along according to plan, content, even happy. Maybe a little dissatisfied now and then, but that seemed . . . immature. Selfish. I had it all. But then the worst thing that happened in my life? Finding out about my parents? It turned out to be the best thing, and I still feel bad saying that, because of everything that's gone wrong for others, but for me . . . ? I can't imagine ever going back."

"Me neither." He moved his hands down to my hips. "I don't want to ever go back, Liv. I said I love you, and I mean that. The thing that I've learned, though, is that when you love someone, you want the best for them. You want them to be happy, and yeah, that's not selfless, either, because what's the point of being with someone who isn't happy?"

My breath caught, and I struggled to say, "Is something wrong? Have I done—?"

"No." He reached up to kiss me. "You've done nothing wrong. Absolutely nothing. That's why I started with the whole 'I love you' and 'You changed my life' and 'I don't want to lose you from my life' parts."

"Started . . .?"

"We need to step back, Liv. To where we began. Being friends."

Now I couldn't breathe. Really and truly couldn't. Somehow, I heard myself saying, "You're breaking up—"

"No. We're stepping back. The two of us. Together. Because it's the right thing to do. Because otherwise, the *three* of us don't work."

"Gabriel? No. If you think—"

"I think we need to find out. I think that's going to loom over our heads until we do. Yeah, Gabriel isn't like that kid in the vision. He's not going to shoot me in the back. He's not Gwynn, either. He's not going to force you to choose. But that's still there. Those parts are still there. Same as the part of me that looks at you and knows that I stole you away before he could get his shit in order. The Arawn part did that. And it's true. When Gabriel told me he wasn't interested in you, I knew that was bullshit, and I went for you anyway. The only reason I won you is because he wouldn't step up. And now you're never going to leave me for him, because what we have is good. Damned fucking amazing good, and you won't give that up and hurt me and risk hurting yourself. So this is where I step back."

I wanted to tell him he was wrong. I wanted him and only him, and there was no tension, no question, no anything else. But that wasn't true, was it?

I looked out at the sun rising over the forest. "So, I guess . . . I guess you'll want me to go home now. That was a goodbye night."

"Or the start of a goodbye week."

When I looked at him, he reached over and fished his

phone from his pocket. He flipped to a screen and held up his list of top ten motorcycle trails.

"One more week?" he asked. "One more trip?" He caught my expression, and his gaze dropped. "Shit, I'm sorry. An amicable breakup is one thing, but I'm asking for the most fucking amicable one in history." His fingers trembled slightly as he put the phone aside. "Sorry. Yeah, that was too much. I didn't mean to . . ." He exhaled. "Sorry."

At this moment, I wanted nothing more than to run. Get the hell out of here, find someplace quiet, and cry my eyes out.

He wanted to postpone our breakup for a week? Go on a trip and act as if nothing had happened? Hell, yes, that was asking for the most amicable breakup in history. It was crazy. Absolutely crazy.

I took a deep breath. A deep breath, and a long moment to think, just think.

Yes, he was asking for the most amicable breakup in history. But that's what I owed Ricky. What I owed *us*. Because as much as this hurt—and it hurt so fucking much—if I said no and ran off, I'd regret it. I didn't want to lose him from my life, and if that was possible, if we really could keep on being friends, this was how it started. By not running.

I reached for the phone, picked it up, and handed it back.

"Your turn this time," I said. "Choose one."

KELLEY ARMSTRONG is the #1 internationally bestselling author of the thirteen-book Women of the Otherworld series, the Nadia Stafford crime novels and this series set in the fictional town of Cainsville, Illinois, which so far includes the novels *Omens*, *Visions*, *Deceptions* and *Betrayals*. She is also the author of the hit crime novels *City of the Lost* and *A Darkness Absolute*, three bestselling young adult trilogies and the standalone YA suspense thriller, *The Masked Truth*. She lives in rural Ontario.

@kelleyarmstrong
www.kelleyarmstrong.com

A sneak peek at *Rituals*, the next book in Kelley Armstrong's Cainsville series

The next morning, Gabriel drove me to work. He'd spent the night at my house in Cainsville. In the guest room, I hasten to add. We'd been up for hours discussing the case. Now as he pulled into the laneway of his office greystone, his topic of conversation had nothing to do with work and everything to do with distracting me from fretting over my parents' appeal. Gabriel had put himself through law school with illegal gaming, and he was finally sharing details.

"Blackjack," he said as we got out of the car. "That was my specialty. It's simple and efficient."

"It's also one of the easiest games to cheat in, isn't it? Counting cards?"

"No one counted cards at my table. Not after the first time."

As we walked around the building, the front door swung open, no one behind it. I stopped short. When I blinked, the door was shut.

A door opening on its own. The sign of an unwanted visitor.

"Olivia?"

I shook off the omen. Given what Gabriel did for a living, we got plenty of unwanted visitors.

"Sorry. Missed my cue," I said as we walked through the front door. "So, tell me, Gabriel, what'd you do the first time you caught someone counting cards?"

He studied me.

"Well, are you going to tell me?" I said. "Or is this one of those stories you tease me with and then say *Whoops, looks like we're at the office already. I'll finish later.*"

His lips twitched. "You like it when I do that. It builds suspense."

"I *hate* it when you do that. It's sadistic. You have five seconds—"

"Gabriel?" Lydia stepped out of the office, closing the door behind her.

He bristled at the interruption.

"Client?" I guessed.

Lydia nodded, and we backed farther down the hall. She glanced toward the stairs, but there was no sign of the other tenants. Still, she lowered her voice as she said, "It's a woman. She claims to be a relative."

Gabriel grumbled under his breath. The fact Gabriel had a legit job made him one of the few "white" sheep in the Walsh family. So, yes, I was sure relatives showed up now and then, in need of his services. Which he would happily give, providing they could pay his fees.

"Prospects?" he said to Lydia.

Lydia's look said this one wouldn't be paying his bills anytime soon.

"I'll get rid of her," I said.

Gabriel hesitated. While he hated relinquishing control, this was the efficient solution. Also, listening to some distant relative sob on his sofa was both terribly awkward and a pointless waste of billable hours.

"The sooner we get rid of her, the sooner we can get to work on our appeal strategy," I said. "I'd appreciate that."

He nodded. "All right. I'll go get you a mocha. Lydia?"

"Chai latte, please," she said.

As Lydia opened the office door, I raised my voice and said, "So, yeah, don't expect Gabriel anytime soon. This courthouse issue could take all day. We need to—"

I stopped short, as if Lydia hadn't mentioned a client in the reception area. When I got a look at the woman, though, I didn't need to feign my shock.

I couldn't guess at her age. Maybe sixty, but in a haggard, hard-living way that suggested the truth was about a decade younger. Her coloring matched Gabriel's, what his great-aunt Rose called "black Irish"—pale skin, blue eyes and wavy black hair. She also had the sturdy Walsh build that Gabriel shared with Rose, along with their square face, widow's peak and pale blue eyes.

Yet already I knew this woman claimed to be a relative so it wasn't the resemblance that stopped me in my tracks.

I'd seen her face before. In the photo of a dead woman.

I had to be mistaken, of course. The dead woman had also been a Walsh, so there was a strong resemblance—that's all.

I walked over, hand extended as she rose. "I'm—"

"The infamous Eden Larsen," she said, and my hackles rose. I am Eden Larsen, as much as I'm Olivia Taylor-Jones. But calling me by my birth name is the social equivalent of a smirk and a smackdown. *I know who you really are, Miss Larsen.*

I responded with the kind of smile I learned from my adoptive mother. The smile of a society matron plucking the dagger from her back and calmly wiping off the blood before it stains.

"It's Olivia," I said. "And you are?"

A smile played at her lips, and that smile did more than raise my hackles. My gut twisted, and I wanted to shove her out the door. Just grab her arm and muscle her out before she said another word.

"I'm Seanna Walsh," she said. "Gabriel's mother."

WELCOME TO
CAINSVILLE

NO WEREWOLVES.
NO DEMONS.
JUST GARGOYLES.

Following the epic conclusion of her internationally bestselling Women of the Otherworld series, Kelley Armstrong launched a brand-new series set in Cainsville, a small town as spookily fascinating as Stephen King's Castle Rock or Dean Koontz's Moonlight Bay.

"[I]mpossible-to-put-down. . . . Why are Armstrong's books so addictive? Because she has an innate sense of how a story should unfold, how much conflict should be on every page, and how much the reader needs to know about the heroes, villains and denizens of Cainsville to move the current book along while also setting up future volumes . . . Bring on the next Cainsville volume, please."

Sarah Weinman, *National Post*

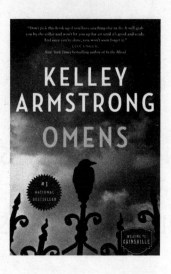

OMENS

#1 NATIONAL BESTSELLER

"I am not a fan of mysteries that cross over into other genres, and I don't like books that begin with infant narrators. So when I tell you that, despite that, *Omens* kept me reading on, you can bet it's a good book. The regrettable kiddo lasts only a few pages and does play a part in the plot. . . . **A clever whodunit with some very nice twists** and the fantasy actually works."

Margaret Cannon, *The Globe and Mail*

"*Omens* is enough of a departure from her previous work to attract new readers, though familiar enough that her fans won't feel abandoned."

Mark Medley, *National Post*